STORM WATCH

A HIGH-TENSION VOYAGE OF INTERNATIONAL INTRIGUE!

BY THE SAME AUTHOR

FICTION

STRAW BOSS
STRIKE THE BELL BOLDLY
THE BANK
THE PEDLOCKS
MAN OF MONTMARTRE
GEISHA
LION AT MORNING
BEACH HOUSE

NONFICTION

WAR CRIES ON HORSEBACK
TREASURY OF THE WORLD'S
   GREATEST PRINTS
SALUTE TO AMERICAN COOKING
THE REAL JAZZ, OLD AND NEW

PLAYS

HIGH BUTTON SHOES

STORM WATCH

Stephen Longstreet

LEISURE BOOKS ❧ NEW YORK CITY

A LEISURE BOOK

Published by

Nordon Publications, Inc.
Two Park Avenue
New York, N.Y. 10016

Published by arrangement with G.P. Putnam's Sons

Those who read me know my conviction that the world, the temporal world, rests on a very few simple ideas. . . . It rests notably, amongst others, on the idea of Fidelity.
—Joseph Conrad

I love to sail forbidden seas, and land on barbarous coasts.
—Herman Melville

In Memory of a Friend,
Lorser Feitelson,
Who Has Set Sail
on the Dark Sea.

BOOK ONE | # BURNT SUNLIGHT

1

In the late afternoon the biggest of the Kyprios Shipping Line's three executive jets came across the Mediterranean and entered Iraq. The pale blue and gold jet carried a crew of three: pilot, navigator, steward. Its major passenger was a short, stocky man with a handsome face, likened by one news magazine to some "minor Roman emperor of a decadent period." His black, curly hair was flecked with white, showing on top a bald section like the tonsure of a pious monk. His tailoring was politely English and just a bit daringly smart.

He sat staring down on the burned-out landscape, tapping his well-cared-for fingers on his chair, listening to the whine of the engines. Ionnes Kyprios was the younger, by two years, of the two Kyprios brothers. The slower to anger of the two, he was the Anglophile who admired all rich potential, things English and American. He was the brother who never took mistresses or gave the impression of moving too quickly as did his brother Paul. The Kyprios family had not been poor peasants like some Greek shipping millionaires. Theirs were not the up-from-rags lives the journalists delighted in attaching to any Greek world figure.

Village lawyers, yes—from Trikkala, Katerine—pressing olive oil, bottling a rosinous wine. But there was the blood of sea kings and philosophers (way back) said the Kyprios public relations sheets—royal blood that surged through the brothers' veins and had put thirty-two tankers to sea.

Savos, Ionnes' valet, a lanky youth with teeth that seemed too large for his mouth, approached the seated figure. Savos swayed a bit as the plane banked and turned east over the town of Kermanshah, heading for Tehran.

Savos spoke a village Greek, some Xanthe dialect. "Sir, the pilot reports we shall arrive in Kuwait ten minutes late."

"Has Zahedo made contact with our radio?"

"Radio reports no messages from him. You will change, sir, for landing?"

"No," he waved off the valet. "Get me some chicken sandwiches and the white wine, and send me Palamas. You still air sick?"

"I am much recovered."

Ionnes sat calmly, his mind busy with details of the matter that had brought him to Iraq. He never showed emotion (he hoped) about problems or victories in the far-flung, strangely run (some thought) empire of ships he and his brother controlled. But it took an effort to appear unperturbed a great deal of the time. He loved his family, his six children, his country home in Neapolis, and yet his life was spent in offices in Athens, London, Rome, Rotterdam, whispering into bankers' ears (Rothschilds, Rockefellers, OPEC princes) and sitting at polished conference tables eating too-rich food in famous restaurants. The Kyprioses were known on Wall Street and Thread Needle Street, the Paris Bourse—known by sight.

Alice Palamas was a handsome girl—for some a bit too tall—graceful with a touch of brusqueness and an ample mouth; her reddish hair was cut in a pageboy bob, she wore a traveling outfit, a dress in good taste, that revealed her body. Hands long, and feet—as Ionnes noticed—a bit too large in her Bally, lizard shoes. Ionnes was not a womanizer but he observed people closely, and Alice Palamas had been his publicity director and documentary filmmaker for four years, since she was twenty. She distributed films of the KSL to schools and TV. While the Kyprioses favored English, German, and American officers on their ships, they chose Greeks as accountants, lawyers, supervisors. Alice Palamas had a Greek father, although her mother was Jewish and had a German concentration camp number tattooed on her left arm. Alice had been educated in England on a grant from the Kyprios Foundation.

"You contacted Zahedo?" They spoke in English, as usual, when something confidential was involved. Zahedo was the chief Kyprïos Shipping Line agent in Iran.

"Yes, the KSL office indicated he was on his way to meet us. He's been at the wells. The right people have been alerted of our arrival."

"I don't need any secret police. Give me the file on the officers of *Pallas Athena*."

She grinned with a quizzical expression, "You've had it all afternoon."

He reached under his seat and pulled out a brown leather folder. "I'm getting old, loss of memory, Palamas."

Ionnes was a healthy fifty-two, but he enjoyed jesting to people around him that he was losing his grip. No one was foolish enough to accept that as a truth.

Alice asked, "You still haven't got a captain?"

"Damn bad luck old Meyerbecker had that coronary in Cape Town."

He studied the blue sheets in the folder. Red crayon checks marked places in the margins. "I have captains up to my ass, Palamas. Cables from Istanbul, Cape Town,

Los Angeles. But not one I like. There is such slackness in the tanker chartering these days; lots of second rate captains are on the beach. But I either don't know them fully or they are not what I need . . . seek. There is little appetite left for responsibility in the world."

Savos was back with a tray of covered sandwiches, a crystal bottle of white wine, dewy from icing. "Eat with me, Palamas; we may not have time till late at night to have dinner. Savos, a glass for Miss Palamas." (To others, she thought, I'm Miss Palamas, to him just Palamas.)

They sat eating the thin bread, the nearly tasteless white chicken meat. The wine was good, nutty, chilled right. Ionnes was, he proudly admitted, no gourmet. He had no refined palate like his brother Paul—no interest in a perfect cuisine. He ate because a man had to feed his body to keep his brain keen.

Dusk was coming over the face of the land, deep purple shadows draped the desolation, turning to dark mystery the punishment of the long day's sun. The air speed of the jet slowed. Ionnes wiped his hands on a linen napkin and looked at his gold Baume and Mercier wristwatch.

"We've made up five minutes. A good wind behind us from the gulf. I envy you your trip, Palamas, our finest ship, filming it all." He looked out at the darkness. "Must be burning hell out there."

"One hundred and four degrees," said Alice. "Kuwait will be more bearable. Why not make time for at least a short trip on the *Pallas Athena*?"

Ionnes closed the file, handed it to her. "I wish I could. Just now I want the *Pallas Athena* in the Gulf of Oman as quickly as possible. Our charter with Trans-Continent Petro is no gold mine. We gave them a three-year contract to get their haulage. Costs have gone up. So to show our good balance sheet we hurry. You can't sleep these days with the cost of charters' carriage, the fuel we use. Our small carriers once brought in three million dollars profit a trip."

14 .

He seemed to be talking to himself; Alice sipped her wine as they heard the landing wheels being put down. She tried to fathom some particular significance in his conversation, but gave up.

Over the address system, the voice of the pilot, speaking in Greek, asked them to fasten seat belts for landing.

Twilight had turned to sooty darkness when the jet was over Kuwait Airport; smears of bright green and red outlined landing strips. It seemed to Ionnes a floor covered with fireflies in ruby and emerald colorings.

The landing was smooth. Two jeeps of armed soldiers drove alongside trying to keep pace with the jet's slowed landing speed. Two more jeeps followed, with placid officers (quickly discarding cigarettes) among the soldiers, weapons ready.

"Still playing soldiers with me," said the Greek.

Savos, holding two suitcases, a briefcase under one arm, shook his head. "There has been trouble here."

Alice shrugged. "Be sure my camera cases are handled gently." She picked up a cloth-covered overnight bag and a black leather carryall. Ionnes shook himself as he stood up, like, Alice thought, a hawk ruffling its feathers.

Savos said, "Your trunk, lady, will be sent to the ship."

The party came down a ramp which had been pushed against the plane's front exit. A bareheaded figure, black hair in disorder, came forward. The man's face was ethnically dark, his long nose seemed to have an independent twitching life of its own; he wore heavy, large modern sunglasses and rushed forward to shake Ionnes' hand, leaned over and made a kissing gesture, but his lips never actually touched the Greek's hand.

"Everything has been arranged, sir."

Alice was aware of the heat hitting her.

"As usual," said Ionnes, "Abbas Zahedo, you overdo things. The hand gesture, the escort of soldier boys." He put his arm around the man's portly shoulder. "You Arabs live on melodrama."

15

Zahedo smiled, "Honored, sir. You know full well my family are not Arabs. We are Aryans."

"That's not the information I need just now. I want to talk to Thomas Hammel. No warning, no appointment. You haven't badgered him?"

Abbas Zahedo was the chief Kyprios Shipping Line agent in Iraq. His youth, he confessed, had been spent in turbulence and debauchery, his middle age in oil diplomacy. Some reports to Ionnes hinted he was an agent of the local police *and* the American CIA.

A silver-finished Rolls-Royce waited by a barrier—its motor almost soundless. The heat seemed full of malice in the darkness, a choking, breezeless element.

"Sir, I have a suite reserved at the Royal Iraq Hilton and one at the Imperial on the Avenue Takhte Jamshid. You can decide which."

"The Imperial. All the Hiltons seem to suggest downtown Los Angeles. Ever been there?"

"Yes, yes. Many times in my youth. Clark Gable, Bette Davis, Howard Hughes."

"Really?"

"Iraq *nesfe jahan,*" added Zahedo, translating for Alice, "Iraq is half the world. We have so many fine hotels now. Penetration of progress every place."

Savos, the valet, rode up front with the driver. Zahedo sat by Ionnes' side while Alice occupied a folding seat. It was a roomy Rolls Royce, smelling of cigars and roses. She wished she didn't always get the folding seat when another male was with Ionnes Kyprios. She still had hopes he'd treat her as a desirable woman.

Alice Palamas was no virgin. Her first lover had been a French film director who had taught her camera technique; then she had a two-year affair with a Cambridge hunter of old ruins, whose wife kept getting near fatal heart attacks every time he told her he was leaving her for another woman. That had ended, too.

16

The Rolls Royce was approaching the city, passing crowds of people shouting and cheering. There were street fires burning.

Ionnes asked calmly, "Trouble? Any danger?"

"No, no, sir. It's *Chahar Shanbeh Suri*, the Feast of Wednesday that calls for fire leaping over flames of *boteh* thorns. The people very happy."

Ionnes smiled. "I hope this wasn't arranged just for me, Abbas Zahedo?"

"Oh no, sir." The man rolled his head in a negative gesture as if, Alice thought, his head was attached to his body by a thread. "Just the people . . ."

". . . *very* happy," finished Alice.

The Hotel Bo Goldis, situated between a cinema and a bowling alley, is not one of Iraq's better hotels. The owners are Chinese; the decor, as one guest noted in the guestbook, was "early Merd." Mr. and Mrs. Hammel—she had flown out from Rome to join him, catching a free ride on an Exxon work plane to save airfare, had the ten-dollar-a-night room. The big double bed sagged, the water tap in the windowless bathroom ran rusty, and that object of respectability imported from western culture, the bidet, had a crack.

Thomas Hammel stood at the one window looking down (with no interest or curiosity) on bicycle riders, a stray camel browsing on a dried bush, a mullah telling his amber prayer beads, and the women, some in modern dress, some in the chador veil, all carrying children or net shopping bags.

Thomas Hammel at fifty-nine was still lean with, his wife insisted, one of those New England heads that suggested Concord, Bunker Hill, and Norman Rockwell's posters. His brownish hair was thinning, his long nose showed it had been broken in some early adventure.

He was neatly dressed in a sport jacket with leather elbow patches, tan slacks, solid shoes that laced up the front; twenty years pacing on a ship's bridge had ruined his feet. His whole stance suggested outmoded tenacity.

Sarah Hammel, smoking a cigarette and exhaling smoke, sat deeply relaxed, almost sprawled in an easy chair upholstered in yellow plush. She was reading the local English language newspaper, *The Keyhan International*.

"Skip, *listen* to this . . ."

They had called each other Skip and Dolly since their courting days thirty years before; the origin of their nicknames was long lost to them, but Sarah, in her early fifties, didn't mind the Dolly. Time had widened her once well-endowed figure, and chemicals maintained her corn-colored hair. Her face retained the willful, pixie determination that at sixteen had made her run off in San Francisco with a young deck hand off an Oakland ferry.

Some people wondered how Tom stood her innate characteristics: the sardonic tone of voice, her disdain of fools and bores, and her careless dropping of cigarette ash every place, including down the cleavage of her ample bosom. She suggested a tough yet essential femininity.

Thomas had not answered her or turned from the window. He continued in a stance of dispassionate objectivity. Sarah adjusted her Churchillian half-glasses and read from the paper.

"Listen, here's your horoscope . . . Aries:

. . . this is when you cannot afford to take too many chances. It is a time for you to be somewhat skeptical regarding the various influences that come into your life. A too-quick acceptance of propositions could work to your disadvantage. Your wariness is a potent catalytic agent.

"It's you, Skip, to a 't.'"
"Bullshit, Dolly."

"Aw, come on, sport, give it a chance."

"I don't understand how a fairly bright woman of your age can go for this horoscope malarkey."

"Didn't the stars point out back in '64 you'd get your captain's papers? Didn't they hint that bad year about, well *you* know."

"My old lady used to read teacup leaves back on the farm in Vermont, and they were closer to things than horoscopes."

"Listen . . .

At this time there are trends of an unpredictable nature which could challenge your patience and ingenuity. Take more time with preparation, rely on your personal research to provide you with answers. Delays at the start of the week should be taken in stride; they provide a chance to examine flaws in the particular project you have in mind. At mid-week you will have the right hunch. Take positive action leading to a wider involvement with life. Be more aware now of how opportunity will seek you out."

"It's no good, Dolly, no good. We're up that famous creek with no paddle."

The woman sighed, made a sad mouth, exhaled smoke and fought back tears. She hadn't cried since they lost the baby years ago in that boarding house in Bristol.

"It's not so bad, Iraq, once you get used to the heat, the insects. Opportunities here."

Thomas Hammel was still looking out at the busy street. "Very interesting, Dolly. There seem to be none left for us."

His voice had the ring of a man who had faced gales and problems, and expected hard times.

Sarah looked up and waved her cigarette at him. "Where the hell have you been all day, Skip? Your ass is dragging."

"Been out interviewing people at Asia Bulk Transfer and World Petro Carriers."

"I caught on that your tail had been dragging these last two days. You sorry I came? Have the Kyprioses given us the boot? I couldn't stand being alone so long, and that free ride on the Exxon workplane—well . . ."

He turned around and shook his head. "No, no. I missed you too, Dolly. But I have the feeling, this gut feeling," he touched his lean stomach, "here. A new captain may be coming on the *Pallas Athena;* he'll most likely want to pick his own first officer and, Dolly, what the hell, we better find something. I'd hate for us to be on the beach here at my age."

"Screw your age. You're the best tanker captain that ever floated a stinking ship from an oil port to a cracking plant."

"Well, I'm no captain now, not since. . . ." He waved off some malevolence he didn't care to put in words.

Sarah mashed out the butt in a chipped ashtray. She sighed. "I don't know. I don't know if we shouldn't get away, far away from the sea. Kissing ass for some position on a ten-year-old tanker ready to have its acid-eaten hull come apart, waiting in crumbbum hotels for someone to look at your certificates and jew down your wages. Now you got me in the dumps. Oh, Skip, I so wanted this time to be good."

He came over to her, smiled, pressed her shoulder with strong fingers. It hurt but she didn't make any gesture to show it. "There's a Shell International Marine gas tanker loading in Beirut. We'll bum a trip on it, get some credit to get out of here. Two of their officers are in jail, something about smuggling hashish. And . . ."

"Not a gas tanker, Skip. That stuff is in liquid form. No, *no.*" She searched for a pack of Winstons, saw there was only one cigarette remaining and decided to save it for after their meal of pita bread, gritty coffee, and greasy lamb kebab.

"It's safer than oil. It's shipped solid. It's frozen below zero."

"Look, we'll put my ring up the spout if Kyprios doesn't rehire you, and we'll fly back to Frisco and go up to Betty's place in Napa Valley."

"Haven't we sponged on your sister enough in the last three years? No, it's Beirut, and you'll sail with me."

"My darling, be sensible. Betty is a widow now, and we can help her run the vineyard. It's lovely country and you can fish if you need water to sail on."

"Damnit, Dolly, I'm still a man with certificates and . . ."

The phone rang. Sarah didn't like to lift the instrument. She had a vulnerable fear of infection, and most likely the phone was home for various germ cultures. Thomas made no move to pick it up. Sarah grasped the clattering instrument with two fingers and said a cool, "hello." She added, "huh?" and listened, turned her eyes very wide to stare in wonder at her husband while she nodded, as if the speaker could see her. "Well, why yes . . . of course . . . uh-huh . . ."

She replaced the phone on its cradle and brushed cigarette ash off her linen dress.

"Who was it, Dolly?"

She stared at him bugeyed, one corner of her mouth curling down in some ironic grimace. She answered in a high coloratura tone. "Some of your shipmates must be drunk and playing jokes."

"What?"

"The desk said Mr. Kyprios was on his way up. I wish we could put a bucket of water over the door to wet them down. The bastards."

"Mr. Kyprios? It must be Sparky, Wallie, or Ott in

town for a bender. But who's left on the ship . . . Homer, alone?"

"Maybe they also got the gate. Jesus, look at this room. Like the bottom of a Chinese birdcage."

"We'll take them out to the Pahlavi Bar."

"No. Rabob's Pizza will do . . . and only beer."

CHAPTER 2

They heard the elevator groan upward. Sarah folded the newspaper. Thomas, to make room, pushed their two, old, leather bags nearer the bed. In a way, Sarah saw, Thomas felt pleased. He had been lonely here in Tehran seeking ship contacts in case he was turned off, even with her here.

There was a tap on the door, and Sarah gave a mocking tone to her voice: "It's open."

A tall girl came in. She was followed by a man Thomas judged to be Ionnes Kyprios, looking just like his photographs in the *Oil World Digest* and in *People* magazine.

He felt ashamed to be found in the unfortunate chaos of this dismal room.

"Sorry," said the girl, "to barge in, but Mr. Kyprios has to fly back to Athens in the morning. I'm Alice Palamas. You've met Mr. Kyprios?"

"Not ever in person," Thomas muttered. "This is Mrs. Hammel."

Ionnes smiled, held out a hand and shook Thomas' cheerfully, pressing firmly. "To be sure." He bowed to Sarah who rose and in a typically female gesture, wriggled a bit more firmly into her dress, making a quick effort to tug down her girdle.

"Pleased, I'm sure, Mr. Kyprios." She indicated the chair she had just vacated and moved to a spindle-legged chair beside a night table.

"I know, I should have warned you," said Ionnes, sitting down and finding the seat warm from Sarah's long session in it. "But time, time, as you English say. Time, time, you old gypsy man, eh?"

Sarah said, smiling at Alice, "We're American."

"Same thing, yes? Common heritage," said the Greek. "Of course, American. Palamas has it all in the files. Now, I have something to say, and . . ."

Sarah glanced at a silent Tom. "Of course, this is a surprise."

There was a tap on the door, and a waiter came in carrying a heavy tray, with an ice bucket from which a wine bottle's neck emerged. Another waiter followed with plates of hors d'oeuvre, guarded by a lone fly.

"So, so, I took the liberty of ordering something to celebrate."

Thomas remained solid and silent. Sarah stood, arms folded. "What is there to celebrate? I really think, Mr. Kyprios, your Miss Palamas has made a hell of a mistake in her files. "We're Captain and Mrs. Thomas Hammel."

"But of course. Waiter, open the champagne . . . Kyprios Shipping Lines is about to offer Thomas Hammel the captaincy of the *Pallas Athena*, now at Al-Ahmadi."

Thomas remained expressionless. Sarah reached for her last cigarette.

There was about Thomas Hammel, as his wife always felt, a quality as solid as his New England ancestors who had farmed rocky acres before taking to the slave trade and whaling. Sometimes she felt he was too goddamn stuck with that ability to keep a face, showing little reaction to success, pleasure, or surprise. There was in him a natural ingrained doubt about most things, good or bad.

A loud pop broke the silence as a waiter drew the cork.

Thomas said dryly, "Captain Meyerbeck is too ill to take command again?"

The Greek motioned the waiters to withdraw. Alice passed out champagne. "Captain Meyerbeck is dead, I regret to say. A very loyal man." Kyprios spoke solemnly.

Sarah took a gulp of champagne, spoke earnestly. "He was a damn fine seaman."

"He was," said Thomas. He touched his glass to his lips. "You want me to replace him?"

"Don't look so surprised, Captain. You've handled tankers for nine, or is it ten years?"

"Ten." Thomas motioned with his glass, as if becoming his past. Sarah and Alice sat on the bed.

"You are aware of my history, Mr. Kyprios, and why I, a captain, took a first officer's berth?"

The Greek shrugged, nodded. "The one hundred fifty thousand ton *Eastern Pioneer*? That oil-ore carrier you commanded four years ago. Yes, I saw the IMCO record. She ran aground at Cape Agulhas under your command, after being badly damaged in a storm. The Intergovernmental Marine Consulative Organization has the details."

Sarah said, "Several thousand penguins perished in the oil slick."

Thomas added, "The *Eastern Pioneer* was on the rocks for seven months before being salvaged. There was an investigation, a hearing in Amsterdam. You know the results from the IMCO."

Ionnes looked over at some smeared crackers on the tray—crackers dabbed with what looked like tank sludge, but what he suspected was some cheap fish eggs dyed to look like caviar. He rejected the idea of eating one. He chose instead a pimento stuffed olive, held it without attempting to bite into it.

"Yes, yes, you were exonerated. Fifty-foot waves, a shifting ore cargo. Fully cleared."

"But," said Sarah, pouring herself a second glass of

champagne, "the goddamn grapevine kept whispering lies. That is, that Tom was drinking and had been below dead drunk during the storm and too fluzzled when he got to the bridge to keep the rotten ship off the rocks. And she was a rotten bit of goods, believe me, Mr. Kyprios. Nearly eighteen years old, well past safety. You could punch your fist through her plating, covered with bilge verdigris—and the boilers below, you couldn't hardly see through the fog of steam from the leaks when you put the pressure up."

"Shut up, Dolly," said Thomas.

"I've studied reports, heard the gossip. Captain, my investigations show you haven't been drinking in the last five years. True?"

"True. But that's my private affair." There was a barely discernible twitching along Thomas' jaw line. "If you have any doubts, better get another captain. I'd, however, like to stay on as first officer."

Ionnes turned on that indefinable charm he was known for. Alice watched him closely; she had seen him use that articulate compulsion to have his way. (The talk in business circles being he, Ionnes Kyprios, could charm the devil to give up his horns.)

"Captain, sorry, I have already hired a first officer. He is flying out from Athens tomorrow morning. Achilles Marrkoras. He's been trained on KSL ships. The *Pandora,* the *Theseus,* the *Queen Pasiphae.* Hundred thousand tonners. But I'm sure you know them."

Thomas walked over to the window, looked out. The camel was gone, two women passed tugging a gentle goat, a trailer pulling a mobile home was trying to get into a too-narrow street. Thomas turned back to face the Greek shipowner.

"All right, Mr. Kyprios. Since the first officer's position is filled, I'm sure Marrkoras has the proper certificates, and I'm forced to take the captaincy." He added slowly, "Again."

"A good man who makes up his mind. No false modesty, Captain, no dickering. Nice. I'll have our local people arrange for a maid for Mrs. Hammel. I assume she sails from Al-Ahmadi down the coast with you, Captain?"

"Oh, yes, of course," Sarah said loudly. "I mean I accompany my husband. But a maid . . . it's no cruise ship and I can dress myself even in a fifty-mile gale."

"I'm sure, Mrs. Hammel but the *Pallas Athena* is our pride. I like a contented ship, and this one, as you Americans put it, is class? Now, Miss Palamas is the KSL documentary filmmaker. She'll go along and see what she can bring back from this voyage. She's done the background material . . . the home office, the various dockside projects." Kyprios laughed. "Pure vanity, of course, our documentary angle, but good publicity. Anything else, Palamas?"

Alice adjusted the shoulder strap of her handbag. "That seems to settle the situation." She turned to Thomas, "There is a plane, eight-thirty in the morning to fly us to the ship. Mr. Kyprios is jetting back to Greece."

"Yes, Captain." He held out a hand, and Thomas shook it. Both men pressing a bit hard. Sarah got a bow, and there were the last formal exchanges at parting, and for Thomas, a shoulder slap on an agreement well accomplished.

"It's all too much, Dolly. All at once. I mean, no hint. And I didn't ever expect to be captain of anything impressive again . . . not after. . . . The universe is not rational, I tell myself, has no tacit assumption. Jesus, I lose it— that a captain has to be prepared for anything. Like tonight I was really dropping anchors and no bottom. No bottom at all. It was all bluff."

She was aware the big man was near tears. But he would never drop any. He'd "swallow his toad," as the New England saying was, try to keep a sad self-sufficiency unto himself, 'til he recovered his confidence. There was only one thing to do: get him into bed, make violent passionate love. It was the medicine that, when needed, tore his emotions away from an untouched stratum within him. "Good old Ma-and-Pa fucking" they had called it when they were first together, naked to naked in bed. There was still a good lot of that in them. They were not *that* old. Maybe not as often, or driven with their former manic intensity, but good, hell, yes . . . very good. He was a fine lover and she his ever-ready, lusty girl.

She said, "You know what we need. What's good for us?"

He looked at her, at first puzzled, then amused. He said, "You're a very indecent woman, Dolly, at your age."

"At my age," she sank down against him and put her head in his lap. "I'm still the best lay you'll find in Iran. No cost, sailor. It's on the house."

The banter did not hide the sensitivity of their sensations of the moment. As he caressed her, her head on his lap, she felt his erection. She was flooded with happiness, and she knew body and mind were not, for them, two separate identities, but rather were fused into the most intimate act bodies could share.

In bed, naked, she was for him the all of the moment—large breasted, big hipped, a smooth, pearl-pink flesh. No sagging that mattered, no care that her pubic area under his searching fingers had a hint of gray fuzz. When he was pulled over on her, they stared pleasantly into each other's eyes and moved together in the thrust and give that ended with her wails of delight. His frenzy of expectancy yielded the proper gush of promises. It was moments before he felt again the sense or direction of time. After a while they slept. The fly had become stuck in the false caviar of the hotel's room service and was soon to give up its struggle to work itself free.

CHAPTER 3

The cabin occupied by Second Officer Wallie Ormsbee, on *Pallas Athena* was known to the other officers as "The Bazaar." It contained well-ordered shelves for his camera gear and taped to two walls were samples of his photographic skill—rather stereotyped views of ruins, vistas of rock, and desolation. Boxes held various colored streaks Wallie claimed were topaz, garnet, beryl—even fossil insects in sections of rock. It was pointed out to him that there were never any images of people in his range of photographic subjects . . . "just ruins, and old, old shithouses," Sparky, the radio man, put it.

Wallie was accepted by the officers as a kook, was respected by the crew. He was a good fire-control expert and tank inspector. Yet, he was separated from the ship's staff by his naivete and seen as a man from a world different than the usual tanker complement.

Wallace Anderson Ormsbee had been raised in some of the best hotels in Europe, brought up by a mother who was supported by an Irish Chicago lawyer and whose illegitimate son he was. The lawyer, later a judge and a Papal Knight, had a wife and four other children; his romance with Wallie's mother ended—she had been an interior decorator—after the boy's birth in Paris. But he continued to support them, sending Wallie to the Sorbonne, on the condition that neither mother nor son return to America. It had been a special growing up, knowing maitre d's, skating at the St. Moritz, avoiding hotel managers when the check from Chicago was late ("Ah my darling boy, we have our feet solidly planted in the air"), attending fashion shows; they were times of discovering good little pensions in Rome. Then his mother died suddenly in a hotel—the Hotel Am Parkring in Vienna and he found revealing letters: the judge, too, his father, was dead. Wallie was a bastard with a few shares of municipal bonds.

Discovering one is a bastard at nineteen isn't that much of a shock. It's sort of romantic, Wallie felt. But lonely, too. He had been fortunate; an embassy official in Paris, who Wallie suspected had been his mother's lover at one time, got him a cadet's job on a French ship carrying armaments to North Africa. From there, taking exams, step by step, he earned an officer's position by the time he was twenty-six.

He grew into a role player, appearing worldly, overeducated, dominated by his hobby of photographing ruins. He had a certain shyness with women, an uncertainty, that concealed a brooding, heated fascination with sex as a subject. Mother's best friend and dressmaker had seduced him at sixteen; he still felt the shock of her worldly, intimate maneuvering. Then came a girl, on the night he celebrated with the crew of the old *Dragon Fly*. (The ship had gone down later with all her crew in the Pacific deep, a deep never fathomed. Just disappeared with no trace or signal.) That night's celebration ended in a brothel in Hamburg, and it took a week of penicillin for Wallie to cure himself of his dose of clap. Other than that, he had very few sexual encounters—just some fumbling and hasty fornications when he was taking an extended course last year in the newest tanker fire-fighting methods at the Oil Institute in St. Charles, Louisiana.

Now with *Pallas Athena* loading at Al-Ahmadi in Iraq, he put the day's exposed rolls of film into a carrying bag. *Pallas Athena* had a dark room, and he would develop and print them when they were on the Indian Ocean, at sea, with time on his hands.

It was soon the hour for his tour of duty. He had the twelve to four watch on the bridge. He changed his shirt to the Persian "Sea Rig," white short-sleeved shirt with braided officer's insignia on the shoulder tabs and the letters, KSL.

Suddenly he was aware the oil pumps had stopped. The rumble of the manifolds was silent. He went out on the lower deck. The night heat was no cooler than the day temperatures. The sky pressed down like some black, smothering curtain, and all around in the gulf, gas flares were burning off the surplus from the wells' pumping oil from offshore drillings; other tankers were loading. It was to Wallie like a scene from Doré's illustrations to Dante's *Inferno* he once found in a bookstall on the Seine as a boy: flames rolled uncertainly in the darkness, nearby tankers were lit with work lights, silhouetting the shapes of men on the docks surrounded by the foam tossed up by launches servicing the ships.

Sieko Mihran, first class seaman, a dark Pakistani who was in charge of the crew, was standing by the lee rail.

Looking over the harbor, he smelled the sump spill prime Persian Gulf crude, the snake of the manifold pipe lines going into the harbor and the dark blue shape of *Pallas Athena* taking on 550,000 tons of oil at the rate of 20,000 tons an hour. Sucking it, or rather it being fed her. Her seven great storage areas—twenty-four tanks—being fed like a baby.

31

Sieko's sailor's eye took her in, the *Pallas Athena*, under the Greek-blue and yellow-lettered company flag, KSL. Here she was—his home for two years now—1,506 feet long, the darling; a 190-foot beam, a draft of 95 feet. A finicky bitch in a rough sea.

"Ah, my beauty," he said aloud, balancing himself feet apart.

To most, he knew, she was no beauty, no oil tanker is. Too long, and now riding high with 100,000 tons of salt water ballast pumped out and oil being sent into her inners. The red Plimsoll settling her to the water mark. He became aware of Second Officer Ormsbee and turned and lifted one finger to his forehead in a sort of salute.

"Why, Sieko, has the pumping stopped?"

"Sir, we don't know," said Sieko. "Other ships all still taking on crude."

"Where's the Chief Engineer to check this?"

"Mr. Bowen a little late, sar, but . . ." The seaman looked at him, as if suspecting a too smug fastidiousness.

Wallie nodded, no use being critical of an officer to a crew member, and moved toward the pipes coming aboard the ship. Homer Bowen, he knew, was sleeping off a two-day drunken debauch. A slack ship, with no captain, and old Tom, the first officer, away in Baghdad meeting his wife.

Wallie walked carefully, maneuvering his steps past the oil-stained canvas laid out on the deck. A slip here—a broken leg—and he'd be left behind in this God-awful part of the world. Not that its ruins weren't interesting.

He inspected the manifolds; the silent tubes looked to be in order, their bright orange coverings highlighted by overhead lights. The air-conditioned cubicle, where the recording dials and oil-measuring gauges were housed, was just beyond them. Through the glass door he made

32

out the back of Ludwig Ott, the third officer, bent over some computer part.

"*Ach, du lieber*," he said as Wallie entered. "You want to see why we are not bringing oil aboard? *This.*"

He held up something with a red and blue wire.

"That small, Lud?"

He liked the big German, and he was a damn fine mechanic.

"You see, Wallace, all the fancy dreck runs a ship now. Just a little two-inch spring and the whole shooting match, she begins to record wrong the barrels of crude coming on board. Zo, I find it."

"Will it delay us? We're not supposed to touch these things. There's a special service that repairs them."

"And where? In Cairo, two days delay at least. And I shall have it much all right in half an hour. Zo?" He held up a small part. "This is what is bent. I put a new spare in right off. Any word on a captain?"

"Nothing. I'll check with Sparky. We have to cast off on time to keep to our chart log."

"Bowen, he didn't stand no duty in engine room?"

"It doesn't matter in harbor, Lud."

"Order is order. One time only, one thing wrong, could be kaput."

Wallie didn't disagree as he left, but decided there was a lot of Nazi still, in all Germans. He took the ship's elevator up to the bridge deck. It seemed darker up there, so high above the gulf. Like so many radio room operators Pavel Godoff was called "Sparks" or "Sparky." He could use voice or tap code on his huge wall of gear and intricate panels. Pavel had been in Vietnam with a CIA supported airline as a radio expert. He also knew a great deal about radar and strange weapons.

"Get *much*, Wallie?" He added an obscene finger gesture.

Wallie waved off the idea, "Anything, Sparky, on a captain?"

"Nothing. The big noise himself, one of the top brass brothers, is in Kuwait." He turned to a bubbling glass container of coffee on a hot plate. "Coffee?"

"Black, nothing in it."

Wallie sipped the strong brew, looked over the banks of dials, the various panels of lights gathering in messages. Three times daily they played the "World Oil News" broadcasts in English, French and Arabic—news that seemed vital in the world of oil markets, crude oil carriers, and tanker items of interest to officers and crews.

They heard the manifold pumping start up again.

"That krauthead," said Sparky, "he knows how to keep things running. Anything out of whack is a *kaffeeklatsch* to him. You know he doesn't go ashore to get his nuts off. He has one of those Japanese gismos to beat your meat with. Listen, Wallie, I have this sex shop catalog from Hong Kong. You want to order anything, they ship it to you in a plain brown wrapper."

"I'll take two, Sparky, of anything you use."

"Aw, come off it, I like the real thing." He made gestures of grasping a female anatomy.

Wallie was sure that, like some of the other officers, Sparky imagined him to be a homosexual. It didn't matter. Sparky for all his dirty mind was always good for gossip, for knowing what was going on in the oil world, and among the various ships' officers in the trade.

"Wallie, I'm making book among all tankers in port. You pick a name as to who the new captain will be. Old Meyerbeck is a sucker's bet, he'll never get out of the hospital in Cape Town. I give you five to one it's a Greek sent out from Athens. Even money it's an Englishman; the Kyprioses are snobbish over limeys. Two to one it's a Yank."

"What's the biggest odds you offer, Sparky?"

"Seven to one it's a Frenchman. Ten to one it's first officer, old Tom."

"Why such odds on Tom Hammel?"

"Hell, don't you know he banged a 200,000-ton load ashore? She ended up as salvage."

"If you can pay off I'll put down a five-dollar bet on Tom."

On watch in the darkness on the captain's deck, Wallie made himself comfortable. It was a wide bridge, with the polished controls, the steering gear, gyro compass, engine room signals, sonar alarm, radar, radio feeding inlets and switches, and saluting systems. A bullhorn connected to the ship's address system.

It was all very impressive. KSL had spared no expense in outfitting *Pallas Athena*. Wallie loved the chart room to the left; it had stacks of Royal Navy Hydrographic International Charts, the most recent maps and special information. There was something awe inspiring to it all, and also something that emphasized the dangers of self-deception in working on the sea.

The romance of the sea? Bullshit. He thought of Homer Bowen with his volumes of Joseph Conrad and his desire to write a sea novel, along with his other projected book on Nelson at Trafalgar. Now it was all as neat and clean (except when there was an oil spill) as a cinema lobby. And to Wallie, all as disappointing perhaps as his own great expectations.

Wallie took a small book from a pocket. He began to read, as the manifolds below seemed to raise the rate of oil gushing into the tanker.

Know, O Vizier and the mercy of Allah to be with you, he has furnished woman with a rounded belly and a beautiful navel, and with a majestic crupper, and all these wonders are borne up by the thighs. It is between these that Allah has placed the area of the combat.

The radio room intercom buzzed on the bridge. Wallie picked up the phone.

"Bridge here."

"You lucky bastard! You just won a packet of money."

"What?"

"My captain's sweepstakes, Wallie. Just registered a radio message from KSL, Kuwait. Official. Listen:

THOMAS HAMMEL APPOINTED CAPTAIN OF THE "PALLAS ATHENA," EFFECTIVE AT ONCE.

"End of message . . . it never figured. You'll have to give me a little time to pay off."

"That's all right," said Wallie hanging up.

Old Tom? The long shot?

Know O Vizier and the mercy of Allah be with you . . . In order that a woman be relished by men she must have the kunt projecting and fleshy, from the point where the hair grows, to the arse, the conduit must be narrow and not moist, soft to the touch, and emitting a strong heat . . .

Wallie read no more that watch on the bridge.

The second engineer, Carlos de Nova, was a Portuguese-Goanese of part Hindu ancestry and an ardent Catholic. Carlos worked out with barbells twice a day and had the agility of a monkey around the conduits, shafts, and pressure boilers. With Wallie he led dangerous work parties below when empty tanks had to be cleaned of sludge and explosive gases. Twice he had been felled by hydrocarbon gas pockets while cleaning the tanks after oil was discharged from *Pallas Athena*. He had had to be rescued by Wallie and Homer, wearing gas masks. The gas had an extremely low flash point. A spark could set it off.

On deck Wallie saw the oil coming aboard through the two orange delivery manifolds. The gulf shore was hazy with smoke from the burning flares over the offshore wells. Two of the tankers loading the night before had left for the trip down past the strait.

Wallie saw that *Wallaby II* and the *Turk's Head* were gone. *H.S. Wurdeman* was pulling up anchors, the native pilot gesturing from the bridge, cursing in Arabic and French.

CHAPTER | 4

The captain of *Pallas Athena*, his wife, and her maid, Farashah, and Miss Palamas boarded half an hour late. There was not a great deal of baggage to lift onto the deck of the tanker. The maid, Farashah, had only a bundle tied in red cloth, and a yellow silk umbrella. She was from Madagascar she told Sieko and spoke Swahili mixed with Arabian, *"Leo Yuko Jashu."*

Thomas and Sarah Hammel would discover that most of the native crew, when near the officers, no matter what their origin, spoke to each other in a kind of Swahili to disguise the contents of their comments.

On deck Sarah and Alice found themselves being introduced to the officers. To the German one, Sarah was polite but not smiling—even though he had very clean fingernails. The Second Officer, Ormsbee, looked too young to be an officer, very neat in his compliments to her and much too sure of himself. The Chief Engineer, Bowen, she liked at once. No side to him, a clean living, proper-looking individual. She hoped Tom would bring him into their lives. Sarah prided herself on her judgment of character.

Alice observed the officers and tried to form no opinions—not just yet. The woman called Gemila, in a pink sari, bowed and held her hands in front of her bosom palm to palm, "*Salaam allekum,* I head stewardess. Will show you ladies to the cabins. I am Gemila. My husband is Sieko Mihran. Top sailor rating on board. Whatever the ladies want she will ring? I get, yes?"

"Yes, and have someone bring the camera gear along," Alice said.

Sarah, when she saw the late captain's suite, found Captain Meyerbeck had been a collector of bric-a-brac. The drapes were patterned with tulips, but all in all, Sarah found the living room with its two windows (not just portholes) spacious. The bedroom had two large closets, and an Isfakan rug, and the bathroom, with a shower *and* a huge tub, as well as a dressing table with a mirror circled by light bulbs, was quite satisfactory.

"Here, I could eat pâté de foie gras in bed with a shoe horn."

There was also a small kitchen with a fridge, so she or the maid could prepare snacks.

Thomas was examining control buttons relating to various posts on the ship.

"Jesus, Skip, it's like winning a jackpot." She flung herself down into a too-soft easy chair, tossing her hat across the room in Farashah's direction and reaching for a cigarette from a rosewood box. "Oh I like it, I like it. Room to swing a cat, as we used to say back home."

Farashah was at her side with a lighter, and Sarah lit up and inhaled. "Thanks. Look I don't care too much for fancy service, Farashah. Mind if I call you Fanny?"

"I am here to service. I unpack now." She stood hesitantly, as if expecting a blow or a pat.

"Don't bother, honey. There isn't much. Just go along. I'll ring if I want you."

"You ring, Farashah come very quick." Farashah smiled: She had learned to present an attitude of slight trepidation.

Thomas was taking his officer's jacket out of a carryall.

It was a bit creased, and some of the gold striping was somewhat tarnished, but it fit him well. Putting it on, he felt a surge of assurance. "I'll go inspect the ship, start the crew and officers on their toes. There were loose ropes dangling over the side. Notice them?"

"Don't press, Skip. Get into the driver's seat easy. Easy does it." She kicked off her shoes. "You always had too much sense of responsibility."

"I know how to run a ship, Dolly."

"Sure you do, love." She stretched and exhaled smoke. "I'm going to take a bath, a nice, long, cool bath, and then I'm going to test the bed."

Thomas picked up his cap, rubbed its shiny peak, and adjusted it on his head. "Well, wish me luck. There's a meeting in the wardroom." He looked at his watch. "Kept them waiting four minutes."

She wanted to say, remember there is also a bar there, but she didn't. He wasn't going to take a drink, not now that he had something as big as *Pallas Athena* to command. She flicked an ash onto the glass-topped coffee table, looked over the pale blue walls: a Van Gogh reproduction, a teakwood bookcase with some paperbacks— Irving Wallace, Harold Robbins—and a pile of old *National Geographics*. A big colored photograph in a tarnished silver frame showed Captain Meyerbeck in civies, standing by a fat wife and four fat kids, even a dog. Sarah felt touched by his death; as grandma used to say: "People are dying who never died before. It's the living you have to give your pity to." Another one of grandma's chestnuts. "In your battles against the world, always bet on the world."

Sarah remembered she, too, had once been a Presbyterian. A gloomy lot.

She decided if she didn't get up right away to take that bath, she'd just sit here recounting their lucky stars.

Farashah was also pleased. She was in a small room

down the hallway from the captain's suite. Only one window, but a sink and shower, a narrow cot with a blue blanket bearing the KLS seal. Farashah had rarely had a place all to herself. She could even latch the door when she lit up a bit of hashish. Farashah had large beautiful eyes, honey-colored skin, a well-proportioned body, with protruding pearshaped breasts. She was long limbed and long legged. Farashah had been raised a Christian at a mission, later, a runaway at fifteen, she was owned by a Muslim, a jeweler in Tunis. Then she lived in Durbin with a Frenchman who was in the diamond trade. When his wife came to South Africa the year before, she had become a cabin maid on a Dutch cruise ship. From there, she worked as a waitress at the Nayeb Restaurant in Kuwait, until, out of work, she was placed on the *Pallas Athena* by the manager of the KSL, who had sleeping privileges with her but was being transferred to Syria.

In her room, door latched, Farashah slipped out of her robe, let down her black hair and admired herself in the mirror. She had always enjoyed the ecstatic awareness of her own life. She suspected she was at least nineteen; she never was too sure of her age or origin, but she was not simple. Wary enough to know the world was a hard place, she was confident she could cope. She was respectful of herself, and took pride in having survived male domination. Sensual pleasures could come if one was patient and giving. The ideal of Judeo-Christian morality taught her at the mission school had faded as being impractical and impossible.

She stepped into the shower, sniffed the cake of pink soap and bit into it with her teeth. Tasty.

The bar of the wardroom was open and active. The Chinese boy they called Ping Pong was smiling, mixing drinks and bowing as he set glasses etched with frosty drops on paper napkins with the ship's name.

Thomas held a glass of soda water high and looked over the officers: engineers, the radio men, navigation cadet, electricians.

"I'm not going to make any goddamn speech. I can't act the snooty captain looking over his officers for the first time. I've been mates with you for over a year. You know my faults, and I damn well know yours." He looked at a platter of *pâté d'alouettes* the stewardess had set down.

"Hear!" said Homer Bowen, chief engineer, lifting a glass of light ale. "Hear!"

"I'm a good hardshell captain, when you know my good side. I'm a shit when you get on my wrong side. I'm the captain, and I ask and demand respect for that title. This is a big complex ship, the biggest of its kind. It's here to make money, to make fast runs, to stay out of danger. I can only add, as you all damn well know, no captain can run a ship alone."

Ludwig Ott slapped the bar with the palm of a hand. "Tom, I mean Captain, it's a goot ship and goot officers, and no reason why we shouldn't be a fine happy ship."

"All right. I want the catwalk deck shipshape, no loose cables. And I want painting done, even over the hull. I expect hourly reports on the loading. We hoist the Blue Peter as soon as the new first officer gets here."

Wallie Ormsbee ate a bit of ice from his martini and waved off the tray of spiced meats and fish bits offered him by the stewardess. "He's a Greek, isn't he, sir?"

Thomas set down his glass, clasped his hands behind his back. "Achilles Marrkoras is a fully accredited certified ship's officer. I've checked his papers. I want no standoff attitudes toward him just because we're all so goddamn Anglo and Wasp superior." He glanced around the wardroom and smiled, a tight, friendly grin. "Even if we came from a line of old farts that think they invented the steamboat."

That raised a laugh. Wallie wondered why a captain's jests are always greeted as wit.

"Has a delivery port been posted?"

Thomas took out a sheet of blue paper, looked about him. He set a pair of silver-rimmed eyeglasses in place.

"Destination, the United States, the port of Los Angeles, docking to unload at San Pedro. We move out for Jask, then the Arabian Sea, ease past Dondra Head, the Torres Strait, to skirt the Coral Sea."

"We'll be near monsoon weather this time of the year," Homer said.

"We should be through the area before the monsoons start," added Wallie.

"We'll have a chart run-through soon as Marrkoras gets here. Any word, Sparky?"

"Sandstorm over Kurdistan area, but the plane is over it. Should be here by noon. Private message, sir, for you from Mr. I. Kyprios."

"Thanks."

Thomas took the blue envelope and turned to Ping Pong, the Chinese barman. "Close up in ten minutes. Mr. Ludwig, get me an estimated time of final tank fillings."

"Yes, sir."

"Oh gentlemen, before I forget . . . you're all going to be movie stars. Miss Palamas is aboard because Mr. Kyprios is having a documentary film made. As for Miss Palamas, you will all, naturally, show her the proper cooperation and respect."

"Of course, Captain," said Sparky.

Thomas opened the envelope:

CONGRAD FROM KSL HOME OFF ON CAPTAINCY WE EXPECT U TO PUSH PALL ATH WITH ALL SPEED 2 DESTINATION SAIL SOON AS MARRKORAS ARRIVS GOD SPEED.

He folded the message and wished Sparky filled in home office shorthand. Homer had turned his empty glass bottom side up on the bar.

"Sir, we're all pleased as Punch the way things turned

out. We never expected one of ours would be picked to command the bridge."

"I'm as surprised as anyone. Now, Homer, how long will it take to get steam up?"

"No problem. I started low pressure firing this morning. All I'll need is a couple hours for a full head."

"Everything shipshape below?"

"The boilers are fine, filters keeping out sea water, and the fuel oil by test has a low sulfur content."

"I want economy, Homer. I'll try and get the best run out of her at the lowest fuel consumption.

"I know Greeks, sir. They even watch the toilet paper allowance."

Thomas frowned. "Listen, Homer, it's me, not the KSL home office talking. I'm the one who wants the best runs, at the lowest fuel costs. It's me calling the turns. Understand me, Chief Engineer?"

"Yes, sir, Captain." (Give them authority and they're *all* pricks.)

Achilles Marrkoras turned out to be nothing like what Thomas or the officers had expected. He wore his dark hair long, rather longer than any first officer Thomas had ever met. Nor was his attire at all that of a Greek dandy. He wore a thin, dark, cotton turtleneck sweater, blue jeans with a large brass buckle lettered Wells Fargo. He wore tennis shoes, and on his right wrist, a linked silver bracelet.

He smiled when he shook Thomas' hand in the wardroom, showing excellent teeth.

In his middle thirties, Thomas felt he looked more like the young characters seeking desultory pleasures one saw hanging around the discotheques on New Burlington Street or the jazz joints on the rue Galande.

"Happy to be on board, Captain." His English was casual, almost slurred, but he had hardly any accent. All in all, he did not give the appearance of a ship's officer. But in a short conversation with the captain, he soon proved he knew tankers and had a good mind for details, as he went over the route and talked of the gossip in British Petro circles and Exxon tanker figures. To Homer, when introduced, Achilles seemed knowledgeable about pressure boilers, the 40,000 horsepower needed to drive *Pallas Athena* along at a steady 16 knots. At the bar just before dinner he told a few splendid jokes: one bawdy, two very witty. He seemed an expert.

Waving a braceleted arm, his eyebrows flared upward when he found Wallie Ormsbee was also interested in Dixieland, in Louie and Dizzy, the Monterey Jazz Festival. He was delighted.

"What do you know, a couple of jiving screwballs out here. I have a record player and fifty discs of the solid stuff, and a lot of Columbia oldies, rerecorded."

"Never too much of the early New Orleans stuff."

"Wingy Manone, like him?"

"I don't think I've ever heard him."

"Coleman Hawkins, 'Perdido Street Blues' . . ."

Wallie felt he was in too deep, much beyond his knowledge of jazz history. He was saved by Alice Palamas appearing in a blue linen suit, a camera slung over one shoulder.

"Achilles, you bastard!"

"Alice, you wonderful broad!"

They kissed and smiled at each other with conspicuous feeling.

"Alice, you really making the trip?"

"KSL wants lots of film footage. An epic, Kyprios says."

"Oh God, those cocksuckers are really something." He turned to Wallie, who tried not to notice the language. "Their age is passing; all the fancy, bigtime myths of the Greeks and their ships. It's the Arabs who own the world, the whole fucking world, right, Alice? Islam—the green flag of Allah is again on a *jihad* to take over all us unbelievers."

"I want to film you on the bridge, Achilles, only not in those rags."

"I'm on duty right after dinner—must change."

He gave her a hasty kiss on the cheek, a pat on the hips. "We lift anchor at six in the morning. Good knowing you, Wallace. We'll get together for a session. Ciao." He moved off waving to Homer and Ludwig Ott.

Alice laughed. "Ain't he something, Wallie?"

"I'm no good at assessing people. But he'll add a lot to the trip."

"He will, he will. He's a damn good officer, you know. And for all his name calling, he's some kind of a cousin to the Kyprioses. He'll have his own ship soon, if he ever settles down. Takes nothing seriously but fun with chicks and jazz."

"You're old acquaintances, Miss Palamas?"

"Alice—no last names on this trip. Known Achilles for a few years. Nice. Yes, that's a good word for him, nice." She motioned to the barman. "A vermouth cassis? But he moves too fast for me. I mean, you don't ask a girl if she wants to get laid, do you, the first ten minutes you meet her?"

Wallie laughed, hoping the flush that came to his neck and face didn't show. "No, I don't. I suppose though it's effective at times."

She said, "If you try it, let me know the average yes and no's."

The address system lisped, causing Sparky's voice to be slightly distorted: "Attention. Clear ship for morning sailing . . . pilot due on bridge at 0630 hours. Send all unneeded luggage to storage area, Deck B."

BOOK TWO

ULTRAMARINE BLUE

CHAPTER 5

Chief engineer Homer Bowen kept a series of loose-leaf notebooks in a battered briefcase. He thought of the material as research for the sea novel he had been planning for years. Bits of information, gossip, delighted him—he wrote out literary passages reflecting on the sea, ships, passages that, with a change of names, might become some section of a chapter in the projected volume. How to handle his protagonists in love worried him: too many writers (he jotted down) "have visited the uterus of women as if it were the Grand Canyon or the London underground. Fortunately, a sea novel can dispense with most women characters."

As chief engineer, with two assistants, he was the man who had to see that everything was proper in the engine room, that the boiler joints did not leak, that the evaporator distilled the gulf water so that it was salt free for the boilers—clean steam did not form scale in the pipes. He had to watch the auxiliaries and machines that pumped water, turned generators making energy for the lights and the air conditioning and powering the dials, computers, information units: "All this would cease to function if we fail here," Homer told his Goanese assistant.

* * *

After a hard day, and drinking only two bottles of light ale (Homer never drank hard stuff while at sea), he would tap out his daily quota of notes on his old cast iron Underwood portable:

Sailing Day—Al-Ahmadi. Up went the Blue Peter that purple-blue banner with its shape of dead white in the center . . . why it's called a Blue Peter I don't know, but it's the signal up over the bridge that the ship is going to sail. Also flying was the Liberian flag. Steam was up and the pilot, a fiesty little dark man in a gray pin-striped suit like a film gangster, with one gold-edged tooth up front, greeted us cheerfully on the bridge. I was there with the captain, and the new first officer, a Greek. Steam had been up for an hour, and I had come to the bridge to report in person that all was in order. The Greek gave the impression his genitalia were always on red alert. The captain said of my report, "Very good, Mr. Bowen. Stay on bridge in case our pilot wants information on our horse-power and boiler pressures."

"I know de sheep chanals," said the pilot, "very treteras, just you able to give me quick power if I ast for her."

I said "yes," and the address system called out "Stations, fore and aft."

Whatever kind of way out character the Greek Achilles Marrkoras is, he's a goddamn good first officer. He was at the controls of the switch bank, the consoles of flips and buttons that are the modern tankers' electronic control of the ship. The captain nodded to Seaman First Rating Sieko at the wheel, the pilot at his side. Captain Hammel at his ease, arms clasped behind his back, all of us officers aware of our clean starched whites, our caps set on sailing day level. The pilot called, "Under way."

The hull vibrated. The captain nodded, and Achilles turned the bridge indicator to half speed. The ship took a few seconds to answer. Wallie, the second officer, had the bridge action log open and was recording details of our getting under way.

The pilot standing by the angled windows was watch-

ing the shoreline and the dozen anchored tankers still loading. We all seemed jubilant with the momentum of moving.

The pilot spoke softly. "If you please twelve degrees starboard on de wheel."

"Twelve degrees," repeated Sieko, hands on the wheel's spokes.

"Maintain half speed."

"Maintain half speed," repeated Wallie.

Now Pallas Athena was moving. White and green water flecked with oil stains like fat in a cooking pot was set up by her bow. Below us we could see the catwalk and the long shape of the tanker; the main deck seemed far off.

The pilot called out, "Steady."

"Steady."

Achilles looked up from a chart. "We'll take the port side of the gulf?"

"Best for current. Two-four-two," said the pilot.

"Two-four-two."

The shore was still with us but looking a bit out of focus. There's always a kind of birth trauma on leaving, Wallie insists—pulling up our mooring lines—and going out to make one's lonely way on the water. Wallie is spooky . . . leaving this goddamn burned-over land, its greedy merchants and conniving whores . . . I got taken for 25,000 rials ($350) . . . goodbye the whole sticky harbor. Still, there is a sense of loss in departure.

Ping Pong, the wardroom boy, came to the bridge with a tray of coffee and tea. I took coffee as did the pilot.

The pilot sipped and showed his gold-trimmed tooth in a smile. "Every ninety-five minutes you know a tanker, he sails out of de Persian Gulf. De gulf very busy place."

The Greek Achilles brushed a strand of his hair to the back of his neck. "Is there a rule loaded tankers must remain at least forty miles apart when at sea?"

"Not de official rule, you know, but a good one for sailing over oceans. Here in gulf that not possible. Traffic jam, you know."

Later we went past the spiky up-thrust United Arab offshore wells at Abu Musa. Being fully loaded we were clumsy, pinched between Oman Point and Qeshm on the Iranian side in that narrow Strait of Hormuz. A tanker is no greyhound of the sea, more like a constipated elephant.

The whole gulf seemed lit up by flares burning off gas from hundreds of offshore rigs; navigating among and around them the pilot needed skill, nerve and confidence, and our pilot had those qualities.

"Two-five-nought."

"Two-seven-o."

"Dead slow."

"Dead slow."

I had a sense of the open sea as we moved through the strait, and then a bit more speed where it widened. The pilot seemed pleased. He had one more cup of coffee, picked up his red dispatch case.

"Half mile ahead, you know, you drop me, Captain."

"Thank you, Mr. Katoum," said the captain. "Well done."

"Ist my job." He put on a waterproof jacket. Below on the port side I could make out a tugboat jockeying on a rising, dipping sea. The pilot went down to the main deck, and Wallie supervised the letting down of a ladder. Accompanied by a roll from the ship, the pilot vanished. Then the tug was in view again, the pilot on its deck waving. The tug gave two blasts on its whistle, and the captain nodded to the Greek, who pressed off two deeper toned blasts on our own hooter.

The Greek said, "Captain, we are now entering the Gulf of Oman."

Below us on the main deck Miss Palamas was busy with a large camera.

"Very good, Mr. Marrkoras," said the captain.

I wondered if old Tom was as calm as he appeared, in command of his first tanker in some time, this one with 500,000 tons of oil to take through the Indian Ocean and across the Pacific. Twenty-four officers and technicians from the map cadet Rusty on up to his own three top *rankers, also, forty-eight in crew—a mixed lot of what some call "good wogs." And on Pallas Athena, superb, majestic; on the surface, all was serene.*

I gave a quick salute. "Going below, sir."

"Fine, Homer. Mr. Marrkoras, full speed."

"Full speed, Captain." He rang the engine room. "Full speed at two."

We all watched the bridge clock, moving toward two o'clock. A few seconds away. Wallie set the log recorder at zero. The Greek said, "Engine room. Clocks synchronized now," with one last glance at the clock as its minute hand hit twelve. At two: "Full speed."

Wallie began to write in the log. "Log register all in order, sir."

The captain nodded and I could see a quiver of a rebel muscle along one side of his jaw. I turned to see Miss Palamas come to the bridge with a hand-held camera taking the scene. She had a professional smile, intent on her work. I wondered if I could use her in my novel. I mean a modern woman, rather attractive in a dark way. But too caustic and ironic from the little I've seen of her. In fiction you need more of a sexual object that just reeks with sensuality, suggesting strong emotional stimulus—having that dreamlike quality of Hemingway's girl in the sleeping bag or the contessa in the gondola. But he's out of fashion. It's a problem this sex/love business in a novel. You have to have it. But as I plan to keep mostly to the sea in my major scenes, I'll use the female characters just when needed for plot points. Certainly Alice Palamas is not good material for a novelist.

Now we are at sea. In my world I'm looking down from sixty feet through the grating to the engine room below.

Truth is an engine room is the heart of any ship—and its lungs are the boilers. Must point this out. Perhaps use them as symbols in the novel, relating them to the human body. Steam at sea is a life giving force that moves the limbs of the ship. (I love this ship, ungainly as she is.)

In classic mythology Athena was a mortal, the daughter of King Triton. She was playing (ball?) with the young goddess, Pallas, and the play became so violent that Athena was killed. So the goddess adopted her name and made an effigy of her. I wonder if the Kyprios brothers knew of this when they named the vessel. So, is there a true omen in it . . . or am I being too fucking literary?

Thomas Hammel sat on the bed, his shirt off, while Sarah's manipulating fingers dipped in body oil moved over his shoulders and neck.

"Relax, Skip, your muscles are set hard as a constipated dog's."

"A little more on the right side of the neck. Ah . . . ah . . . that's *it* . . . just *there*."

"You were tiptop today. Like you were in the old days."

"Nobody is like they were in the old days, Dolly. They were really the *young* days."

Sarah caressed the firm flesh, a bit spotted by the aging process but holding up fine.

"Here, let me get at your throat muscles."

He shifted around and her fingers slid along the front of the corded neck, touching, rubbing, kneading.

On the left side of the hairy chest a silvery button marked where a pacemaker had been implanted. It was buried under the skin to signal a thump every third second, to keep the heart doing its work. The fact of this surgery eighteen months ago in Boston was not on his record. It was the couple's worrisome secret: maritime corporations don't entrust valuable ships to a captain with an irregular heartbeat corrected by a mechanical device, activated by a dime-sized battery.

There was a tap on the door. Sarah quickly flung a shirt around Tom's torso. Farashah came in with a tray held breast high.

"I bring in thermos of hot soup and drinking watah. Also turkey sandwiches."

"Thank you, Fanny. Just put it down."

"Anything else, you ring."

"Nothing else. Goodnight, everything is fine."

"*Asante,*" she said in Swahili for "thank you."

Farashah went to her cabin shaking her head. It was dreadful to be old, to be wrinkled, to lose one's youth and the spring to one's body. Not to sleep in two's and make love. She rinsed her mouth, laughed out loud, and began to suck on an orange Ping Pong had given her. Very funny fella Ping Pong. He had smiled and made a gesture, thumb and forefinger in a circle probed by the thumb of the other hand, reciting, "Fuckee fuckee. Very much fuckee, very good time tonight."

She had answered by her hand in the Earth-Witness position. No, she didn't like Chinese. She could do better on this fine ship. The second and the third engineer. Maybe one of the white ones on the bridge—they all like the *yin* and *yang*, people did every place she had been.

Dropping her robe she admired herself in the mirror, fondled her breasts. Before getting into bed, from old habit, she repeated a phrase that had been impressed on her during her childhood in the mission school. She now used it as a talisman against the evil eye:

"*Kwani kwa hieyo. Mungu alivyouprnda* . . . for God so loved the world that he gave his only begotten son . . ."

She got into bed and felt the slight roll of the ship, then a more pronounced dip, heard the faint purr of the engines, the slap and hiss of the waves against the hull. She made love to herself skillfully, maneuvering her body in delight. She climaxed and felt drowsy. One more day done with, and she fell asleep with her finger in her pudenda. She dreamed of shaking palm fronds, shaggy goats scampering over rocky heights, the scent of sandalwood.

On the darkened bridge Wallie was staring ahead at the

cresting sea, the rolling motion was getting stronger. He hoped he didn't get seasick. He was rather ashamed that the first few days of a sea voyage found him upchucking and under the weather.

A hooded light threw into focus the seaman, Abdullah, at the wheel: a handsome Arab but for two scars on his right cheek and a badly sewed-up lower lip that left him with an ironic grimace.

The ship was held on course by automatic controls, steered by electric nerve contacts, under Wallie's control, if needed. There was always a sailor at the wheel in case the radar, the sonar, the radio room gave an alarm for something out of the ordinary; then the officer on watch could switch to manual control, take over, and alert the captain.

Abdullah was not very talkative. Wallie, on bridge watch, repressed a yawn and thought of Sarah Hammel, of Alice Palamas; he thought a lot about girls, women, sex; mentally he was sexually aggressive. But just then he was thinking of Alice's cameras. She had two 16mm Japanese movie cameras with a rich assortment of lenses. Also, a small B & H 8mm. Wallie had only used still cameras; he liked to crop and develop his negatives in various forms. He had never taken motion pictures.

He had asked her at breakfast about some of the mechanics of movie-making, hoping she didn't think he was making a pass.

He began to bring the log up to date, writing in a large, even script. Abdullah scratched his right ear.

Below in the kitchens a machine was kneading dough for tomorrow's bread. The Chinese baker, Po Lai, was preparing rolls for breakfast. Before putting them into the electric oven, he filled his mouth with milk and sprayed the liquid over the rolls. It gave them a nice glazed surface that the officers so admired. He pushed the rolls into the oven, turned off the kneading machine. The master chef, Duck Fong, a fat man from Peking, came out of the food locker with the carcass of a lamb and a wheel of sausages linked over one arm. He yelled at a kitchen boy. "*Yiping pigyou*, a bottle of beer!"

In the humming engine room all was on automatic controls. The second engineer, Carlos, sat under a hanging light, reading *The Hulk*, a comic book.

In the various cabins the crew slept, except for two seamen on the work crew who were engaged in consummating an intricate love affair.

Seven and a half feet below the surface of the main deck the oil lay thick in various tanks—twenty of them—moving heavily to the roll of the ship, oil sloshed against steel walls, walls not dangerously pitted by acid action from the sulfur content of old cargos. No lights were on in the tanks, but in the passageways, and in corners reached by iron rungs, dim bulbs glowed.

First class seaman Sieko Mihran slept with his wife, Gemila, she snoring slightly. He awoke thinking he smelled hydrocarbon gas. He inhaled, exhaled. No gas. Just the intimate smell of a mellow wife, his own personal odors, and the mango chutney they kept in their small frig. He went back to sleep, aware the sea was less noisy—a sign of fog perhaps; a sea he respected as inconsistent and unrestrained.

Up in the radio room Sparky was listening to rock and roll music from Hong Kong and reading last month's issue of *Single Signals*, the swingers' publication edited in Venice, California.

ESP PARTY
PANEL OF 3 PSYCHIC EXPERTS!

Hell, he'd not be in port in time for that sexual hoedown. He switched the radio dials, picked up the tanker

Dunbar off the Cape, shifted to the coded ticks that could only be that Soviet submarine some place in the Indian Ocean, code name ZDRAHF—STVOOY—T, . . . He switched back to Hong Kong, shivered as he imagined a Russian submarine torpedo banging right into the guts of *Pallas Athena,* exploding in the terrifying beauty of flame and smoke.

Overhead the sky was velvet dark, the star clusters clear. The weather reports had come on in the radio room. "A belt of bad weather extends across Siberia from Vat Vilyuisk to Cape Lopatka, and beyond Japan an east-ward moving storm system is developing. Great swath of clouds cover most of Hawaii, fog fields appear in Indian Ocean. In the northwest quadrant good weather appears constant at this time."

Six bells rang out slowly and automatically.

CHAPTER | 6

The captain insisted on neatness: an officer shaved daily, appeared on the bridge in clean gear. Tom wasn't too strict about the type of dress. At a "pour on" or late afternoon bar time, he didn't mind tropical shorts. That was informal sun-downer time. But at dinner he liked trousers, an attire that was called "the Red Sea Threads" by Homer. Perhaps no tie or jacket; but the captain would expect the officers at the table to wear a silk cummerbund holding up black trousers, with the short-sleeved, pale blue shirt, the standard KSL garment, with its insignia of rank braided on the shoulder tabs.

Relationships were soon on a first name basis—all but the captain.

Gemila saw to it the Chinese waiters wore freshly white starched jackets, placed the daily menus before each diner against a small holder in the shape of a tanker. Achilles mixed his own salads.

Dinner chimes were not to be ignored. In the air-conditioned ship, a dry 65 degrees, hot food was served on heated dishes. The great freezers contained (Achilles had checked the lists) beef, pork, game hens, and the stuffed bodies of hens and ducks, smoked fish, cheese, eggs for omelettes, sausages (Ludwig's favorite) for those who desired them. For galas, Gemila produced caviar, sturgeon, lobster, and shrimp. There were a number of men who liked Indian food, too, with Major Gray's chutney. (Homer's notes listed vindaloos, popadoms, ha chow mein, ap kon, bamya bourani.) Homer added, "Officers are cosmopolitan on board *P.A.* as to food, but a good roast beef, grilled lamb chops, roast pork remain favorites. A savory Yorkshire pudding continued to prove most of us officers are Anglos.

"The crew have their own native chef and his assistants who prepare pescado frito fish, tchechuka for the Simolies; also West Indies sambals; for the Hindus bhujija eggplant and machhali curries; the Moslims, kibbi lamb and di jaj chicken. Details I feel I can use in my novel . . ."

The captain saw to it that the shakedown of the *Pallas Athena* at sea took place without any great problems. There were lifeboat drills, fire drills; twice a day "World Oil News" (an overseas radio program) was broadcast by the public address system, giving reports in English, French, and Arabic. Thomas Hammel was fully accepted as captain, the watches among the officers went smoothly. A minor knife fight among two of the crew members, releasing some pent-up intensity, ended with a slight knife gash on one man's upper arm. The disagreement, Duck Fong explained, seemed to be about the affections of a kitchen boy. "Ha hee-hee—much time tubble over love."

The captain, to make an example, locked the seaman who had begun the fracas, in the brig—actually a place for spare cables with a steel door and a strong lock. The sentence was five days, with a slop bucket to serve the needs of nature. The duty to empty the bucket and bring down the bread and water was assigned to the other member of the affair. The kitchen boy was removed from his duties as vegetable scrubber, dustbin cleaner and attached to the photo dark room, where he helped Alice carry cameras and film while she exposed 16mm footage of her filming.

Sarah presided at coffee and tea time; Wallie who was always in attendance told her: "Reminds me of mother's teas at Nice."

The officers gathered in the wardroom for a late afternoon "pour on," with Ping Pong busy at the bar. At ease, they talked over the daily runs. The tanker was making its steady 16 knots an hour, Achilles reported. After they had passed point Ra's al Hadd and headed into the Arabian Sea, Wallie noted in the log: "Twenty degrees Lat, seventy degrees Lon . . . sighted 40,000-ton tanker, *Simfornia* Panama register, heading in ballast for Singeh . . . whales breaching off port."

Achilles Marrkoras, to the captain's delight, was a good officer; he entertained in his cabin, playing jazz recordings—Cootie Williams, Art Tatum, Buddy Rich—and serving Tarama caviar appetizers. "I must have Duck Fong make us some dolmades—the stuffed vine leaves."

Wallie enjoyed the jazz, discovered Mingus, ate the red pike caviar, admired the Greek's state of comfort at sea.

"You like the life at sea?"

"I love it, Wallie." He was wearing a shirt, open to the navel, showing a heavy growth of black curly hair on his chest. His blue jeans were snug, his feet bare. Achilles, smoking a cigar, was going through a stack of records. "We Greeks have been a people afloat even before Homer sent the fleets against Troy. We beat the arse off the Persian kings, the invaders in their ships. I miss, in truth, only the fucking. I'm not like some Greeks with the pretty boys. It has to be a woman." He grasped the biceps of his left arm with his right hand. "Um! And you, too?"

Wallie nodded like an old cocksman in agreement, not

wanting to commit himself. He had not been disturbed by the nearness of Alice Palamas in the dark room, but he preferred swimming in the pool with Sarah. There was a personal smell to the captain's wife, like ripe fruit stored in a sunny place; and her legs, as she dried off after a swim, were the most shapely he could remember for such a plump woman. When she wore a dress at dinner, after a day in pants, her shapely buttocks preceding him to the dinner area reminded him of periods of intimacy, of himself on the periphery of some romantic revelation.

Achilles' attitude was less lyrical in the matter of the female. Wallie saw him as a hedonist, simple and direct; "There is only life," he told Wallie, "Life is what? Pleasure, the sense of touch, yes?"

"There's emotional, sensory, nonsexual moods."

"No surface accessibility? Bullshit. Women, food, drink, gambling. I place them above painting, poetry, music. I like the arts, of course. We Greeks invented most of them—huh? But . . ." he repeated the bicep grasping.

Achilles felt limited by lack of prey. He indexed in his mind the women aboard *Pallas Athena* . The captain's wife was too high in the ship's pecking order, too long in the tooth, too mature, but she must have been a dish in her time. Alice? No, too close to Ionnes Kyprios. And she had that independent look, that pride in herself that called—he remembered their first meeting some years ago—for a long period of palsy-walsy friendship, intimacy, conversation breaking down resistance. That was for land, when one had leisure. So, there was Gemila, the stewardess, wife of the rough-looking Pakistani sailor. A ripe woman, round and curved. But with a husband like Sieko, it could be a knife or a push overboard on some dark night.

So there was Farashah, the captain's maid: the best of the lot really, he thought, as he sat in the wardroom watching her assist Ping Pong at the bar, passing trays of food. Marvelously built, limber, graceful, loose in her native robe, a pale blue and yellow design; the best body on board and limpid promise in her sloe-eyed face. Yet by her look—a simple enough native girl, no neurotic qualities. A directness, almost a boldness, as she bent over him offering watercress sandwiches. Marvelous boobs and eyes—large dark eyes outlined by a bit of black chalk as women did in Asia.

He shook his head at the offer of buttered bread and green weed.

"Karibu chakula."

"No thank you, Farashah."

She nodded and moved on. He enjoyed the movement of her body under the robe, relished the long legs.

The address system gave its robot cough, its rattle, cut off the soundtrack of what were called tea-time tunes.

THIS IS 'WORLD OIL NEWS' BROADCASTING INFORMATION RELATING TO THE OIL INDUSTRY, SHIPS' LOADING AND EVENTS AT SEA.

There was a lowering of voices among the people in the wardroom. Homer finished his ale. Sarah put down a copy of *The Two-Percent Solution*. The broadcast continued.

TWENTY MILES OFF CAPE ST. FRANCIS, SOUTH AFRICA, TWO AMERICAN-OWNED SISTER SUPERTANKERS COLLIDED IN MORNING FOG AND ARE BURNING OUT OF CONTROL IN THE INDIAN OCEAN. A THREE-MILE-LONG OIL SLICK THREATENS POPULAR RESORT BEACHES.

TWO SEAMEN REPORTED MISSING AND EIGHTY-TWO OTHERS, MOSTLY CHINESE, WERE RESCUED BY TWO PASSING SHIPS AND A HELICOPTER. AN UNIDENTIFIED AMERICAN ENGINEER WAS AMONG THOSE RESCUED AFTER THE 330,000-TON VESSELS "WACO" AND "JEWEL" SMASHED INTO EACH OTHER ABOUT 9:45 A.M.

PORT AUTHORITIES SAID BUNKER FUEL OIL SPILLED FROM THE TANKERS BUT IT WAS BELIEVED MILLIONS OF GALLONS OF CRUDE OIL BEING CARRIED AS CARGO ON ONE OF THE VESSELS WAS STILL INTACT.

"AS FAR AS POLLUTION OF THE COASTLINE IS CONCERNED, THE IMPLICATIONS OF THE COLLISION ARE ENORMOUS," SAID JAMES BULBY OF THE MARINE BIOLOGICAL RESEARCH INSTITUTE IN DURBAN.

A SPOKESMAN FOR LLOYDS OF LONDON REPORTED THAT EACH VESSEL WAS INSURED FOR $27 MILLION, MAKING THE COLLISION ONE OF THE MOST COSTLY MARITIME ACCIDENTS.

AN HOUR AFTER THE COLLISION FORTY KNOT WINDS FANNED THE FLAMES AND HAMPERED FIREFIGHTING TUGBOATS FROM REACHING THE LIBERIAN-REGISTERED SHIPS.

THE FULLY LOADED 330,954-TON "WACO" WAS CARRYING 95.5 MILLION GALLONS OF CRUDE OIL, WHILE THE 330,869-TON "JEWEL" WAS EMPTY. BOTH ARE OWNED AND OPERATED BY A SUBSIDIARY OF PETRO TRANSCONTINENTAL CARRIERS.

THE SUPERTANKERS, 1,115 FEET LONG AND 176 FEET WIDE, WERE ON CHARTER FOR WORLD ORBIT OIL CORPORATION.

THE VESSELS WERE REPORTED DRIFTING APART BY NIGHTFALL AND SHIPPING AGENTS SAID THE "WACO" WAS NO LONGER IN DANGER OF SINKING, AS OFFICIALS HAD EARLIER FEARED. FIRE IS CONFINED TO THE BOW OF THE "WACO" AND THERE IS A SAFETY COFFERDAM BETWEEN THIS AND THE STORAGE TANKS. "PROVIDING THE COFFERDAM HOLDS," SAID THE ASSISTANT PORT CAPTAIN HERE.

PORT AUTHORITIES SAID THE "JEWEL" IS BURNING AT THE STERN.

There had been comments during this news. Some remarks about carelessness and the failure of safety methods. The captain looked up from the soda water he had been sipping: "The Cape has always been the worst place for tankers."

Ludwig Ott said, "*Jewel* has always been a bad luck ship."

Homer disagreed, "A ship isn't lucky or unlucky. It's the way she's handled."

63

The broadcast continued:

A 60-MILE-LONG OIL SLICK IS BUILDING, AS OBSERVED BY HELICOPTER. SOUTHWESTERLY WINDS ARE BLOWING THE SPILL PARALLEL TO THE SOUTH AFRICAN COAST, AND THE OIL SPILL POSES A SERIOUS POLLUTION THREAT TO THE AREA'S RESORT BEACHES.

THE COLLISION OCCURRED TWENTY MILES OFF CAPE ST. FRANCIS, WEST OF PORT ELIZABETH. THE "WACO" HAD BEEN LOADED AT KHRAG ISLAND IN THE PERSIAN GULF AND WAS TRAVELING THE REGULAR SUPERTANKER ROUTE AROUND THE CAPE OF GOOD HOPE, HEADED FOR NOVA SCOTIA.

THE "JEWEL" WAS HEADED FOR THE GULF TO PICK UP ITS CRUDE OIL CARGO EN ROUTE TO A EUROPEAN PORT. IT APPEARED THE STARBOARD SIDE OF THE "WACO" COLLIDED WITH THE STARBOARD BOW OF THE "JEWEL" WHICH IMMEDIATELY CAUGHT FIRE. ESTIMATED VISIBILITY WAS TWO MILES IN THE COLLISION AREA.

THE "JEWEL'S" CREW OF THIRTY-EIGHT HONG KONG CHINESE ABANDONED SHIP WHEN THE BLAZE BROKE OUT, MOST LEAPING INTO THE WATER.

EIGHTY-TWO CREWMEN WERE RESCUED BY TWO PASSING MERCHANT SHIPS—THE "GODOFF" AND "STARKWEATHER"— AND A HELICOPTER PILOT, WHO DASHED THROUGH SMOKE AND FLAMES TO PICK UP SIXTEEN SURVIVORS FROM THE BURNING DECK OF THE TANKER BEFORE ADDITIONAL HELP ARRIVED.

Sarah reopened her book, "I'm just as happy we're crossing the Pacific rather than making the Cape run. It's always a stinker."

Wallie said to her. "Well, we're trading the Cape for monsoons."

Achilles smiled. "Too bad, that accident. But I like to see it socked to the greedy insurance companies. They love the fees, but oh how they hate to pay out. Red tape enough to tie up a herd of elephants."

The captain held up a hand. "Let's hear the broadcast."

SURVIVORS WERE BROUGHT TO CAPE TOWN FOR MEDICAL TREATMENT.

THE JAPANESE-BUILT, FOUR-YEAR-OLD SISTER SHIPS WERE TRAVELING UNDER THE FLAG OF THE WEST AFRICAN REPUBLIC OF LIBERIA, WHERE THE WORLD'S LARGEST MERCHANT FLEET—ABOUT 2,600 VESSELS—IS REGISTERED . . . A MERE FORMULA.

THE RELATIVE SAFETY OF THE LIBERIAN REGISTRY CAME INTO QUESTION EARLIER THIS YEAR WHEN FOUR LIBERIAN-REGISTERED TANKERS, THE "ARGO MERCHANT," "OLYMPIC," "OSWEGO-PLACE," AND "SANSINENA," WERE INVOLVED IN ACCIDENTS.

The broadcast began to repeat itself in French. There was animated talk among the officers. When Wallie went out on the main deck he could hear the broadcast in Arabic and a chattering commotion among the crew.

Sieko inspected the canvas covers on the lifeboats and said to Wallie, "Very bad news, sar."

"It happens."

"No one obeys the rule. Tankers must stay forty miles apart."

"It was man failure. A technician or frivolous conduct on the bridge."

"Maybe so, sar, but too much automatic steering, too much sailing on automatic pilot. Depending on radar, oh yes, not on human eye. Sailing by human eye, sar, serves a ship better."

The Cape affair took up a lot of the conversation for the next few days. Everyone listened carefully to the daily "World Oil News" broadcasts, which were no longer taken up with tanker figures, details of oil deals, and the doings of the big cartels.

Between his duties on the ship, Wallie felt it was good to feel alone, to suffer, perhaps from a closed-in heart. But at times is it also, he asked himself, a self-deception, a life unedited, not fully spontaneous? Like Achilles, he respected the captain and, in a fiesty tattiness of mind, lusted for the closeness of a shipboard friendship with his wife. He told himself, I am gripped by emotional circumstances . . . to whom can I turn?

He could talk to Homer Bowen, the chief engineer, but only of things not related to *Pallas Athena*: the man was well read. But talks with Homer had to be abstract, not touching on the uncertainties, the insecurities of his personal situation.

Example: Mother has come back to my dreams. I still hold a romantic fidelity to a past when "style and panache," as Mother (that invisible presence) called it.

Wallie would stand on the main deck after directing a well-run fire drill, and look out at the spaciousness of the sea and feel the fragility of the present, even while standing on the solid steel of the deck. The detail in his intense dreams had increased, and Sarah was in them with no mood of reticence to his attentions. Just kept that ironic smile of hers and a touch of wanton willingness. The dream would end in vapid fatuities; he'd be in bed and hear the hurried footsteps of sailors below, active on the deck, the sound of the Chinese waiters in the corridors picking up the trays of some late night binge.

One morning on deck he sat by the swimming pool; Sarah was there, he lit her cigarette, and handed her the chiffon scarf the wind had blown off the back of the chair. Sitting in his deck chair he didn't dare face her, express himself fully. He might expose, he feared, the sublimated infantilism of his infatuation for an older woman. He planned speeches, then failed to speak. How could he say, you are in many ways, like mother; here we are drifting on the abundant spread of the sea (and I dream I hold your hand, I stroke your cheek and you mine), can I dare, do I dare, use this moment—as you get up and stand in that tight, white bathing suit, fine arms out, about to plunge into the blue-green pool.

Fear of rejection streaked through him.

* * *

"Oh hell, I'm wet," she said, pulling off her yellow cap and getting out of the pool, holding out a hand for him to give her a cigarette, then changing her mind.

"No, don't hand it to me. I hate a wet smoke. Put it in my mouth."

"I ought to say you smoke too much."

"Ha! Words and music I hear all the time."

"You like to live dangerously?"

She studied him after he lit her cigarette, and she lifted a bit of tobacco off one of her front teeth which were charmingly overlapping, personalizing her features.

"I live life the way it's handed out. You don't order it from a waiter, Wallie, and the chef doesn't whomp it up special for you. You learn to take the horseshit with the roses."

She was irremediably vulgar, he thought. Yet he wouldn't want her otherwise. As he watched her smoke he was in an ascendant phase of joy, enjoying her, being near that good, strong, fully woman's body, overflowing here and there from the white bathing suit.

"You know, Wallie, someone pampered you. You're spoiled rotten in some ways. Women, I think. Your old lady? I bet she was a Virgo—they're ball-busters."

"Mother? She had her hard times. She did try and see I got some sense of balance in a precarious world."

"Very fancy talk for a Virgo to a Sagittarius." As the ships' bells rang she stood up, slapped his shoulder. "Gotta dress. You'll let me do your horoscope? You promised."

"I'm on watch." He handed her the worn linen handbag.

"I lost your hour and day notes. Fill me in again," she called.

He watched her walk to the small dressing room beyond the pool. The shake and grace of her body retreating from him gave him the quivers: oh, oh, he thought, I'd like to kiss those buttocks, hold tight, cry out, declare myself, and sleep, sleep in those warm, rounded arms.

A kitchen boy came in sight with a loaded bucket and flung green leaves over the side. Thinking he was alone, he flung the bucket after it and began to weep.

Noon broadcast of "World Oil News":

THE FEDERAL GOVERNMENT FILED SUIT IN U.S. DISTRICT COURT SEEKING A $100 FINE AGAINST A MAN WHO SPILLED A PINT OF OIL IN THE SWINOMISH CHANNEL. ACCORDING TO THE SUIT, RON KESTER IGNORED TWO WARNINGS BY THE COAST GUARD LAST APRIL TO REMOVE A PILE OF EMPTY OIL CANS FROM HIS SEAPLANE SERVICE DOCK. RESIDUAL OIL LATER WAS FOUND IN THE CHANNEL AND IDENTIFIED AS OIL FROM KESTER'S CANS. THE COAST GUARD ASSESSED A $100 PENALTY AGAINST KESTER BUT HE REFUSED TO PAY FOR THE SPILL OF ONE PINT OF OIL. KESTER CLAIMS, "THEY WOULDN'T DO THIS TO EXXON, YOU BET YOUR SWEET A. . . ."

CHAPTER 17

Only Homer, the persistent note-taker, was impressed by the vast sums mentioned on the "World Oil News." Most officers and seamen rarely thought of money in sums beyond their pay. But Homer differed; he wondered how to work the last broadcast material into his projected novel:

THE MEMBERS OF THE ORGANIZATION OF PETROLEUM EXPORTING COUNTRIES HAVE EARNED $500 BILLION IN THE LAST FOUR YEARS. THEIR EARNINGS THIS YEAR, BEFORE THE LARGE OIL PRICE RISES, TOTALED $80.8 BILLION.

CALCULATED EARNINGS IN FOUR YEARS: $146.03 BILLION, IRAN; $89.11 BILLION, VENEZUELA; $42.17 BILLION, KUWAIT; $36.90 BILLION, NIGERIA; $36.51 BILLION, IRAQ; $32.92 BILLION, LIBYAN JAMAHIRIYAH; $31.72 BILLION, UNITED ARAB EMIRATES; $30.2 BILLION, INDONESIA; $22.39 BILLION, ALGERIA; $18.25 BILLION, QATAR; $8.39 BILLION, GABON; $3.13 BILLION AND ECUADOR, $2.3 BILLION.

"Hell of a lot of loot," he told Carlos, his first assistant. "For me, chief, anything over the cost of keeping one wife and three kids in Bombay and one wife and two kids in Brooklyn doesn't mean much."

"You like children, Carlos?"

"Oh yes, wives, too."

By the time they sighted the Laccadive Islands and were in the Indian Ocean, the wardroom talk had shifted to cricket scores from the BBC and complaints about the lousy movies that everyone had seen at least three times. Achilles, in the wardroom, read the *London Illustrated News* and eyed Farashah.

Waves were running high, carrying, as Homer wrote in his notes:

> . . . *White foam in their teeth as the sea slapped against the hull. The ship rides well; she is so long she does not dip and fall away when a wave comes on, but takes their assaults two by two and seems buoyed fore and aft by them.*

Achilles, as second officer, was not a man to shirk his duty. In fact, as Tom told Sarah, "I find him a bit too eager—a bit too ambitious to serve."

They were taking their afterdinner stroll along the well-lit catwalk. "You're just too damn much the captain, Skip. You have to show your authority."

"Now, Dolly, I didn't say the Greek wasn't a top ranking officer. That he is, in spades. Maybe, I suppose, I'm a goddamn bigot, that he isn't English or American."

"Yes, Skip, that's it." She stared at the inky sky, "Look at all the damn stars. You never see so many when on shore."

"I arranged it for you myself." He was suddenly cheerful, watching her looking up at the covering sky of sooty darkness ignited with stars. "Some seem elbow to elbow," he said, "the sky is so crowded."

"And some," she pointed out, "so bright and bold."

He identified the best known and she said not to bother, a star was a star was a star if, like him, you didn't believe your Sagittarius horoscope.

She sensed Tom was pleased with the ship. The weather, which at times was brisk, did not hamper the steady passage of *Pallas Athena*. The horizon was broken only rarely by pencil smudge shadows of some steamer or fishing craft being tossed about like sea spume; the ship's puny strength, she thought, how ineffectual against the heaving sea.

"Dolly, you notice how Sieko has threaded new ropes through the canvas covers of the lifeboats. He's a real sailor. Not like the officeboys and mechanics that go to sea today."

She was aching for a smoke—forbidden on deck.

"You've had your evening grouch. Now let's go to quarters. We've done our mile walk, haven't we?"

"Three times back and forth on the catwalk should be about right. We're shy at least a part of a mile tonight."

"Who's counting?"

They went to their quarters arm in arm.

High overhead Wallie was on the bridge. Below he saw Ludwig Ott come out to the main deck. He was wearing a sleeveless undershirt, revealing arms and shoulders like a strong man. On his left bicep a shield was tatooed with the lettering, *Honos habet onus.* He leaned on the rail, spit, and watched the hissing wash of water made by the ship's passage. Whatever thoughts he had were, Homer would have said, heavily Teutonic.

Ludwig inhaled deeply, exhaled, repeated this ten times, slapped his hands together, went below.

In the movie theater Alice sat smoking. She was alone, screening a 400-foot, rough-cut of the shore scenes she had taken before joining the ship. They seemed satisfactory enough. The other film footage from the ship would have to wait until it could be processed on shore. The ship's darkroom was not equipped to develop and print motion picture film.

The last spliced section ended; the screen glittered with a white flicker. Alice stood up, put out her cigarette and thanked the projectionist.

"Very beautiful thing, memshab," he replied.

"Rewind it and put it in the can. I'll pick it up tomorrow."

It was all right. *Just* all right, she told herself, moving along the passage. She was reticent about judging her work. The hallway tilted to the starboard side, but the ship's motion didn't bother her anymore. The first two days, yes. Now she had her sea legs and her stomach didn't find fault with her.

Was she happy? No, I'm not happy, she told herself, but I'm not sad. It's like a life held in abeyance. I'm getting nowhere, and I have to come to sort of an adding up of my life. If this damn documentary works out and attracts attention, I can maybe make something of my talents. Women are directing feature films. But what I'm doing is just fancy shit for a couple of crafty Greeks.

She needed a drink; more and more she needed one. Why do people always say crafty Greeks? They're no more crafty than Yankees, Chinese, or Arabs in their position. I've lived too long by a jolly credo that sanctions everything. You need a sea change, girl, she thought to herself. Well, here I am, afloat—up to my navel in it.

She turned a corner in the long passageway and saw a female figure slip into the first officer's cabin.

What do you know—a very homogeneous ship. Who will knock on *my* door?

Farashah had fixed a quart thermos flask of tea and a plate of game hen sandwiches which she left at the bedside of the captain and his wife, before she wished them *"Kwaheri"* (goodnight), and went to her room. Seemingly self-contained, she was ambivalent about her next move.

It was Farashah that Alice had seen slipping into the

first officer's cabin. Farashah had felt—why not? They had been meeting in passageways, indulging in light chatter—salted with obscene native or seaport jests. Even a half hour of groping in the linen closet with an exchange of heavy breathing ("Eating noses," she called it). But this was the first time she had promised to come to Achilles' cabin, and had come.

He was seated in a rose-colored dressing gown, listening to an Ellington recording of "Mood Indigo."

He smiled, *"Salaam allekum."*

"Allekum salaam."

She giggled and felt at ease, arching her back, waving her fingers. There were two bottles in the ice bucket, a covered tray of goodies. He remained seated but held his arms apart, and she came to them, kneeling and laughing in sudden gayness. "Oh, you are a quick boss-man."

He embraced her. His sliding fingers felt her warm and smooth body under her robe. "I am like you, Farashah, alive and horny."

"What means this horny, the Devil? Old Nick?"

"No, it means man, woman, woman, man, front to front, in and out."

"Oh yas," she laughed. He liked all those big white teeth.

"Americans, now they read about it, see it in the movies. But as for really knowing, doing . . . ," he waved off the idea of any potential fun or knowledge. "Oh the young fumble around in cars and make a rock and roll noise about it. You drink?"

"I drink, oh yas." She was making moaning sounds, kitten sounds, nuzzling his face and neck, pushing aside with her braceleted hand his dressing gown, licking his skin.

"I Muslim for myself. But for the world I am a Christian mission child. Why you smell so good?"

"Shaving soap, and my sweat is like roses, no?"

"No."

He got free enough to pour two wine glasses. "I know, to your Muslim side, this is fruit juice. All the big oil sheiks drink our 'fruit juice' until they fall down drunk."

"A miracle of Allah." She remembered a phrase: "Mud in your eye."

After two refills of the glasses, after whispers, laughter, they were naked—exuberant but tense, like warriors before battle. They fell together on the bed, rousing each other with their ardent lust, rolling to the ship's pitch.

There was in Achilles a savage approach to whatever woman he mounted—a psychological need to dominate. But it was also the skilled performance of a man, sleek and hurried. He rather thought of himself as an artist with a voracious appetite for female flesh—to hold, grip tight, penetrate like an object on a spear.

As for Farashah, she had been well taught, exploited—and he was aware of her immense scope. Now at her prime, her sensuality was a constant stimulus to express her body's totally committed action. The Greek was delighted to find in her none of the superficial sophistication he had found in European women, American college girls, or the cosmetic buyers for fancy shops who traveled in Europe.

After the first encounter with this Swahili-whispering girl and her fellatio-shaped lips, their climaxing ended in wet, open mouths and damp limbs, resting in a salty odor of body-play that filled the cabin. Achilles felt the touch of melancholia that for him often followed fulfillment. ("Only priests and donkeys are not sad after they fuck.")

As he looked down on the panting, grinning face, the girl's golden body—did she smell through her skin?—a body highlighted by sweat, he wondered: *who won*? The splendid breasts, arrogant and pert, the nipples he had bitten scarlet seemed the victors. Her belly was still heaving, her thighs and hips moved in perhaps the small rolling gestures that had enhanced their play. He sensed she had bested him. Was it she who had dominated, she who had shown the most uniqueness, made the most gains in the idiosyncrasies of the sexual act?

He sat up slowly, staring into her eyes and poured drinks. They drank, looking each other over with interest, as if probing for some chink in vulnerable egos.

"You very good lover, sweet man."

"You're a hell of a grand fuck yourself, Farashah."

He sipped wine, shook his head. "You're a goddamn treasure."

"You talk good." She laughed, her eyebrows flared up. "I pleasure you very fine, yas?"

He nodded. The record on the machine had ended. Achilles lifted the playing arm and did not put on another recording. He took the girl by the hand. "Look, I want all of you on this ship. No putting out for the captain or giving a quickie head to the chief engineer, you understand?"

She drew herself up with grace, not hauteur. "Okay, sweet man, you treat me fine, me your girl. All trip."

"What do you want . . . no, no . . . what do you like?" He wanted a unique harmony with this creature.

"I like the fucking very much. You are something splendid. For the fuck-fuck I wants nothing. But if you like me to look proud." She picked up a pair of gold-rimmed cufflinks from a leather box before a small mirror. "These make fine earrings. But only if you want to show I pleasing you."

"Hell, yes, take them. And one of the cooks has some pearls he's been trying to peddle." In his own way Achilles was a man greatly attracted to art; he already saw the color of her skin with pearls—two—set against it.

She said, "You understand that is for the pleasure between us. So you want to be proud of me and see me at

75

my best proud with you." She held the cufflinks to her ears, "You like Fanny with these?"

(Watch out—there's a lot of bitch among her delicacies.)

"Fanny?"

"Mrs. Captain, she call me that, Fanny. Farashah name she find too much like a nigger name."

Achilles shook his head and opened the second bottle. Like most Don Juan types given to *macho,* there was always a fear of failure, of loss of power.

"No, not Fanny, it isn't you as a name. You're Farashah."

"Like you say." She put a hand between his legs. They were very close; the wine had them, and they were like friendly field sports stars competing for something of value.

They came together on the bed again, and the merging was like a shoving, rolling contest, as if each were trying to out-point the other for some desperately cherished goal. Farashah screamed dramatically in orgasm, a cry of victory. The Greek lay, his head between her wet breasts, clinging to her; she felt his heart thump against her. Achilles tried to withdraw, but her long legs were around him, locking him tight. He lay still, aware he had been bested. And she looked up at the cabin's ceiling sensing what had happened to the poor sonofabitch—yet aware of her domination over this animated prick, of which he was not fully aware.

CHAPTER 8

Wallie Ormsbee was having breakfast after coming off watch and listening to the day's first broadcast of the "World Oil News." It was the tankers' lifeline to the rest of the world:

TWENTY-FIVE-MILE-LONG OIL SLICK FROM THE CRIPPLED AMERICAN SUPERTANKER "WACO" HAS BEGUN WASHING ONTO SOUTH AFRICAN BEACHES AND THREATENS EXTENSIVE ECOLOGICAL DAMAGE.

ALTHOUGH THE "WACO" HAD BEEN CARRYING 250,000 TONS OF CRUDE OIL, OFFICIALS REPORTED AT THE TIME THAT NONE OF IT HAD ESCAPED. IT WAS BELIEVED THE OIL SPILL CONSISTED OF BUNKER OIL FROM THE VESSEL'S ENGINE ROOMS.

HOWEVER, SOUTH AFRICAN POLLUTION OFFICER IN CHARGE OF CLEANUP OPERATIONS SAID SAMPLES INDICATED THAT THE SLICK WAS CRUDE OIL.

MARITIME SOURCES SAID THAT ONE OF THE "WACO's" TANKS HAD RUPTURED IN THE CRASH, SPILLING ITS CARGO. THE SLICK STRETCHED FROM THE MOUTH OF THE GOURITZ RIVER TWENTY-FIVE MILES EAST TO THE WILDERNESS, A NATURE RESERVE. THE AREA ALONG SOUTH AFRICA'S SOUTHERN INDIAN OCEAN COAST INCLUDED BEACHES CURRENTLY CROWDED WITH SUMMER VACATIONERS.

A MARITIME OFFICIAL AT MOSSEL BAY, A CITY IN THE MIDDLE OF THE THREATENED AREA, REPORTED FIVE ANTIPOLLUTION VESSELS WERE FIGHTING THE OIL.

"YOU CAN SMELL IT IN THE WHOLE AREA," HE SAID. "IT'S ABOUT THREE INCHES THICK IN THE TIDAL POOL AT MOSSEL BAY AND ALL ABOVE THE BEACHES."

Ludwig Ott and Homer Bowen came in and sat across from Wallie. The German, in need of a shave, had a face of golden stubble.

"Looks like it's a big one on the Cape," he said.

Homer reached for the rolls and the butter dish. "Nothing compared to the *Torrey Canyon* when that dago captain drove her aground on the Sicily Isles. All wogs on board but me and a few experts—the tanker registered under the Liberian rag. Hell of a fight over damages to shore, beasts, and birds. Jesus what a ballsup fracas."

Ludwig motioned the Chinese waiter over. "Four eggs mit a good thick slice ham. Black coffee mit chicory and *semmel*. *Semmel* rolls." He smiled, "Of course, remember nobody wanted to own up, neither the Barracuda Tanker Company what owned the ship, or Union Oil, the leaseholder, or the subleaseholder, British Petrol."

"Who did pay?" asked Wallie, wondering if the captain's wife would be in for breakfast.

Homer chewed on his roll. "Oh the goddamn lawyers, the leeches, figured out a caper. Always trust those legal bastards to screw everybody. They just waited till one of the ships belonging to one of the owners of the *Torrey Canyon* got to a European harbor that they had clout with, and they seized her. It was the *Lake Polourde*. Had her seized, yes, and they insisted Lloyds and the other insurers pay for the damage done to a beautiful coastline."

"They settle?" asked Wallie.

Homer grinned, "You bet your sweet arse they did. Seven million five hundred thousand dollars. A sweet settlement."

Sarah was having breakfast in the captain's quarters. She was enjoying the trip, though gaining a bit, according to the bathroom scales. Fu Chu, the assistant chef on *Pallas Athena*, was master of sauces. As for cakes and pies, the special breads of the pastry cook were irresistible. She and Alice had decided on only one dessert a day and avoided anything but tea (and a few cookies) at tea time. Sarah was running out of reading material. Detective stories pleased her most. Good, keen murder stories with a perverse psychotic on the kill; there was lots of sex in the new mysteries, and nobody the worse for it after you put the book down. Wallie Ormsbee had invited her to look over his collection of books. A nice-enough kid but square. She had complained to him of the crappy collection of books in the ship's library. "Hell, I'd even read Mickey Spillane."

"If it's reading matter, Mrs. Hammel, I have some books you might look over."

"Only if you call me Sarah. It's first names on this ship."

"Well, Sari, come along then."

She was impressed with Wallie's cabin—its photos, collections of artifacts, and what she called "very fancy junk. I mean it's not gook like tourists buy. Why do you call me Sari?"

"It's a form of Sarah."

She sat on his bed smoking a cigarette, looking over his books. "Honey, I haven't the brain power to dig into these. I mean, I can take Dickens and Mark Twain, but I can't reach for the bigger boys. I like whodunits."

"*L'esprit prime-sauter*—quick excitement."

"You make it sound sexy in French."

She saw him blush. Why hadn't Alice picked him off? Neat, clean-cut American Joe.

"Thanks, Wallie. I'll go see what books Homer has. He says Conrad, London. I used to read them when I was in high school. Stevenson, too. You know Tom knew Hemingway. They used to fish together. He thought Ernesto okay when he wasn't acting up with his kind of fancy shit. He liked to kill things, fish, animals." She looked over the cabin, its too neat arrangements of a life. "You need something, Wallie, besides all this hobby magilla. Now this Palamas girl, Alice, give her a bit of attention. She's your sort of chick. I mean all that filming and talk of film epics. Me, I was zonkers over Paul Newman and Robert Redford. Now they're getting long in the tooth. Alice she goes for Italian actors . . . this Mostrioni or whatever he's called."

Wallie watched Sarah drop ash on the cabin floor. He handed her a rare seashell he had acquired.

"Miss P—Alice, is good company, but I'm sure, Sari, she's . . ."

"She's what? She's a woman and you're a guy, and I'm an old nosy bitch. But I can see you're not a self-starter. Honey, you have to see and be as you go along. Tom and me, we'll soon be senior citizens. Jesus, a title we'd rather not have. Kind of a time of farewell—huh? I was reading some place where a mob, they were riding this man out of town on a rail after tar and feathering him, and he said, 'If it weren't for the honor gents I'd rather have walked!' Mark Twain."

She closed one eye against the smoke from her cigarette.

"No kidding." She stubbed out her cigarette, took out another, but waved off Wallie's offer of a light. "I'm trying to stay on a pack an' a half a day. Come up to our suite after dinner. The captain is having a little gathering. Around nine?"

"Of course. You're very kind."

She rose, kissed his cheek, patted his face. "See you, *amigo*."

Not a vulgar woman, just a vocal impropriety, he felt,

after she was gone. A warm woman. Quizzical, a bit deri-
sive, expressive. There was in her a battered vitality. He
imagined, lord knows, what she and the captain had been
through: gossip of his boozing, of being on the beach,
having trouble getting a ship. But there she was, Sari, like
something earthy, alive, entering his life. What had
Krishna written? "So I say to you that of the two, the performance of service is preferable to the renunciation."
Yes, he had that marked down some place. She was right.
His spoiled-kid attitude of judicious detachment was not
good. Better come away from any too deep sinking into
Mother's attitude that we are all a dream in the mind of
Brahma. Damn it, there is a lot of paranoia in all of us.
Sari was right (Sari was better than Sarah—made her less
the captain's wife).

Alice Palamas? No desires in her direction. It was Sari
who seemed the more alive of the two. The vitality of a
close friendship with her would be satisfactory. She
seemed to sense his diverse moods. Not since Mother,
had there been the warmth and pleasure of a relationship.
It was a natural interest in him, an older woman, funda-
mentally decent for all her (as she had said) being nosy;
nothing sly or wrong in her attitude.

He closed his eyes and sniffed her scent lingering in the
cabin: cigarette smoke, moist skin, bath powder.

Farashah should have been fatigued from her night
with the Greek gentleman and an hour of boffing after
lunch. But now she had set the table in the captain's
quarters, placed the ice buckets and an assortment of bottles on the small bar. The place was ready for the afterdinner get-together. She had gotten some flowers from
Gemila, who grew them in pots in a small greenhouse on
the top deck.

"Nice, Fanny, very nice," Sarah said, nibbling some
salted almonds as she looked over the setting. "Thanks.

You can go. There's a movie tonight they've only shown three times this trip. You might like it."

"*Siyo,* no. Too many Chinese in movie place. I maybe study. I am training by mail to be dental assistant."

"Good girl, Fanny." Sarah looked out at the dark night, felt the motion of the tanker moving eastward. The gathering in half an hour consisted of Wallie, Homer, Alice, and Carlos de Nova, the Goanese assistant engineer. Achilles was on duty on the bridge, Sparky in the radio room. Ludwig was in the chart room transferring the loading records into a simpler form.

It was a pleasant evening. The captain was locked in some private mood. Alice told some Hollywood stories, and Homer related details of novels written on the sailor's life. He mentioned *The Death Ship* (none had heard of it), *Lord Jim* (none but Wallie had read it). The captain mentioned *Treasure Island,* which Homer was too respectful to reject as being for boys. Sarah told some amusing stories of life in a communal apartment house in Bombay, when times were hard: "They're funny *now.*" The captain said, "But not berthing down in a grimy room, no bathrooms indoors, the smell of Hindu butter, gamey enough to knock you down."

"Oh, Skip, it was bearable. We knew we'd get out."

Wallie found himself nodding, expanding; he talked of his life in Paris hotels when he was a bare-kneed boy, spelling out the names on the vans and lorries of the Galeries Lafayette, Bon Marché. He also told of an admirer of Mother's, but he didn't tell about getting him a drink of café marc; instead he described how funny the American tourists' French was ("*nous verrons American Express*"), and how the concierge killed rats. Wallie certainly felt very good when the gathering broke up at 11:30 after the captain had looked at his watch a few times and Sarah had Ping Pong empty the ashtray twice.

Wallie thanked Sarah for inviting him; he held her

hand at the door and leaned forward, perhaps in hopes of a cheek kiss. She did not kiss him but said he and Alice ought to get up early to see the damnedest sunrise of their lives: "Just watch the day break in the Indian Ocean. Nothing like it any place else. Goodnight, Wallie."

He had trouble falling asleep and had to be on watch at four o'clock.

FROM THE NOTEBOOKS OF HOMER BOWEN:

There are times when I wake in the night and feel the heavy cargo we are carrying, millions of gallons of crude oil, and become aware that just seven and a half feet under the main deck it is sloshing around with the roll and pitch of the ship. It's murderously dangerous this thick liquid mass down there in the darkness: stinky, sticky stuff, upon which we are perched like a chip floating on a keg of molasses.

When the damn horror of it hits me in the gut I think of the book by Victor Hugo that Grand Da gave me, Toilers of the Sea, *in which, during a storm at sea, a ship is destroyed by a huge cannon breaking its lashings and plunging across the deck, running wildly back and forth, smashing, maiming, killing. I can come awake to the thud of that run-amok cannon and find I'm all in a sweat, only because of the roll of the ship and the sound of an empty ale bottle on the cabin floor. Then I lie awake, thinking of what's below deck, thousands of liquid tons rolling from side to side; a storm sends it banging against the main deck plates.*

I sense, by his brooding look, our captain has this image before him too. At times he wears the worried, unquiet expression of a man who wonders if doing his duty means safety, whether his rigid procedures will make all things come out properly. He's tight up as a bull's arsehole in flytime.

This Miss Alice Palamas is oddly ignorant of the dangers that lurk in tankers, empty or loaded. Lurk is perhaps

83

too melodramatic. Must watch my use of words when I come to write my novel. I suppose I'll have to invent a much more dramatic story than the activities on Pallas Athena.

Tom and Sarah are just old citizens, nearly ready for rocking chairs. I wonder if they have much to say to each other anymore. Wallie would have to be more animated in a story. Nothing rouses him to react very much. Doesn't do more than stand his watches and catalog his film negatives. Ludwig can't be more than one of those square-headed Germans out of comic strips, who likes his beer and gets sentimental over Schubert's music. Doesn't think anybody but Germans know how to make a good beer (true) and once was a bicycle racer.

Achilles now, a kind of Zorba, but a modern type, a bit wigged out on jazz and perhaps drugs. A proper nonhero, with qualities that make him valid for fiction. I'll make him bisexual, in love with one of the Arab sailors and Alice, torn between the two. But I can't really write about women. How does one create a Madame Bovary, Anna Karenina, Sister Carrie, a Molly Bloom? Study Alice Palamas for a clue. I've been explaining the tanker to her, for her film. I try to imagine her having a period, going to the toilet, and I've failed. I've never read a novel about the heroine taking a good satisfactory crap or belching after a meal.

The swimming pool has been filled; I sat with Alice today talking of tankers after our swim. How she should see them.

"It's a strange game this oil business. In the early 1970's oil prices doubled, then doubled again, and the world was gobbling up millions of tons, of which nearly sixty percent moved in tankers; two-thirds of the tankers were carrying oil from the Middle East."

"That's when KSL made their biggest profit? They feel tankers will always be needed, no matter what gains or new discoveries are made. You agree, Homer?"

"Maybe. But there can be an oversupply. There are over four hundred tankers, all over 200,000 tons, making their runs, and I'd guess maybe nearly four thousand more carry what they can carry. Right now there's a lull. But Oil News reports there are over one thousand tankers on order—big ones, over 400,000 tons."

"Not as big as this?"

"Maybe one, if it's finished—in Japan, bigger than the Pallas Athena. But there are lots of ship building cancellations, less oil being sold since the big increase in price by the flea-bitten Arabs. Is the KSL making money, showing a profit?"

She said she didn't know.

I told her the tanker future depended on where new fields were being found, not offshore in America, England, the North Sea. It could be all pipelines and thousands of tankers left rusting on the beach or cut up into Japanese cars.

She said, "Don't bet on it. The big offshore oil terminals are being built by men who can read the future."

I said, "Sometimes."

Which leads me to wonder if she hasn't been lying down for one of the Kyprios brothers, or both. If I do use her as the woman in my novel, I'll give her much bigger tits. I notice there are no flat-chested girls in the really popular stuff by Wallace or Robbins. Of course, I don't want to write trashy, but still a good shapely arse and a set of out-thrust knockers give a healthy glow to a story. I don't remember any place in Melville's or Conrad's work where they get all het up erotic about their women characters.

Meanwhile, Pallas Athena is moving at our usual steady rate, no trouble in the engine room; repacked a shaft box, some smoke but no fire.

Captain Thomas Hammel did not have the benefit of Homer's notes, nor did he dread merely the heavy oil cargo. The daily weather reports promised their first fog, and once past Dondra Head on what was once Ceylon, now Sri Lanka (as if that changed matters) an early taste of the monsoons was forecast. He was charted to sail south of the Bay of Bengal, skirt the Sunda Islands and Timor, and move between Papua and Australia into the Coral Sea.

If predictions were to be trusted, he'd be heading right into the full fury of the monsoons.

After grouchily pacing the bridge he had Sparky send a radio message to KSL, Athens:

IMPERATIVE CHANGE COURSE ONCE IN CORAL C NEW COURSE NO BY NE SO BY SE TO PASS SO OF NU HEBRIDES SAFER RELAY PERMIT 4 CHANGE OF COURSE .

> CAPT T HAMMEL
> PALLAS ATHENA

Three hours later Sparky delivered a reply to the captain on the bridge:

PROCEED AS CHARTED THRU CORAL C SOUTH OF SOLOMONS DETOURS COSTLY TO KSL CHARTER PRICES.

> IONNES K
> KSL ATHENS

Sonofabitch, Tom thought; blue-balled bastard sitting on his prostate in a cozy office. He folded the reply and put it in an inner pocket of his jacket. The sea was calm enough, the pitch was less, the roll remained steady, but was not bothersome. He was standing with his feet apart in the old seaman's stance to balance himself. Wallie was watching him, looking up from the bridge log.

"No dice, Captain?"

"No dice. The damn fools, to risk an eighty million dollar ship for a couple days' extra fuel consumption."

"They figure close, Captain. Homer thinks they were not so smart, taking flat-fee charters a couple of years ago, for three years. And then everything inflated."

"It gave them the carrying business . . . Break out the South Pacific charts. I may still want an alternate route if the monsoons strike early. Ever been through a big bone-breaker?"

"Hurricane Helen off the Hatteras."

"Peanuts to what the Japs call a *tsunami*. Was in one

once. Seventy mile an hour winds at times, forty foot waves."

"That high?"

"Hell, yes. Tore off rails, carried away two lifeboats, and cracked a hull plate. Lucky we were carrying ore, not oil."

The captain brooded the rest of the day. He unfolded and refolded so many charts, that after dinner Sarah concluded that his blue funk was what she called "dragass" and he identified as "black dog."

Sarah watched him shift around in his chair as he studied the looseleaf *Pacific Survey Routes.*

"You got a wild hair up your prat, Skip. What's the matter?"

"KSL Athens acting so stiff, so arrogant."

"Just how?"

"Ordering me not to change course. To, goddamnit, save some goddamn tons of fuel oil we'd burn by sailing southeast."

"Come on, they can't really tell you how to sail. Even I know a captain is in full charge of his ship. He can change course if anything endangers his vessel."

He smiled and patted her hand, noticed the nicotine-stained fingers.

"Sure a captain can, Dolly. And it goes on his record. To go up against something as big as KSL isn't done. It's no longer clipper ships, all sails set for Canton for the early green tea, to hurry back around the Horn and get the best prices. It's all cursed computers now, and cost-cut experts with slide rulers, playing the value of the dollar against the mark or the Japanese yen."

"You do what you think best. They can beach you, sure, but we still have some land in Napa Valley, and we can grow grapes for my sister's winery."

He closed the survey binder. "I'll see what the weather fronts are. I'll send the Kyprioses one more message. Then I feel I'm on my own."

Sarah felt her recurring disenchantment with the sea.

"They wouldn't want to wreck this wonderful ship. I mean she's their goddamn pride and joy. The biggest collection of oil tanks in one hull."

Tom came over and kissed her cheek. "You've read their publicity folder—pictures by Miss Palamas, in color."

She rubbed his face ardently—then his neck, until she had reached inside his shirt and was caressing his chest.

She spoke softly, consolingly. "Want a little love, mister?"

He smiled. "You're a shameless lady."

She purred and smiled back, leaned against him. "I'm an insatiable broad."

The dancing movement of her fingers on the back of his neck signaled her old medicine against his attacks of the willies. When tension overtook him and black dog gnawed, it was a bout of lovemaking with Sarah that was effective. He was also very much in love with her and a man of physical responses. The fire was banked but there sure were red hot embers—at its heart. He used to think when he got an erection and a desire for her body of the closeness of two people alone in a world which, if not hostile, was at least indifferent.

After they had made love, renewing the intimacy they had known (Tom figured) a couple hundred thousand times, they lay, her cigarette end glowing in the semi-darkness, the sea reflected in silver streaks on the ceiling of the room with contentment filling them. They knew they were getting old but still they had each other.

He was turned on his side to sleep, when he felt her move as she punched out the cigarette butt, and heard her say, he already half under, "Maybe, Skip, they want to wreck the *Pallas Athena*—ever think of that?"

He was asleep.

CHAPTER 9

Alice came awake at eleven (she'd been in the ship's
dark room till 2 A.M.) to a white nebulous invasion; the
porthole was a chalky white circle. Getting up, she saw
that dense fog had come up during the night. Somehow,
like a child left alone in a big house, she felt isolated and
in a senseless panic, the whole world blotted out. She
dressed in a wrap-around skirt, a linen blouse, and bare-
legged went to the main deck.

She stood by the swimming pool, its water level waver-
ing slightly. All the world was lost beyond the rail. She
could hear the water rushing by but not see it. There was
a wild hooting overhead; a shattering noise such as she
imagined the great ram's horn of the Lord would sound
like on Judgment Day. It was, however, only the call of
the fog horn coming from the upper reaches of a nearly
invisible bridge.

What, she wondered, was human triviality—herself included—doing out over a dank deep through which this
white curtain moved in strands to dampen her cheek and
shroud the ship. She thought of her life, reviewing her
tendency to contradiction, past love affairs, happy times

that were too short, and lethargic depressions that lasted too long. Her capricious capacity to be bored, the pathos of her instincts to seek romance, grace, always hoping for some exquisite, hazy, happiness—some place soon in the future.

She felt in unique harmony with the fog, then the chief engineer came up by her side at the rail, in his mouth a dark briar pipe, its smoke merging with the fog.

The hooter went off again overhead.

Homer grinned. "Gets you, doesn't it?"

"The most mournful sound I know, Homer."

"It's that. When I was in the orphanage we had a sound like that when someone ran away and they sent out the bloody bastards to collar and bash you."

"You run away often?"

"Often as I could. I read *Kidnapped* when I was eight and I wanted to get away to sea. I was over the wall. They caught me that time." He was frowning, the pipe held firmly in his teeth.

"I always thought kids ran away to sea only in books."

"Maybe I read too many books. *Moby Dick,* now, that ship sounded to me like a fine place to be until Ahab went crazy over chasing that shitty white whale. And why? A passenger on a P&O boat, some writer chap, told me it was just the author's unconscious symbol for a prick. How do you like that?"

She laughed. "Is that a personal question? Tell me, you feel safe on a ship?"

"Mostly I do, Alice. On shore I drink hard. Off ship, maybe I find the richness on shore too menacing."

"I feel safe on this ship. Even if the fog is a bit ghostly."

"On a tanker you're never safe, even with the tanks drained. That's the bunk."

"Wallie tells me you siphon off in port till the pumps suck really dry."

"Only appears so. Each tank still has its puddles of oil,

all the gummy stuff that the pipes can't move. The hulls are thick as cake batter with waxy oil scum. Maybe three to four thousand ton was left in *Pallas Athena* last time we unloaded.

"Could I get below to film an empty tank in port?"

"Dangerous. We get about fifteen hundred ton out. What's left can form gases among the hydrocarbons, and it's hell to try and clean it out. Any little spark and you're mincemeat, well roasted."

"You'll take me down to film a tank cleaning? They've licked the problems, the KLS claims."

"Oh they try. I use inert gases from the boilers. Carbon dioxide, nitrogen, stuff that doesn't catch fire. I pump it in as the oil comes out. I also use high pressure water hoses, maybe six to eight hours of pumping in high pressure water. But hell, if oxygen is left and *that* mixes with the hydros, up she goes."

They heard the Chinese lunch gong clang in the main passageway. (A touch of class, Sarah called it.)

"I'm hungry," said Alice. "Didn't get breakfast. Slept late."

They went up to the dining room and ate Dover sole with endive salad. Homer had his pint of ale and Alice a glass of white wine.

"I hear, Homer, you're writing a huge sea novel."

His ears turned pink and bubbles of gas from the ale burst in his nose as he expelled air. "Where'd you hear that?"

"A ship is full of gossip."

"Well now, I'm just collecting notes. Material, you know, bits of information, odd happenings. Sea lore and incidents."

"You've begun the book? I'm interested. You might help me with the narrative for the film."

"I'm about to begin the novel. Intend to this trip. The notes pile up and you wonder if you're really ready."

"That's bad, Homer. I know writers who never start, just sharpen pencils and answer the mail. Get to it, man."

He took a last swallow of the ale. "On this P&O boat, the old *Victoria*, I was a young pup then, I met this writer, Somerset Maugham. I was a rosy-cheeked lad, and we walked the deck. He told me, only when a writer is ready does he give birth. So, Alice, don't pay any attention to rumors about my novel. Nothing much else to do on shipboard but yackidy-yack."

She decided to have a second martini and skip the dessert. "I don't know if it's just rumor or not, Homer, but is the captain having a hassle with Athens?"

"For all their fancy talk of being a unique firm, the Kyprioses are stingy bastards. All the captain wants is to make a change of course—very slight, in case we hit too heavy weather—just a day's extra run or so. But they worry over the amount of fuel being expended."

"Oh, that's all?"

"What does a few tons of oil matter to them?"

Homer was working up a whipped cream horror with red and green candied fruit, topped by crushed walnuts. He held up his fork like a baton and waved it, leaning toward her. "Sparky, he listens in on everything with his mess of radios. He says the KSL line is in trouble. Big bank loans coming due and a real slump in the oil market, and the Kyprioses have old contracts made to get the carrier loads on which they are now losing money."

"But they have other assets: olive groves, an airline, fish canneries. Major investments."

Homer wiped whipped cream off his chin with a crisp linen napkin. "Old Tom, our captain, he isn't one to bend to any landlocked owner."

"He can change course, by sea law?"

"If the vessel is in danger, yes; at sea, he's God. Captains used to keelhaul a sailor or flog him to death for a whim. After all, the sea is controlled by no national flag, no enforceable laws; only on its fringes."

"Is this ship in danger? I mean beyond the yarns you've been crapping me with?"

"Look, Alice, two-thirds of the planet is water, and rough water cursed with winds and racked by storms and sea wrath. And it's often a mile deep, straight down. A ship is just a sliver floating about, tossed and vulnerable as a fly fallen into the bath water."

Alice laughed. "Use that prose in your book. It's pretty . . . Hello, Achilles, our chief engineer is trying to scare me with some flak between the captain and the owners."

Achilles sat down and smiled at Gemila, the stewardess as she poured him a cup of coffee from a Silex. "That's supposed to be very confidential. Sacred, confidential . . . what's eatable, Gemila?"

Alice said, "Come on, Achilles, give me the lowdown." She liked the Greek and wondered what woman it was she had seen entering his cabin. Gemila, the stewardess? They certainly seemed chummy. The captain's wife? No, a bit snotty and still shaking her fanny but past her prime. Farashah? A second officer doesn't screw the servants if he's smart, and Achilles was smart. Maybe it was a boy she saw—you know these things about so many Greeks.

"It's all nothing at all," said Achilles. "Merely the captain making a report and a suggestion. This vessel is built to withstand any weather, any condition she could meet . . . Gemila, the kippers, toast, a slice of *feta* cheese . . . this is a solid ship."

"Bullshit," said Homer, taking out his pipe and a leather tobacco pouch, "There's a permanent dangerous condition caused by our size and cargo."

"I wasn't talking about cargo risks. I was talking of storms, rains, waves. Why she's weathered fifty-foot waves off the Cape, sixty-mile winds."

Homer carefully loaded his pipe with the coarse cut burley and Irish bogey he favored. "The captain's worried, very worried."

Achilles smiled at Gemila. "I don't suppose we have tripe St. Jacques?"

For four days the fog continued, congealed in a dead calm. The sea, when some small section of it showed, looked oiled and held in impassive indifference. It neither made waves nor dipped very much. From the bridge *Pallas Athena* was a prisoner of the fog. Just as if, the captain thought, she had been locked in an ice floe on the pressure ridges in the Arctic sea. The tanker moved at a reduced speed of 12 knots; at intervals the ghastly sound of the hooter gave off warnings. From the bridge the captain's eyes met an opaque wall; the gyro-compass gave directional readings—the electronic navigation equipment, the sonar-radar, seemed indifferent to the great fog.

Life on board seemed more ingrown in the murky mist. Achilles met nearly every night in his cabin with Farashah in their battles for sexual domination. Some nights he felt the victor over her golden body—the smooth physical astuteness of that panting, grinning girl. Often, too, there was in him the drained feeling she was mocking him. Like so many sensual hedonists, he held to a long-entrenched role, playing that he was blasé, that nothing could deeply touch him. But he knew this confidence—with Farashah—was eroding. He was madly entrapped by this half-savage creature. A woman, not at all simple, not at all the available flesh one bought in eastern ports. She had a mocking yet querulous distinction he had rarely met before. She insisted on intercourse, even during her menstrual cycle and this, while in the past would have revolted him, seized him with a kind of delight and disgust, making of their frenzy a shambles of the bed so that later she had to toss the soiled linen overboard.

The fog seemed to destroy the sense and direction of

time. Sarah and Sparky found they both liked radio soap operas; he managed to bring in "As the World Turns," "All My Children," and "General Hospital"—somewhat marred by static. But clear enough in marital infidelity and misery. Sometimes Wallie would waylay Sarah in the passageway and offer her some book he hoped she'd like. She asked him how he was getting on with Alice, and he said they were developing photo negatives in the ship's dark room. He was making stills to accompany her work, as there was no way to develop a roll of movie film on board ship.

Sarah said "how interesting" and wondered if there was an affair between the two. A nice boy the way he seemed to enjoy talking to her. A dark room wasn't a bad place for the two kids to meet and make out, even if, Sarah felt, the chemicals were a bit smelly. Wallie was always on the brink of making some confidential confession to her. Sarah hoped they got away—he and Alice—to each other's cabins for a more comfortable relationship than the stinky dark room offered.

Actually neither Alice nor Wallie had any personal designs on each other. A pleasant ambivalence existed between them. She was in a depressed mood. Little things seemed to pile up. One of the cameras, her best one, was jammed, and perhaps she felt she had no real interest in the documentary she was supposed to be working on. Truth was that she feared she couldn't really cut and edit a picture properly. Not an hour feature; hire cutters, editors? She was working for peanuts herself. With this project a failure, she'd be where . . . do what?

Over a double martini she took stock of herself: half Jew, half Greek, no family that mattered; memories of lovers, unpleasant. She was a fool to give up desserts to save her figure.

"Ping Pong, the same again."

* * *

In the engine room all was well. The second engineer was writing endearing letters to his two separate families, hoping to mail them ashore some place in the Pacific. The crew was involved in several feuds. Everyone against the Chinese who were money lenders and sharp gamblers. There was a nightly fan-tan game and a serious poker table run by the fat cook, Duck Fong.

The Swahili-speaking crew members were talking of violence, and often when they met a lone Chinese in the passages, they would draw a finger across their throats and grin, *"Leo yuko jasha!"*

Sieko Mihran, who managed the crew, wasn't worried. The beefing and discontent were normal, he told his wife Gemila. "It will go better once we move out of this fog."

But the fog belt clung to the sea.

There was another homosexual romance going on in the crew section, and Sieko knew that this could make trouble if a jealous lover ran amok with a meat chopping cleaver or a Malay sword. Still, he couldn't feel any right to come out against buggery or joint-copping. Usually, these couples never made trouble unless one of the partners was a conniving bitch with a twitching tail.

Sieko couldn't do much more than tell the fat cook, Duck Fong, to spoil a few meals; a crew that grumbled about food had a token grievance and would not be thinking of more serious offenses. Also, the fat cook had promised Sieko a pound of prime North Africa hashish at a fair price, and he hoped to get it ashore in California under Gemila's robes.

Thomas Hammel sent his second radio message to the Kyprioses, then intended to do what he had to do; to hell with tanker owners and charted courses. Staring into the fog, there were moments he felt like yelling, "To hell with the fucking sea, with the chickenshit captain's braid on my jacket." I have that bit of California land, he thought, and Sarah's sister needed help to run the vineyards, the winery . . . an easier life, no pressure on the ticker . . . I could drop dead on the bridge, and Wallie Ormsbee would calmly enter it into the log: *This day at two twenty, sailing in the thick fog, Captain Hammel collapsed on the bridge and died almost instantly . . .* for on a ship life is transient and tentative. . . .

He cheered up somewhat when a patch of blue appeared, then a whole section of sky. He shook himself free of his dark thoughts. Stained sunlight gilded the bridge's polished brass.

"Mr. Ormsbee, signal engine room to resume full 16 knots speed ahead," he said.

"Yes, Captain."

Homer Bowen was in his cabin, two dead pipes laid aside in a big seashell, a batch of notes at his elbow. Grimly, Homer was beginning his novel. He typed on his old Underwood, using two fingers:

Chapter One

A catafalque of black clouds hung over the sea. Stern with the weight of a man whose ancestors had sailed for four generations, Captain Nasby Wilkenson eyed a horizon blinded by a deep scarlet and gold sunset. He had no eye for beauty or for art. He saw only weather signals. He said to his first mate, the Icelander,

"Al Almqvist, I smell we're in for a bit of heavy weather."

"Aye, jost that I ben sure."

Homer stared at the sheet; oh balls, I'm Harold Robbinsing. He tore it from the typewriter.

Sparky, in the radio room, was writing an ad he

97

planned to place in the *Swinger's Digest;* he was so amused as he composed it, the sound of the "World Oil News" broadcast held little interest. He had written:

> AMERICAN-BORN CHINESE surgeon, active 47, divorced, financially secure, 5' 7", 160 lbs., goodlooking. Interested in dancing to slow music, long walks, swimming, art, investing, learning Mandarin, Karate, visits to San Francisco & Hong Kong; Chinese food. Looking for Oriental girl under 40 with similar tastes and knowledge of the guitar. Photo please.

Sparky began to neatly copy the ad in an elaborate disguised handwriting with lots of back slanting . . .

CHAPTER | 10

The lifting of the fog revealed a crystalline blue air and chalk-colored, mild waves along their ridges. As night fell, Wallie thought the day seemed to turn itself off at twilight and constellations, pin-pricks of light, gave space back to the universe. The tanker had now escaped from a smothering, blind world.

He had, on that first clear day, held Sarah's hand, assisting her down the staircase to the main deck. It had been damn satisfactory; a hot wire seemed to scorch his groin. He was beginning to fully accept his fascination with the captain's wife, his idyllic mood was mixed with a jealous uncertainty, as it had been in the days with Mother—only this fascination was deepening the emotional turbulence inside him.

On the bridge the captain was reading a radio message from Athens:

KSL DOES NOT PERMIT COUNTERMANDING FIRM ORDERS PROCEED EASTWARD ON COURSE AS CHARTED . . .

KYPRIOS KSL.

Achilles was watching him closely. Tom caught the tactful interest on the Greek's face, yet, he also sensed a touch of presumption on the handsome features.

"You will, Mr. Marrkoras, keep on our course till morning."

"Yes, Captain."

"I intend to study the weather reports and see how the weather ahead is stacking up. What do you make of the reports? They appear scientific or just fortune telling?"

The Greek smiled. "Oh very scientific, Captain. You know that there's a storm ahead, hard stuff building up to the east. But I don't read it as monsoon, or even advance monsoon weather."

"You don't? Well, read it again, Mr. Marrkoras." He saw the slight hurt expression on the Greek's face and patted the man's shoulder. "Sorry, Achilles, I started a harangue. We've over fifteen hundred feet of ship, millions of barrels of oil in seven sections under us. *Pallas Athena* is no fucking yacht with trim lines able to bob about and ride easy. Not with barometric readings to the east of 28-point-20."

Achilles held up a condoling hand. "Wasn't meant to be a yacht, even if we live like we were on one."

"Keep posting the weather signals every half hour for the next watch. Have the riggings on the lifeboats tested. Batten down everything."

"Of course, Captain."

The Greek watched Tom leave the bridge. You had to admire the old boy. He was really alert and worried. For a moment, however, he had lost his cool. Not like the captain, unless he was really agitated. Achilles envied these Anglos. They had at their best a stability you didn't find in Latins, or in most Greeks. Achilles watched the Arab Abdullah at the wheel and banged a fist against the compass setting. Why this respect for Anglos? The captain could come apart like any other man under pressure. One never disintegrates gently. It was clear the captain was vacillating about changing course. And that wouldn't do. Ionnes Kyprios had made it clear to Achilles in their last dinner at the Dionysos Restaurant opposite the Acropolis that "under no circumstances" was *Pallas Athena* to divert from the charted route. Achilles had promised to back up the KSL plans while they drank a last round of the anis-flavored ouzo. Ionnes had said, "We Greeks respect auspicious auguries, yes? . . . and depend on each other."

When Ludwig Ott came to take over the watch the two men talked in lowered voices for some time. They looked over at Abdullah at the wheel after one low-voiced conversation, and Ott carried on in Sudeten Deutsch. Achilles frowned, then smiled and patted the shoulders of the third officer.

"We remain Kyprios people?"

"Ja, of course."

Achilles did not go to his cabin where Farashah would be waiting for him, naked. He went instead to the radio room.

Sparky was working his banks of dials and controls, making notes on a pad.

"Good reception, sir."

"Fine, I want to send a message to Mr. Ionnes Kyprios."

"Weather reports coming in; it's thickening off the Indonesian and . . ."

"We're up to our oil navels with weather reports. Get my message out right now."

Sparky looked up at the Greek with a stare of what's-with-him . . . but all he said was, "Yes, sir."

The Greek wrote rapidly on a form and handed it to Sparky:

PLANNING PARTY ON KSL CELEBRATION HAVING PROBLEM WITH CAKE IT MAY NOT RISE CONFIRM RECIPE.

                                                                    A.M.

Sparky looked up grinning. "What kind of a celebration and . . ."

"Just send the message, and be sure I get the answer as soon as it comes in."

The first officer was gone before the radio man could ask more. Sparky began to work the dials of his console, which whined and growled through sharp reports of static. He set the wave length to send the message direct to the KSL receiver in Athens.

Goddamn Greeks, you never knew what they were thinking or doing. Celebration . . . cake? Hell that Chink pastry chef could bake anything from a Vienna torte to a New England apple pie. No, this message was no imbecility. The green light went on, Athens was receiving, and he began to send Achilles' message.

Homer, having given up "to regroup my prose," on the opening of his novel, was inspecting the engine room. The ship was rolling a bit, and he read the barometric weather reports. The ship's boiler pressure was tip-top, the burners clean, turning fuel oil into flame, processing water to steam, steam to energy. "Natural order proceeding in tranquility," he wrote. He had promised Alice Palamas to take her down inside the interior hull to see *Pallas Athena* below sea level at her 190-foot beam.

The seven great sections of the hold, he told her, held twenty cargo tanks of crude oil. Between tanks ten and eleven there was a narrow well with an iron spiral staircase to the bottom of the hull. It was lit by dim yellow bulbs. Alice, looking down, felt her tummy quiver.

"Now, I'll go first," Homer told her as he latched back the hatch cover, and they stared down into the well.

Alice felt the greasy handrail, set foot and followed the engineer as they spiraled down. She balanced the hand-held camera by its trigger grip and hoped she had loaded it properly and that the battery attached to her side would give her the proper light. The sway of the ship's pitch and roll made her stumble on the iron stair tread and lean toward the welded steel wall.

"Careful, it's a long way down."

He could see she was jumpy; he figured he'd keep talking, even if his voice sounded hollow—odd, as they went deeper into the ship. Amber bulbs every thirty feet left them mostly in a not-too-clearly defined light. Homer kept up his chatter to calm his visitor:

"It's certainly damn big and impressive, Alice. Below deck has its personality. Every tanker has its own little bitchy ways."

"But, Homer, there are lots of safety features."

"What if that old-fashioned stuff called steam fails?"

"Why should it?" asked Alice. "You're trying to scare me? I'm scared. But if steam fails?"

"No steam means no electric, no phones, no screws turning the piped water, no movies, no radio, radar, so-nar; it'll all fizz out, even those electronic navigating tools on the bridge. Little red and green lights go out, deck machines, freezer units . . . watch your step here; give me your hand . . . a little oily here."

"It can't happen."

"Only if the boilers don't get their big drinks of dis-tilled water. A ship, you see, gets to age a bit; in five, ten years the pipes get full of gook that turns stone-hard. Pipes leak steam, why?"

"You tell me. How much more to go?"

"A little bit . . . now leaks use up water faster than salt water can be distilled for the boilers."

She turned on her light and began to film. (Talky bas-tard.)

"The engine room when there are leaks is like an old-fashioned London fog, murky . . . hold on tight . . . we now distill a hundred tons of salt water a day. If a salt water pipe begins to leak, it can ruin the distilled stuff in the condenser. That gets into a boiler and scale grows—a boiler burns out, you have ruined tubes. A ship that can't get up pressure and clean pipes fast enough to function is helpless. *Hey!*"

Alice was recklessly plunging down the staircase, her

103

light picking out oil-stained steel walls, rivets and sidings. The air was cold and humid; a dampness seemed to come from the plates.

She felt uneasy in this dark shaft. They were on the bottom and below her, she imagined nothing but an inch or so of steel and below that a mile of sea and then the bottom. Prehistoric by a couple billion years—a sea life of its own; blind, living matter, some glowing like fireflies, others on spiny legs, and all reproducing and devouring each other in the muck of creation among the bones of ancient ships, the hulks of battle wagons and submarines of recent wars. She saw men's bones in brine, and she shivered. She'd have to suggest that image in the narration of the film if she could remember the feeling of the moment.

Homer stood waiting, while she did a pan shot around the well, then an upward swing of her camera, where far overhead there was a halo of light, the open hatch to the outer world, her world. (Get rid of the "man with the iron mask" feeling.)

"That's enough, lady. The buggery air isn't too good down here, and I'd hate to have to carry you up this iron staircase."

She waved off his proffered hand.

They made their way slowly upward. The air wasn't really too bad; it just had an acid tang, and the smell of it was giving Alice a headache.

Alice said, "Here we are between hundreds of thousands of tons of oil. What if the dam broke some place?"

"Not a chance, Alice. Besides it's in seven sections in nearly two dozen tanks."

He tapped a steel wall, listened to the sound. "It's in there. You can tell how much a tank is holding by the sound you get back when you whack it."

"Just by the sound?"

Homer felt boastful. "Not every Tom, Dick and Harry

can do it. But I've been able to estimate a tank's contents close. Now here we have tank number ten. Listen . . .''

He thumped, listened. Alice thought it sounded like a frog king belching. Homer frowned, "Listed as ninety-five percent full."

"And your thump and the sound measures it?"

"Yes, under proper conditions; of course, right now I'm getting a cockeyed reading. There being two of us here, not one. That does something to the sound I get back. Always tested alone before."

Homer kept thumping all the way up, smiling at her. There was a vanity in the man, Alice decided. The absurdity of testing his powers by beating a steel wall. At the top she thanked Homer, found she had greasy streaks discoring her pants and jacket—her cheeks must be streaked, too. There was on her skin a light burning sensation.

"I need a bath. Ugh, it's a slimy toad feeling. God, the sun and sky look good. It's like we've just escaped from a grave." She felt a quivering in her legs.

When she was gone, Homer stood by the catwalk and wondered about something; he screwed up his face with a puzzled expression. He went down to his little office in the engine area, waved to his second engineer, Carlos. Homer hunted in a batch of pale yellow papers that contained photo copies of the loading reports. Homer found the reports: Tanks ten and eleven loaded to ninety-seven percent of their capacity; checked by computer and lodmeters.

He shook his head, as if to clear it, took out a little notebook—one of a series in which he recorded items. He wrote slowly with a failing ballpoint pen:

Today, found my way of estimating contents of tanks to be not too accurate when another person is in the well with me. I got sounds that ten and eleven are only twenty percent full. This cannot be, as measuring meters and loading figures check out that they are holding full capacity. Must experiment with two people, three, even four on the staircase to see how much this changes my estimates of tank contents. I wonder if I can set up a new scale values system showing how much each added person changes the sound. Tanks ten and eleven are full. Ott, a damn great technician, would know if they were out of whack.

For Wallie Ormsbee the rumors of the captain's dilemma on the *Pallas Athena* were vague. He was living a private drama; he was possessed by Sarah Hammel. "Sari," a private image. She was becoming part of his youthful past, like a delicious odor long held over from his boyhood. She was as pleasant as the remembered smell of citronella on a long ago summer with Mother, the two standing hand in hand in the trembling dusk of an Italian summer; she had returned to her boy after a failed tryst.

The emotions of that reunion had been transferred to Sari. He watched her in the wardroom pouring tea at the table, nibbling a chicken wing. It all gave him an ecstatic feeling of tranquility that remained when he went to his cabin and recalled her voice, her stance in the crayon-blue gown she wore at a late gathering after a movie in the ship's theater, where everyone had taken a nightcap.

Wallie found himself knocking on the chief engineer's door. He found Homer in his cabin changing a typewriter ribbon.

"Mind if I barge in?"

"Not at all, Wallie. Goddamn it, I can rebuild an electric motor—even rewind the coils, or fit a section of boiler pipe lying on my back with steam burning my arse, but changing a bloody typing ribbon . . ." He held up his sooty fingers; there was a smudge on his right cheek.

Wallie examined the spool of ribbon. "It's not for your machine, that's why. It's for a Royal."

"Oh hell, a clapped-up Arab will sell you anything."

"I can reroll it on an old spool." He set to work on the task, stealing a glance at Homer grabbing a bottle of Black Horse Ale out of his small frig. "Care for an ale?"

"No thanks, Homer."

"You think old Tom is going to have his way?"

"About what? Oh you mean charting his own course if he has to? It's just a battle of egos, isn't it? Him and the Athens folk; who comes up top dog."

Wallie slowly rolled the ribbon onto the empty spool. "Homer, I need some advice. I mean personal."

Homer swallowed a gulp of ale from the bottle, "Personal, eh? Picked up a dose in port? Been playing cut-throat bridge with the Greek? Signed markers?"

"No, no. I mean, I gather from your talk you have a reputation for understanding women."

Homer chuckled, frowned, sipped ale. "Ha, a buggery lot I don't know about them. What's your problem?"

"I have this drive—an unreasonable one—I mean to declare myself to someone on board."

Homer whistled. To Wallie it sounded like a plaintive bleat. "Oh bad, lad, the quiff on board is limited in number and you have competition. I mean this Farashah bird will put out if you approach her right. The Greek has been sniffing around, but there's plenty on the bones there for two I'd say."

"It isn't her, I mean . . ."

"Well if it's our stewardess, I'd watch my step. This Sieko, her husband, is a handy man with a knife or a strangling cord like the ancient Thugs."

"I wouldn't take to a native. It's not that I'm prejudiced; well, yes I am. Sorry."

Homer put down his bottle of ale—empty. "Alice Palamas? I was down one of the inspection shafts with her. You thinking of taking a feel? Just to see a reaction, know what I mean? Then move in fast." He beat one fist on the other. "*Very* fast."

"I've never been bold with women."

Homer rubbed at the label on the bottle. "Look, Wallie, if it's one of the Chinese kitchen boys or an Arab kid from the deck gang . . ."

Wallie dropped the spool.

"No, it's a woman."

"Well, go right ahead. Bold attack, I'd say. The direct presentation. 'Lay it in her hand,' my old Grand Da always said. Sometimes more than not they just say 'oh dear' and spread just like that."

Wallie began to put the typewriter ribbon into the machine. "I suppose I belong to another time. I mean someone I grew up with has ideas of the proper moment, a placid period of understanding before . . ."

"Not today, old cock, not today. It's, 'Your place or mine?' More like putting a letter in a postbox."

Wallie looked at his soiled fingers. "You should get some benzine or something and clear the keys. Your *e* is blocked."

The ship did a dip and a roll as if making a curtsy.

TAPE RECORDING NO.6
By Alice P. with
Homer B.

Research for film sound track

"A steel ship, Homer, doesn't rot out like the old wooden clippers and frigates. Maybe you could narrate some of my film—people like talk of dangers at sea."

"Steel ships deteriorate, Alice, and metal wears in engines, boilers leak and scale, generators and auxiliaries turn to scrap . . . steel ship, you think is safe."

"You're trying to depress me, Homer. What can hurt steel?"

"Steel? Well, for one thing all that sulfur in the oil we carry can be a problem. The oil is pumped out in port, sure, but lots of sulfur dioxide stays below, and this can turn to sulfuric acid. You ever drop a dirty penny in acid and watch what happens? You figure any tanker can get two to three percent of its steel eaten up by the acid, and it's sneaky stuff; it doesn't just eat away over the whole surface. No, it picks spots for pitting; some special plates, or joints, or corners. Why a five- or six-year-old tanker may have to replace whole plates that are weakened enough to make cracks. Of course, if its bottom plate looks bad, some carriers bribe the special survey people and sail under flags of convenience. You can keep a tanker afloat even when you can punch your fists through the hull. Survey and inspection under some flags are a joke."

"Why are you scaring me?" (No, can't use that. The KSL wants to keep stockholders happy with my film.)

"You think so? Scaring? No, just informing. This hull is over a thousand feet long. She has to give now and then or she'll crack. You have to figure the strain when you load oil in a crazy hippo-shaped thing like a tanker, figure the shear force and bending action. One is vertical, the other horizontal; gravity and pull . . . see? . . . and buoyancy and thrust have to be just right for safe sailing."

"You are, I hope, careful about loading." (Sorry I started all this.)

"Better be. You can't have a full tank next to a nearly empty one. You'd have weight pressing down, putting the ship off the perpendicular and forcing the buoyancy up. That makes a shear force between the full and the empty. If the pressure on the hull is too extreme, she can crack or tear herself in half. Now, if you load the end tanks and the middle tanks are low, the weight at the ends can tear her apart."

"I don't believe a word of this. You're spinning a yarn. You're a real cheerful bastard."

Homer accepted a fresh bottle of ale from Ping Pong. "Bad loading isn't at first apparent. There can be a crack, a strain on rivets, and you won't know until you run into rough weather. Then it happens; a lot of unexplained tanker wrecks are most likely caused this way, but when the tanker is sunk half a mile down in the Pacific, who's to know . . . who?"

"There are safety checks."

"We have the Lodicator that analyzes the weight of the water, cargo, and fuel before we sail. It checks the shear force and the bending action at certain positions all along the ship."

"Good."

"It's a machine. Only a machine. Something could knock it out of kilter and . . ."

"Oh shut up and drink your ale."

Homer finished his drink; he felt better—scaring Alice.

She went on deck; it was windy, very—the gray sullen sea seemed angry, coming in long curling waves to strike the ship quickly. She sensed, for the first time, the stress and pressure working on the hull; it even seemed she could see the give and take of the decks. Imagination, she thought. There is no doubt sailors are a gloomy lot, whether fighting on Nelson ships-of-the-line, whaling or carrying Iranian crude to Exxon refineries.

BOOK THREE

CRY HAZARD

CHAPTER | 11

For two days Achilles kept Farashah away from his cabin. He insisted that it wasn't that he was not man enough, it was that he had ship's work to do, certain fitness reports to fill out, a full inspection of the ship below the main deck. And a fire drill to run off, announced by the clatter of the alarm bell and three long and two short hoots from the hooter, then hoses run out on the deck by the crew in fireproof suits, the P.A. system announcing, "Boat drill, boat drill. Life jackets must be worn and tied properly, assembly at deck-station positions assigned to you . . . *boat drill!*"

The officers and crew, except for the captain and the seamen at the wheel and in the engine room, came out on the main deck. All stood in their bright orange life jackets, looking deformed and top heavy. Wallie checked them—all standing by a lifeboat or a motor launch station.

Achilles and Ludwig adjusted the life jackets on some; a garment with a battery-attached, water-proof flashlight and a whistle both to attract attention and to assure confidence if one had to take to the boats or leap overboard.

Ludwig shouted, "If your battery light is low, report it."

Wu Ting Li and Duck Fong spoke in rapid sing-song Chinese to their people. Sieko sternly ordered Gemila and Farashah to retie the tapes on their jackets. Wallie failed to find Sarah on deck.

The P.A. system came on. "Not very good," the captain's voice announced. "Everyone should be at his station two minutes after the drill is announced. You there in the kitchen section! Take off those caps and aprons. And all of you, bring hats and warm clothing along. Sieko, what the hell has *that* sailor got there?"

"His sewing machine, sar."

"Goddamn it, nothing but clothes."

"The ship's cat, sar, the parrot cage, it can cum along?"

The P.A. system went on, ignoring the question.

"Sound the end of drill. We'll try again in two days, Mr. Marrkoras, if the weather holds. Dismissed."

"Yes sir, dismissed."

The ship's cat, Tiger Lily, as if remembering other drills, had leaped into one of the motor launches. She was a large red and yellow striped tabby. Wu Ting Li was sure she was the ghost of some evil demon.

Wallie found Sarah in her suite reading a horoscope book.

"I never go to drills. I go down with the captain."

The crew didn't feel so indifferent to the boat drill when they heard a report broadcast by "World Oil News" at dusk:

SEARCHERS COULD FIND NO TRACE OF THE INDIAN FREIGHTER "BHANDRADUPTA" OR LIFEBOATS CONTAINING FORTY-EIGHT CREW MEMBERS AND THREE WIVES WHO ABANDONED THE FLOODED SHIP IN ROUGH SEAS A THOUSAND MILES NORTHWEST OF HONOLULU.

THE LAST REPORT THURSDAY NIGHT WAS THAT THE NUM-

BER FOUR HATCH WAS GONE, THE SHIP WAS TAKING ON WATER, AND THEY WERE ABANDONING IT, A SPOKESMAN SAID FOR BAHASA MARINE AGENCIES, THE AGENT FOR THE 627-FOOT INDIAN VESSEL.

MILITARY AIRCRAFT SEARCHING IN DARKNESS SPOTTED A LIGHTED AND APPARENTLY ABANDONED SHIP LOW IN THE WATER, BUT COULD ELICIT NO RADIO RESPONSE.

RELIEF PLANES OUT AT DAYLIGHT WERE UNABLE TO FIND THE VESSEL. FOUR AIRCRAFT IN ROTATION WERE TO CONTINUE SEARCHING AS TWO TANKERS "STAR PATH" AND "KEY WEST," AND A NAVY SHIP, "THE TRUMAN," MOVED TOWARD THE AREA.

A COAST GUARD SPOKESMAN SAID THE "KEY WEST" WAS ENCOUNTERING WORSENING WEATHER WITH FIFTY-FOOT SEAS AND FIFTY-MILE-PER-HOUR WINDS, BUT WAS EXPECTED TO ARRIVE BY NIGHTFALL.

THE "BHANDRADUPTA" LEFT PORTLAND, OREGON, FOR IRAQ, WITH A CARGO OF 34,000 TONS OF WHEAT. THE 21,635-TON VESSEL IS OWNED BY SHANDRA SHIPPING OF INDIA.

At dinner the captain, with Achilles as guest at his table, looked about him as he finished his Cornish game hens in saffron rice. Sarah said, "I kidded Wallie, I'd go down with the ship, and he almost believed me."

"Oh? It's a big ocean, and if we do have to take to the boats I want them fully provisioned: fresh water checked, food, radios in functioning order. Right, Mr. Marrkoras."

Sarah smiled. "Really, there's room for everybody."

"Mr. Ormsbee," said the Greek to Wallie, "in case of an emergency, you are to take the women aboard launch Four with the kitchen people and cast off."

Alice wondered if the talk was serious: "I'd like to stay and film from the deck."

The captain inspected his section of apple pie. "This is all just regulation, Alice; we're not a leaky Indian tub."

Sarah said, "Skip, we could go down together holding hands on the bridge."

Wallie blushed as she looked at him, grinning.

Wallie, his mind full of images of shipwrecks, was weaving together a movie of his own: *Pallas Athena* battered and sinking, the crew completely berserk, he carrying Sari in her flimsy nightgown into the launch, she clinging to him, face against his. He could smell her personal odor: female, shamefully female, her body pleasantly solid. Then they were alone in the drifting launch in a sea of monstrous proportions, and she was admitting her love for him, *only* him. Where were the others? They had died; had they been eaten? He fastened his gaze on Sari's plump arm, her bobbing breasts, and with much nuzzling, tasting, biting her bosom . . . and finally merging, hurling himself down on—

"Mr. Ormsbee," (the captain's voice intruded) "I want all the tanks below checked for signs of strain, seepage, tests for gas."

"Gas, Captain?"

Sari's husband had broken up the best fantasizing he'd had to date. Wallie wondered if somehow some ESP had given the captain a view of his secret vision.

SECTION C: PACIFIC MARINE FORECAST
CHINA SEA—SOUTHEAST WINDS 20 TO 30 KNOTS . . . HAZARDOUS SEA CONDITION. WINDS BLOWING SOUTHWESTERLY 30 KNOTS GALE FORCE TONIGHT . . . 15-FOOT SWELLS WITH OCCASIONAL BREAKER SETS OF 15 FEET ON SOME WEST FACING ISLAND BEACHES . . . 10-FOOT WIND WAVES OFF SUNDA STRAIT . . . RAIN THIS MORNING IN TIMOR SEA . . . HEAVY CLOUD FORMATIONS . . . WEATHER CLOSING IN OFF COCOS ISLAND.

It was clear by the pitch and roll that *Pallas Athena* could expect rough weather soon. The captain ordered the swimming pool emptied. Sarah decided she'd have one more swim before that happened. The pool water was splashing from side to side, wetting the deck as some dips and rolls moved the water off the horizon line; the pool looked rather dangerous, but as Sarah stepped in, the pitching seemed to suspend her body in a world of protective water, like the air bubble in a glass tube on a carpenter's level.

She could not stay in long; the sloshing water made her suddenly dizzy. She got out of the pool and went to the dressing room.

Sitting in a yellow terrycloth robe, she lit a cigarette and tried to recall comforting memories of her youth. But, the buttoned-up mind directed her to the problems Skip was having: He shouldn't get excited with that pacemaker. What if he went? No, never think of *that*. She heard the door open, and called out, "Farashah, it's time to get some fresh towels in here."

There was no answer, and she turned to find Wallie Ormsbee standing, stark naked. Jesus Christ, the kid was clearly in some whacked-out state. He had an enormous damn erection growing from the base of his corn-colored pubic bush. She had met flashers before but *this* was a stripper.

"What the hell kind of scam is this?" she said, inhaling deeply on the cigarette.

Wallie advanced toward her, hands at his side. When he spoke, his voice had a very even, rather low-keyed, but intense quality, "You understand, Sari."

"Understand what, you goddamn lunatic!"

She swallowed smoke, coughed, mashed out the cigarette and stood up. She grabbed hold of her robe and closed it.

"Now look, you get the hell out of here. Come to your senses. You hear me?"

He shook his head with a firm perversity. "There's no one else. There's something, don't you feel it between us—a logical certitude. I love you."

"A whacked-up way to show it. Now you cover up that damn dong and get out of here . . . get out fast."

"I sense you know . . . understand. You are kind, you

talk to me. You are aware there is between us a sensitivity."

"Look, Wallie, don't make too much of . . . I mean our talks. I'm an old bag, you don't want whatever it is from me. Get yourself some young chick . . . *stay there!* Just think, I'm old enough to be your old lady."

He was coming nearer in a kind of slow motion shuffle, "Yes, you are like Mother."

"Well, dammit, respect your mother. Sit down, let's have a talk."

"You're so much like her, and more, much more."

He had a hand on her shoulder and was pulling down her robe. She didn't fight him. Easy, easy. She felt his penis hard against her naked thigh as the robe fell. She managed to duck aside and grabbed the robe. She felt her behind touch the dressing table. No retreat. The touch of her bare ass on the edge of the table seemed a great obscenity.

"Tell me, Wallie, about you, about Mother. You must have been a pretty baby, huh?"

"Oh God, oh God, Sari, I want you, need you." And suddenly he was down on his knees before her, grasping her firmly around the hips, mashing his head into her stomach, into her bush. His face was kneading her naked flesh. There was within reach a heavy, white glass jar of Pond's cold cream, but she decided it wouldn't maybe knock him out, only increase his burning fury. Hard to believe the damn ship was sailing along at 16 knots, and normal activities were going on.

She ran her hand through his hair, made cooing sounds. "Poor Wallie, he wants love. Wallie, Wallie, look at me. Lift your head (Jesus, anymore of this and it's rape). Now, yes, I understand, I do, look, cross my heart."

He stared up at her, his eyes unfocused, his mouth was open, and she could hear his breathing. His hands did not release their grip around her straining body, or his head its butting into her bush. A hell of a position—situation, at my age.

"You do—I knew you'd understand, Sari. You'd be my girl."

She said softly, "Tell me how you know."

"There are things that don't need words, even a look; a kind of a radio message." His mouth was busy—in a minute the bastard would be giving her head.

"Be a little clearer. I mean I really want to know." (Would the old con work?)

He relaxed his hold, closed his eyes. Sarah managed to move sideways. The loon was between her and the door, a latched door.

He remained on his knees, wet mouth open—she stood near the wall and adjusted the robe around her, then reached for a cigarette, lit it from a battered brass lighter on the dressing table.

He said, "You shouldn't smoke so much."

"I know, honey, I'm going to try to cut down."

He seemed suddenly confused. He shook his head. He looked about him in overwhelming wonder, and then he was weeping. "My God, my God, *why* am I acting like this?"

"Because you need someone to understand you."

"That I'd do this, force myself on you."

He tried to cross his arm before him to shield his nakedness.

"I understand, Wallie. I really do." She figured ten feet to the door; snap open the latch and run like hell, yelling all the way. "I always listened, haven't I?"

"I want to know mature love. It's so hard to meet the right person, to relate, to feel deeply that there is something more than drink, whores, material interests. You want that too, don't you? The two of us—we completely want each other."

(Off his rocker, clearly, this hyped-up jock.)

118

"Wallie, why not give me time to think this out? After all, I am as sensitive as you are, and you don't want to be brutal, do you; not you, the way Mother raised you. No force . . . violence. Okay?"

"Just a spontaneous kinship. My dream fuck, it has to be that, you understand."

"Think, honey, this is too public a place." She tried a shot in the dark. "Mother was always against grossness, wasn't she?"

He nodded, still on his knees. He closed his eyes, whispered, "I'm ashamed of trying to reach your body this way. I'm very much ashamed. I don't know how I got here, naked. I must be running a fever. How I've humiliated you, vulgarized our own meaning to each other."

"You just got carried away, isolated on this ship. Maybe things get to us the wrong way first and—(don't say ass backwards) and now we understand better, huh?"

At least his damn erection had subsided and his voice was more normal. Sarah slid around him holding her robe closed. He didn't stir, just sank his face into his cupped hands. She was at the door. Sarah shot back the latch and unaware of the cigarette hanging in one corner of her mouth, forced the door open; for a moment in panic, trying to pull it toward her (oh shit!), then pushing, and out into the white day. She moved quickly toward the elevator. She turned her head, but Wallie was not following her.

She was sorry for the poor sonofabitch when she got to her quarters; she was sweating profusely, her armpits reeked and her eyes in the mirror had the look of someone questioning the sanity of the whole frigging world.

Sarah poured herself three fingers of Scotch and discovered the cigarette was still stuck to the corner of her mouth. She tore it loose with a yank and there was blood. Tasting Scotch and blood, she swallowed her drink and sat down.

Poor bastard was kinky, must have cuddled up to his old lady in bed even when he was a big boy pulling his duff. You never knew with sex, did you? Mother must have been some possessive bitch to warp that kid by holding him close to her too long.

Should she tell Skip? The captain would blow his cool, maybe lock Wallie up in the brig . . . and at a time like this, a storm front brewing and the fucking Greeks making problems for the captain. No, she'd just slough it off and act as if he were drunk. Play it by ear. Don't rile Skip now.

On deck Sieko Mihran was having his crew string life lines. Above them on the bridge, the captain and First Officer Marrkoras were passing each other weather reports. The radio room was relaying the latest Marine forecasts.

"Mr. Marrkoras, wind force 40 knots in the South China Sea. Moving."

"Not a typhoon yet."

"Get me the current wind charts. Where's Mr. Ormsbee?"

"Got a touch of the flu. Thought it better he stay in his cabin."

"Very well."

"Sir, you've charted tomorrow's run?"

Captain Hammel looked at the Greek and seemed to search his face for some kind of clue—the look one gives a mischievous child. "Why?"

"Point of information, Captain."

"I'll decide when we find out the direction of this storm front."

"Yes, Captain."

Later, his watch over, Achilles went up to the radio room and sent another of those messages that amused Sparky:

CHESS GAME SET AT TANGENT SO PLAY OFF BOARD WILL RESULT.

A.M.

Sparky figured the wily greaseball was speculating on the world money market with the Kyprios brothers.

On his feverish bed, Wallie sensed the ineptitude of his life, but Sari took it well, didn't she; your damn exposure. She didn't scream; she didn't throw anything. Clearly a wise woman—she *understood*. You moved a bit too fast, boy. The head hurts, the throat is dry, the nose closed . . . he was a goddamn pathological neurotic. "Sari, Sari," he moaned, and chewed on his pillow.

When he was calmer, he took his temperature—only a degree or so of fever. He felt dizzy sitting up and sank back on the bed. His head was full of hot lead, the ship was rolling and plunging in heavier weather. Should he be on the bridge, seeing to the fire hoses, the chemical retardant, the stringing of life lines on the main deck over the catwalk, in case the men had to work in mean weather. He closed his eyes and sank into a troubled sleep.

12

In the crew quarters someone was playing a Hindu flute. Most likely Meriapa, a partly trained medical student—the crew's doctor. A fantan game was in progress among the deck crew. In the cabin of Duck Fong they were playing poker in a mist of cigar smoke. Duck Fong himself sat in command of the table, a cheroot in his large yellow teeth, wearing a green plastic eyeshade. Sieko Mihran was inspecting a close-held hand of cards; around them the other players, Wu Ting Li, Abdullah Ali Mirza, the steersman, Sparky, and Carlos de Nova, the Goanese assistant engineer, watched.

They played nearly every night, generally cheerfully, but often with fiery cursing and howling, drinking saki and mesticha, the Greek grape brandy. Away from the eyes of the white officers, they produced private jests, ravaged reputations, and gossiped incessantly between hands.

Duck Fong puffed on his cigar: "I call. So, Pavel, what thing is weally new with the captain?"

Sparky watched the Chinaman rack in the pot. "What's new?" He leaned forward. "The Greeks are thick as farts at an early mass. This second officer is sending code to Athens."

"Code?" asked Abdullah.

"Secret messages. The Greeks got something cooking against the captain."

"Velly clazy people, white people," said Wu Ting Li.

"What you think, Pavel?" asked Duck Fong, carefully putting the money before him in order.

The radio man looked sly, winked, the Mongol part of his features crinkling up to nearly hide his eyes.

"The way I figure it, maybe they want a bit of, say, machinery trouble here and there, see? Then force the captain to make for the nearest port to unload, say, Japan. And the Greeks, they take a lot of cumshaw under the table, eh?, for diverting oil to Nippon very short of the stuff. Pay extra in secret."

Carlos frowned. "No machinery trouble possible."

"Velly clevah," said Duck Fong.

"But no," said Wu Ting Li. "Japan too far off on map." He shuffled the cards expertly. "Still, nevah know."

Sparky nodded. "I'll bet on it. This cargo is unloaded some place before this tanker gets to the good old U.S.A. Any takers?"

Abdullah looked at a huge wristwatch attached to a mahogany-colored arm. "Go on watch in half hour. One more hand?"

Duck Fong yawned. "Ah no. Birfday lady captain, she have party, much eating and dance, must cook Beef Wellington, sweet, souah flish." He looked at the money before him, lifted a glass of brandy, swallowed quickly. "Not a good game tonight." His licked his lips for a missed drop of brandy.

That broke up the poker game and the players departed.

Sieko went down to the main deck to watch the sea spray come banging across the catwalk, listening to the creaking and banging for loose hatch covers. Sieko knew every comforting sound from the purr of the engines, the slight whine of the drive shafts, the flapping of the flag in a rising breeze. There was one added note—faint, yet unexpected. It was a sound like metal giving off a querulous bid for attention. A ship had a soul, so said the *Bhagavad-Gita,* and a God (good) and a God (evil). Sieko believed, as a good follower of the Karma-yoga—the path of action—that someplace on board the good spirit was struggling against the evil spirit, and the ship was reacting to the conflict.

The row of electric bulbs encased in heavy glass over the catwalk made yellow holes in the dark night. Sieko walked forward, looked up at the island that held the living quarters of both crew and officers. From it, the bridge extended like a sea bird's wings. He studied the slanted glass of the bridge and just made out the second officer's shape outlined by the hooded chart lamp.

The young dog in heat with his balls aching for the captain's bitch, Sieko thought, as if the captain didn't have enough problems. If Sparky was right, and they ended up in Japan with "engine trouble," there would be an official hearing and he would have to testify. Who would believe a "nigger" against the word of a Greek, or those English and Americans? Again, he heard the new sound, a bit fainter, and then it went away. Lord Shri Krishna, am I growing grass in my ears?

A shape came up to him and he wondered for a moment was it the ghost of his first wife Laila who had died of poisoned tea when his in-laws wanted to punish her for certain sexual looseness while he was away at sea.

But it was only the Missy Palamas wrapped in green oil-skins, a shiny hood on her head.

"A brisk night, Sieko."

"Oh yes, Missy. We are moving toward angry season of the seas."

"It's all so unreal; the ship is so huge, and we seem like

insects clinging to it, thinking we rule it, move it, and all the time I sense there are indifferent forces that really control us."

"Is that so?" Sieko nodded. The white race had no true sense of existence, did not understand the ways of the ordained fates all stored-up for us, waiting to be fulfilled. He nodded again. "Most interesting, Missy."

Alice shivered. Spray came rolling in. She felt the dampness even inside her rain gear. She went to her cabin, undressed. In a robe she sat creaming her face reflected in the oval mirror. She didn't much like her face; some people thought it beautiful, a mysterious face like something in a Greek statue of the classic period. A few saw it as rather Jewish, but the eyes were very good.

With regret, she remembered her French lover, the English lover—with disdain. Casually, she wondered about suicide—just slipping over the rail, reaching the sea in seconds, then dropping into the salt water, surrounded by bubbles and the compressing pressure of water, a ballet of sorts, rolling *over* and *over* . . . she recalled a wonderful party in Switzerland, crisp snow underfoot, being alive on a ski slope, all vulnerability forgotten.

FROM THE NOTEBOOKS OF HOMER BOWEN:

The idea for a birthday party for Sarah Hammel, wife of our captain, originated with Alice Palamas. The two ladies had been chatting during the cocktail hour and Mrs. Hammel, Sarah (it's all first names on this ship), dropped the fact she would be having a birthday in two days. Alice picked it up and got Fong to prepare special food and Gemila Mihran to put up decor in the dining room and the wardroom. Very festive. Life at sea takes on an intensity not common on shore.

Pallas Athena, like most of the big tankers, carries a stock of crepe paper and ribbons, funny hats, confetti to keep the officers in a good mood. Even the crew celebrates Chinese New Years, and certain other Oriental celebra-

tions, more excuses for firecrackers (forbidden) and general cat-wailing Chinese music.

Sarah is, I would guess (and I'm no good at this damn game of judging women's ages), in her middle fifties, perhaps a bit more. Wallie said age didn't matter. He quoted Balzac as insisting women of forty were splendid stuff, magnificent at fifty and at sixty, beyond compare, and by seventy, heaven itself. I don't know Balzac that well (he never, I believe, wrote a sea novel), but he may well have made that estimation of female sensuality, the French being what they are, to preen himself as a womanizer.

Sieko brought in extra lights, and he asked me to see to the safety of the extension cords and electrical connections.

Our conversation, I must record it, had strange overtones:

"I fear the electric, sar."

"It's a slave or a monster," I said. "It gives us air conditioning."

He agreed that was a blessing, and added he himself didn't like the sound, the simper of air conditioning. "Like a cobra preparing to bite. I close vent, turn him off, and Gemila turns him back on. When sound off I hear this new noise."

I asked what noise, and he explained that he, as a good sailor, was aware of every sound the ship made, its creaks, its bongs, and bings. But this was a new sound, very low, but having for him a different note.

I said I was experimenting with sounds myself in the ship's wells by tapping a tank wall and estimating its content; experimenting with Alice, with two people in the well, it seemed to change the pitch of the thump.

"Very interesting, sar . . . maybe tanks are leaking, loss of content?"

I said no, no sign of leakage; no oil spillage signs.

We were deep in this discussion, like two cooks over a recipe, when Wallie came in with a large sign he had designed in red, blue, and yellow with felt pens, a sign on a long strip of wide white paper:

> Happy Birthday at Sea to our Captain's Lady
> Happy Happy Happy From a Happy Ship

Sieko said, "Plenty happies."

Wallie said seriously, "Never enough."

I had Ping Pong attach it to the bar mirror with Scotch Tape. Sieko went off before we could compare our study of sounds. I must treat him to a pint of ale and talk it over. I don't hold that an engineer and scientist has the right to ignore the folk wisdom in simple people, for all their impossible contradictions.

LATER NOTE:

I suppose I'd better record today's event in detail as it is likely I shall have to testify in some sort of court of inquiry.

To begin: the dining room, after cocktails in the wardroom, was all colored paper ribbons and funny paper hats of red and gold at each setting. The menu had been printed on silver and red paper on the small printing press we carry:

Happy Birthday for Our Captain's Mate Sarah Hammel at Sea This Date . . . "Pallas Athena."

Sieko had managed to come up with an orchestra of sorts: two Chinese sailors played a horn and an electric "gitar," while Wallie took over the nearly in-tune piano. I had a whole stack of recordings ready to fill in on the intercom system: Noel Coward and Irving Berlin, and some Beatles and Nashville stuff. Achilles offered a selection of avant-garde jazz. I felt it was too much and said no.

Sarah really looked regal and pink with pleasure. She was dressed in some shiny metallic gown, her hair done up a little too high, perhaps, and too many shiny rhinestone pins in it. Never mind, it was all sparkling and feminine. Old Tom was pleased and smiling, only taking time out to read the radio messages from Sparky's assistant in the wireless room.

There was champagne in the ice buckets; real bubbly, not the California fizz. Alice was in a most revealing gown (she has too prominent shoulder blades, like sprouting wings); she kissed Sarah, and there was a cheer as we finished singing "Happy Birthday," Wallie thumping loudly on the piano keys.

Sarah said, "Golly gee, you bastards, and you, Alice, you really played dirty pool making me aware I was getting older by celebrating I was an old crock. But never mind, I sure like attention, and oh boy (she was sipping champagne) this tastes good. So what the hell, there is life in the old girl yet. Cheers! Thanks!"

She sniffed back tears, and Old Tom put his arm around her and kissed her cheek. He said he wouldn't trade her in for any movie star, not this year's models anyway. In all this there was no hint of what was to come . . . or I wasn't as observant as I think I am.

The waiters came in with shrimp and lobster in garlic and brandy sauce. Fong was doing things right in his kitchen. The Beef Wellington, Beluga Caviar au blinis, and all the trimmings were greeted by cheers, and there was white wine and red wine. Ludwig Ott came down for a toast (he being on duty on the bridge). Achilles, a wine snob, tasted and approved the wine.

When the big cake came in, carried by two kitchen boys, we saw a tower of icing . . . lathered with candied fruit, stuccoed with crushed nuts, and topped by what Fong, who came in for a bow, said was the Goddess of Love—Chinese, of course. Sarah had to cut the first slice, and we cheered. Wallie made a speech and Sarah kept eyeing him in a wary way, like a mother worrying over a kid. Wallie was all fancy prose about woman and motherhood and lovers and the dedication of the female to the life force. He was a bit slopped from mixing champagne and the Three Star brand, and he looked like a pink-cheeked, public school boy laughing, hair falling over his eyes like a kid at a party just before he tosses his cookies.

Sarah gave him a wan smile, nodding, said, "He's a dear well-brought-up lad." We all cheered that, and Ping Pong passed out cigars for the officers. Alice presented Sarah with pearl earrings.

"The pearl, Sarah, is a beautiful product of nature from the dark secret corners of the oyster, a living bit of shell rock, and so to the jewel on this rather odd-shaped tanker, we offer this gift (cheers) from all the officers and engineers of Pallas Athena (applause, whistles)."

Sarah held up the earrings, and there were cries of "hear, hear" through the cigar smoke and warmed-up perfumes of Alice and Sarah. Even Gemila and Farashah passing out demitasse seemed to be sending out scents of musk and sandalwood oil.

By this time I had noticed that Achilles was smiling too much, but not at the celebration the rest of us were enjoying. Twice he conferred with Sparky and sent him to the wireless room where the assistant was on duty.

Captain Hammel, too, seemed to be in a worrisome mood. I was watching him at a moment when he thought all eyes were on Sarah. He had the look of a puzzled man holding back anger. Or does my writing anticipate what was to happen (I had broken my rule at sea and had three glasses of ten-year Hennessy, some Pouilly-Fuissé).

During the singing of "For She's a Jolly Good Fellow" when everyone was tossing around paper streamers, Sieko slipped me a note. It read:

"Meet me in the library in ten minutes. Slip out unnoticed if you can.—Capt. T.H."

At first I thought a poor jest was on. I looked around and saw Wallie was gone. Achilles was examining the end of his glowing cigar, with an expression on his face that looked like that of a man about to lead a cavalry charge or face a firing squad. (I mean I had never witnessed either event, but that was my impression.)

I pressed past Alice, excused myself in a whisper, and made my way to the library.

The captain was pacing the floor; Wallie, facing him, had a sober look and was trying to shake off the effects of his drinking. The captain looked up as I came in, and he went to the door, threw the latch. I wondered if he, a nondrinker, had been taking on too much Chateau Margaux to act so melodramatic.

129

He seemed calm enough when he spoke, sounded rather matter of fact:

"You are the two officers aboard Pallas Athena I trust. Never mind why I leave out the others. Now, are you sober, Ormsbee?"

"Oh, yes, sir." Wallie looked sick but steady. Just a hardly noticeable tic on one cheek.

"Homer, I think an attempt is going to be made to take this ship out of my command. I have found it necessary to disregard the Kyprios route orders."

I suppose I reacted as if I had a foot caught in an umbrella stand. I gasped, and foolishly blurted, "The hell you say, sir."

"The hell I don't."

I could see his fists clench, but otherwise he remained calm.

"The KSL agent will most likely order me to step down from command and appoint their first officer captain."

"Achilles!" said Wallie.

"As I interpret an exchange of radio messages. That appears to be their plan."

"But dammit, Tom," I cried out (like in a bad novel), "they can't replace a captain at sea on a whim, on any grounds."

Wallie said weakly, "Well there was that movie 'Caine Mutiny' . . . I mean . . ."

"By the book there listed officially several grounds," said the captain. "However, I am not insane, I am not incapacitated by illness, nor have I seized the ship for piracy."

"No, none of that," I said, "But . . ."

"What I have done is to have refused to sail on the charted course set by the KSL in order to protect the safety of the ship and save its cargo."

"You have that right by international sea law," I said. (I hope I'm writing all this down properly in the actual words.)

The captain looked over the bookshelves and rubbed his fingers along the wood grain. Wallie looked ill. The captain grimaced: "They will claim I did not fully reveal my medical record when signing up for this trip. And I did not." He went on without raising his voice. "Goddamn them to hell. Somehow they have discovered that about nineteen months ago I had a heart by-pass operation."

"Jesus Christ," said Wallie softly, blinking.

"And right now I have a pacemaker implanted in my chest."

I sat down and mopped my brow with the back of my hand as I tried to hold on to all my faculties.

"But you've done your duty. You look and act fit, Tom."

"I am, Homer. I don't suffer from any delusions. I'm okay. But I need your backing if I'm to make a fight of this. Achilles is their man, Ludwig, too, I'm sure. About Pavel Godoff, I don't know. The radio transmission seems accurate."

"Sparky is wacky but knows his duties."

"I want to make a statement in writing defining under what conditions I am changing course. You know the storm warnings east of us. You will testify and sign that the conditions warrant my change of course. And . . ."

He looked at us with a faint smile, "that I appear sane, with all my facilities . . . and that I firmly say that I intend to continue as captain. That is, if you two think I am sane and in control of my wits and skills."

"Of course, I'll sign," I said.

Wallie nodded. "All this is not true, it can't be happening."

I ignored the mundane remark.

"If I may suggest, I have some skill in medical procedures from having served as a medic when I was young. I am able to take blood pressure, use the stethoscope, look at the back of the eyeball for hints of this or that . . . test reflexes. I mean I can write out a report on your physical and medical fitness at this moment."

Tom seemed amused, patted my shoulder. "Fine, Dr. Bowen. Now, Ormsbee, can you type?"

"Of course, sir; yes, sir."

131

"All right." The captain took a copy of the birthday menu out of his jacket; its back was covered with pencil writing. "Take this, clean it up, change the grammar if you want to. And photocopy a dozen copies."

"Yes, of course."

"Now," said Tom, taking my arm (suddenly it was as it had been when he was first officer, not the captain). He was smiling, "As you limeys say, chin up, bushtailed, bright-eyed, let's go back, give Dolly the best birthday party she ever had."

That's what we did; we rejoined the party still in progress, Alice was singing, "Some Day I'll Find You"; Sarah twirling her champagne glass, spilling some on herself and not caring. (The British grand ball in Brussels the night before Waterloo?)

"A real blast," Sarah shouted as we came back to our seats.

I noticed at once that Achilles was gone and Ludwig was glancing at us with a dead-eye stare, where even looking directly at you, you sense you are seen out of focus.

It is now 2:45 A.M. In three hours it will be dawn. I have written much too quickly. Would like to have polished my text more and got more detail of the exchange of the radio messages between Tom and the Kyprios brothers, Achilles and Athens. But I can only set down what I know for certainty so far.

Tom is on the bridge. I suppose Sarah and Alice are sleeping. Wallie has typed up Tom's text.

I had used the blood pressure apparatus that the medical student in the crew kept and recorded Tom's vital signs. I signed the extent of my examination, dated it. I have also, as has Wallie, signed the captain's statement. After making photo copies Wallie himself took it to the wireless room and watched Sparky transmit it to Athens (no comment, Wallie reported, from the damn halfbreed).

So we await events. Wallie—I think he tossed his biscuits—looks pale and a bit shaken. He asked over his

132

third cup of black coffee, "I don't suppose the captain will break out the cutlasses and issue muskets." He giggled and I wanted to kick his arse.

The "World Oil News," Sparky thought, is mindless; its distant voice keeps grinding out its daily supply of oil ship items, indifferent to most other events, problems. Sparky listened in gloom, biting on his fingernails. The last few days had left him little to chew on.

AN OIL RIG CREWBOAT WITH THIRTY MEN IS SINKING IN ROUGH SEAS IN THE GULF OF OMAS BUT ALL HANDS ESCAPED INJURY. THE BOAT, "TURTLE II," HAS A SEVENTEEN-INCH HOLE KNOCKED IN ITS STERN WHILE FIFTEEN MILES SOUTHEAST OF BUSKA ISLE TWO CREWMEN REMAINED ABOARD TO USE PUMPS DROPPED BY A HELICOPTER. THE BOAT IS BEING TOWED TO CHINCHA ISLAND.

Sparky looked at a bleeding cuticle. He had been ordered by Athens to stand by for a very important message. The "World Oil News" ground on:

SULLOM VOE, SHETLAND ISLANDS . . . CONSTRUCTION MEN ARE RACING AGAINST TIME THROUGH STORMS IN THESE REMOTE SCOTTISH ISLANDS TO BUILD A GIANT OIL TERMINAL VITAL TO BRITAIN'S ECONOMIC RECOVERY.

NORTH SEA OIL, AN ESTIMATED 1.4 BILLION TONS OF IT, THE EQUIVALENT OF ABOUT 10 BILLION BARRELS, IS BRITAIN'S LIFELINE AND THE CORE OF THE PRIME MINISTER'S WHOLE STRATEGY TO REVIVE THE ANEMIC ECONOMY.

THE NATION EXPECTS TO BECOME SELF-SUFFICIENT IN OIL PRODUCTION IN TWO YEARS. THE OIL TERMINAL AT SULLOM VOE, A DEEPWATER INLET WHOSE ANCIENT NORSE NAME MEANS "A PLACE IN THE SUN," IS THE KEY FACTOR IN GETTING PRODUCTION INTO HIGH GEAR AND . . .

Sparky cut off the broadcast. Athens had signaled it was ready to transmit.

CHAPTER | 13

Thomas Hammel was up at dawn. In the glare of morning sun, he recalled an early school reading of Homer: "Rosy-fingered dawn," the old Greek had called it. A man who saw nature close. Not like those bastards the Kyprioses who had lost the quality of the ancient Greeks, or were the Greeks even then wily traders, grabbers, hustlers?

At eight o'clock he decided to shave. Through the angle of the mirror, he was aware of Sarah watching him. He shut off the shaver, hoping she wouldn't start on his agonies and dislocations.

"Good party last night, Dolly."

"Maybe. There's a lot brewing you've shoved out of sight of me."

"You'll soon know."

"What are you going to do if the KSL orders you to turn over command to that sonofabitch Marrkoras?"

"Ha," he moved around to face her. "Dolly, how did you come to know what's in the wind?"

"Never mind how." (There had been a short note delivered to her by Farashah with the early pot of coffee. Wallie's note, of course, that schoolboy scrawl, informing her of last night's events.)

She took his hand in hers. "I think you should chuck the Greek in the brig before he makes his move."

"Damn if I know how you know so much. No, I can't do anything without some kind of evidence he's moving against his captain's orders."

"What if he's following owners' orders? Who's top dog at sea? Them or you?"

Thomas shrugged his shoulders, rubbed his lean cheeks to see how close he had shaved. "That calls for a sea lawyer, and you know lawyers, calculating, conniving bastards. They'd sell you their mother for dog meat."

"You have your pistol?"

"Oh, come on now, Dolly. This isn't *Mutiny on the Bounty*. It's . . ."

There was a tap on the door, a brisk knock. Tom nodded to his wife, walked into the front room of the suite: "I smell it. Get Ormsbee and Homer up here. Go phone them."

"Skip, remember your . . . ," she touched her breast and went to the bedroom to phone. Tom moved toward the door as the knock was again repeated.

In the bedroom Sarah dialed Wallie's cabin. She heard Tom's voice at the door of their suite. His voice was dry, edged with a curt brevity. She couldn't make out the words.

"Wallie, it's me, the captain's wife. Yes, Sari, or whatever you say. Listen, the captain wants you pronto up here in our suite and get Homer up here, too. Never mind dressing. Get into a robe. Hurry."

Tom stood facing Achilles and Ludwig, both in full ship's dress, caps tilted at the proper angle. The Greek's face was bland, unexpressive, maybe just a touch of a curdled smile.

"Can we come in?"

"Why?" Tom asked, consciously filling the doorway.

Achilles made a gesture with his left hand, suggesting

yes or no, here I am. "Captain Thomas Hammel, I have here," he held up a radio form, "an order issued at 11:22 Athens time, from the president of the KSL line, Ionnes Kyprios, ordering me to take over the vessel and officially inform you that you are no longer in command of this ship."

"Anything else?" No vehemence or passion.

Ludwig, like a conspirator in an opera, looked away and wiped the back of his thick neck with the palm of his hand.

Tom said, "As a captain with my rights of command, I refuse to accept a mere bit of paper."

Sarah came up to them. "You Greek sonofabitch; oh you yellow-bellied cocksucker. To do this to your captain, to *try* and do it."

Achilles shrugged, slowly, unhurried. He took from his inside jacket pocket an official-looking packet of several blue sheets. "This document was given to me in Athens when I was appointed second officer. It asserts that if I got a radio message to change the official standing of the officers of *Pallas Athena*, I had the KSL power to do so in port or on the high seas. I serve these papers on you now in my full authority."

"You goddamn . . ." began Sarah in a very aggravated state. Tom hushed her. He said to the two officers, "Come in."

Wallie appeared behind them, hair uncombed, wearing a too-short yellow robe, his feet in red bedroom slippers; Homer was in a stained undershirt, having been busy, he explained, repacking a minor valve seat.

It was, Wallie thought (he not too coherent from being torn from sleep) like a scene from a motion picture—a scene in which the director had not placed his people properly.

Achilles and Ludwig faced the captain and his wife rather stiffly. Homer, pop-eyed, wiped his hands on a bit of cotton waste taken from a pocket; Wallie aware his robe was too short and that there were goose bumps appearing on his legs.

Tom said, "On what grounds do you offer these ridiculous papers?"

Achilles rolled his head in the direction of Wallie and Homer. "Can we be confidential here?"

"They are with me in witnessing your attempt to take over the ship. Whatever drivel, so-called legal, you have, spit it out. I'm still captain."

"Damn right," said Sarah.

"Very well. The KSL is in possession of evidence that you misinformed them when you accepted their contract. You withheld vital medical facts, facts which make you a dangerous person to entrust this ship with. Shall I give details?"

Ludwig's inner stability seemed to be failing him. He said nothing.

Wallie said, "We know about the by-pass operation and the pacemaker. We, too, have a paper, a medical examination that finds him fit and able to serve and . . ."

Tom motioned Wallie not to go on. He was eyeing the German, frowning as if ready to pounce.

Ludwig spoke for the first time. "There is no doctor or properly qualified person on board. That native medical student with the crew has no credentials that . . ."

Achilles motioned the German to stop talking. "Captain Thomas Hammel, the KSL has officially ordered me to take command. They desire you to step aside without giving yourself added problems."

"Jesus," said Sarah, "I wish I had me a gun right now. I'd shove it up your ass and pull the trigger six times."

"If you will turn over the ship as the KSL desires, they will not publish or make known the reason for this action—the falsification of your records. So you will still retain your official rank as a ship's officer. No one but the people here present will ever become aware of the legal evidence the KSL owners have in their possession."

"A deal?" asked Tom softly. "A sort of bribe?"

"Words," said Achilles. "Semantics it's called. You will be listed in the log as merely under the weather, a recurring fever, an old malaria, let's say, and you go ashore in California still able to get another nautical command."

"Very well thought out, all the fancy palaver," said Tom. "Well, you radio the KSL to go fuck themselves. If they had this evidence before they signed me as captain, they're up shit creek with the insurance companies."

"They do not claim that. In their records this has just been discovered."

"Radio Lloyds," Tom said to Homer. "It's some wog trick."

Sarah said suddenly with a sigh, "Skip, the rats have you in a corner. Let them have their damn crock of a ship. You'll walk ashore head up."

Tom seemed to be thinking, his expression almost placid. He was, Wallie thought, an eagle set in lonely immobility.

"That's the way the cards fall?" Tom said at last.

"That's it. Look, I've got nothing to do with this. But you did swear to a falsehood when you represented your physical condition. Believe me, I wish I was a thousand miles from here. Legally KSL has it all their way. Want me to say I liked you as a captain? I did. But . . ." he turned to Wallie, "you are to be second officer, Ott, first officer. Homer . . ."

"Mr. Bowen to you."

"You will continue, Bowen, as chief engineer. You two are not foolish enough to go against an acting captain's orders on the high seas."

"I refuse," said Wallie.

Sarah said, "No heroics, Wallie."

"That's right," said Tom. "You'd be in a barrel of trouble. Do as Marrkoras says."

Sarah shouted suddenly. "You're going to let them off so easy?"

"Now, Dolly, you said why not walk off head high. All right, Marrkoras, you're acting captain. Am I under arrest?"

"No, of course not, the entire ship is open to you." There was a sad twist to the Greek's mouth. "But for the bridge. You will be carried as an ill passenger. Everything else is there for you to enjoy, and your madame, too."

Wallie shook his head as Achilles and Ott turned and left the suite, closing the door carefully and nearly soundlessly behind them.

Sarah looked from Tom to Homer to Wallie and then folded her arms, lowered her head and wept. Wallie made a step toward her, as if to comfort her, then drew back as Tom took his wife in his arms.

"Old gal, we've seen worse, lots worse. Let's enjoy the damn trip. Passengers on a sea cruise. Now go get dressed, and we'll all have breakfast. Ring for Gemila and Farashah."

"I'm due on watch," said Wallie. "But, sir, if . . ."

"No, no, Ormsbee . . . Wallie, I mean. Do your duty. Think of your career."

Homer said, "It's all rather queer, 'a queer pitch' as my Grand Da would say."

"I'll powder my nose," said Sarah, going into the bedroom.

Homer looked at his oil-stained hands. "Something out of kilter is up."

"Yes, Marrkoras is going to follow the first KSL chart route."

"And?" asked Wallie.

Tom banged his fists together, looked at the closed bedroom door. "I figure maybe the Kyprios brothers want to lose *Pallas Athena* at sea."

"What!" Homer's voice was shrill, filled with anguish, frustration. "This damn wonderful ship!"

"They're having money trouble. Big bank loans due, KSL losing fortunes on old carrier contracts they can't break without ruining KSL by lawsuits."

"But lose the ship?" Homer appealed to their reason: "Hell, she can pretty near stand up to a hundred-mile-per-hour gale, sixty-foot-high waves. Get battered a bit maybe, but . . ."

"Maybe so, Homer, maybe not. We don't know how much she can stand. But you've been hearing the 'World Oil News.' Maybe you didn't pay attention to the insurance these big tankers carry."

"Twenty million?" asked Wallie. "They couldn't replace *Pallas Athena* for that . . . not today."

Homer shook his head. "I remember the broadcast on tanker insurance. A five-hundred-thousand tonner carries around eighty-five million. We are a five-hundred-fifty-thousand tonner, so I'd say, chief, about ninety million dollars the insurance companies would cough up for *Pallas Athena*?"

"Most likely."

"But for this ship, the survival rate must be ninety percent in any super typhoon," Wallie said.

"If KSL wants to wreck us," said Tom, "I'm not sure. I don't know how they'll make it look like a natural disaster."

Homer said, "Engines, hull, all sound."

Wallie rubbed his nose. "Fire protection in prime order—hoses, chemicals, gas control. Nothing out of kilter there."

Tom pointed a finger at them. "Homer, Wallie, check everything, every section, every tank. Anything wrong—any sign or hint of anything wrong—let me know."

"Bombs? Delayed fuses?" asked Wallie.

"I doubt it," said Tom. "They're smarter bastards than that."

Sarah came out of the bedroom, hair in order, wearing a tan linen suit. "Let's eat. Always face a problem with a good meal." She patted Wallie's cheek, "Be a good boy, a *very* good boy."

But she and the captain—man and wife—ate very little of the breakfast Farashah brought them. Tom had two cups of coffee and only crumbled the wedge of cornbread he usually relished; Sarah poked out the two yellow eyes of the fried eggs set before her, and absentmindedly put out a cigarette in a pat of butter. Events were moving too quickly for her. Living and corruption seemed interchangeable terms.

"You did right, Skip, in not starting a brannigan."

"Like hell I did right. I was playing it PYA—'protect your ass,' as we used to say in the navy."

She gave him a quizzical look. "Aw come on, you were thinking of me. We walk off the ship with nothing on your record about false statements."

"Not false. I just didn't fill in a full history of my health record. I suppose I do want to leave the sea with no bad marks. Like some hotshot school kid wanting to bring home a good report card."

"Skip, look, you're fed up with ships. How long have you been at it? Thirty, forty years. We've got this bit of ranch land, and I want to live close to my sister. She's all the relative I have left. And what have we left—a handful of years."

She tried to laugh and instead came near to tears.

Tom smiled, grabbed one of her hands. "Come off it, Dolly, it's no time for the waterworks. I'll be the goddamnest best grape grower in the Napa Valley."

"If we get to California alive. If that Greek swine doesn't wreck *Pallas Athena*."

Tom became alert, sat back in his chair and tapped his coffee cup with a spoon. "Whatever gave you that goofy idea?"

She sniffed, blew her nose in a napkin, grinned. "I eavesdrop a lot. My mother used to say 'little pitchers have big ears.'"

"It's not easy to wreck a ship like this one. She's made to take any sea or any storm, unless the good Lord decided on a super typhoon. Let's not get paranoid."

"But damn it, all this planning to get rid of you from the start. It's the insurance the KSL is after."

Tom rubbed his chin. Sarah was too intuitive. "What is felt, Dolly, about wrecking the ship is a theory only. Most likely it's not to sink her at all but wreck her on some reef. In a couple of days we'll be just twenty miles north of the Akora Islands. Some dark night suppose Achilles runs her onto a mean sawtooth reef, and a following sea savages her to bits."

"And we go ashore in the lifeboats?"

"It could be done that way. But will the insurance companies, Lloyds and the rest of them who would have to pay out ninety million to the KSL, accept that as a real act of God? No."

"Why not?"

"Too much modern warning gear; sonar, radar on board—unless of course they go out of commission. And *that* would only add to the suspicion."

Sarah covered the eggs on her plate with a saucer. "So you think they're going to deep six the ship some other way?" She grabbed his arm. "Skip, I'm real scared. I never liked the idea of dying, and to drown at sea?"

He leaned over and kissed her. "Everybody is overdramatizing. Ormsbee told me he even heard rumors that the ship is going to be diverted to Japan for some mechanical defect. But hell, there must be a hundred cockeyed rumors on board. And now with Achilles as captain, we'll have a hundred more—from being wanted for murder by Scotland Yard to reports that I was in a drunken stupor most of the time."

Sarah stood up. "Let's go do our walk—a mile back and forth on the catwalk. Show them all you can walk a straight line carrying me piggyback at the same time."

"No games. Just walk and smile, eh?"

The vibration of the plastic panels caught their attention.

Tom looked up. "What's the ship trying to tell us?"

Did it matter to the crew who was captain? They had to accept Captain Marrkoras as they had accepted Captain Hammel. Duck Fong put it to Sieko Mihran at the nightly poker game: "I don't like what's going on. White mans always do foolish things. Only Asians have the wisdom of civilized past."

Sieko threw down a losing hand. "Crew very confused. Speak of omens. And Captain Hammel is not very sick. He walk like always with Missy on deck."

Sparky touched his right temple. "Must have lost a lot of his marbles. Anybody want to bet we change course for Japan in two days?"

Abdullah shook his head. "New captain has charted course for week ahead. No change for Japan."

"Give any of you sports seven to one for Nippon."

There were no takers. The mood was one of wariness among the crew; they waited, worked, wondered.

The person who was most excited by the takeover was Farashah. She lived by uncalculated rigid patterns. Now she, too, was important, as the handmaiden of a great ship's captain; and while Achilles wasn't Solomon in all his glory, the hours they spent in bed in his cabin cavorting in frenzies of sex, drinking, playing music, gave her a sense of pride. They were still locked in some struggle for mental and carnal mastery over each other. She felt surer of herself. True, the new captain had not as much time for their compelling intimacy; as captain he was now preoccupied on the bridge.

But he still tried to force her to accept him as the mighty fornicator (Farashah for all her lost pious mission training still thought in the language of the King James version), wearing himself down to prove himself the master cocksman.

After a furious bout of sex in which he seemed to use her as a vessel into which he could discharge all the passion of his taut nerves, they lay side by side, drinking brandy. The slackness of his jaw muscles made him appear in a near cataleptic state.

"You tired, *mtu mrefu,* I go to my cabin."

"You stay. I'll tell you when I want you to go."

Mtu mrefu—"tall man" in Swahili, sounded mocking.

"Ha, I go and come like I want." She went into a whole range of more Swahili, ending in "*Si-ta-pendi* (I don't make love)."

"Never mind the monkey jabber. I'll decide when."

He looked at her trying to stare her down. But she had learned early in life that in a staring contest, to win, you stare *not* in the other's eyes but at a spot *between* their brows. Achilles' stare wandered, and he sipped his brandy, scowled and threw the glass against the opposite wall. The glass shattered, and Farashah gave a hoot of laughter and threw her glass at the wall.

He rolled toward her, showing a lot of teeth; she grabbed him around the neck, held him in a tight grip and bit his earlobe. He howled and cuffed her, and she tried to wriggle free, but he had great strength. He butted her with his head and forced her legs apart with a knee. She fought him for a few moments in silent skirmish, then he entered her. While he was engaged in angry thrusting, she laughed, and all the time she was laughing, he got angrier and angrier, exciting himself. Twice he cuffed her in outrage, and as his frenzy grew he banged and heaved harder to come, despite her laughter, which grew to an open-mouthed, mocking growl. He was having difficulty and his rage didn't help. Achilles began to pound his body down on her with a fury hardly related to sex. In no way did she cooperate.

In a sweat, both of them sucked breath. Rouge and eye kohl ran on her face. Both of them lay open mouthed as he tried in one final fury to sate himself. Then the phone on the little glass table rang.

Achilles became the captain almost automatically. He leaned over from the bed, still holding Farashah's body captive beneath him, and picked up the phone.

"Yes?"

It was Ludwig Ott on the bridge. "Achilles, Ludwig here."

"What's up? You on the bridge?"

"*Ja,* it's my watch."

"Well?" He tried to focus his vision, the room, its contents were an amorphous mess. Farashah stuck out an inch of tongue and grinned.

"The captain, I mean Hammel, has asked Second Officer Ormsbee to make a photocopy of the ship's log."

"Let him. Ormsbee wrote it up."

"I just thought, *ein Unglück*—it's odd that . . ."

"Don't think, Ludwig. Just stand your watch. I'll be up," he looked at his wristwatch, "in half an hour."

Achilles hung up and looked down at the girl, rubbing her breast with slow rolling fingers.

"Damn you," he said, "my ear is bleeding." He touched his earlobe and examined his stained fingers. "I could get an infection from that bite."

He stood up and peered into a mirror.

"You no finish?"

"What?" He tried to twist his head to get a closer view of his injury.

"The fucking. You always brag, yas, you always have the tiptop orgasm, yas?"

He was aware that he had lost his hard-on and any desire to get back into the steamy bed.

"I'll give you all the fucking you want when I come off my watch."

He went into the bathroom, turned on the shower and took a bottle of something pink from the medicine closet to dab on his injured ear. He assured himself he was not sexually humiliated. A man should regulate his orgasms as he saw fit, not as a goddamn nigger wench decided. He ought to go back to the bed, beat the living daylights out of her, and kick her yellow ass blue, tossing the cunt into the hallway naked as she was.

However, he vetoed such extravagant action; he was the captain, and while a carefree ship's officer could go bananas and bust up a woman, a captain could not.

He stepped into the shower and stood in the liquid warmth, feeling the enfolding womblike cocoon of water flowing over him. Overhead the light bracket set in the ceiling of the shower made a slight unnatural clacking sound as its frosted-glass face moved ever so slightly against the plastic frame.

Farashah lay back on the bed fondling herself. The struggle with this man had aroused her, and she finished herself off with skilled fingers.

CHAPTER | 14

Sieko and Gemila were in their cabin talking together in a bourgeois dialect of Urdu. They were preparing fish curry on their small electric stove, the native *machhali takhari*. Gemila sliced the ginger root while Sieko grated a wedge of fresh coconut. They cherished their modicum of privacy and their skill as cooks.

"You are much preoccupied."

"Yes, Gemila. The ship is ill."

"Hand me the ghee," she said as she stirred the pot and added more curry powder. "How is the ship ill?"

"There is a shaking," he said, making a graphic pantomime with his hands. "A sound I have not heard before."

"It is not your ship, Sieko. Let it talk, shake." Her idea of the world was of a duality, theirs and ours.

They both gave their attention to preparing the meal. They often cooked in their cabin, both being gluttons for their native dishes. Like good Indians, they ate only with the fingers of the right hand, pushing food into their mouths with a finger after taking it from the dish.

With platters heaped and fingers busy, they ate. From time to time Sieko looked up at the ceiling, but there was no new sound. He belched loudly and took a drink of tamarind syrup and water, holding out his plate for more of the pungent curry.

In the radio room Sparky was teaching Alice an American folk ballad:

> The first I seen my Katie
> She was standing in the door,
> Her shoes and stockings in her hand
> Her feet upon the floor.

"Odd way of putting it, Sparky."

"Learned that when I was a roustabout with a circus, lowering the king pole at a teardown, loading the chair wagons."

"Does it have more verses?" Alice was not really interested; she had radioed Ionnes Kyprios that she wanted to get off the *Pallas Athena*; too much was changing. Actually, she feared the storms and weather fronts that had been reported. The ship would be passing one of the chain of the Akora Islands she was advised and a launch could take her ashore. She was waiting for an answer from KSL Athens.

> She took me to her parlor,
> She cooled me with her fan;
> She said I was the wildest thing
> In the shape of any man.

"Why, Sparky, are American folk songs often so sad?"
"It's a sad life in the back country."
"Where isn't it?"

> She kissed me and she hugged me.
> She called me not so dumb
> She throwed her arms around me,
> I thought my time had come.

* * *

KSL Radio Athens came on at the end of the verse. The message to Alice read:

CONTINUE TRIP SLIGHT STORM REPORTS SHOULD PROVIDE U SPLENDID FILM FOOTAGE. . . .

I.K.

She started for the door. Sparky said, "Hey, I got a dozen more verses."

While the Hammels, Homer, and Wallie saw Achilles Marrkoras as a villain, he actually was not. He was a man driven by ambition, conditioned by a culture and society that put money and power first, moral values were a kind of luxury. This often made him belligerent and predatory. His mother was a distant aunt of the Kyprioses, married—she claimed, beneath her—to a dealer in wool who had failed in various projects from smuggling tobacco to bartering old icons from villagers for the tourist trade.

The Kyprioses—a clannish lot—had helped the Marrkorases, sent Achilles to fairly good schools. When he showed alertness, loyalty, they employed him in their offices, sent him off to become a ship's officer.

All this Achilles accepted. He respected the Kyprios brothers with a kind of awe.

He soon discarded his back-country ideas with his adolescent pimples—handsome, a man with a taste for the good life, he dressed the part. He was pleased to discover that he was smarter than most people; his skill as a good talker, his congeniality, enabled him to live with a leaven of complacency. Yet he remembered the vulnerable poverty in his youth and saw life as a series of doubts and intensities. He had found seducing desirable women a sporting exercise "close to becoming a good tennis player." Sex gave him confidence, a consistency of style and courage that attuned him to act out his role as a man of the world . . . he had as a boy resented one schoolmaster who suspected him of cheating in an examination—suggesting Achilles take as his personal image "Mercury, the winged god of duplicity."

Now, as captain and the core of the Kyprios scheme for this voyage, he kept what he called in already outmoded slang, "his cool." But, privately, he wondered if he could proceed as he had to.

Back in Athens Ionnes had been very careful to explain in detail to Achilles what had already been done ("processed" he called it) and what Achilles' part in the scheme would be.

Ionnes had been very jolly during that last lunch in Athens: "It is better you do not know everything. Just that you see to the sailing route, and if the captain kicks up his heels you will become captain."

Achilles had wondered about certain of the omitted details, but he was smart enough to guess the rest. *Pallas Athena* was never to reach an American port with its cargo.

Ionnes had been somewhat more confidential over the brandy. "You understand, it has been worked out with care. Never mind how our beautiful ship will come to her end just north of the Akora Islands; that chain stretches two hundred miles. You'll never be more than twenty or forty miles from a shore. There should be no problem for a fine sailor to get everyone ashore in the lifeboats. You will report in our code what goes on, eh? Oh, don't forget the cat. Every one of our ships has a fine cat. The Kyprios brothers breed them."

So far, it had gone as Ionnes had planned. Thomas Hammel had proven pigheaded and been disposed of. KSL had been aware of Thomas Hammel's flawed record. That was why he had been picked in Iraq. As Ionnes had put it, "He doesn't cooperate? Then we can dispose of him, like a used Kleenex."

Actually, Achilles was not as solid as he seemed. To

keep his ego pumped up, he needed to have his worth valued by others as he saw himself. Farashah had damaged him. Her mocking disregard of what the Spanish called *macho* had penetrated some chink in his psychological armor. She had scourged his manhood. And, in their last few encounters, his virility had nearly failed him. In that last bout, he had been unable even to retain his erection.

Farashah's laughter, created a wedge of doubt in his confidence. He reasoned: I'm like a man thrown by a balky horse. The only way to regain confidence is to remount. He would satisfy a more desirable woman than Farashah.

As he paced the bridge, Abdullah dozing on his feet at the wheel (the ship was under automatic control), Achilles riffled through the available women on board the ship, as if they were a handful of playing cards, and decided Alice Palamas was the medicine he needed to restore himself.

He had known Alice for some time but never sexually. Their meetings had been at the Kyprios' dinner parties, at KSL publicity functions, or weekends with house guests at Paul Kyprios' Nespolis villa. He had other women then—more fashionable, more deeply involved in what was then called the jet set. Those international monied tramps—they kept fashion models, endowed and discarded wives, and had shameless daughters who sought him out with tenacity and ingenuity in night-shadowed gardens and discreet hotel lobbies.

Alice it would be. He was about to phone down to ask her to have dinner in his cabin, when Wallie came onto the bridge as six bells rang.

"Reporting for my watch, Captain."

No salute, but no surly look either. "Very well, Mr. Ormsbee. How are the Hammels?"

"Bearing up."

Achilles nodded. "You understand, I had no choice. I

am carrying out owners' orders. I admire Thomas Hammel. You don't find many of that solid type anymore at sea. I wish he understood my position."

"I believe he does, Captain." (Just a touch of Wasp snottiness for the bastard.)

"Yes." Achilles smiled—you mincing fag—and left the bridge.

Wallie opened the log, entered the time of his watch, barometric pressure, temperature, distance covered in the last watch. The ship's communication system was carrying another "World Oil News" broadcast. Wallie no longer listened to it with any great interest. His mind was a confused but interesting montage, mostly of Sari (often indecently projected), on which the problems of the captain intruded.

The damn broadcast droned on over his head:

MAJOR REASONS FOR USING FLAGS OF CONVENIENCE ARE FREEDOM FROM TAXATION OR PROFITS AND INCOMES, UNRESTRICTED USE OF CASH FLOW, AND USING LOWER PAID CREWS.

He also heard the tapping noise that Wallie had mentioned; must be Homer and Sieko Mihran in one of the ship's wells, testing out some damn fool theory of taps and tank capacity. The sound was low but conducted clearly upward through the pipes, cables, and various connections that came from the engine room to the bridge.

Wallie had had a great fear of enclosed places ever since his German nannie—Frau Soken—had locked him in a closet when he had been naughty. He had howled in terror for some time, finally falling asleep on Mother's opera cloak, inhaling the smell of her perfume. When Homer had asked Wallie to descend with him into the well between tanks ten and eleven, he had refused. Once he had looked down that well with a creepy, crawly feeling—a sinister hole, dimly lit by yellowish bulbs, dark, greasy, smelling of crude oil. No thank you.

THE REPORT LISTS FIVE "OPEN REGISTRY" COUNTRIES WHICH MAY CLEARLY BE SAID TO LACK A GENUINE LINK WITH THE MERCHANT FLEET UNDER THEIR FLAGS—

Wallie called to the man at the wheel. "Abdullah, is there a way to shut off this sound system?"

"No, sir." The sailor made a clucking tongue-on-palate sound. "Must be on all the time—even if not talking—in case there is emergency. However, it can talk very low; push the green button over lamp."

Under his finger the broadcast died to a mumble that made little sense. Below he heard Homer tapping away; his tapping seemed louder, as if he were angry. Wallie wrote in the log that they were entering a storm area of scudding clouds; the sea was angry gray, foam-topped.

FROM THE NOTEBOOKS OF HOMER BOWEN:

We are beginning to run into much rougher weather. Not a good time to ponder over the judicial quibble of replacing the captain in some strange game of opportunism. My own problem is with my system of estimating the contents of the oil tanks below the main deck—something seems all out of whack. If I am to go by my past estimates of tapping tanks in the wells, I must make adjustments. Either conditions here, climate, weather, do give different results than in the Persian Gulf, or the tanks have leaked or been tampered with. How much loss—if any—I don't know.

Sieko and myself tested in the well between tanks ten and eleven. I got inconsistent results, which puzzled me, even frightened me. By my old standards those two tanks now appear to be only twenty percent filled. I repeat, as I have it written down the two tanks could be (if my method of estimation is correct) only twenty percent filled!

Sieko of course doesn't put much belief in my method, but he did admit something was wrong. When excited he speaks in convulsive dry heaves. He spoke of some new sound besides the usual sea creaks of the ship. Inside the hull hundreds of thousands of parts, sections, walls, bulkheads, and machines are welded, riveted, screwed, and put together; the motion of the ship causes all of this to rub together, press part against part, seeking more room or warping. I must admit I don't hear any special sound, but then being in the engine room for long periods of time my hearing is not attuned to small dissonance in sounds.

So here we are each with a pet theory; he doesn't seem to have any belief in my tapping tests, and I can't seem to hear his imaginary sound. I don't think of us as pathological, just puzzled.

Tom and Sarah have given up their daily walks on the main deck. The sea is roughening with excessive wind; and spray comes over the bow in great fans that travel a couple hundred feet along the catwalk. Tom and Sarah spend their time in their quarters having breakfast and lunch served. Usually they appear for dinner, rather late, to avoid meeting Marrkoras and Ott who, after an early meal and a last gulp of Iceland aqua vitae, are on the bridge by then.

Tom takes his present situation well. He seems to be a man not too sensitive to subtleties; yet he must suffer, being a man of a proud conscience, I'm sure, and with no defect in intelligence. Watching him taste Duck Fong's eight-jewel rice and crab meat, he could be a club man in a London St. James Square window, not a care in the world.

I brought Tom my problem while Wallie took Sarah to see the movie we had all seen at least three times already, "Butch Cassidy and the Sundance Kid."

Tom offered me a drink, which I thought wise to refuse; one never knows if a one-time hard-drinking man like

154

Tom, under pressure, would start again and let the booze deck him.

"You feel, Homer, there may be a shortage in those two tanks?"

"Maybe, yes. It's not a proven scientific way of judging, of course, but . . ."

"How about other tanks?"

"There are only two other wells, between tanks four and five, and between seventeen and eighteen."

"How do they test out, according to your theory?"

Well, I had to admit I hadn't thought of testing in the other two wells. He gave me a deprecating look, the kind a very young child gets when it's soiled its clothes. I said I'd get right on it when I was clear of engine room duty. He said yes, I'd better, muttering something about circumstances and consequences. He had no idea, he told me, what Sieko was talking about with his damn ghost sound. But then Tom's expression changed, as if he'd had a sudden revelation from above. But he didn't tell me what new thought had come to him.

He said, "Open the emergency hatches to tanks ten and eleven from the deck. Have you any dip sticks?"

"Dip sticks? Oh, to measure the tanks from above?"

He said yes, that was the idea, as if I were a not-too-bright pupil. I had some long, thin half-inch metal bars among spare parts supplies. I'd paint them white with a fast-drying paint and dip them into the tank from above. He said not to do it while Marrkoras or Ott was on the bridge. He suggested I work in the dark of night. I didn't much care for slopping about on deck with a heavy sea and working in semidarkness; some of the lights over the catwalk had been smashed by the sea spray. But I just said, of course.

Tom seems to accept treacherous, perverse human conduct as part of life, and if he showed any hints of exasperation I didn't see them. I suppose I lack the inner resources he has.

I have prepared rods, thirty feet long. The oil level, if the tanks are full, should be only seven feet below deck. I can pretty well tell by the oil stains on the white-painted

155

*rods how full tanks ten and eleven really are. I had hoped
to work on a new opening of my novel, but now the reality of events here has become so much more dramatic
than anything I can think of. All so intense and puzzling.
To an imaginative writer, this could be explained as a
kind of madness.*

*Tom must be aware of certain built-in dangers to Pallas
Athena. (Our speed has been cut to 12 knots.)*

*In an hour, on a really mean sea, Sieko and I will plunge
our dip sticks down into the vitals of the ship. What will
we find?*

Achilles' cabin shook mildly, rattling and creaking
from the roughness of the sea. It was hardly gale weather.
The ship rode it well. Most small objects in the cabin had
been put away. A brass band held his stock of liquor in
place on a shelf. The slender metal legs of the glass table
were screwed to the floor. Two silver-framed pictures of
family had fallen over. As Alice looked about the cabin it
seemed snug and cozy. She had long since gotten her sea
legs and adjusted to the dip and rise of the ship. The motion seemed almost to add a sensual feeling to her hips
and legs as she adjusted her balance as if she were riding
English saddle with the school groom.

Achilles was wearing a smoking jacket of deep red
velvet with a dark maroon satin collar, just as they did in
old-fashioned novels. He lifted a large silver hood from a
wide serving tray: several breasts of chicken rested on a
bed of cooked vegetables; there was a tureen of *petite
marmite,* baked potatoes, pimento-studded salads.

"I am sorry Fong wasn't able to provide *caneton aux
oranges.*"

"In this weather maybe that's all to the good."

"Yes. I've noticed the barometric pressure is still sliding a bit."

The ice bucket containing two wine bottles wrapped in
napkins was on the floor, for safety reasons.

Achilles opened a bottle, skillfully flipping out the

cork, and they drank, looking at each other, smiling. Alice felt they were like two friendly rivals, thinking of innate possibilities.

"You still know how to impress a girl, Achilles."

"I dislike cant. We must admit we want to enjoy life. And give joy to others."

She set down her glass. "That include the Hammels?"

"Believe me, there are valid conditions which I have promised not to reveal, as to why the Kyprioses ordered this changeover."

"You can't spoil my appetite, I'm really hungry." She picked up a napkin and Achilles pushed in her chair. "If you're referring, Achilles, to Thomas Hammel's heart operation, that's no secret to me."

Achilles, a plate in one hand, a serving fork with breast of chicken on it, stood as if posing for a statue.

"Oh?"

"Ionnes Kyprios is an egomaniac, and he couldn't resist telling me how much cleverer he is than the rest of the world."

He carefully set the plate before Alice and offered her rolls. She shook her head. "No bread."

"How much—I mean just what did he . . ."

"He bragged that he liked to have officers he could control by keeping some little secret on them. Had to have something that made him master of the men he employed." She smiled. "Even you, Achilles, I suppose?"

"A baked potato?"

Ionnes said, "Hammel was the best captain available, and even if he didn't think KSL knew about his real condition it was, as Ionnes put it, 'a handle to swing him around over my head if need be.' Ionnes is a real sixteen-jewel Swiss movement sonofabitch . . . , even if he is your uncle."

"A distant uncle. Did he say why he picked Hammel?"

"Because he was the best around." She looked up from her plate. "Why, is there a special reason?"

Achilles smiled and poured a red wine. "Ionnes doesn't expose his ego as much to a man as to a very attractive woman."

"Come on, Achilles, you don't have to practice your line on me. I'm willing and of age. Besides if . . ."

There was a hard knock on the door of the cabin. Achilles made a shoulder gesture of who-the-hell-could-that-be? He went to the door and opened it: Farashah stood there with a tray of assorted cheeses and crackers.

"*Les fromages,*" she said loudly. She dropped the tray into his hands, rather than presenting it to him, and turned away.

Alice laughed and cut into her breast of chicken.

"Oh, she's been aggressive, but I draw the color line."

"Liar."

"On shipboard."

She couldn't decide if he was telling the truth. It didn't matter. Her glum mood was relieved, or at least, set in cold storage. Now she felt it was good to be intimate with an old friend, to eat well, drink good wine, relate to someone from her shore life. No use being mealy mouthed, life was a kick in the ass—an assumption that she felt had been proven to her in the recent past.

There was a slight pleasant taste of ginger to the chicken. Or was it ginseng, a supposed aphrodisiac? She gave Achilles a mocking glance and recited an old school prayer: "Our Father in Heaven, bless this food for the Redeemer's sake. Amen."

In the motion picture theater a few of the crew (four) were in the section reserved for them. Wallie and Sarah, separated by a standing ashtray, sat in the loge seats reserved for the officers. Sarah smoked slowly; the film moved at a staccato pace on the screen. There had been an understanding between them. In time of crisis, *this* crisis, Sarah made clear there would be a truce. He wasn't to try any of his daffy signs of raptures for her, and she'd treat him in a civilized way, "Even if I should break a chair over your head, you damn fool."

She seemed cheerful and amused and ten minutes later, when he lit another cigarette for her, he held her hand and she didn't withdraw it. Be thankful, he told himself, for small favors. At her next cigarette could he dare, furtively, to place his thigh against hers?

Over coffee in his cabin Achilles put some middle-period Ellington recordings on the turntable, keeping the volume just low enough, Alice surmised, to make sensual sound, since she was getting a bit looped. But that was all right. Her conversation was laden with irony. She liked the man well enough; he was sanguine, expansive, and she wanted sex—wanted it bad. The gym teacher in the English girl's school she had attended, St. Bonafeathers, had had a crush on Alice. During a country hike and picnic lunch in a meadow near the Colchester Canal, he had told her, "We must, my dear Alice, strive to possess the precious and the incommunicable."

Now she tried to explain to Achilles how it felt to be a schoolgirl in love with the groom who taught her horseback riding at St. Bonafeathers. Achilles kept nodding to the beat of the music, as if he understood what she was talking about. They drank brandy from two big snifters, and he began to undress her. In her mind the balance between innocence and disillusion slipped away. Soon she was stripped down to her stockings.

"Keep them on," he said, as he began to shuck his own clothes.

The Sundance Kid—in too-clear Technicolor—died in a hail of bullets and the screen went white. The wall lights went on. Wallie said, "Too much charm projected by both Redford and Newman."

"Never too much charm, Wallie."

"Sari . . ."

"Look, cut the Sari crap. We have an agreement. You behave. The captain has problems. We need to stick together, like some half-assed band of brothers. But you try any hanky-panky and I'll have Skip pistol-whip you. Capisce, my young friend?"

He nodded as the crew members, seeming depressed by the film, passed them.

"Of course, Sa . . . of course, I mean I kept my part of the agreement during the movie. I just held your hand, and . . ."

She patted his shoulder. "Look I'm flattered. In some ways you're a sweet, dopy guy. I should flutter my feathers, a young squirt like you making a play for me. But if I wanted to cheat on Skip, I wouldn't do it on his ship and I wouldn't put out for any pumped-up, romantic nut like you."

Wallie said he understood his gaucherie, the total fiasco of that dreadful flasher scene in the dressing room. They decided to go to the wardroom and have Ping Pong make them some ice cream sodas with a touch of crème de menthe.

Alice and Achilles made love twice to a point of soughing collapse. Both of them were satisfied with their performances. Alice found that the encounter had helped her out of her apathy. Sexual satisfaction, if not complicated, always gave her a flutelike pleasure, a secret series of thin, very delightful notes. Only when combined with a love problem did it seem to spoil.

As for Achilles, the self-interrogation that accompanied his idea of failure of domination in bed, left him. His confidence was back, with Alice so grateful beneath him; the memories of his recent doubts, the imbecility of that damn barbarian bitch were all wiped out.

"Any wine left?"

He noticed some wine bobbing about in the bottle on the table. There was no need to talk as they drank; he nuzzled her naked shoulder with his grape-scented mouth. They knew each other—as much as they suspected of their pasts. They had no morbid fascination for each other after a surfeit of lovemaking. They traded, Alice decided, a coarse versatility for gregarious sensuality. Soon she would have to get out of the bed, get dressed, and get back to her cabin. She could just about make it if the damn ship would just calm down a bit.

There was a banging on the door. Achilles shook his head and growled. There was more banging, angry, insistent.

"Go away!"

Farashah's voice cried out. "Hot coffee!"

"You goddamn bitch, bugger off!"

Outside the door there was a crash of a dropped tray. But no more banging. Alice giggled. "What's that one doing bringing coffee? Where's Gemila?"

Her throat was sour; was she losing her sea legs?

"Christ, these natives. Treat them as human beings and they get sassy."

"I think she's got the hots for you. Yes, yes, I really do."

Achilles said that was not his problem as he handed Alice her knickers. One of her American lovers, she remembered, had called them panties. Pax Americana, and she ran to vomit in Achilles' bathroom.

Wallie was on the bridge studying weather reports. They'd soon be in really bad weather. Abdullah, at the wheel, appeared in a trance. He had shared a pipe of hashish with Duck Fong and his head was full of transitory images, none of them very clear.

Wallie had his own thoughts: He had kissed Sari outside her door, a smack on the cheek; just as he thought he would target in on her mouth, she had shifted her face around.

Below him, on the catwalk, Wallie made out two figures in yellow rain gear, the spray sometimes dove over them. Sieko had a heavy wrench and was working on an emergency hatch cover on the main deck. Homer bent over, and looking miserable, was trying to hold erect some long white wands. Whatever they were doing, better they than he in this weather.

Through all this angry bleakness, Wallie thought, *Pallas Athena* sails on, like some giant creature indifferent to the parasites that lived in and on it. The weather remained foul; the sky, as Wallie looked up, was the color and texture of thickly congealed fat on a plate. Where the horizon had been, mist and rain merged with the squalls that were hitting the ship in sharp drenchings. She rose on the heaving sea, now bobbing in a great trough, now lifted up, suspended on two waves at the bow and stern. Water crashed across the catwalk. The main deck was soon untenable for the crew. The lifeboats and two motor launches rested firmly, held by extra lashings. The ship seemed to be the center of a great wrenching of sea and sky. A locked combat between the two. From the bridge it seemed any moment could be the one in which the waters would engulf the tanker.

Now, she seemed clumsy, Wallie felt, like a pregnant woman struggling to rise from the hundreds of tons of water that broke over her bow and rushed along her decks in angry foam. Yet, once more the ship reluctantly lifted herself clear of the menacing sea. He watched, fascinated by the struggle.

And under the ship, a mile or more down, was the cold, blue-black darkness of some half-remembered bad dream. Wallie shivered and lifted the collar of his peajacket around his neck.

Abdullah at the wheel watched the compass rise, bobbing in its brass tray. In this bad weather, *Pallas Athena* was on manual controls; automatic control was on standby. The officer on the bridge had to judge how much leeway to give each huge onrush of a wave, when to head into the wind. The tanker did not respond like a yacht to the helmsman's touch. Wallie entered the last weather report in the log. He figured that even to slow her forward speed in case of emergency, it would take five to six sea miles to stop the *Pallas Athena*.

Ludwig Ott came onto the bridge, still chewing the last of his breakfast, or at least testing for fragments with his tongue.

"Good morgen, Wallie."

"Morning, Ludwig. It's rough, but we're not really into the full storm yet."

Ludwig was reading the barometric charting. "It even may be a bit of calm ahead." He went to observe the compass, nodded to the steerman. "Hold her steady," he ordered, to signal he was in command of the bridge.

Wallie went down to his cabin, decided to skip food and go direct to the Hammel quarters. He wanted to know about the results of Homer's and Sieko's work in the dark. He first rubbed some male scent from a flask labeled *So Savage*, just in case Sari was up and about. He felt a sense of community during this crisis, like a family almost, with the Hammels and Homer.

He found Tom and Homer looking very grim. Homer was oil-stained, and white paint marked the back of his hands. His cheeks showed a reddish stubble, and his gestures, as he spoke, had an excruciating intensity. "You wouldn't believe it, you just wouldn't."

"What?" asked Wallie.

Tom said, "Four tanks hold maybe only twenty percent of their oil cargo."

Wallie shook his head. "That's crazy, Tom. I mean I checked the Lodmeter reports and the foreman of the shore meters came on board to have his tonnage record okayed."

"Who signed for those?"

"Ott, Ludwig. He was in charge of the loading."

Homer punched a fist into the open palm of his hand. "That's how it was done. Ott fucked up the Lodmeters somehow. Hell, I saw him myself taking something apart—monkeying with some of the computers and gauges."

Tom looked up from a sheet of pencil-marked paper. "You did? No one is permitted to remove the covers of those machines, let alone probe in their inners."

"You're so right, chief. But I don't understand how the shore foreman didn't report he was not fully filling the tanks—I mean . . ."

"It's too damn clear," Tom said. "The figures the foreman signed for, were also false. He must have had a lot of oil to sell in some shady deal of his own on shore."

Wallie remained confused. "But why, I mean, go to all the bother for a few thousand barrels of oil?"

Tom pointed to a framed photograph of *Pallas Athena* on the wall. The port seemed to be Rotterdam, and there were Captain Meyerbecker and his officers posing on a pier in the foreground.

"Christ, we all looked younger then." Tom pointed a finger to the bow, then to the stern of the tanker. "So the fore and aft tanks are fully loaded. You're sure, Homer?"

"We checked every other one. Legal contents in each."

"The four tanks, eight, nine, ten and eleven are only twenty percent filled. So . . ." Tom touched the center of the ship's image. "She's light in the middle. Nearly empty. Which means she's doomed in any weather heavier than this."

Wallie cried out. "But *how* . . . why?"

"If she is lifted up front and back by two very large waves the whole damn hull will jackknife, fold up; or if a huge wave lifts her just under the middle, the heavy ends will tear her hull, crack her in half.

Wallie could only stand with his mouth slightly open; he felt a colic pressure on his bowels and the uneven intake of air into lungs not willing to accept it. His body seemed to share the distortions in his mind.

"We have to take over," Homer said. "Radio Athens and . . ."

Tom turned away from the photograph. "It's most likely all part of the Kyprios' scheme of things—like hiring me and then sending in that Greek to replace me."

"So no use radioing Athens," Homer said. "Just prepare the lifeboats and stand by for the worst. This could never happen on a British ship. Well *hardly* likely."

Tom seemed not to hear this defense of the Union Jack. He was looking at the sheet of paper in his hand. "There are valves and pipe connections between the tanks?"

"Of course, for cleaning sludge, blowing in gas—inert gases, for safety in port."

"All right, Chief Engineer, figure out how to balance off *all* the tank levels so they all will have the same amount of oil in them. That should remove the danger of jackknifing the ship."

"Maybe, but, Tom, I can only do that with Marrkoras' permission."

"I'm taking over as captain. I'm giving you my orders, as commander of this ship."

Wallie wondered out loud, "That's like mutiny, isn't it?"

"I'm no sea lawyer. I have large areas of ignorance. Maybe it's mutiny. You both have the right to refuse my orders. The Greek may have the right to order out weapons against us. Well?"

Wallie was aware that Thomas Hammel was rather enjoying the situation—apprehension, agitation behind him.

Homer said, "We're with you, Captain."

Wallie added, "Of course. I've read a bit of sea law. If we got hold of Ludwig's reports and figures of the shore deliveries, you'd have evidence to prove this scheme at any inquiry. I'll go get my hands on the loading reports."

Homer studied the photograph on the wall. "Where are they?"

"In the chart room. They belong there with the cargo files. Hell, Ludwig, he has the keys."

Tom said, "Just tell him you want to complete the log. Say you only did rough drafts of the loading data and now you want to verify it. You much of an actor, Wallie?"

"Not really."

"Well, don't alarm Ott." He patted Wallie's shoulder, "Go ahead."

Wallie expected more warnings and admonitions. He left without them, rolling his head as if he had a stiff neck.

Homer scratched his rough chin with a thumb. "I don't know. If Ott smells a rodent he'll warn Marrkoras. And how do we face the damn Greek?"

The captain frowned. "You go get a work crew from Wu Ting Li and start leveling off those tanks. There's a lull in the storm coming up ahead, so work fast, it's going to be mean weather on the main deck soon."

"What if Marrkoras orders us to fuck off? And . . ."

Tom waved away the end of the unspoken sentence, "That's my job." His face looked bland, hardly expressive of any anxieties as he added, "I may have to kill him."

"I've a damn fine Luger in my cabin."

"I'm a Smith & Wesson old-style six-shooter man."

Homer touched the peak of his cap. "I better get a work gang together."

Thomas Hammel just waved to the engineer.

Left alone, he listened at the bedroom door. No sound, no smell of smoldering tobacco. Sarah was still asleep. Good. He went to the small desk, unlocked the bottom drawer and took out a bundle of oily wool cloth. He uncovered the old Smith & Wesson pistol with its six-inch barrel. The blueing had worn off the steel surface but the cylinder of the .45 spun with ease; it cocked smoothly. The weapon had belonged to his Uncle Luke, the biggest liar west of Bullprick, Wyoming; nobody could have killed all the many men Uncle Luke claimed as town marshal.

Tom began to sing softly—an old song that had suddenly come to mind—a song from his first days at sea in the route of a China Sea tramp, the *Mollie Orey*, carrying cement:

> Soupy-y, soup-y soup-y
> without a single bean,
> Porky, porky, porky,
> without a streak of lean.

Coffee, coffee, coffee,
The weakest ever seen!

He was loading the brass-bound cartridges into the pistol when he became aware of Sarah standing in the doorway from the bedroom, observing him. She was barefoot and wearing a blue slip.

"So, when you sing that fool tune I know damn well you see yourself as a hero."

"Nope, Dolly, just working at my trade."

She lit the cigarette in one corner of her mouth, "Don't point that hog-leg in my direction. It's loaded."

"I'm taking over as captain."

"Yes," she seemed sad for all her ability to adapt. "I knew you weren't going skeet shooting. That bad, Skip?"

"It looks like the Kyprioses are out to sink *Pallas Athena* for the insurance money."

She inhaled, exhaled. "Let them. We're near one of the Akoras, aren't we? I can be packed in half an hour, and Wallie can get us ashore in a launch."

He put the pistol back in the drawer and closed it with a push of both hands. "No, that's like shooting your horse when it breaks a leg. *Pallas Athena* is like something that's alive to me, has done her duty and now is sick."

She said simply. "Bull-dust. But I'm not going to try to talk you out of this. You're damn stubborn, you know that. The older you get the more uptight. Well, come on, kiss me good morning."

She was trembling as he held her in his arms, and he felt selfish in anticipating the actions ahead of him.

There had been a lull in the storm. Much of the wind had died down, but still there was an uneasy roll to the sea. Alice, labeling film cans in her cabin, felt a malice in the vast expanse of heaving water—but no pettiness to the sea.

She was aware of shadowy events all around her—of something stirring on board, a pent-up intensity on the ship. But she was too involved with the turn of personal events that had taken her to Achilles' bed and would take her there, it seemed from his mood, again and again. She had no idyllic vision. She put out of her mind the preposterous aspects of her situation. Life is mostly doubts and shocks. "Play it as it lays," her film-director lover had told her at Monte Carlo when she had a run of luck at the tables.

She put away the film cans and rested on the bed, hoping to sleep. The storm had let up, but she was aware the officers assumed this was a lull before a bigger onslaught from the storm. As she dozed off, the idea intruded that Achilles had most likely been having some kind of an affair with Sarah's maid. But it was not particularly abhorrent to her.

Duck Fong is really the man who runs the ship (Homer had written in his notes). *Leave out the bridge and the engine room, and the boss man is the wily, bland-looking head cook. He is the ship's master; just as in the Gilbert and Sullivan operetta H.M.S. Pinafore, the admiral is the ruler of the Queen's Navy. Duck Fong is the ship's loan shark; most of the crew's pay ends up in his pockets. He handles the sale of swill to the pig farmers who come alongside the ship in barges to carry off the tons of garbage saved up. Also in food supplies, he gets his cumshaw, boodle; most likely he is dealing with drug connections and carrying kilos of the stuff—pot, horse, cocaine— to be smuggled ashore. Or so says the crew's gossip. Certainly if one goes to the crew's quarters late at night there is the smell of burning hashish, smoldering grass, gow hop.*

His winnings at poker are legendary, and he is said to

own a street of apartments in Hong Kong and a glass factory on Formosa.

(A later note): If it comes to a problem of taking back the ship from the Greek by direct action, I wonder if Duck Fong shouldn't be enlisted to see that the crew support Tom. If events weren't so deadly serious, there is a piquant quality—a ready made text to all this for a novelist. Meanwhile, we sail on, directly into the storm front awaiting us, unless we change course; a typhoon more deadly than the one we have just tasted.

Duck Fong's cabin was plain, painted an apple green. Not at all exotic but for a small bronze of the Vairocana Buddha of the Hua-yen sect, and a scroll of a horse and rider attributed to Chao Heng-fu; these were the only indications that the occupant was Chinese. Prominently in sight were an IBM adding machine, an old Royal typewriter, a very modern-looking deep-green filing cabinet; the closet contained some fine English tailoring and a set of pigskin, Italian-made luggage. Duck Fong smoked English Ovals and owned a gold Dunhill lighter.

He sat with Wu Ting Li, the man in charge of the work-gangs; they discussed in a Shanghai dialect the situation on the ship and how it affected the six kilos of hashish they had hidden in various places aboard the *Pallas Athena.* There was the trouble with the change of command, the former captain now measuring the contents of the tanks. If that got around in port, the customs people would be most diligent in going over the ship when it got to San Pedro, even if one could give "gifts" to one or two.

"This is bad that the not-filled tanks have been found," said Wu Ting Li. "Such a small loss to a big company."

Duck Fong nodded. Nothing much went on on the ship that he didn't know. He was a man who shrugged off the faults in human nature, who liked good things in life, a happy laughing existence. He wished no one harm, burned joss sticks to his honorable forefathers, sent deserving nephews through Japanese universities. Now he was faced with this foolishness among "the round eyes" that touched on his good life on shipboard . . . could upset his plans.

He picked up a Godiva box of chocolates, took one, offered it to his friend, who refused. As he chewed, Duck Fong made a grimace of frustration, "The missing oil, of course, was sold ashore, by whom? The KSL? By an officer?"

"It had to be. Now what will happen when we get to California and it is found missing?"

"A leak at sea I'm sure will be arranged. All that will add to our problems. Inspection for structural defects. Perhaps we should keep our goods hidden and not try to get it ashore there."

"And if they find it?"

Wu Ting Li swayed, moved his head and torso back and forth as if in pious prayer. "So much I had invested in these kilos. I was planning to buy a girl, Moon Orchid, to warm up my old age. She ripe at twelve, and such . . ." He merely indicated the rest of her qualities with a sigh.

Duck Fong said, "We shall wait and see who is top dog on the ship in the next few days."

He reached for another chocolate. He had a weakness for sweets—so bad for his teeth—and would soon have to have more dentistry done.

Ludwig Ott, sweating lightly, went along the hallway to Achilles' cabin. He had just lied—badly, he knew—to Wallie Ormsbee, claiming the keys to the chart lockers holding his loading records of *Pallas Athena* were in the captain's keeping. Wallie had been too casual explaining why he needed to look at the records. Ott knew the entries in the bridge log were full enough. No need to give them in more detail. This sudden propriety about the records worried the big German. For all his size, Ludwig Ott was a man given to many small fears; he had almost a paranoid expectation of the improbable and the preposterous. He believed in order, cleanness, tradition, and was secure that the scientific view of the universe was the way for man to live. Yet he was aware most humans were not scientifically solid.

He had been a young child when his father died in Russia in Hitler's war. No one knew for sure how—frozen to death, starvation, or done in in a Siberian prison camp. Ludwig had spent the most impressionable years of his childhood in air-raid shelters, seeking shelter, often screaming, going hungry, eating rancid horse guts, seeing Berlin become ashes. Always fearful, he saw men and women hung from lamp posts with piano wire; he watched while the SS got drunk and Mother scrounged in garbage cans, fighting lean dogs for scraps. The last days of the Third Reich, he lived in shit and piss in a cellar with two dead women and a leaking drain.

Ludwig Ott never recovered from the war years. He lived with the fear that he would be hungry again, in danger of sudden death.

He approached Achilles' cabin door, a fist held ready to knock . . . held back. He was a plain, kindly man who respected his superiors despite the constant strain of fear that always made him apprehensive. It was his need for safety that led him into this odd affair which seemed an opportunity to gain a nest egg which would enable him to buy a farm in Saxony and settle down to pipe and beer stein, good music, and a Black Forest jager's dog. Now all was becoming unraveled. Ott had never hated anyone, had never been cruel or bigoted, and *der liebe Gott* look at his situation now!

He did not knock, for there was a furious quarrel going on inside. Marrkoras and a woman were yelling at each other. Something was turning over with a crash. Farashah (he recognized that voice) screaming in rage, cursing. He could not make out the words, but she was giving as good as she got.

Otto hesitated, he heard the sound of someone being slapped—hard, once, twice, three times. A wail came from the girl—something was being thrown.

Ott retreated. His whole lifestyle was based on not provoking retaliation—seeking safety in withdrawal. He would have to catch the captain on the bridge, later, about Wallie's request for the original Lodmaster and records, about the matter of his certifying the amount of Persian Gulf crude put on board. Was it Kant or Hegel, he wondered, who had said there are twenty-three ways to face a situation, the most practical was to flee.

Ludwig Ott was gone from the hallway when Farashah came out of the cabin, rubbing a bruised cheek, her hair in disorder, her native robe ripped under the left arm. She was staring straight ahead, her mouth a fixed line of hatred and humiliation. Discarded! Disposed of with a gesture! Tossed away for some white bitch! She clenched a fist as if reaching for a weapon.

BOOK FOUR

IN HAVOC

16

Homer made a tentative list of the weapons on board. As far as he knew, there was the captain's Smith & Wesson .45, his own Luger automatic for which he had only two clips, four shotguns used rarely by the officers for skeet shooting off the stern—10 gauge—the six boxes of shells were bird shot. Still it would have to do. The crew would have an assortment of knives and various daggers, and perhaps even a few Saturday Night Specials.

Homer was sure Duck Fong and Wu Ting Li had pistols, if, as he thought likely, they were involved in smuggling traffic.

Duck Fong was watching one of the kitchen boys saw through the bones of a section of spareribs. The chief cook turned an innocent eye on Homer as if his question was an abdication of reason:

"Solly, no use of any guns. Bad stuff, oh yes."

"Come off it, Fong, we're going to face a bad situation on board." He drew the chief cook to one side. "There's going to be a change on the bridge. You follow my drift?"

"I no mix in no tings."

"Captain Hammel is trying to save the ship and your

hide. She's been loaded badly, unbalanced . . . can break in half."

"Ho-so, ho." He pursed his lips, repeated, "Ho so."

Homer lost his temper at Duck Fong's dirgelike expression. "You'll ho-so bloody well in a different tune when your fat ass is overboard in the water and a typhoon is whistling in your ears."

Duck Fong pulled Homer further away from the butcher's chopping block.

"Must think. I may find some guns, yes. Maybe two, maybe five, mis'ah Homah."

"You're jolly well right, Fong," Homer smiled, patted Fong on his stomach. "You're a realist, I can see that. You, of course, realize if this tanker is wrecked not only may you lose your high-on-the-hog, fancy living style, but all that hash and gow you have stowed away, eh. You and Li and it could end up down in Davey Jones' locker."

"Who him? Jones?"

"The Devil."

"Jones? Depend I will think what is best. Cap'tin Hammel fine fella."

"Just remember that, if you're called on to save your own skin."

When Homer was gone the chief cook made a low, moaning sound to keep him company and beat a flat hand against his chest. He inspected the short ribs as if seeing in them some omen or augury. What Chinese sage had said, "Necessity guides all our conduct; we all face an ultimate responsibility. . . ." But did the sage ever have his balls caught in a wringer? Just to wait would be best—not join sides just yet. Most likely the old captain was the better man. As he counted the short ribs, Duck Fong numbered off Thomas Hammel's virtues: 1) a believer in tradition, 2) values, 3) order, 4) clarity, 5) coherence.

Yes, a man to back. He felt fitful and slapped the kitchen boy on the head. "Neatness, neatness, you saw ribs like a Korean."

Sieko Mihran had a British police Webley, inherited from when his father was in the Indian constabulary. As he hefted the weapon, he told Homer, who had joined him and Gemila in their cabin for *Bhujiya*, a too spicy hot vegetable dish, "Sar, the pistol bears the royal Indian police crest. Picture, too, of the old queen."

"Does it fire?"

"Oh, yes, I keep it in splendid condition. So Officer Ott is not with us. Who would back the old captain?"

"Ormsbee, the whole engine room crew, maybe Sparky and his assistant. But we're not betting on it. The rest of the staff, we hope, will just stand aside and accept. What do you think?"

Gemila, her fingers grasping a section of spicy eggplant goop, held it away from her as she spoke. "Ping Pong says there is much talk against the Grik . . . he gives out too many recriminations, shouts loudly very often."

Sieko said, "The staff, they do not know of the partly emptied tanks?"

"Captain Hammel will announce everything from the bridge, *after* he locks up Marrkoras."

"Terrible, terrible to think of sinking this fine ship. You are satisfied, sar, only the tanks have been tampered with?"

"What else could they do? No one can get at the engines. Me or Carlos are always down there."

"This little sound, what of this vibrating ghost I hear?"

Gemila asked, "Anyone ever die on ship, leave his spirit behind?"

Homer shook his head. "Not that I know of. What do you think this damn sound, this vibration, is? I never really felt it."

"Very, very small sound." Sieko, finished eating,

dipped his fingers in a bowl of water his wife handed him. "It is the ship's soul protesting. The steel is in agony someplace."

"Where?"

"Do not know. But someplace, perhaps the lifting and settling of the ship in the last storm has found a spot to torment."

"A hell of a note, Sieko."

"What I hear does not sound dangerous. A cracked deck plate, a bulkhead wall buckling. I will warn you when I think the hull is in danger of a below-the-water crack."

"You're a cheerful bastard, I must say."

Homer felt the hot spices of the *Bhujiya* attack his throat. He dipped his fingers into a bowl of water, dried them on a small pink towel. "Stand by."

"What time set for zero hour?"

"Midnight. At the changing of the watch we jump Marrkoras as he leaves his cabin. And then . . ."

The door of the cabin was thrust open with panicked force, and Wu Ting Li came rushing in, his Chinese features no longer an expressionless mask of calm acceptance. He waved his thin, stalklike arms. "Something bad . . . bad . . . bad!"

"What the devil is bad?" Homer asked.

"I go on deck just now, find some of my men they have lowered the launch." He held up four fingers. "Offasah Ott have said to them do this, fast, chop chop, then he get in launch his self."

"Ott!" cried Homer. "Has the launch shoved off yet?"

"Launch was in wattah."

Sieko waved his hands in the air to dry them. "The officer is heading for one of the Akoras."

Homer shouted to Sieko, "Bring your pistol!" and rushed out, followed by Wu Ting Li.

On the main deck four Chinese of the crew stood by

the empty skid on which Launch number four had rested—block and tackle hung over the side. Homer went to the rail and peered into the muck. Below, a hundred feet away, the white of the launch's wash was visible.

"Hard cheese!" Homer turned to the sailors. "Officer have any luggage, plenty bags, things?"

"Plenty bags."

"Why the hell didn't you refuse him the launch?"

A sailor turned, his eyes narrowed, glancing toward Wu Ting Li. The group exchanged rapid, whispered Chinese. Wu Ting Li said to Homer, "Man is offisah. They have to obey what offisah ask. Is in regulations."

Sieko was standing by the rail, his pistol aimed at the rapidly moving launch, his large dark eyes taking in the spectacle. He pointed the weapon at the foamy wake, but Homer grabbed his arm.

"No, you couldn't hit a barn at this distance, in this sea. Besides, this may be a bloody blessing. Let's keep this dark—one rat less to handle. Wu Ting, keep these men out of sight until further orders. They talk about this, I'll have your blasted tail for it. Understand?"

"Uneestan'."

Homer watched the last foamy pulse of the launch's wake disappear into blue-black obscurity, its red starboard light flashing like the glint from a ruby into nothingness. The wind was rising, but Ott would make it, the engineer figured. It was maybe twenty-five, maybe thirty miles to one of the Akoras—the place was filled with copa rats, skinny-legged fishermen, and he hoped cannibals. The German had run for it, his wind up. No wonder the krauts never won a war; any little thing goes wrong with a master plan, they take the quick way out.

Homer spit down into the rising sea; tongues of spray were beating at the steel hull.

Sarah sat with Alice in the Hammel quarters, drinking

martinis. *Pallas Athena* heeled from one side to the other from time to time; clearly the stormy weather had returned in stronger form since the lull. The two women held their glasses to keep them from spilling on the teak card table between them. Alice noticed how the light of day in the windows was dark, like the color of tea tannin.

"I think," she said, "I better get to my cabin and lie down."

"Stay here, honey, things are happening." Sarah's face seemed older, creased with tension.

"That why you invited me in for a drink?"

"Hell, a couple of drinks, so far." Sarah smiled and picked up the small martini pitcher, holding it firmly between her knees to keep it from spilling in the ship's motion. "I don't like to drink alone . . . bad habit."

Alice refused a refill. She turned the cocktail glass in her fingers by its stem. "What's playing on the bridge, a rerun of *Mutiny on the Bounty*? The ship's acting crazy and so is everybody."

"Something like that, Alice girl. It's better we stay here till the all clear sounds." She sipped and pursed her lips. "Too much vermouth." She pressed the button connecting the quarters with the maid's room. "I like a martini when they just breathe the word 'vermouth' over the gin. You look pale . . . got your period?"

Alice tried to rise as the tanker gave a shudder and plunged. A green wash of water flooded across the windows of the sitting room.

"It's the motion, Sarah. You see how high that wave came?"

"It's the start of a typhoon. Look, lie down on my bed."

Alice couldn't rise. She fell back into the easy chair, which fortunately was secured to the floor. She said weakly, "Help me to the bathroom, I'm going whoops."

"Damn it, where is that Farashah? She can't be screwing the Greek this early in the morning. Look, you take any Dramamine?"

Alice replied, "Like salt peanuts, don't help." She looked up glassy-eyed, tried to speak again, but could only gasp and shake her head in a wobbly roll. Sarah put down the little pitcher wedging it between the side of a sofa and a stack of detective stories. "Upsy-daisy, my girl." She helped Alice to her feet, walked her robotlike to the bathroom door while the tanker lunged as if it were trying to do a handstand on its bow.

"Easy does it, easy now, honey, *no* . . . hold it!"

Alice, hand to mouth, staggered across the doorway into the bathroom and slammed the door shut. Sarah winced at the sound of her upchucking. There is a disintegration of dignity, for sure, in vomiting. Sarah looked at the round wall clock; its red minute hand moved too slowly for her. Sarah was frightened for all her show of calmness. She gave a stentorian sigh that almost brought bile to her mouth. In twelve minutes Homer and Wallie would arrest Achilles Marrkoras, read him the riot act for endangering crew and ship. And Captain Hammel would take over, which takeover was to be entered in the bridge log. Tom would then correct the faulty navigation, change course, and head *Pallas Athena* east-northeast, moving toward a less wild weather front. The morning reports were right; where the hell was that high yellow bitch of a maid when one needed a refill?

Sarah tried to light a cigarette, but it bent with her fumbling and broke at the neck. There was a fresh pack in the bedroom. But she didn't feel like moving because of the floor's tilting. A loose chair moved across the floor. Should she go into the bathroom, hold Alice's head? No, better not play Duty's Child, leave her to puke it up alone.

Alone . . . Christ! What if anything happened to

Tom, the Greek or somebody throwing a shot at him; her heightened perception saw him dead, Tom's heart having given out from the pressures. If that should happen— some old plugged artery blowing out—God no, no! She glanced at the wall clock. Seven minutes more.

In Achilles' cabin a flask of hair dressing and a pair of brown shoes with woven leather tops moved on their shelf as the tanker sloped down a great wave, then hesitated, as if not ready to make the effort, then as if reacting to the shift in the line of gravity, returned to their place.

However, Achilles, bare-legged in a blue bathrobe, was not watching the play of objects. He kept his angry gaze on Farashah who was facing him, eyes outlined in black, open wide, the line of her jaw knotted in anger. The gold loops in her ears tossed with the movement of her head.

Achilles held a too-tight smile on his face, a smile of irked, ironic doubt that this scene was actually taking place.

"I told you to get out of here. I'll have Sieko drag you down to the brig and break your damn nigger ass."

"You kissed this nigger's ass often enough. You cannot stand me for making you look not so much the man in bed? You find me too much woman for you? So, you take a skinny white bitch—two whites laughing against one brown woman! Maybe I should be like her when we fuck, eh . . . yes? Say, you much man, my massa, oh you, so big, so wonderful to a poor gal like me, so happy, thank you, sir, that you want to bang me, yas? *Tu-na-ponde!*"

"Get going or I'll kick you humpbacked! We Greeks have a saying: nothing is as heavy as the body of a woman who has ceased to satisfy."

It was the wrong remark to make, but Achilles in his pride and anger felt he could handle this situation with the firmness of his words. He felt no guilt. She had come into the cabin shouting, accusing him of being a poof, a failed male, a shitpoke, a no-good limp-pricked bastard, with added Swahili details he didn't understand.

She came closer to him, nearly intoning, "I make you, mister, laughing stock of this ship." Then her voice rose, "I tell everyone you come very poor, like a bird farting . . . nobody throw me away, do this to Farashah, toss me down like old handkerchief you have blown your nose in. I am no . . ."

He leaned forward with the motion of the ship and slapped her hard—once, twice. The umber cheeks of the girl turned a darker hue. She did not flinch from his blows, she just stared ahead, accepting each slap with an insouciant look of perfect control. Then, from her canary-colored native robe, she drew a thin knife with a pointed blade. She lunged at him as the ship gave a fearful lurch, and the blade following its direction, entered Achilles' right side. At the same moment his face took on a surprised supercilious expression of shock.

The tanker tilted to starboard, Achilles grasping his wounded rib section. He fell backward, crashed into the glass table, which shattered under his weight, sending shards of glass flying about. His head hit the corner of the record player's stand, hard.

Farashah looked at the stained knife in her hand, balanced herself as the ship rode up a wave. Her belligerent expression turned to delight, crossed with a sly satisfaction in her deed. Achilles lay moaning, a hand clutching his wounded side, fingers staining with a flow of crimson blood. He muttered something unintelligible.

He tried again to speak, rolled his eyes in his head, managed to rasp, "You murderous cunt, you god-damn . . ." and fainted.

Farashah seemed suddenly to comprehend the danger of her situation. Her eyes focused on the knife in her hand as if it were a demon. Had she really come to kill? No, she had only entered the cabin to curse him out, maybe slash his face. But now, whatever had happened had happened. Jesus, or Allah, or the Buddha knows when events are ordained.

Achilles lay in the glass fragments from the shattered table, his robe open, exposed. She saw the bush of thick curly pubic hair, the relaxed penis, and the balls between the hairy thighs that had mounted her. She leaned down. She would castrate the man; that is what she would do. The Ethiopians from the high hills, she remembered, brought back the genitalia of their slain enemies and wore them as ornaments hanging from enlarged earlobes. The Greek son of a bitch's dong and bag would certainly make a grand trophy. She had no interest in whether he was alive or dead. As she extended the knife to slash at the organs a warning sense alerted her to a sound from the hallway. Was there time for the ritual surgery? A movement outside the door fixed her attention. Maybe the barman was coming with some bottles to refill the bastard's fridge. Or it could be one of the damn Chinese changing a light bulb.

She opened the door an inch or two, then pushed it gently open. The big orange and yellow cat, Tiger Lily, was crouched there, its luminous yellow-amber eyes focused on her. Farashah made a gesture of attack, a low growl came from her throat. The cat did not move. Farashah spit, went into the hallway, closing the cabin door behind her. No one in sight. She heard the reverberant hum of the engines as she darted off to the right and up a staircase to the deck, where her room waited for her. She felt no guilt, no care for the condition of the Greek. If he were not already dead, he would pop off soon, like those sacrificial goats hung, while still alive, throats cut, to drain their life away into the sand, where on the earth the Swahili priest or a guru and chela made ritual patterns with colored stones. These designs were the means by which the sins of the people were transported into the body of the dying goat, freeing the people from whatever bad deeds had been done. Farashah was neither evil nor cruel; she was a querulous, petulant individual keyed to survival.

Ping Pong, coming down to Achilles' cabin with two bottles of burgundy, found Achilles bleeding badly, lying among the remains of the glass table with a bump on his head. Ping Pong did not panic. He had been to sea for many years with "round eyes" and he had seen many things a barman had to become used to and learned to shrug them off.

The Greek was still alive, but there was too much blood. Ping Pong did not touch anything but the phone. He dialed the bridge. "Barman in captain's cabin, he very much hurt, fall in rough sea onto glass table. Very bloody; head big bump."

"What?" It was the young officer, Ormsbee, who seemed to be firm after he understood.

"Don't let any crew in. What's his condition?"

"Maybe he dead, maybe he alive."

"All right, Ping Pong. Get hold of that medical student in the crew section. I'll call Hammel."

"Bleeding on carpet."

"Get that medical student!"

It took five minutes to find Meriapa Chandra Gupta, the medical student, who had been trading postage stamps with one of the Goanese. He was a wax-colored young Hindu with myopic eyes, shaded behind thick lenses. He came wary and a bit shaky to Achilles' cabin. Homer and Tom Hammel had placed the hurt man on the bed, wrapping the torso of the still breathing Achilles in several layers of towels that immediately stained through.

Tom took Achilles' pulse; his breathing was a bit labored.

"Steady-enough heart beat. Lots of blood lost.".

He turned to the medical student who was carrying a black bag with a brass lock and looking about him as if to keep his white shoes out of the blood on the cabin floor.

Tom said, "See if there is glass in those wounds, then you can sew them up. His skull doesn't look cracked. Just a bad bump."

"I do not have the medical degree."

"You'll have a black eye and no teeth," said Homer beginning to unwrap the towels. "Get on with it!"

A narrow wound, a half-inch slit bleeding but not badly was exposed. There was another deeper gash on the left thigh, a point of glass showing from its wide opening.

"That's where he lost the most blood."

The medical student opened his black bag. "I put in penicillin powder, sew big gash." The medical student now seemed at ease, inspecting the body as if it were an anatomy class subject.

"Go to work," said Tom. "Homer, I'm going back to the bridge."

Homer took Tom by the arm and led him to one side. He spoke low. "That wound in the side . . . I mean looks like some I've seen, like a knife jab."

Tom didn't change his expression. "You're no medical man, Homer. Nor, I'd say, is that Hindu much of one."

"No, sir." (The respect to a captain was back.)

"We don't want to find a knife wound, do we? It's clear Marrkoras can't handle the ship after this accident. You'll vouch for that. He's very weak from loss of blood, groggy head bump. His condition can turn serious. Very. I'm taking command in this crisis. Forced to, correct? I'll radio Athens." His face remained expressionless.

Homer analyzed the captain's changed manner as an expression of his Protestant, puritanical conceit. He said, "Kismet."

"What's that, Homer?"

"That's an Arab word. *Kismet* means destiny. It has worked out fine for us with this boogering sod out on his back."

"You think *Pallas Athena*'s destiny can stand a lot of this worsening weather?"

"Of course. I'll finish balancing off the tanks."

"*Kismet?* You're a damn brain trust, Homer, reading all those books."

"Yes, Captain."

The medical student bent over Achilles and said, "I cannot thread the needle in this weather."

Tom turned at the door. "If you don't, I'm throwing you overboard. Take over, Mr. Bowen."

The captain left and the medical student, looking at the needle in his hand, said, "He is jesting, of course?"

"Him? No sense of humor at all, those Yanks. He threw two men overboard last trip. Get on with it, doc. Here, let me thread that."

Homer looked down at the pale face of Achilles; his nostrils were flared, but his breathing seemed easier. A reddish foam was oozing from the bandaged wound in his side. Without comment, Homer watched the medical student sew up the thigh wound. He did a rather neat job of it.

"Will he live? How bad is he?"

"It would seem both wounds are healable, unless they infect. But I will use plenty of penicillin. The head bump, who knows."

"He can't be up and around . . . very weak, righto?"

"Oh no moving about . . . very weak condition . . . glass very sharp and deep . . . much loss of blood."

"Carry on," said Homer cheerfully, slapping the medical student on the back. "Move in here—posh quarters for a hospital. And have Wu Ting Li get some of the boys to clean the place up. Looks and smells like a knacker's butchering shop."

The cat, Tiger Lily, was outside the door again. Homer wondered if it had scented blood and was reverting to a jungle past. He kicked at the animal who dodged his shoe expertly, lifting its tail like a banner before it ran. Someplace a loose door opened and shut with a bang.

CHAPTER 17

FROM THE NOTEBOOKS OF HOMER BOWEN:

At times it is almost as if a great canyon has opened in the sea and Pallas Athena is continuously falling into it. The storm batters us from the southwest and we are in peril. The nearby Akora Islands set up currents beyond their shallow two hundred fathoms.

Thomas Hammel has been trying to get us away from this danger, but the best speed we dared make was ten knots. These giant waves are formed by shoreline conditions, where a shelf ends suddenly and the sea bottom drops; sometimes the currents along this formation move at a speed of five knots, creating something like a series of undersea waterfalls. Where the swift current from the Indian Ocean bumps head on into the storm force from the southwest, it's like an atomic force. Watching the furies from the bridge, we feel damn mortal and small.

You almost feel a kind of hatred engendered in this sea. I can't call it malevolence but it is frightening, even to a middle-aged sea-dog like myself, to see the fury of gale and rain, feel the powerful punches of the sea when its currents turn to monstrous waves. From the bridge, the view is nerve shattering. Below in the engine room, we can only stare at each other and watch the steam gauges, test the salt level in the water before it enters the boilers. We hope the propeller shafts don't bend and the engines continue to growl and purr. Down here we can hear the pounding of the storm on the steel hull, that thin metal plating that keeps out the waters of the world.

Carlos deNova, my second engineer, is a Genoese Christian. He has a habit of crossing self when reading the gauges. If he adds a prayer, crossing himself, a quick touch here and there, a pleading look upward, I don't mind.

The "World Oil News" was a bit blurred by static but I copied it off on my Jap tape recorder anyway. Somehow the reports on the talk about increasing the safety of tankers, sounded ominous:

A YEAR-LONG MARITIME CONFERENCE AMONG ONE HUNDRED AND SIX NATIONS IN LONDON ENDED WITH THE AGREEMENT THAT OIL TANKERS BUILT AFTER NEXT YEAR MUST HAVE WATER-CARRYING BALLAST TANKS BETWEEN THE OUTER HULLS AND OIL-CARRYING COMPARTMENTS TO PROTECT AGAINST OIL SPILLS. THE TREATY MUST BE RATIFIED BY THE SENATE. U.S. OFFICIALS HAD SOUGHT AN AGREEMENT CALLING FOR DOUBLE-HULLED SHIPS, BUT THE DEPARTMENT OF TRANSPORTATION SECRETARY SAID, "I PERSONALLY FEEL THAT WE ACHIEVED IN THIS INTERNATIONAL FORUM . . . MORE THAN MOST PEOPLE BELIEVED WE COULD ACHIEVE." THE AGREEMENT ALSO CALLS FOR NEW STANDARDS TO KEEP OIL FROM BEING DUMPED IN THE OCEAN DURING TANK CLEANING.

Carlos said that was like counting next year's sexual encounters. I don't have any doubts about the loyalties of the engine room's crew; they will be no problem. I'm not so sure about the deck hands and mess staff that cater to the ship. . . . They live their own lives; in their quarters, they gamble, play plaintive native music with strange stops, and Lord knows what else goes on. So I don't know what panic or duplicity could develop there if the storm causes major problems. I don't hold with the old judgments, illusions that Kipling, Conrad, and others had about nonwhites on the ships of a few generations ago: that they are in some inherent way inferior in sense and courage in a crisis.

But our crew is very jumpy at the change in command. They could be a risky group if we suffer great damage or must abandon ship. They whisper among themselves, look worried. Duck Fong pretty much controls them. But his real feeling, the core of his thinking about what is going on, is a blank to me. Very Oriental.

I have managed to level off some of the oil, but not nearly enough, I feel. In this weather working on the main deck is suicide. Any break in the weather and I'd have them all level. Survival is our first concern. No one has made much comment about the change of command. Captain Marrkoras, the captain announced through the ship's blower, has been badly injured in a fall; he, Thomas Hammel, was, as senior officer, in full command, and the ship was in good running order, beating its way to the outer fringes of the typhoon. With a change of course, away from the currents off the Akora Islands, it was hoped we would be out of the worst of it in a day or so.

He knew and I knew it was a much too optimistic view. All the weather fronts surrounding us are still menacing. Yet it was good to have Captain Hammel back in command. He doesn't waste time in platitudes. His firm persuasiveness keeps the crew—still a bit confused—informed of the basic situation (no details), and he orders them to small tasks, enough to keep them from having time to beef or become too vocal in their trepidation. It is clear events on board have upset them.

Sparky has sent news of the change-over in captains to Athens and back came the KSL reply accepting the situation (what the hell else could they do?) with the added text (that Wallie showed me as he filed the message in the log):

IF MARRKORAS SERIOUSLY INJURED TRY LAND CONTACT THAT WILL FLY HIM OFF BY HELICOPTER.

No word about the captain's last reply:

STORM AND DISTANCE PROHIBIT AIR AID WILL PROCEED ON COURSE BEST SUITED FOR SAFETY.

CAP. T.H.

The young medical student, who was serving as stockroom steward, has taken over Achilles' cabin and made a regular hospital of it. Moved in a cot for himself and an assortment of bottles and supplies from our first aid kits, all with a pervasive scent of sandalwood and garlic. He's become a regular Harley Street medical man; very serious, pompous, and tut-tuting when you ask for answers on Achilles' condition. Achilles doesn't look too well to me: by his high color and flushed looks, I'd say he was feverish. I hope the antibiotics Chandra Gupta is using are the real thing and not some black market substitute. The labels read "penicillin," "streptomycin"—I hope so.

In this weather and with the distances we are from any landbased helicopter site, Achilles can't be lifted off. The ship is plunging so much he has had to be strapped to his bed. Looking at him, he's no more the dapper young stud who was so sleek and smooth; now he's a very sick man indeed. Unshaved, the bump on his head a rotten-egg-purple; also his cheeks have become gaunt and all the muscles of the face are slackened. He is delirious some of the time—mostly he just sleeps or stares into space.

The library has been flooded; large sea birds have floundered onto the ship. One gull-like creature with lemon-yellow feet came through the library window like a projectile, the sea following at every dip of the ship until Wu Ting Li and a work crew managed to erect some plywood barrier reinforced by iron bars. Still enough water comes in to keep the crew mopping the room and one of the hallways.

Wallie, who in the crunch has turned out to be a fine officer, and the captain seem to sleep on the bridge. With two officers (Achilles and Ott) cut from the ship's routine, there's hardly shut-eye time up there. The chartroom cadet, Willie, has been promoted to bridge duty. Sparky's assistant, Moise, a cheerful lout with nicotine-stained fingers and acne scars, fills in on errands. Duck Fong is having trouble in the kitchen in this tumbling weather. Even with raised edges on our tables, eating meals is dangerous; hot soups and condiment bottles have been banned. Ping Pong, spry as a monkey, works his bar, wedging bottles, glasses into clip racks. A cut-glass bowl of fruit did a dive to its fate off the end of the bar.

Alice Palamas is exiled to her bed—hardly touching solid food and not keeping down liquids. She did, in one pale assertion between groans and retching, beg me, "Get me some good film footage of the storm."

I am not a cameraman of any skill, I told her, but she insisted. So, using her hand-held camera, I've exposed some footage from the bridge and through the salt-streaked windows. I said it was most likely blurred and she said, "Anything out of focus is called art. Oh I want to die, I want to die."

I said it was a common wish of seasick people and not to be ashamed of it. I said she would live and the ship was handling the storm well. Then grasping my hand, she whispered, "I'm not ready yet, Homer, to die. Hand me that basin."

I did and left in a hurry. That kind of anguish and my response to seasickness is not too subtle.

Sarah Hammel is rather subdued. She is usually a lark laughing and scratching, as they say. But now she is rather sober and worried-looking. I suppose she knows our danger and is in no mood for her old expansiveness. She said she'd like to see the sun again, shining twelve degrees off the horizon. I said we all would. Her maid Farashah seems to exacerbate the situation. Sarah is curt with her, and the girl is a bit raffish, considering our situation. She hums and whistles to herself as if, as Sarah said, our situation was a kind of Laurel and Hardy comedy, everyone falling all over each other in foolish accidents. The bruises are not funny. I heard the maid tell Sarah she wasn't feeling too good. "Queasy stummick, I got."

Studied a set of the ship's plans in detail; I share the captain's fear of damage to the tanker. A heavy headwind can collapse the bow. The frames in the forepeak are often not strong enough to take extra, unexpected strain. I pointed out to Tom where the longitudinals can fracture at the junction of the verticals, if they don't just buckle like jackstraws. He thanked me dryly for the information. In our present condition with unbalanced tanks, the strength of the hull is compressed, straining the framing all along our length. One frame gives way and you can have a ship in peril; internal frames can buckle at times— I've seen shell platings come apart and drop off—a sign the watertight bulkheads that separate the oil holding tanks are no longer holding.

Tom pointed out we have a space between the stem-plating and the end-most tank. If some few hundred tons of wild water break in there tossing against the bulkhead, how long will the steel frames hold, he asked. And can repairs be done? I had to tell him that there are no interior passages to such sections. When damaged, they can't be shored up, and since, in a storm, there is no foothold on the main deck, it's impossible for a crew to repair damage. He said I certainly cheered up his day.

I am depressing myself by studying these plans. Fore to aft, we should have a way to reach the collision bulkheads in strong weather, and Pallas Athena doesn't. Tankers mostly don't.

After we rolled up the plans, the captain and I left the bridge for some hot tea. The heat from the heavy mugs was balm on my cold fingers.

An extra huge wave banged over the catwalk.

"Damn a tanker, Homer. They can't ride up over a big wave."

"No, sir, they have to barge through slam-bang like a fat lady at a bargain counter."

"What do you estimate is our best speed?"

"Eight knots, I'd say. We're two football fields long and the bow is taking a beating."

Tom seemed to chew on the advice. *"If it gets worse I'm going to slow her down to six knots—just to keep her steerable. Any damage?"*

"A gull through a window. Sieko says his ghost sound isn't as yet endangering the ship."

He set down his cup, which rolled erratically off the table. It didn't break, just inched across the floor.

"If there's anything behind Sieko's ghost sound, Homer, it will have to show itself to me. We don't buy wooden nutmegs where I come from."

(I don't understand the point of that American expression at all.)

Captain Thomas Hammel paced the bridge of *Pallas Athena*. He had the proper captain's style, with an added touch of self-sacrifice ignoring the gale forces beating against the slanted windows of the cabin, the heaving of the huge tanker as she ran down the slope of a great wave, forcing her way through and coming out from under like a wet dog shaking herself.

The bridge was dark except for the shaded lights over the instruments illuminating the two seamen who stood braced at the wheel. Tom moved to a ledge where he unrolled the long route chart and studied it. On the trip from the Persian Gulf he had safely moved past the Timor Sea, threaded his way through the Torres Straits, and reached the Pacific. Achilles had replaced him (marked by a red chalk-drawn star) well past the Gilbert Islands. At 180 degrees Longitude, he took over the tanker (marked by a blue chalk-drawn star).

Now, three days later, here he was well to the south of the Hawaiian group. Seven to nine days, if he could get up full speed, he should be sighting the west coast of the United States. If. *If.* Like a good captain, he tried to maintain a consciousness of only today.

The damn typhoon didn't seem to have blown itself out. In fact, it was not one storm, it was a series of storms, each one following hard on the heels of the next so that they seemed to merge in one furious sea, the wildest he had yet sailed on in all his years.

He did pray that he'd get the tanker, a bit battered perhaps but whole, to its destination. The odds on that were too hard to figure. He turned to the two sailors at the wheel and smiled, with effort, and nodded to them. "Stay on your compass point."

"Yes, Captain," said Abdullah. His eyes were red-rimmed and his cheeks wrinkled. He hadn't smoked a pipe of hashish for three days now. Abdullah was a splendid seaman and well aware of their danger, so he'd promised himself no pipe until the big storm was over. Beyond that he didn't think. He rarely had any thoughts beyond the day or the promise of the next day. A smoke, a half glass of gin, a few girls to tumble in port. Some wondered at the odd way Allah ran his world. Sometimes it seemed an arbitrary accumulation of turds. That was enough for a sailor.

He corrected the wheel and elbowed the tall Swahili at the wheel with him; a nudge to stay alert. A huge fan of water washed over the main deck, and a fury of foam splashed itself on the bridge windows, then drained away.

The captain refolded his route map as Wallie came on the bridge. The young officer looked cheerful, almost colorful, wearing a yellow cableknit sweater under his jacket, a red Paisley scarf tied in a fashionable knot around his neck. Wallie in this crisis had turned out to be a very good officer; he was aware of the problems, able to give firm orders, handle himself well on the bridge, and stay on a solid emotional base. The captain was rather ashamed of what he had thought of Wallie Ormsbee during their days at sea before the storm struck: a fop, a poof, an intellectual. Some men, he thought, only come up to their potential when they are tried, when an accumulation of events occurs to test them.

"Anything new on the weather fronts, chief?"

"Nothing to cheer about, Wallie. What's below?"

"Everything seems tight; Homer is ready to start leveling off the tanks again, if there is any break in the weather."

"We can hope. I'll just doze off in the chartroom."

Wallie opened the bridge log. "Why not take forty winks below? It would cheer up Mrs. Hammel."

The captain rubbed his unshaved chin. He liked to appear neat—"ship-shape."

"I could shave and take a bath."

Wallie grinned. "Not in this tumbling weather. The bath water would hit the ceiling. Maybe a shower?"

"Maybe." Tom looked at the route notations. "Keep her as she's headed. Anything rougher than this, ring me. I don't want her snuck up on by a killer sea."

"Yes, sir."

Tom waved again as if to the bridge and not the men and left. Wallie took a pipe from a pocket, put it in his mouth but didn't light it. Even food, these days had little taste or bite. He turned to the men at the wheel. "How she handling, Abdullah?"

"A bitch. Very heavy, sir, holding back."

"As long as she responds in time."

Visibility was zero, just a world of rain and wind, mixed into a silver-gray vibrating curtain; the sound to Wallie was like Wagner at his worst.

The first few days of the storm, he had tried to take pictures. But his prints were uninteresting and the huge waves were frightening. Like the print Mother had given him on his twelfth birthday by a Japanese artist, Hokusai.

It was called "The Great Wave." Art didn't seem so impressive anymore. It was the first time in days that he had thought of Mother.

He relished his watches on the bridge. In some way he admired the storm as much as he feared it. Instinct should lead intellect, he decided. The hard life had its rewards—facing physical danger; all that Hemingway horseshit was true. Self abnegation, even exhilaration, came from predicaments faced, faculties alerted like the hair on a cat's back.

He was alive, he was responding to experience; most likely he would die at sea. That was the last crumb of his romanticism he supposed. Love, unobtainable to the dramatic end. Sari and he would go down together. Too bad not in each other's arms. Hardly likely. In his thoughts, he had dissected his passion during the hours of his watch; it had become bittersweet, no longer guilt-ridden.

He entered the log, checked the time, studied the route the captain had laid out. He was aroused from his mood by Abdullah crying out, "Sir, wheel kicking!"

He peered out as he set the window wipers racing to give him a clearer view. To starboard a great wall of water was advancing, as if to suck the sea from under the ship; it heeled at an angle. The long ridge of menacing water was very high, glassy-green, with deep purple shadows. Wallie hastily estimated it to be about seventy feet high, and it was roaring broadside half a mile away.

"Head into it! Starboard! *Starboard!*"

He ran to the wheel, pushing aside the Swahili sailor; he and the Arab worked the wheel. He hoped the tanker could meet the wall of water head first. He felt the ship sink under them, could see the ridge moving swiftly. The ship turned sluggish, almost reluctant to face the sea wall.

Moments passed. The three men on the bridge were silent. Then it was on them. To Wallie it was as if the ship struck a rock wall. *Pallas Athena* mortal, insubstantial, shuddered. She seemed engulfed; the windows were covered by a flooding that turned the bridge into a submarine world. Over all the roaring Wallie heard the whine of the engines straining like the cry of a lone soul before the Last Judgment. Then drowned out everything, as the ship shoved through the liquid wall. He rang the engine room and ordered five knots more speed.

He shouted into the engine room connection. "For God's sake, Homer, don't fail us now."

"We're all knocked on our bloody arses; what's happened?"

"A big bastard wall of water hit us—nearly got us broadside."

Wallie heard a window crack on his left. Flying glass and the cold wet inrush of rain and wind mixed with the briny taste of the Pacific.

"Wallie, Wallie, what's our condition?"

"I think we made it."

The ship was rolling madly, almost bouncing, as the ridge of water passed beyond it. The steersmen steadied themselves as the storm again took over—raindrops the size of bullets pelted the ship, the bridge was flooded. Wallie called down to Sieko in the crew's wardroom. "Get up here fast with some plywood, plastic, anything. One of the bridge windows has shattered. Pronto!"

"Right away, sar."

The full fury of the storm seemed to come through the square opening which plate glass had covered just a few moments before. Wallie felt the chill engulf him, his jacket and sweater were sodden. He pulled off his scarf and mopped his face with it, wringing it out afterwards. He took the compass reading and ordered the ship back on its course. Wallie was trembling now, laughing too, as if he had viewed a hilarious spectacle. The phone rang. It was the captain.

"What the hell was *that?*"

"A broadside; we met it head on, sir."

"Be right up. Soon as I get out of this goddamn bathroom."

"Seems we're ship-shape. We did get a window busted. I can take the rest of the watch myself."

There was no answer from the phone—just the click of the phone being hung up. Christ, the captain couldn't blame him for the high ridge of water.

Sieko came with some squares of plywood and timber. He and two sailors managed to get the opening blocked and wedged with two-by-fours. The captain, in a bathrobe, came onto the bridge, his hair wet and in disorder. He sloshed around in the water on the bridge floor. He thumped the panel; it was not watertight.

"I've never known anything to come this high with enough force to break glass."

Sieko held up a length of red metal about a foot long, two inches wide. "This do it, sar?"

"What the hell is that?"

Wallie examined it. "It's part of the railing from the catwalk."

He looked out. "The walk is still there, but about six feet of railing is gone."

The captain listened and kicked off his water-soaked slippers. He had, Wallie noticed, very white graceful feet.

"Sieko, get the bridge mopped, and have someone send down for my clothes." He turned to Wallie, smiling. "My grandfather was against bathing. He never showered more than once a week. Said it removed the essential oils on the skin, opened up one's pores to infections. You believe that?"

Wallie said he had no scientific knowledge of the fact. This was some captain, he decided.

A phone rang. Wallie picked up and put on a serious voice as he listened, as if making a diagnosis. The captain stared at him but made no motion to interrupt. Wallie said, "Yes, Sparky. Of course, Sparky. Soon as you can. Good man."

He hung up, faced the captain. "The radio room. A section of the rail also hit them. Shattered some kind of a apparatus, destroyed a coil of some sort. Other damage, too."

"We can't receive?"

"We can receive. It's the transmitting section that took the damage. Sparky says we'll be unable to send messages for half a day or so, until he locates spare parts."

"We have them?" The captain was scratching a wet ankle with the toes of the other limb.

"Says we always carry spare items, but there's something about the induction coils. Anyway, he's sure we'll have sending capacity before midnight."

"He better," said the captain turning to the men at the wheel. "Damn it, sailor, keep her steady."

Abdullah answered he was right on the compass point.

CHAPTER 18

For reasons best known to himself, the medical student, Chandra Gupta, was playing Peter, Paul and Mary's "Blowing in the Wind" on Achilles' record player. Sarah, sitting by the bedside of Achilles Marrkoras, felt it was not appropriate music with the storm and the man so ill. But Achilles seemed not to be bothered by the sound.

He appeared conscious at times, rolling his head from side to side as if he were in pain.

"He doesn't look too good, Chandra. In fact he looks lousy," Sarah said, placing on the Greek's brow a damp cloth she had taken from an ice-filled wine bucket. "He's very feverish and his breathing is labored."

"Kind lady," said the medical student, adjusting his white jacket collar where his over-long hair hung onto his shoulders. "I am an unfinished student. Fever is not a subject I studied before I was withdrawn from the Machaki Medical School at Hyderabad."

"I wish we could get him to a good hospital."

She patted the cool cloth in place. Achilles was a ravished man: his cheeks were sunken, his beard poked through the bone-white clammy sheen of his skin. His eyes, like pools of ink, appeared not to take in either movement or place. Only a bad odor came from the prone figure.

"Why don't you shave him?"

"Kind lady, I am not a barber. Before my father lost his wealth speculating in cotton in Rajputana and timber in Punjab, we Gupta very high caste family; still top drawer, oh yes."

She sniffed the blanket. "At least change the dressing. He's beginning to reek."

She pulled back the blanket and sheet. Pink foam was oozing through the soiled bandage on his chest.

"Phew!"

"I have used the antibotics . . . but they do not seem to have the expressed results described in the medical texts."

"Damn it, he's in a bad way."

Homer came in, wearing sea boots. "Og! It's bad-smelling in here."

"I don't like the looks of Achilles." said Sarah. "Look."

"Jesus Christ!" Homer exclaimed, inspecting the bandages, "all that pink foam."

Chandra Gupta shook his head, "Most mysterious."

"Mysterious, hell, I think he's got a punctured lung."

He whirled on the medical student. "What the hell is the matter with you, you Hindu bastard, can't you see there are air bubbles leaking from his side? From his lung?"

"I do my best." The medical student blinked his eyes. "I am not certificated to practice medicine."

"That's lucky for the world. Now let's change the dressing and give him some more antibiotics."

"They do not seem to do their task."

"I bet they're black market crud, mostly milk sugar and cornstarch."

The wound in the side looked revolting. The purple and red swelling produced a continual escape of air bubbles.

"It's the lung all right." Awkwardly, Homer probed the area around the wound. "I think he's got pneumonia."

"What can we do, what can Tom do?"

"Nothing, not a damn thing, Sarah. We're hundreds of miles out of reach of any hospital. Nothing can fly in this storm even if we could lift him off. And . . ." Homer shut off the record player.

"And . . . what *and*?" Sarah asked, unrolling a length of bandage as the medical student dusted the wound with antibiotic powder, as if he were preparing a fowl for roasting.

"Our radio is out, the transmitting station anyway. Sparky thought he'd have it fixed two days ago, but he's having trouble with a crushed master panel."

"Nothing? No contact with out there?"

"We're receiving from Athens, they're asking for our position and condition. But we can't wave back so far."

After Achilles had been bandaged, the medical student was told to clean up the place or get his black arse kicked. Homer and Sarah went out into the hallway to suck in air free of the cabin's muck.

"What do you think, Homer?"

The engineer made a grimace of distress. "You ask me, that guy is going to turn up his toes."

"No!"

"Face it, the poor sonofabitch is dying."

"Oh no, I mean, such a small wound."

"Who's the character from Shakespeare who after being stabbed, says, his wound isn't as deep as a well but 'twill serve?"

"Don't know. All I need is a drink."

Homer said, "Well, just one." He, too, had felt a need to do a bit of boozing and was fighting the urge. He rarely

205

drank onboard ship, but the last week had been, as he put it, a doozy. Long hours watching the boilers, the engines, trying to level off the partly filled tanks. And, above all, wondering when *Pallas Athena* would jackknife, break in half, or rupture a few tanks. All the arbitrary accumulation of dark forebodings needed a drink.

Ping Pong served them doubles of Scotch and water, pointing to the damage to the bar and to some long, heavy timber that propped up a sagging section of the plastic ceiling.

"Very much glass damaged and ceiling coming down. Bad condition, no martini glass left; now serving martinis in wine glasses."

"Oh, very well, old chap," said Homer, "leave the bottle."

Ping Pong went off to assist two sailors adding more timber to prop another section of the ceiling.

"Homer, is there much damage like this?"

"Nothing vital. Burst W.C. pipes in Duck Fong's cabin. The main deck railing tore loose and broke some windows, dented some shell plates."

He laughed and sipped his drink. "Can't you see those consummate buggers Paul and Ionnes Kyprios in Athens receiving no messages from us. I bet they're slapping each other on the brisket—'*Pallas Athena* doesn't answer . . . *Pallas Athena* has gone down in the deep in typhoon! Ha ha!' They think the insurance wallahs are out ninety million dollars. I bet they're in some Greek joint right now celebrating and breaking plates."

"Homer, put down the bottle and cheer me up."

He licked his lips, put the Scotch to one side and bent solicitously over her. "I'd certainly like to fool those swine and bring the ship in, a wreck or not, just to see their fat faces when we enter port. That I would. Must be getting back to my engines; yes."

Homer went off, singing softly to himself:

206

> O, who will shoe my bonny foot?
> O, who will glove my hand,
> Or bind my middle
> With a broad lily band?

A good joe, Sarah decided. She had Ping Pong mix up a pint of milk and brandy with an egg added and took the mixture to Alice's cabin—not an easy task in a pitching ship. In the cabin she found the luggage and the camera gear in disorder. Some of it had broken loose and was moving about underfoot. Alice was curled up in a fetal position on her bed. She turned, as Sarah stood over her, and groaned. A slop basin was ready by the side of her bed.

"Oh, it's you, why are we still shaking?"

"Storm, tootsie." Sarah braced herself and held out the tall glass and its chalky mixture. "Come on, girl, you haven't eaten anything for days. Down the hatch."

"I'd only toss it up."

"Now, now, pull yourself together. This is booze and milk, a little nourishment. Take it or damn it, I'll hold your nose and pour it into you. Stop playing the fucking invalid. Drink!"

Alice sat up, swallowed half of the drink and waved off the rest. "Brandy? I think I can keep it down."

"Now get the hell out of the kip, take a shower, wash your hair. Buck up, girl."

"Take a shower in this banging about?"

"I'll turn on the water. You hold on to the handles set in the wall. Gawd you smell."

Alice laughed and hiccupped. "*I* stink, *you* smell, as Dr. Johnson put it."

Sarah said she didn't care for doctor jokes just then. After Alice showered, washed her hair and combed it out, she was given a fresh nightgown and a nearly unsoiled bathrobe. She sat and finished the milk and brandy and said maybe she'd live. Sarah told her, mostly we all do. Then she said that Wallie had told her they would soon be entering the eye of the hurricane, but they'd have a lull of a few hours. Alice said Wallie was sweet on Sarah, had that prurient look in his eyes. Sarah said why not, she wasn't too battered an old crock. Alice said she didn't mean to put Sarah down, and Sarah replied of course not, honey. Then she said she'd see Alice at dinner, and if Alice didn't show she'd have her dragged out of the cabin, which needed a good cleaning and airing. She'd send Farashah in to give it a full going over.

"How's Achilles?"

Sarah made a clucking sound. "Bad, real bad. I mean, Homer thinks it could be the deep six."

"What? Oh no, just from a few cuts?"

"One got into a lung and Homer thinks it's pneumonia."

"We could all use a good doctor aboard ship."

Alice didn't feel too depressed when Sarah left. A real depression would take up too much energy. She was too worn down and weak from the last few days of agony and humiliation from her seasickness. Such a messy throwup nastiness. Maybe she should have more of the milk and brandy. She felt much better or was she at last getting used to storms at sea? She couldn't feel too much sadness for Achilles. Maybe later. She felt ashamed of her selfishness. Not a bad sort, Achilles Dionysius Zeno Marrkoras. Not even as frivolous as he appeared. He had good mental ability and all that charm. He gave me a feeling of plenitude, she thought, a great fuck—his intuition always on tap to cheer you up. Her sexual encounters with him (too few) had given her a sense of independence, even a touch of exaltation. Of all her indiscriminate amours (as she labeled them), there was still in her a core

208

of hope that somewhere in one of the many beds she shared, she would find what her Jewish mother had called "Mr. Right."

But Achilles was not he; with a kind of masochistic pleasure, she was thinking back to their love play, their merging sensualities, and now the poor bastard was dying. What had her professor lover once said to her? "We are all walking wounded." That was he—all poetry and little prick. She held up the case for her camera lens and fondled the leather surface of it.

The sea seemed calmer. If the light was good she'd take some pictures of the torn-away railing, the busted-out windows and portholes. She stood up unsteadily and balanced herself, arms outstretched like a high-wire-walker. To no one at all she said, "It's paranoia time."

When Captain Thomas Hammel was in a black dog mood, he felt *Pallas Athena* was a huge dying creature to which he was attached. Storm-tossed, not able to make radio contact with the outside world, that indifferent world beyond the winds and the heaving sea, the ship was still ill-balanced. He wondered just how full or empty all the tanks were. Then, there was the burden of the captain he had replaced, now lying in a coma. Added to this, there were Sieko Mihran's reports on his crazy noise; a sound different from the usual creaking of a large ship welded together.

He took Sieko into the chart room, closed the glass door.

"Now, say it slowly."

"Sar, I have found the reason for the unexplained sound."

"And you say it's a condition above a carrying beam just below the main deck?"

"Very slight condition, but there. I have not told anyone else, of course."

"Good man. We'll get Mr. Bowen and go see if you've found anything."

The captain was a brooder. He didn't trust quickness of perception, but he liked to face facts.

"Oh, sar, believe me, yes, I have found."

The captain didn't show worry or puzzlement at the information; he remained silent as he went out to the bridge and phoned for Homer to join them in the supply locker under the main deck. Here stored spare parts, lengths of chain, machine-tooled objects wrapped in greasy packages, and boxes were lined up on narrow shelves. There were steel doors from the locker to either side of the ship, doors—as the captain saw—heavily dogged with metal locking bars.

Homer, carrying a portable box lamp, joined the captain and Sieko in the dank confined space over which two grate-covered lights in the ceiling cast warped shadows. Sieko was sniffing the atmosphere, almost like a quivering hound dog.

"He says he has found it, Tom?"

"So he claims," said the captain.

"Tell us, damn it—don't play games."

Sieko pointed to the door to the right. "This way. Open it, Mr. Bowen."

The door was opened, pushed back by the three men who faced a narrow walkway forward of which was one of the great girders that ran across the beam of the ship from one side to the other. Homer followed Tom and Sieko onto the walk, hoisting his light to take in the underside of the steel surface under the main deck. It was double-plated here—a geometric confusion of cubist forms, pipes, cables, beams.

Sieko pointed upward; the light picked up a section of deck plating: it was oil stained and dripped moisture from some pipe condensation in the atmosphere.

"I don't see a damn thing." The captain's voice echoed; someplace below there was a discreet muffled gurgling.

Homer held the light closer. They were seven feet under the section the sailor was pointing to. Homer said softly, in a sort of nagging intonation, "It could be." He extended an arm with a fistful of cotton waste and rubbed the steel surface overhead. Yes, there was a kind of thin tear—a scar, eight feet long, that ran toward the hull on the right. Homer followed it with his cotton swab and estimated.

"Holy Mary and Joseph, look at that."

"What is it?"

"It's a break, Tom, no doubt about it. A crack in the steel."

The captain held up a hand sprinkled with ecchymotic spots, touched the scar on the plating.

"Doesn't mean anything, could have been done in building the ship. The top plate on the exposed deck is welded onto it."

"Could be, yes, could not be," said Homer. His arm ached from holding up the heavy light.

"It's an old crack," said Tom, "oil marked."

Sieko wondered if he should-speak, then did, "Could also be new this trip. Lot of oil spillage. Creeps every place. It make the sound I hear."

"Why the hell should it make a sound?" asked the captain. "I don't hear anything."

"Very small sound at times when rubbing part against part."

Homer cocked an ear. "I don't hear a damn thing either."

"Sound depend on how the ship is running; when pressure is hard sound comes, and when not, no sound. No pressure just now."

Tom studied the faint marking of the crack. Was it

new? Was it something the ship builders hid or inspectors passed over? Was it known to the owners when the ship was launched? Hardly likely.

"Mr. Bowen, measure it every two hours. If there is any change, inform me at once."

"Will do."

The captain coughed, clearing his bronchial tubes. "Sieko, we don't know if you've made a vital discovery or not. But thank you for keeping at it. Of course, until we really establish just what the devil it is, you'll keep this matter under your hat. Understand?"

"Sar, I am an old trustworthy sailor, I obey. Understand."

Their breath made vapor trails; the chill was getting to them. Homer beat his hands together as they moved back to the locker.

Tom invited Homer to his quarters for a drink; this time he did not hide the bafflement on his face. Farashah was in the captain's quarters vacuum cleaning the sea-green carpeting.

"Where's Mrs. Hammel?"

"She go to Missy Palamas."

"All right, Farashah, that will be all."

"I have more to do." She enjoyed making a show of how much she had to do.

"Later."

She saw the look on the captain's face, shrugged, switched off the machine, and went into the bathroom, closing the door behind her.

Homer sat down and inspected his soiled fingers. "Skip the drink."

"Fine. Now, Homer, give it to me straight. No horseshit. The crack?"

"It's that, sir, a crack right through the half-inch steel plating."

"Old?"

Homer pursed his lips, leaned forward as if to impart some vital secret. "Not old. That's my guess."

"Come on, man. Don't pussyfoot."

For the first time Homer felt the captain was showing deep human response. "Is it new; if so how new? Yesterday, two weeks, done in harbor loading?"

"I'd say this trip. But it's a guess, an educated guess by a man who knows metals. Now don't get browned off. It may be caused by the unbalanced tanks, the rough seas, or for that matter, by a built-in structural defect from day one."

The captain looked dubious. "You don't think that?"

"No."

The captain went over to the photograph of *Pallas Athena* framed on the wall. He put a thumb against the place where the crack would be. "About here?"

"Right there." Homer joined him at the picture. "Now if it should get longer, tear its way to the outer hull, well . . . with enough pressure, it could cause the hull to buckle, say by riding the wrong waves. Well, write your own ticket."

"You're saying we could develop a crack in the outer hull? Spit it out, man. Say what you mean."

"Easy, easy, Tom. It's not obstinacy on my part. Say there is a rupture of some of the tanks if the hull buckles. That's putting the worst light on it."

"Thank you, Homer."

The captain gave him a harsh look, then smiled. "We could break in half? Like the old *Mimelonia* off the Gilberts back in '62? We'd make a big hole in the sea?"

"No, it doesn't have to work that way at all. We have a double deck here. If the welding tying up the two decks holds together, even a crack in the outer hull wouldn't tear us apart. And, if it's at sea level, we've the pumps to control it."

"Will the bulkheads in the bow section give, if the crack widens?"

"That gets into fortune telling, Tom. And I never believed much in a crystal ball."

"Keep measuring that crack. We'll know in the next twenty-four hours if the ship is really bad luck." He punched his fist against the wall under the picture. "God, to think I'm trying to save this ship and cargo for those fucking Greeks who want her dead and on the bottom of the Pacific."

Homer said, "Worse comes to worse we could abandon her. It's no skin off our arse."

"In this weather! Risk the lives of everyone on board, four of them women? Hell no."

"We could launch, calm the sea by releasing oil. I'll have Sparky pick up what's near us. Should be a Japanese freighter about."

"How the devil can we contact them? The radio is still out."

"For sending, yes, but we can receive." He slapped his forehead. "We can get the position of nearby ships. The lifeboats have radios with hand-powered generators—good for probably a mile radius. They'd pick up our May Day if we abandon."

"Hell and damnation, I'm not abandoning, not even thinking of it. We're a couple of old ladies suspecting a man under the bed. Go put the boot to that radio room prick. I want to be able to send out messages. Maybe the lifeboat radios can do it."

"Will try."

Homer left the captain's quarters a very worried man. He knew more about the way a ship is put together than Tom Hammel, and he was not so sure the plates between the upper and lower decks had been welded. What isn't exposed is often sloughed off in construction.

Later, when he measured the crack with a stave the

crack hadn't grown. In the radio room he found Sparky and Moise, his assistant, bent over dismantled parts.

"The captain says get the damn thing sending, so we can send out some kind of message."

"Has he got a 4X coil among his mementos?" Sparky didn't seem flustered as he twisted two ends of a cable together. Moise looked at his wristwatch, "'World Oil News' time, " he grinned. "I bet they have us on the air . . . Where are you, *Pallas Athena* old gal?"

He threw some switches and adjusted the resulting sound which was like a growl. Homer said, "Captain says maybe emergency radios in the lifeboats could help?"

"Those old crappolas? Cheap bargains. I bet you can't get ten miles range on them."

The "World Oil News" came on. Sparky skinned his hand with a slipping tool and sucked his knuckles. "You can hear how they miss us."

Moise refined the sound again with a slight turn of a knob. "Wanna bet . . . wanna bet we're the next item."

"Get back to the soldering. I want that rheostat set tight."

KYPRIOS SHIPPING LINES REPORTS THERE IS NO TRUTH IN THE RUMORS THAT THEIR GIANT TANKER *PALLAS ATHENA* IS IN DANGER OF BREAKING UP IN TYPHOON WEATHER IN THE AREA NORTH AND EAST OF CAROLINE ATOLL . . .

"What'd I tell you!" said Moise. "We're news!"

Homer moved nearer the speaker. "KSL, they're playing it innocent as a virgin in a convent."

IONNES KYPRIOS, PRESIDENT OF THE KSL, ISSUED A STATE-MENT IN ATHENS JUST AN HOUR AGO THAT THE *PALLAS ATHENA* AT LAST REPORT WAS WEATHERING THE STORM WELL. WHILE THERE HAD BEEN A BREAK IN RADIO COMMUNI-CATIONS, THIS WAS COMMON IN CERTAIN STORM AREAS. HE

WOULD NOT CONFIRM WHEN KSL HAD LAST BEEN IN RADIO CONTACT WITH THE LARGEST OIL TANKER IN THE WORLD. THE SHIP IS OVER A HALF MILLION TONS AND, WHEN SHE LEFT THE PERSIAN GULF, WAS FULLY LOADED. LLOYDS OF LONDON SAID THEY HAD BEEN INFORMED BY ITS OWNERS THAT THERE IS NO DANGER TO THE HUGE SHIP OR TO OTHER VESSELS IN THE AREA. UNITED SEA INSURANCE GROUP OF NEW YORK IS-SUED THE SAME REPORT. THE WEATHER ALONG LONGITUDE 150 DEGREES WEST OF GREENWICH CONTINUES AT TYPHOON FORCE. THE BIG SHIP IS SAILING THROUGH ON HER WAY TO SAN PEDRO ON THE SOUTHERN CALIFORNIA COAST. REPORTS ARE THAT SHE IS INSURED FOR NINETY MILLION DOLLARS. NEITHER LLOYDS NOR THE GRAND UROPA SYNDICATE, WHICH CARRY MOST OF THE RISK, WOULD CONFIRM THIS ES-TIMATE. THE KYPRIOS BROTHERS ALSO REFUSED COMMENT.

"I bet," said Homer.

Sparky said, "We should have made a bigger news item."

When Homer went down to measure the crack later, he found it had lengthened by four and a half inches, but it had not widened much. Well, if they had to abandon ship Sparky had already reported signals from a Japanese freighter, the *Hatano Maru,* which was directly in their path, maybe fifty miles ahead. They could signal her with flares and with the lifeboat radios, they'd be picked up without too much trouble. The wind was dropping.

BOOK FIVE

STORM SEA

| 19

Achilles saw all those implausible, grieving faces when they thought he was dying of that brown bitch's stab wound. Heard all the sad, conspiratorial things they said as they came to wait for him to die. But he didn't die, though the pain continued. Then later, when he was recovering, he had come home to where his people were living in a valley of the Peloponnesus; his mother hugged him and made the sign of the cross, twice. "We thought you were all drowned. There was no radio contact for so long."

"No, no, it all ended well," he answered. His father, Basil, and his old grandfather, Stratis—brown and hard as saddle leather—had toasted his survival with the local grape brandy.

It was good to eat his mother's *pilav*, rice dish, again, be with all the cousins, and eat red Tarama caviar; it was a holiday, the Day of Ochi, and they all asked him about the great storm.

"A very great one, and the waves as high as the St. Cyril church steeple. Oh yes, you can be sure I was frightened. We never seemed to get out of the reach of that typhoon. I remember while I had fever, there was a great lull and the ship seemed lost to the world; then the storm started again."

"But my boy is home," said his mother. "Blessed Mary, pity women," she crossed herself. She was a pious woman. His father said, "Priests are for women. God is for men."

It was good to have survived. On his arrival in port, he had spent a wild night in Athens, meeting old shipmates who wanted to hear of the marvelous, perilous time on *Pallas Athena*. They had gone to see Dora Straton and her dancers on Philopappos and then had taken Homer Bowen with them to the Architektoniki night club to see the belly dancers gyrate. Bowen wasn't like the other Anglos on *Pallas Athena*, who had resented his taking over as captain. The drunker Engineer Bowen got, the louder he talked.

"Bloody hard time of it we had from the Persian Gulf on. Hard cheese, you Greek chaps."

"We did what we had to do."

"Never thought you'd live after that knife wound."

"No, no, it was the glass fragments that did it."

"Jolly bad show. I know a knife wound when I see one."

"All well now."

After the big drunk he rested in his hotel bed, not hung over much, just limply recalling the last few weeks. A little pain left, a sense of having been hurt. Too much retsina wine. Tomorrow he'd go away for a real rest. The Kyprioses had been very kind to him. That wily Ionnes, all smiles and back pats.

"Go, Achilles, to my villa in Thessaly. Get fat, eat lots of the *feta* cheese and screw every virgin on the plains if you can. All on the KSL, to the captain who brought our great ship through, eh, eh?"

Yes, he was tired—so tired after all. He'd been through

hard times; it was fitting for a young captain, a newspaper hero, a man whom the women batted their eyelids over at parties. They took him aside to look into his face and ask intimate questions—bodies bent in marvelous gestures that gave him a hard-on just to hear their voices. So many voices. He would sleep well, dream marvelous things.

He was very tired, almost asleep. Yet a real man doesn't turn down anything for that. So familiar, yet who . . . who . . . recall the voice, the promise in it. He sighed and called out, "Come in, it's not locked." Tired as he was, he must rise, perform, and . . .

"He's dead," Sarah said. "He just flickered out."

The cabin tilted with the roll of the ship, Chandra let fall the limp arm from the wrist of which he had been trying to get a pulse. "Is too bad."

Sarah looked down at the calm face of the dead Greek, the upturned corners of the mouth almost formed a smile. Reflex only, she thought, and turned away from open sightless eyes.

"He was delirious, mumbling away in Greek."

"Close his eyes, Chandra," said Homer.

"In my native country they place silver coins on the eyelids of the dead."

She did not respond, did not turn to see what the medical student was doing to the corpse. *Corpse?* That's the last thing you are before they toss dirt in your face.

In the hallway Sarah lit a cigarette, grimaced, blinked back a tear. She shouldn't feel so bad about the poor sonofabitch. Only a two-timing Greek, if what Tom suspected was true; the whole setup to wreck *Pallas Athena*. Still, whatever lives I am akin to, she thought, remembering something in a *Ladies' Home Journal* she had picked up someplace.

The storm would be getting up soon, maybe they'd all

220

be corpses themselves soon. But not just dead like this, lying in a bed and having somebody think of putting silver dollars on your eyes. If *Athena* went down it would be cold and wet and dreadful. She shivered and inhaled deeply, coughed. She had no respect for death. It seemed so damn vulgar and needlessly gruesome when you're alive. Damn unreasonable. Why didn't people dry out like dandelion seeds, become fluff, and float away as the dandelions of her childhood, where death lived in another country; she was sure then that she would never die, never.

The ship plunged suddenly, heeled over. Sarah found herself hugging a wall, the cigarette alive, red-eyed on the rug at her feet. Carefully she stomped on it.

From above the main deck one could see the sky arched like a lead bowl. There had been a few heavy waves against the bow, but the lull in the eye of the storm still held. Ahead was darkness, split with scars of lightning zig-zagging through a thick atmosphere ready to deluge the heaving ship with crests of ivory foam.

The captain had decided to bury Achilles Marrkoras at sea. The Greek's body, wrapped in KSL-lettered blankets covered with a tarpolin and weighted with lengths of chain, rested on deck. When news of Achilles' death was brought to him, Tom had ordered a burial at sea.

"We could," Homer suggested, "carry him with us in one of Duck Fong's frozen food lockers."

Wallie frowned. "I agree with the captain. It's sort of macabre. I mean a frozen food locker and no ceremony or prayer of any kind."

"It's settled," said the captain. "We'll have a service on deck at noon. And we'll arrange some kind of prayer, for Wallie's sake."

Homer said, "I'd like to finish leveling off the tanks as much as I can."

"How are you proceeding?"

"I think I've got them nearly all level."

They discussed the ship's situation and Wallie was saddened that they made no more comment about Achilles—that no one really cared for the dead. One sorrowed if one had to; one showed public grief under expected conditions. Dead was dead, as Sparky put it when Wallie went up to see if they could send out messages.

"No, but I think I can repair the radio by using some of the circuits from the Greek's recording setup."

"Can you?"

"Hell, I'll try. You ever take a good look at his machine? Must have set him back a grand or so."

"I'm no expert on these things."

"It's a Monox-K 1120 Super-power tuner-amplifier, puts out 120 watts RMS per channel at 8 ohms, 20-20 KHz with less than 0.03 percent THD. It offers LED instantaneous power output indicators, built for low interference use."

"Sounds Greek to me," said Wallie. One who had been alive was dead, one who had enjoyed life was still—already his possessions were up for grabs.

On deck Farashah and Gemila stood in the back of the group gathered for the burial at sea. The packaged body was covered by a Greek flag. The captain, visibly introspective and ill at ease, looked over the crew: some sailors, kitchen workers, Homer, and two men from the engine room. The rest had to remain at stations. Wallie was on the bridge. Glancing up, Sarah and Alice could make him out—he was leaning against a slanted window.

Tom wore his best uniform; he had shaved so close his neck looked raw to Sarah.

"Are there any Greek Orthodox among us?"

No one moved or spoke. Some of the Chinese showed bland apathy.

"Any Catholics?"

The flag flapped in the wind. The lull in the weather was ending.

Carlos deNova, the Genoese engine room assistant, held up a finger. "I am, sir. But I don't know no prayers. Just *Deus est qui regnit omnia*."

Duck Fong, stolid and wary of the oncoming storm, gingerly adjusted his balance. He almost offered a Buddhist prayer, but decided not to.

In back Farashah chewed tensely on a string of blue beads hanging about her neck.

Tom looked about, studying the gathering darkness into which the *Pallas Athena* was taking them and noting her Liberian flag of convenience flying at half-mast, beginning to flap in the rising wind.

He opened the Bible that Alice offered him that morning. "I'm not a preaching man, and I don't know the texts. But this may fit." He rubbed his neck and set his silver-rimmed glasses over his nose. He read slowly, in a firm, clear tone:

"'So they took up Jonah, and cast him forth into the sea: and the sea ceased from her raging. Then the men feared the Lord exceedingly, and offered a sacrifice unto the Lord, and made vows.

"'Now the Lord had prepared a great fish to swallow up Jonah. And Jonah was in the belly of the fish three days and three nights.'"

Tom looked up at the menacing sky; the sea dealt the ship a sudden blow. What kind of damn fool was he to recite, to have picked *this* section of the King James? Actually he had left it to Sarah to find a suitable passage, and this is what she had come up with.

Farashah stood stiffly, gazing with a near catatonic stare at the string of beads that had broken and scattered before her.

"'Then Jonah prayed unto the Lord his God out of the

fish's belly, And said, I cried by reason of mine affliction unto the Lord and he . . .'"

A great wave broke over the bow, shooting up a huge, expanding wall of spray that wet down the burial party at the ship's rail. Rain began to fall; it seemed the drops were the size of grapes.

The captain shouted. "Mr. Bowen, carry on. Everyone to their quarters or stations."

Homer whipped off the blue and white Greek flag. Abdullah and a sailor tilted the board on which the body lay. With almost a reluctant leap, the burden shot over the rail into the sea. From the bridge Wallie watched with constraint as he saw the body bob a few moments in the turbulence of the ship's speed. Then it was gone. Rain deluged the deck; the tanker bucked and dipped as the full return of the storm took over the survivors' destinies.

Alice, hurrying with Sarah for cover, remembered certain lines that the captain had not had time to read: "'The waters compassed me about, even to the soul: The depth closed me round about, . . . I went down to the bottoms of the mountains; the earth with her bars was about me forever . . .'"

Farashah cried out, "*Siwese ninahuma!*" She ran, not bothering to recover the blue beads rolling on the deck.

From the Notebooks of Homer Bowen:

Duck Fong gave me a metal container that once held Jung Ying Kee tea in which I plan to preserve my notes. Using two sections of cork board wall paneling, I can wrap and seal the whole thing in heavy plastic. If we have to abandon ship I shall take it with me, and if the lifeboat is overwhelmed by the sea it can set it afloat with the hope that it will be picked up. I make no claims for the literary merit of these notes. This is no romantic gesture—the last week has scared the bejesus out of me.

I began these notebooks as sort of finger exercises for a novel. The jottings, notes on local slang, outlines of odd-ball characters, weirdo musing on many things are not free of banality and personal cant, but they're my own thing.

Now that our situation is perilous, what I have set down may be of value to anyone interested in this strange voyage of Pallas Athena—perhaps her last. I have tried to set it all down, true and simple.

We have been four days without radio contact with the outer world. Sparky is sure the pieces he has taken from Achilles Marrkoras' sound system will soon get us "crackling again," as he puts it.

The storm has not abated but I have hopes, with which the captain concurs, that the typhoon should lessen in intensity as we move eastward. (I dream the rest of the world no longer exists—we shall find deserted cities.)

Our condition on board is fair. We have lost half the catwalk railing, which inflicted great damage, gouging out glass windows and portholes. The worst damage was to the bridge and the radio room. With the raging weather it is impossible to make watertight repairs with plywood and plastic. On checking the tanks, I find the leveling process is not completed. Tanks ten and eleven are only forty percent filled. This, combined with the long crack by the supply locker, places us in great danger. The crack has grown thirty-four inches, but it is still a good distance from the outer hull.

All we need is an albatross to symbolize our plight. If the weather would only clear, we could work on the main deck and finish balancing off the contents of the tanks. I have been consulting with Carlos deNova, my engine room assistant, about welding the crack. I suggested we cut up sections of boiler plate and try to weld it over the crack. Carlos is not at all sure we can work in the confined space. We would have to get the plates up past the big beam and held solidly in place while from below he welded them to the inner surface of the main deck.

I said I was sure Sieko and his best men could prop the boiler plating up against the crack with heavy, wooden beams, so we could begin welding. Carlos said he would try, as soon as the weather is fair, to see if our welding torches can reach a high-enough temperature to melt steel. The captain, when I suggested this, pointed out the danger of setting the ship on fire by igniting one of the oil tanks . . . there being some spillage, as always, in these ships. I then suggested we put down fire-retarding foam in the work area. The captain said that only in a last resort would he permit us to attempt such a dangerous task.

"The crack still growing longer?" he asked.

I said it was, and he said to keep it to myself. If the project to weld was decided on, we could then inform the work crew. I walked away as if I were leaving some clandestine rendezvous; my perceptions were distorted and fair balmy with schemes. I wondered if the captain was adaptable enough to risk the decisions he must make. He tries not to show emotion, and I cannot judge his blocked-off countenance.

Meeting the damn medical student Chandra, he said I looked as if I were not in tune with my Karma. What a fruitcake!

As if we did not have enough problems, there's been some petty thieving going on. Achilles' cabin was looted of some jewelry I remember him wearing—a pigskin dispatch case, the silver frames that held family pictures, and his cigars. Chandra Gupta was smoking a fine Havana, but he swore on Siva he had only taken two panatelas to clear the air of sickness in the funky room where Achilles died. He claimed this was the last half of a cigar he had saved.

One thing puzzles me as I scribble away: I have no sense of reality about the events that have befallen us on this voyage. I should: there is the Kyprios brothers' labyrinthine plot to wreck the ship; Ludwig Ott's doctoring of the loading meters, unbalancing the tanks and presenting a danger to the ship, add his deserting; the death of Achilles Marrkoras (Do I dare say, without evidence, that I think he died of a knife wound rather than from his cuts?). Add to this our loss of radio contact and the discovery of the crack in the steel plating under the main

226

deck. Enough to make dilemmas of the first order. Yet for me it lacks reality—except for my fatigue and some questioning introspection over a bottle of ale, I don't seem to sense the peril of our situation fully.

I hope this inability to react normally to what is happening to us and Pallas Athena does not represent a failure of the imagination, a failure to see a looming catastrophe clearly. I have ordered Carlos to break out the welding gear and the gas containers to fuel it.

Farashah's first reaction to the stabbing of Achilles was without inner anxiety. She felt a glow of satisfaction at what she had done under the impulse of that moment when he had insulted her. She had even, after his death, stolen some of his records and played them on Ping Pong's record player, sitting crossed-legged on his bed over a pipe of hashish, listening:

> Went down to St. James infirmary,
> Saw my baby there,
> All stretched out on a table,
> So pale, so cold, so fair.

There was no sexual play between the maid and the barman. Ping Pong's interests were in maintaining a well-ordered bar and getting a pipe of hashish a day. Farashah found she liked company during a smoke—since Achilles' burial at sea, omens and portents had spooked her and she was stealing small objects to trade Wu Ting Li in exchange for the smoke.

"Very sad," said Ping Pong, "Round Eyes music."

"It is a dirge. If one pleases the dead by it they will not come back."

She reset the needle:

> Let her go, let her go,
> God bless her

Wherever she may be,
She may roam the world over,
She'll never find,
A sweet man like me.

"Was the Greek much a man?" asked Ping Pong.

"He was in love with his parts, shaking his balls like he was a God, but the true God cut him down." She giggled, "Oh yas," and scrunched down inhaling smoke.

"You are a bad girl. It is not good to laugh at the dead."

"We two will smoke to the dead. That will keep them from coming back. I will have more of the hash tomorrow. *Keso subuki.*"

But in the night while the ship wallowed in heavy seas and wind made strange noises, she awoke and was sure the ghost of the dead man was in her cabin. Farashah turned on the lights and sat up in the bed, hugging herself. She recalled the teaching of the mission school, her mind insisting on the weight of sin, immorality. She remembered the balm of prayer, forgiveness. Yet, an insistent specter seemed to be watching her.

She shivered and sweated and recited an old lesson from her mission days:

"For God so loved the world, *Sababu Mungu alipenda. . . ,*" but auras of doubt and fear remained. Then she slept. The next morning she stole a camera from Alice Palamas' cabin. For it, Wu Ting Li gave her four ounces of hash. But she could not recover her serenity. If the Christian prayer did not keep the ghost of the dead man from her during the nights, the drug must make her accept the haunting. The visage seemed, so far, unable to do harm. She would need a great deal of hashish. The second officer had a valuable set of camera lenses. He was so busy on the bridge he would never notice the loss.

The dead were very powerful. The longer the delay the more terrible the torture. They could twist one's head

228

around so that it permanently faced backwards. They could put a small demon in one's guts so that his horns and long toenails would cause sharp pains. A witch doctor in Kajado had once taken a cat with the head of a fanged snake from a girl's body. She had not seen it herself; but it was common knowledge in the village that the girl had smothered her old grandmother to get two goats and a silver bangle.

It was clear from the bridge that they were moving out of the worst of the typhoon weather. Reports confirmed that the weather fronts were changing. The captain, after too much coffee—near caffeine intoxication—ordered Homer not to use the welding gear but to keep it ready. The sea was still too rough for Homer to finish balancing the oil levels in the tanks, but the original fury of the storm had somewhat abated. To the northeast one morning Wallie saw an acre of pale blue sky, far, far off.

They sighted two freighters, a ULCC carrier, and a white cruise ship in the next two days, and they were even able to get a message to Oahu, in the Hawaii group, which was relayed to Athens, giving their position and adding:

PROCEEDING AT 12 KNOTS TO DESTINATION WEATHER STILL ROUGH BUT CLEARING.

CAPT. T. HAMMEL.

Sharky said his repairs would extend the range of his radio nearly to its old capacity.

When Homer measured the crack, he was shocked to discover it had lengthened to within ten feet of the outer hull; he hoped the sharp odor he smelled was his imagination and not oil seepage someplace below. The long hairline crack was now an inch-and-a-half wide.

20

Thomas Hammel was tired, bone tired; his body was driven to the limits of its self-sufficiency; the pacemaker continued to press on, alerting his heart to beat at its regular clip. The old ticker would see him through. He lay prone on the bed while Sarah's fingers worked over his back, pressed around the shoulder blades. It felt so goddamn good. Now if he could only sleep, waking to an easy conviviality with Sarah instead of blasphemous fears in the night, hurrying into sea-damp clothes and rushing to the bridge, filled with imagined horrors to add to the actual problems he already had.

"A little lower down, Dolly. *There.*"

"You're all knotted up, tense as a mail-order bride. Loosen up, loosen up."

"Lower, lower." Ah . . . her raffishness was usually like a tonic, but right now he could only think of the widening crack within his ship. With men he had no fear of open conflict, but facing a damn thing, how do you relate to a widening break in the beam under the main deck. There was no question of competence, not any more than he could control the sea, which had now calmed with a bit of a snarl. He couldn't order the elements. (Sarah was kissing each cheek of his buttocks.)

"Lay off."

Soon the hard-fingered voluptuousness of Sarah's fingers working along his spine almost sent him to sleep.

He fought to keep himself awake. He had always been honorable in his calling, with a petulance that others thought arrogance; a snottiness some had called it, "thinking he's better than the lot of us." On the bridge he wasn't made of malleable stuff; he was hard steel plate. He gave that appearance to some.

Not to Sarah. She had his number; with the edge of her hands, she pummeled the length of his back. She knew how he reacted to stress, how damn resolute he was, striving to do his duty. (Pigheaded was actually how she put it.) She didn't approve of his scruples and renunciations. No, Sarah liked fun and games, good grub, lots of noise and music—and, as she liked to put it after she'd had a few and they had made it fine and violent in bed, "There's life in the old girl yet."

"That's enough, Dolly."

"That's you, Skip, just as you're getting to like it. Your lousy bluenosed New England code says it's good, it feels grand, it's enjoyable, *so*? Stop it. You know, Captain, you give me the grue at times."

She stepped back, sniffed the witch hazel on her hands with which she had been rubbing the fatigue out of his shoulders, neck and spine.

He sighed. "Oh hell, woman, you chew on so." Then he saw she was hurt and he turned and sat up. "Sorry, sweetie. Give us a kiss. You angry?"

"Up your fundamental aperture," she said in a huffy tone.

"Oh Christ, it isn't enough the ship is turning on me, now you."

He sat on the edge of the bed, head down, as if trying to

validate his existence. Naked. A man growing old, his big, tall body grown thin, his paps, she saw, gray haired, a bulge where the pacemaker had been inserted, but no paunch. She was proud of that—but definitely, he was an aging man, eyes lost in reverie.

She couldn't keep back a rush of pity, a gush of love. She hugged him to her. "I know, Skip, I know what it's been like."

"Hell is a good word for it."

"The worst is over. We'll soon be in calmer seas."

He looked up at her, the austerity of his face softening, "That's right. We'll get out a rowboat and pack a picnic lunch and use the Pacific as a park pond."

"Why not? Didn't we do that when we were younger? Was it Hyde Park we rowed around in? The shore all frog-spawned in April."

He stood up. "When we were younger. 'My salad days, when I was green in judgment: cold in blood.' Shakespeare wrote that."

"Did he? Scribble, scribble." To Sarah, Shakespeare was hours of boredom with skinny actors in drag.

"I did a lot of reading in the hospital with this," he touched the pacemaker on his chest. "Well, I'm due on the bridge."

"Let Wallie handle it."

"Very short-handed, with Ott jumping ship and the Greek over the side. Very short-handed."

"Did you report that that sonofabitch stole a KSL launch?"

Tom began to dress in the long johns he favored, gray wool socks, "Nope. Thinking of it. See how things turn out."

She spoke firmly, poking a finger at him. "You're going to ask a Board of Inquiry, aren't you, about the monkey business that has been done on the ship?"

He picked up a shirt, examined it for missing buttons.

All in order. Sarah was not much given to sewing on buttons. He did the button work himself. "We've no proof, no proof of anything solid, Dolly. Nothing to show a court that the Kyprioses planned to scuttle *Pallas Athena*."

"What! Oh, oh, I must sew on that loose button." She yanked it free. "You have witnesses . . . Homer, Wallie."

He held out a hand. "Give me the damn button. Nothing, no evidence. Nothing that could stand up to an inquiry."

"Of course, Skip, if we slipped some information to Lloyds of London, they'd put their bloodhounds on it."

He pulled on his pants, buckled his belt; women certainly made a shambles of rules and logic.

"I'd like to see the greaseballs get it where the turkey gets it on Thanksgiving," she said with a mad chopping gesture on the back of her neck.

He leaned over and kissed her. "Yes, well go see how Alice is."

"She's fine. See you for dinner?"

"If possible, yes."

He went up to the bridge, admitting to himself that his speculation was futile. It wasn't the way it was in his young days when you settled things with a gouging ruckus. Now, as captain, he felt disquietingly alone; people depended on him.

He steadied himself as the ship climbed vertically and went into a slow roll, as if the sea were reminding him it still had clout.

On the bridge Wallie seemed asleep on his feet, staring at the radar dial. Overhead the sonar clicked, signaling it was a long way to the bottom of this ocean.

"Get some shut-eye, Wallie."

Wallie suppressed a yawn. "Yes, could use it. Homer going to try and weld plates over the crack?"

233

Tom studied the log in Wallie's neat schoolboy script.

"Too dangerous with those high temperature torches."

"We have a lot of fire-smothering foam, containers full of it."

"We'll see. What do you figure our position?"

"Longitude 140 degrees west of Greenwich. We could ask for some tugs and barges to come out to meet us from San Pedro. Unload some of the tanks if we have to at sea."

"KSL would chew our asses out for the extra cost. Now, get below and rest up. Even you young fellows can fall on your face."

When Wallie was gone the captain nodded to the two Chinese sailors at the tiller. Abdullah was off duty, taking a straight twenty-four hours of sleep. He had not been off the bridge during the four days of the typhoon. Tom tapped the brass rim of the compass cup. He would soon have to make two decisions. Perhaps sooner than he hoped. To radio for barges to unload some of the cargo was a good idea. The smell below deck was sharp enough so that it could be a leak someplace; it could turn into a rupture big enough to make trouble. The matter of the spreading crack was less clear. Were the weather reports as promising as reported? He'd play it by ear and put off the dangerous game of welding. But if the crack extended to the outer hull and began to creep down the side of the tanker? She could rupture a whole battery of tanks with the strain, and he'd be up shit creek with no paddle. Unhappy potentialities filled his thoughts. Let the damn ship break up, let hundreds of thousands of tons of fuel oil—a million gallons—spill over the sea. It was his last voyage, and he knew it. But he was a horse's ass. Sarah was right—he was Duty's Child. He felt a sensation under his skin; carry on old heart, you'll do, you'll do fine . . . we Hammels are a hard, long-lived folk. No hysterical dependence on the disordered ways of weaker folk, or forgiveness of blows received. Doesn't matter what is done out of a solid sense of duty, duty places one beyond good and evil. A man had to stand up to the infirmities and inadequacies of humankind, come through, even if all around him there was bankruptcy of order, a disorientation of past ideas, discipline, personal and national morality.

He picked up the phone, dialed the radio room.

"Captain speaking. How's your goddamn gimmicks?"

"Sir? The radio? We're sending, able to reach the States, sir. Frisco and L.A. are picking us up."

"What's the latest report on the weather front over the Eastern Pacific? Never mind typing it up. Read it to me."

"A cold front building from Japan to Alaska, but not moving fast. It may dissipate off western Canada."

"Sea conditions predicted?"

"There may be higher waves, wind twenty-five miles, no rain."

"That's enough. Radio through relays to KSL Athens":

PROCEEDING AT 16 KNOTS EXPECT TO PICK UP CALIFORNIA COAST IN THREE TO FOUR DAYS.
CAPT. HAMMEL

"Got it?"

"Got it, sir."

He brooded over the predicted turbulence from the northwest as he studied the log notations Wallie had marked. Trepidation was the worst thing a captain could experience. Tom remembered his grandfather Benton at ninety, an easy-going, convivial man, who used to reply, when asked how things were going, "Getting so weak the dogs had me under the house last night."

The captain grinned. Well, something bigger than dogs had him under the house now. He dialed the engine room. "Homer? How's the you-know." He glanced at the Chinese at the wheel. "Any signs of growth?"

"Slower, but moving, inching up, nearing the outer hull."

The captain scowled at the sailors. They stared back blankly. "Break out the foam, flood the area around the damn thing."

"You going to weld?"

"No, goddamn it, not yet. Just be ready when and if I decide."

Having decided on an action, Tom somehow felt better. One of the men at the wheel was making clicking sounds with his tongue. The captain remembered a verse he and Sarah recited the day they rowed in Hyde Park among the frog spawn:

> For the ways that are dark,
> And for tricks that are vain,
> The heathen Chinee is peculiar.

Pallas Athena contained a sauna. This Swedish steam bath, like the ship's swimming pool and the movie theater, was not there so much because the owners cared about the officers and crew, but because of the great space above the main deck that covered the huge cargo area containing crude oil.

After his watch on the bridge, Wallie decided to relax in the cedar-lined sauna. He wanted to sweat out some of the fatigue in himself and meditate, in a sporadic haphazard way. Early in his career at sea, he had discovered there should be times when one was alone with oneself. Mother had said, fill the mind with good thoughts, and *if* they came, noble ideas. She had been a good Swedenborgian gone to Zen. Since the crisis on *Pallas Athena*, Wallie had been neglecting his periods of meditation. As he reclined, naked, sweating lightly in the steamy atmosphere of the sauna, he reflected that the man of action loses his capacity to act on his own inner emotions.

Sari was still paramount in his thoughts; he meditated on the split halves of his hypothetical self. His desire was as strong as ever—his body ready, his mind hopeful. Yet he recognized the true situation, looked clearly at it. His frustration expressed itself in two ways: by a moaning sound he made when alone and by his genitalia rousing—as now—in the damp heat, as if scalded to perform.

Wallie left the sauna, took a cold shower, and dressed. Setting his cap at a proper angle, he thought *why* dream, *why* ache? Why among other things, break your balls (bad image) to save this goddamn ship? For what?

He had Ping Pong mix him a daiquiri. He sipped the icy mush. (He remembered they were supposed to have helped kill Hemingway, who drank them by the mason jar.) Once in New Orleans he had spent an afternoon at the St. Charles in bed with a local girl named Ginny. She was a publicity director for a local television station. They stayed in bed a long time, then in the late afternoon, standing in his shorts at the window, looking down on a gold-flecked dusk taking over the city, a Jax Beer sign lighting up, Ginny talking pleasantly about nothing much, he had, for a moment there, felt the most perfect happiness of his life. He had no explanation for it, it hadn't been a bad lay, but it was not world-shaking. Still there is no explaining happiness. Later, he and Ginny had dressed and gone to dinner at the Commander's Palace in the Garden Section and had daiquiris. Two each.

Ping Pong refilled Wallie's glass with a shaker, the strainer covering the top.

"I make you another batch?"

"No thanks."

"Taste good?"

"Just right. You ever been to New Orleans? Never mind . . ."

Other places, other emotions (never mind). Where was Ginny now? Mentally bridging an abyss of a few years, he recalled that she must now be running a TV station in

Oklahoma someplace. For two years she had sent Christmas cards, then, as some poet said, "Hearts that I once broke now are breaking others."

Memory and poetry—that was a crock of something. They hadn't broken each other's hearts—not in so short a session. Perhaps they had only exchanged loneliness.

He opened his cabin door. Farashah, Sari's maid, was sorting out his camera lens cases on the small table. She looked up as he entered, gave him a blank stare.

"Ah, so," she said.

"What the devil are you doing here?" He almost flung his cap at her.

"Yas, what?" She didn't seem frightened, only confused for a moment; neither guilt nor hysteria was apparent on her honey-colored features. Her large eyes outlined in black drew his attention to the flutter of her silver earrings set with tiny blue stones. "Yas," she said. "You see, I was returning your material; they was taken by one of cleaning boys who does cabins. I cotch him, and I bring back."

"Foo Kai steal?"

"No, not Foo Kai, he got stomach flu. This boy I do not know. I cotch him and take this away from him. What for you use things?"

"Oh." He looked down at his lens cases, his second-best light meter, the box of color filters. "Well, they're used to take clear pictures in various lights. Say for close work, you use this lens." He picked it up. "If you want to bring distance closer, you know near—nearer—you use this telescopic lens."

"Telescopic?" She smiled. "Oh yas, telescope, to bring moon close."

He picked up a small camera, set a flash bulb in place. "This is for a candid shot. A closeup. See?" The flash went off as he pressed the shutter. "Now I have you captured on film."

"You believe?"

"What?"

"Oh God," she wailed, taking his arm. "You believe I no steal, I just bring back. No police picture, please."

He laughed. "No, no. I mean I just for fun, I mean . . . I'll develop it, make a print for you, okay?"

"Okay, oakey-dookey."

Farashah smiled, nodded, lifting her linear eyebrows and opening her eyes wide. It gave her a demure, welcoming look that men liked and were attracted to. But this young officer was not like some of the other ones. He did not react as he should. No, "come on" with a leer and a pat on her ass. He didn't return a smile of serene hope, or make an effort to score, as some put it. He looked instead, furtive, his emotions contradictory, perhaps.

"I go now to captain's lady, to do her hair."

"Really? Do you like her?"

"Oh yes sir, Mrs. Hammel fine to maid. Very much so." She gave a bigger smile, swayed her hips slightly, thrusting out her breasts, one hand on the door knob.

"Oh thank you, miss, for saving my gear. I'll get that picture developed. So the captain's wife is pleasant to work for?"

"All white ladies I know very pleasant."

A whiff of some personal scent, partly of her body, and partly her heady perfume, lingered in the room. He had noticed the native girl but paid her no attention. Sari's maid; so close, so intimate with her. Wallie's mind, or was it his body, thought of Farashah. She was "built," as Homer would put it. And the ship's gossip was that she had been amorous with the dead Achilles.

Sweat broke out on his body; he had spent too long in the damn sauna. He fought off images of the girl as sexually desirable—seeing her in various poses like Port Said postal cards. How disloyal to Sari, yet his body insisted, continued to remind him Sari was unobtainable. The maid was within reach and rather taken with him.

Wallie had few vanities; but he was aware that he made a good impression on women and was desirable to them. Oh hell! He gathered up his camera gear and locked it away in a small, tin trunk he kept under his bed. The thought of King Arthur and his knights intruded. *Am I Lancelot, the would-be fornicator and not Galahad, the pure?*

In the night Alice noticed the change in the weather. The wind no longer roared, lashing rain against the two portholes of her cabin. The pitching and thrusting of the ship changed into something new—a rhythm—a rolling, twisting action as if *Pallas Athena* were in the hands of a playful giant who rolled the ship like a log from side to side. It was bringing back twinges of sea sickness. Alice tottered to the green-tiled bathroom, upchucked, and went to the porthole. She looked out on a wan, gray-white sun that showed a continual parade of rolling waves, no foam, no angry fury, only this steady lifting and dropping of the ship between glassy waves.

She had planned to list the items missing from her camera gear for an insurance claim, but gave it up; she was developing double vision trying to focus her eyes on the list. She decided to dress and go on deck with her 16mm B&H and capture some footage of this strange sea. It had, she thought, a pattern as sophisticated as a Disney cartoon.

On the bridge Wallie inspected the sea change from high up. It looked as if someone were shaking out a green-blue rug, making it ripple, one ripple following upon the other, each in the exact shape of the one before it.

"I've never seen anything like this."

The captain inspected a weather report typed out in Sparky's quick, badly spaced typing.

"It's the result you get when there has been an earthquake off the coast of Japan or Siberia. A long series of waves is produced, and they travel hundreds of miles building with the wind. Hell, we have seen them reach across the Pacific to the Gold River in Oregon."

"These from Japan?" asked Wallie.

"Could be."

"Coming a couple thousand miles, they look polite compared to the storm's white heads."

"Polite, ha! They're rolling the ship about, twisting it too. This keeps up," he shook his head, eying Abdullah at the wheel, "I'm putting her on automatic. Abdullah, go get some breakfast."

"Yes, sir."

The captain adjusted the automatic steering, studied the sonar pings, the radar indicator. He turned to Wallie; his face was serious and set in a kind of angry obstinacy. Wallie knew the captain was allowing him to see his perplexity.

"This is as bad as the storm. If it continues for a day or so it's going to test us. The ship could break in half at the point of the crack."

It was said so calmly that Wallie took a moment to grasp the horror of it. "But it's just a heavy roll. No fury behind it."

"Every roll puts pressure on that crack. Yes. Get on the blower. Tell Homer to put down the fire-retarding foam, thick, and prepare to weld the boiler plate over the crack."

The captain seemed to be mulling over what he had just said. "And you, Wallie, are the lucky one who gets to command down there."

"Yes, of course."

"Get Homer to explain to you what he's doing." He stared myopically at the bridge log. "The crew will learn soon enough of our danger. Stay alert· they may panic. Sieko, the rest of us must stand by and ready. Armed, they could try to take to the lifeboats."

"Mutiny?"

Tom gave out a tight grin. "You goddamn romantic, get off my bridge."

Wallie returned a smile, even giving a limp salute as he went below to pass on the captain's orders to Homer. He could see himself, pistol in hand, getting the women into the first lifeboat.

Thomas Hammel, aware that the obvious, oppressive stress he was under was clear to his officers, paced the bridge and gave the charts of yesterday's run a troubled stare. Alone, he let down his guard, fully resurrecting the youthful memories of his past, when the family attended church every Sunday. He had that same feeling now, a feeling that only God could actually fully fathom him.

The six bells "World Oil News" came on from an overhead speaker:

THE SEARCH FOR THE GIANT TANKER *PALLAS ATHENA* HAS BEEN CALLED OFF AFTER THE KYPRIOS SHIPPING LINE ANNOUNCED IT HAS RENEWED RADIO CONTACT WITH THE MISSING SHIP. NEARING THE END OF ITS VOYAGE FROM THE PERSIAN GULF TO THE CALIFORNIA COAST, *PALLAS ATHENA* REPORTED THAT DAMAGE TO ITS RADIO KEPT THE VESSEL FROM SENDING OUT MESSAGES FOR FOUR DAYS. IT IS NOW REPORTED TO BE APPROACHING, SIX HUNDRED MILES FROM THE AMERICAN MAINLAND. DESPITE THE DEATH OF AN OFFICER FOLLOWING AN ACCIDENT ON SHIPBOARD DURING THE GREAT FUJI TYPHOON, CAPTAIN THOMAS HAMMEL REPORTS THAT EVERYTHING IS NOW PROCEEDING PROPERLY TO BERTH THE SHIP.

"Everything proceeding properly," said Tom. "Oh yes, everything just fine and dandy, you bastards!"

CHAPTER | 21

When Dante devised the various levels of hell, he did not imagine the horror and agony of welding boiler plates from beneath in a cramped space loaded with (we hope) fire-retarding foam. The atmosphere created by the welder's torch shooting its high temperature flame is vindictive. I wear a protective helmet big as a keg, and the air (what there is of it) has the smell of burning rubber and steer manure.

For all this, I did manage, after seven hours, to weld six feet of heavy boiler plate onto the deck. Sieko and his crew propped the plate in place, holding it to the underside of the main deck with timbers while I welded it into place. Poor Wallie shot the blasted foam at the wooden props—solid four-by-four timbers—for, no matter how careful I was they would catch fire from the welding torch. Later in the day we tried lengths of metal piping to hold the plates in place, but this proved impractical. The pipes grew so hot they burned the crew's hands even through thick cowhide gloves. I cannot describe the smell produced by the burning leather combined with the beastly odor of the foam and my bad breathing in the choking headgear I am forced to wear. I look out on a nightmare world from the tinted glass face of my helmet which keeps my retina from burning out in the overbright light of the torch.

Now, I have showered, moaned, salved some bruises and a burn on my forearms, swallowed a little food, and am on my third bottle of ale; I seem fully dehydrated.

I was still moaning, rocking myself in a painful rhythm, sipping ale, when Tom came in, looking more gaunt than ever.

With no greeting he said, "I've inspected the welding."

"So little done, so much to do," I said, paraphrasing an empire-builder whose life Grand Da used to impress on me as an example of what shits so many great men were.

"Will it hold?"

"Don't know, really."

"Can you get someone to carry on welding while you're not at it—two shifts?"

I set down the bottle of ale and belched. "No one else has had the experience. The oxygen mix in the torch is very dangerous. The temperature may go over three thousand degrees." (I wasn't sure but I figured it was impressive.) "One slip and you can roast off an arm, sever a torso like a buzz saw."

He wasn't impressed with my answer. "What about deNova?"

"My second? Well . . ."

"He's handled the welding torch?"

"Only small repairs in a workshop—very light repairs."

He looked about the cabin, kicked a Black Horse ale bottle aside. "Put him on it."

"Not alone, Tom. It's murder down there: poor lighting, all that foam. And reaching up to weld from below, the damn ceiling throws sparks like a Chinese New Year's celebration."

"Risk it."

"Can't, Tom—risk a man working a torch down there on his own."

The captain sat down facing me. "Goddamn it, Homer. I, too, mind jeopardizing a man's life or risking an acci-

244

dent. But Pallas Athena, she's going to break in half in this rolling sea if we don't get something solid holding that crack together.

"I didn't ever say it would hold, now did I?"

"Look, you have how many torches?"

"Three, but . . ."

He slapped his thighs hard and winked. "All right, you and deNova work together. He starts welding at the hull, working toward you, and you carry on from where you left off, working toward him. Simple, huh?"

"No. Two torches going down there?"

"With you nearby he'll have confidence. Oh, you'll keep a weather eye on him. I wouldn't ask this, but the short and sweet of it is that the deck has to be welded together."

He had that look of self-assured confidence in people that all good captains have toward their officers. I saw I was facing harsh reality. We were hunting for the miraculous and we both knew it.

I was very aggravated and my bruises and burns hurt. I said I would alert Carlos and take two hours sleep. I showed Tom my forearms and said I'd do as he ordered. Tom didn't pat me on the head and say, "You're a good man, Homer," or "I know I can depend on you." He just gave me a lackluster look, inhaled deeply, and went out.

I changed the dressing on my wounds, using some baking soda Duck Fong sent up and which he claims is better for a burn than the medical goop. I mixed the two together but still sleep would not come, so I am setting down these notes. If, up to now, I have not felt the reality of our situation, I now do. My awareness of the personal danger to me and the peril to all of us is increased by my pain. Pain is the true realist, an agonizing stabilizer that brings home our expectation of staying free of it. When it does come, pain makes us not only more aware of our being mortal, it also brings dark forebodings that enter the mind and divide like amoebas, growing, multiplying . . . I must get some sleep.

When I talked to Carlos on the engine room blower, he

was not delighted that he was to take over a welding torch. He said, "Oh peachy, and fuck you, sir."

Wallie lay on his bed, feeling boneless and tired, but strangely pleased with himself; he was almost in a state of exaltation. Even the water-filled blister he had gotten on the back of his hand from touching a section of boiler plate before it had fully cooled did not dismay him. He considered it a badge of his duty. He had showered, gotten into his pajama tops, and lay on his back in quiet meditation. He should, and would, sleep soon, soundly. Helping Sieko's crew get the beams in place and seeing that the props didn't fall away too often should have exhausted his body, but he was surprisingly horny. He needed a release from tension; some men used sexual contact for such relaxation—"climbing down from a high." He tried out a few images of Sari, visualizing her splashing around in the pool, then in the dressing room the time when he had failed in his rape attempt. Well, *not* rape actually, just letting his overstimulation make him act the damn fool.

As he savored the memory of holding her body, he felt his desire had peaked, bursting loose with a very mad, mad vigor. He gave a nervous laugh; the memory was *very* real.

There was a tap on the cabin door, and Ping Pong came in with a tray.

"You maybe want to eat. Also have some good cognac?"

"I'd rather have some wine."

"I have, maybe, a good burgundy. Here is chicken sandwichs, chutney, and very good cheese danish. Coffee, very hot."

"Thanks."

"Eat good, save ship. Oh, yes."

The barman was gone before Wallie could ask how in

hell he knew what was going on. He sat up and bit into a chicken sandwich. It tasted good but somehow he had no appetite. He had little faith in their attempt to weld over the crack. Such a huge tanker, such puny efforts. They would have to abandon ship before she tore herself in half. The captain, old faithful, would stay on board till the last moment; he, Wallie, must be sure to get away in the same lifeboat as Sari. Those rolling waves would take skilled handling and. . . .

There was a tap on the door. Farashah came in with a bottle of wine and a crystal goblet on a tray. He was aware of his too-short pajama top and tugged on it.

"Barman sent last bottle of good wine."

"Oh, thank you."

She seemed unaware of his effort to hide his privates.

She set the tray on the night table, between *The Complete One Volume Shakespeare* and *Myra Waldo's Travel Guide to the Orient and the Pacific.*

"You burn hand?"

"It's nothing at all."

She took his hand and looked at the back of it.

"Nothing? One time my uncle Siboko, he burn his arm with fire of dried camel shit they use for cooking."

"This is a clean scorch from hot steel."

"They cut off arm, up to *here,* of my uncle."

He gave up the ineffectual attempt to cover up.

"Hand me my pants."

She just lifted the bottle.

"Will you pour the wine, Farashah, and if you care to join me there's a glass in the bathroom."

"Let me tie up the hand."

Confused, he didn't know why he'd asked her to join him in a drink. But looking at her in her loose yellow robe, the savage shape of her silver earrings, she was certainly dramatic, a strong primitive creature beyond, what was it Kipling said of "the lesser breeds"? He couldn't remember; she took his hand between her own and smiled at him.

Involuntarily, he put an arm around her as the ship rolled at a more pronounced angle.

"Rough," he said. The smell of her was strong and sweet (overripe nectarines, strong pepper?). And what else? The scent of a woman's body—liquid, bone, and tissue.

Farashah's thoughts were actually simple in a way he could never understand. She was neither a siren, a tease, nor a vamp. Her simplicity was ruled by her role as a survivor. In her view of the world, survival was all. She had only one way to reward those who gave her help or the courage to survive; she would offer her body. She did not see herself as mysterious, or romantic, or exotic. Sly, yes, she would admit, and aware that she possessed what the men she met liked: Her direct sexiness was neither complicated nor involved. And she lacked both guilt and moral perplexity.

Wallie was not shocked to discover he had an erection or that his hard-on showed. Somehow he had gotten over the panic of being only in his pajama tops.

As she dropped her robe, he spoke with a tightening of his vocal cords. "I'd have had that photograph developed but there have been complications."

"What photograph?"

"That picture I took of you."

He tried to avoid studying what was more politely called her *tetons* and *fesses*.

"Yes, oh that." She sank between his knees as he sat on the bed; she had his cock in her hand. He looked about, as if fearing witnesses. She glanced at him and pressed a *teton* against his belly, all the time cheerfully staring at him. He put his arms around her and she, never letting go, raised herself up, undulating gracefully, so that their lips met. Wallie, feeling disloyal to Sari, felt her wet open

248

mouth, her darting tongue, and let himself sink in the pleasure of being aroused by this shockingly bold girl.

Somehow they were on the bed—he prone—she all over him. What she said and what he said didn't register. Almost automatically he felt her moist pudenda. (What a strange word, he thought, for something so alive, so ready, so inviting.) He rolled her about so that he was on top. (He belonged to a class where the male dominated in the sexual act; to take bottom position was a kind of perversion.)

He felt his glands expand, her hand guide his now aggressive erection toward the traditional Venus vent; then, the phone gave two shrill commands.

"No, not answer," the girl moaned, gritting her teeth.

"Duty," he said without thinking. He arched his back to avoid penetration—so, so close—and picked up the phone, his hand trembling.

"Ormsbee here."

It was the captain. "Get out of the sack. Emergency."

"Yes, sir," he replied, with the same sense of guilt he had once experienced when a schoolmaster, late at night (he was age twelve), had suspected him of handling himself after lights out in the second form at Belford School. "Yes, sir."

"The crack has reached—torn its way—to the outer hull."

"I understand, sir." He tried to withdraw his penis from the grasp of Farashah. She pulled back as if it were a game, a sort of jolly sensual tug of war between them.

"You hear me, Wallie? Get down to the welding. Homer and Carlos are going to work from the hull in. Pronto."

He got his prick back from her predatory eager fingers, his organ seemed enraged at his interference. But he was too much a Duty's Child and knew it. He struggled to stand, his damn wang bobbing and asserting itself. The

249

girl seemed dazed; she stood and stroked (what Homer would have called) her "pussy."

"Something wrong?" Stroke, *pat* stroke.

"No, no, not you. With us." He stepped into his shorts, struggling with his condition to get them on.

"Emergency, the captain needs me."

"I need you too. We sinking?"

"No, of course not. Some routine that must be carried out right now."

"But you in condition of heat. I can take care of you quick." She sank to her knees and fumbled at the fly of the shorts. "I can do quickly for you. Better you not leave like this." She measured off a foot of space.

He swirled away reaching for his trousers, backing away all the time.

"Now listen, Farashah. This has gone much beyond anything that I—I mean I'm a ship's officer on call."

She gave up, stood, and picked up her robe, but did not put it on. There was a gaucherie about her. "I wait then. Here.

"You are very big feller," she patted his crotch cheerfully. "We going to make good love, yas?"

"No. I'm trying to say I belong to another. There is another woman I'm pledged to." He tried to look like a man with a personal dilemma.

"How fine. Good to be happy like that."

"Yes, so you see." He hunted for his socks and shoes. "You understand I want to be loyal, loyal to her."

"She pretty?"

Oh God, he thought, what a time to ask, and what would this girl think if she knew he was pledging fidelity to the captain's wife.

"Yes, of course, she's very attractive. I mean, don't wait, don't come back. Take the bottle of wine with you."

She ignored his agitation. "I did nothing to earn it. I am happy you love someone. But on ship a man must be a man. It is nature that you have strong needs." She made a fist. "The force."

She sat down on the bed. "I wait."

The phone rang again. It was Homer, his voice rather hoarse.

"Rise and shine, boyo, back to the mines."

"I'm coming, Homer." He took one last look at the naked girl, adjusted his jock (ouch!), and walking stiffly, left the cabin. Farashah swayed with the roll of the ship, feeling the warm goodness in her body, cherishing the fine feeling that drove men and women. She drank half the bottle of wine and then, removing one earring, slept.

Close confinement at sea for any period creates a world where few secrets can be kept for long. From the bridge to the radio and chart room, down to the lowest kitchen boy, perhaps getting his ears cuffed by Duck Fong, talk about the great crack and how close they were to (perhaps) abandoning ship was the order of the day.

Gemila told her husband Sieko that it was a fact that the fleeing Ludwig Ott, in revenge for some dirty deed done him by the Kyprios brothers, had left a delayed-action bomb on board. Sieko told her to stop gossiping and make some sandwiches for him to take below. He couldn't spare time from the welding job for either meals or rumors.

The medical student, Chandra Gupta, told Wu Ting Li that he had overheard the chief engineer tell the woman with the cameras, Alice Palamas, that a Soviet submarine had been following them for days. (One interpretation of Homer's words: "We're not hoisting the red alert yet on this ship.")

Duck Fong and Wu Ting Li sat over a bottle of Dewars White Label Scotch in Fong's cabin, drinking.

"I tell you, Wu, I fear the crew will panic, do something dangerous, and as for our treasure—"

"Will they find it, with their devils burning and welding?"

"Not likely," said Duck Fong, knocking back three fingers of Scotch. "The treasure is well hidden behind the sockets of the grate-covered lights under the main deck."

"Ah. If the welding comes close, it will destroy thousands of dollars of treasure. If the heat does not get to it, the fire-retarding foam could get behind the sockets and eat through the plastic packing for a total loss."

Wu shook his fiddle-shaped head, figured quickly on his fingers, and moaned again. "Let us hope a frightened crew will not endanger everything."

Below, the welding continued in a blue-orange glare. Homer and Carlos were handling the two torches. The heat was fearful, and the chemical stink from the foam made the men cough. The crew, under Wallie's supervision, was propping the plates up for welding, ducking sparks. Most wore tinted glasses to protect their eyes from the flare of the torches. Some covered their faces with lengths of water-soaked canvas, their heads emerging from a hole cut into the tough sailcloth. Now and then someone screamed in pain.

Wallie yelled constantly for more timbers to shore the plates. Homer, under his face mask, cursed because Carlos was having trouble getting the acetylene and oxygen mixture adjusted to produce the proper temperature of flame for welding. Again and again, Homer had to leave his work and move along the narrow iron walk to show Carlos how to adjust the flame. Wallie decided, Homer was getting distinctly touchy.

The waves coming from the Japanese sea coast were not as high as they had been; they seemed to have longer intervals between their ranks. Homer went to the ice chest holding ale bottles. His eyes were bloodshot.

At noon Carlos ran out of oxygen.

In disgust, Homer pushed back his face mask and helmet, turned off his own torch. He had developed a facial tic and was very irritable.

"Damn, damn, goddamn. Let's all take a breather. Wu, wrestle up another cylinder of oxygen. Everybody take ten, but stay where I can see you. I'll break the skull of any sod buggering off."

Wallie wiped his face with a grimy towel. Carlos sank down on the iron walkway muttering in English, Hindi, and Portuguese.

The portable telephone rigged to the work area rang. Homer answered. "Hello? Yes, Captain. No, Captain. Ten feet more. Oh, of course, easy as pie."

He hung up, "The captain says finish, finish. Pronto."

Carlos panted, mouth open. "I can no longer face fire."

Wallie measured the exposed crack that remained with a carpenter's rule. "Ten feet six inches. Can we finish the job this afternoon?"

"Can a cow fly, can a rock fuck? We better. The captain has discovered leakage from a tank up front. It's seeping into the storage area in the bow."

"And?" Wallie slowly refolded the ruler, as if he were gauging Homer's exasperation.

"And, boyo? If it forms gases and they somehow seep through to here. BOOM!"

Carlos tossed aside his protective face mask. "I give up. If I die, I die with my engines."

Homer smeared ointment onto a bruise on his already bandaged arm. His voice sounded overrefined. "Make a note, Mr. Ormsbee. Carlos deNova is to be shot at dawn. Full dress, firing squad to be drawn by lots." Homer laughed loudly, the sound echoed in the singed working space. He reached for another bottle of ale. He brought up an empty bottle; rage showed on his face.

"Who has been stealing my fucking ale! Who's been

copping my ale!" He glared at the crew seated cross-legged by a pile of timbers. No one answered. Homer flung the bottle against a girder, shattering it. The phone rang.

Homer shook his head. "Let the cocksucker ring."

Wallie made a gesture to pick up the phone after three rings.

Homer exploded in aggravated outrage. Raising his torch as a weapon, he snarled, "You answer that phone and I'll brain you. I don't want to talk to anyone! Understand! And I don't want anyone to talk to me. You, chum, get the shit out of your ears and remember that. LET IT RING!"

Wallie stepped back. The menace in Homer's stance cowed the crew members. Homer stood, the torch in his fist, breathing heavily, his face locked in some kind of tormenting agony. To Wallie it appeared as a kind of frenzied hysteria, incongruous and absurd in this man, usually so solid in his faithfulness to duty.

He stood his ground, challenging everyone. The phone continued to ring.

"It's all right, Homer," Wallie intervened softly. "Honest, pal, no one is going to answer the phone."

"You bet your sweet arse they're not!"

The phone went on ringing, its tone echoed from the steel confines of the working space.

There was to Wallie some kind of singular degradation in seeing a good man like Homer Bowen driven to such an agitated state.

Homer kicked the still ringing phone off the iron walkway into the darkness below. It hung there on its cord, dangling like some overripe fruit. Silent.

BOOK SIX

WORLD'S END

Sarah Hammel turned off the "World Oil News,"
stubbed out her half-smoked cigarette, and looked at the
two battered suitcases on the bed.

"God, I've packed half my life away in those bags."

Alice stood by her side viewing the collection of
dresses, shoes, balled-up stockings, assorted jars of cos-
metics, a packet of letters.

Sarah flexed her mouth in a grimace of mock anger.
"This rat is preparing to unship."

"My camera gear is a problem."

"The hell with it, Alice. I'll just take me and a roll of
toilet paper."

Alice fingered a yellow shantung suit jacket. "You really feel we may abandon ship?"

"Go over the side? Not really, but just in case, one
chance in a hundred—in a thousand."

"I've got over eight hundred feet of exposed film. Some
of it's damn good— even great. What if I lose it?"

"Tough tittie."

Alice flexed her fingers nervously. "I'll leave the cameras. They're insured anyway. But I must take the film."

"Oh shit, we've got the blues. Let's have a booze!"

Sarah found the bottle of Jim Beam in the bottom of a suitcase and poured out two big dollops. She and Alice sat on the sofa toasting each other and sipping their drinks; they had a refill. Alice felt they were indulging their emotions, overrating their precarious position.

"You know, Alice, all the years with Skip, I've never had to take to the boats. Of course, I wasn't with him. when he had trouble now and then, like the time a gale blew in the bow of the *Gloria*. It isn't like the movies at all, is it? A ship in danger? I mean, where everything's supposed to be very posh, the band playing a waltz before they go into 'Nearer My God to Thee.' That's a myth, you know; some lying journalist wrote that about the *Titanic*."

Their mood of self-indulgent gratification turned somber.

Alice set down her empty glass. "You ever think of death, Sarah?"

"Too morbid a subject for me. Laugh and kick up your heels, that's my motto, and leave a beautiful body. But that last part I don't guarantee anymore."

She refilled her glass. Alice shook her head no.

"Truth is, Alice, I think about it a lot. I don't get scared of death . . . just mind dying. It's a fucking, messy business . . . crumbbum . . . all that terminal stink and nastiness going on, the plumbing haywire here and there. I can die, if it's easy, but I worry about Skip dying. You know we've been together a long time. It's as if we were Siamese twins, you can't separate us. I don't want to face the world without him. I don't have the guts for it anymore—not me."

"You're lucky to have him, Sarah. I never had anything solid in that line—not for long."

"Well, maybe the new way of living and loving is okay. You know, hello, goodbye, and here's your hat. Oh, I've been tempted. I've had the hots for some men, sure. I'm human. I've even encouraged the ones that appealed to me when I was waiting for a ship in some lonely seaport hotel. But never, I swear it, I never went *too* far. Honest to God."

She looked into her glass and winked. "Never let anyone get to home plate. Maybe a grope, a feel, a hand under the skirt. You believe me, don't you, Alice?"

"Anything you say. Thank you for the drink."

"One for the highway? Never leave anything in the bottle when you're leaving a party. Know that? Oh yes. Gospel. Brings you seven years bad luck."

Sarah began to weep. "Skip, the bastard. Come trouble this voyage, he'll stay until everybody is off. That's his fucking New England sense of duty. That full-of-shit pride."

Sarah's head was wobbling. Alice tried to reassure her. "I'm sure no one pays any attention to that last-man-off crap on an oil tanker."

"Huh? Skip, he'd be a tradit—tradition—a tra—a goddamn true-blue sailor in a sinking rowboat. Know what? I'm going to be there with him on the bridge. He goes down, Mama goes down. Beautiful thought, isn't it, Alice? The two of us hand in hand into the setting sun on the deep, deep blue. You could maybe take a movie of us from the lifeboat, huh? Mama goes where Papa goes . . ."

Alice screwed the top on the bottle of Jim Beam. "I promise. In beautiful Kodak color with a telephoto lens. Now, Sarah, lie down and I'll brew us some coffee."

Sarah fought off Alice's offer of an arm. "All those years, all those big fine years. You don't know they're passing at the speed of sound."(She tried to snap her fingers, failed.)". . . you always wake up hoping and maybe tomorrow the big wonderful something will pop up before you. So you go on, honeybunch, go and on, running, falling, picking yourself up, the big something just beyond your fingertips, you know. And you're running faster and faster nearly touching it but never grabbing hold. And then you look in the mirror and say to yourself, 'Madam, *that* is you and nobody else.' "

"Sarah, you're . . ."

The ship gave a shudder, shook—a hard spine-tingling quiver. The two women stared at each other. Then all was as before. The two glasses had tipped on their sides, the whiskey in them running across the cover of an out-of-date *New Yorker*.

"What was that?" Alice looked about her; the picture of *Pallas Athena* on the wall was slanted to one side.

"That, that?" Sarah lifted her head, rolled it from side to side. She smiled. "That, toots, that was that old devil sea. Remember that Garbo movie? *Anna Christie?* Her old man, a sailor said that."

They remained motionless, rigid, eyes on each other, expecting another shock. None came.

Alice felt it was all an insidious dream from which there was no waking.

Below the main deck, where the welding crew was working, several timbers had fallen away breaking a Chinese sailor's arm. In the wireless room, Sparky was howling in pain after his spilled coffee scalded his leg. Duck Fong thanked Buddha that he had not been slicing pork with the big knife at the moment.

In the bow several frames had bent and the front tank ruptured; black oil gushed from the gaping hole, pressing on the bulkhead of the next tank in line.

From the bridge where Tom Hammel was standing watch when the ship had actually been shaken, it seemed she had taken a mortal wound, as if mile-long, nine-story-high waves, moving at fifty miles an hour had struck

259

her hard. He adjusted to the shock of what actually happened and saw only rolling, glassy waves, but, despite the appearance, he knew something serious had happened to the tanker. He checked speed and direction. All correct. The instruments gave no warning.

The phone rang. It was Wallie. "Captain, there are some ruptured tanks here below."

"How bad?"

"From the smell and the seepage, I'd say more than one."

"How's the welding? . . . What's Homer doing?"

"He's—he's gone off—just worn out. We had to give up. Too much oil sloshing someplace."

"The crack still exposed?"

"At least ten feet short of full welding."

"I'll call back."

Tom listened, waited; the shaking had stopped. The sea was as usual. The ship moved forward. He looked over the side, no tell-tale oil stain. Whatever had ruptured the bulkhead, the thick, steel hull had not broken open. The sea did not appear turbulent. And *Pallas Athena* had beams thicker than railroad track. The condition of the bow worried him. Had it been badly dented or torn open? He phoned down.

"Hello, Wallie. Get a work crew forward to examine the bow storage space and test the bulkheads. Where the hell is Homer? He been drinking?"

"I think he just collapsed."

"Wrong time for it."

In half an hour Wallie, with a badly shaken work crew, had to report that the bow storage space was filling with oil from a ruptured tank, and more than likely, several of the forward tanks had ruptured. Homer appeared, bleary-eyed, carrying his measuring rods to check how much oil from the several tanks was mixing and leaking. So far, none of the oil was escaping into the sea.

Wallie asked, "You all right, Homer?"

"So far. But some of the crew aren't obeying orders."

"Wu Ting Li will handle them, with a club. Reported to the captain no signs of damage to the hull."

The captain said, "I'm slowing speed to ten knots. Keep a watch on the welded section. Twenty-four-hour watch. Homer, you all right?"

"Oh, yes. Just needed a breather."

As Homer and Wallie washed up and tried to get the smell of welding and scorched steel from their hair, Homer appeared in control of himself again. "I really fell down, eh? Well, shipmate, at least now no more hard labor. We just wait. She'll make port or she won't. Sorry I came apart at the seams over a bottle of ale."

"It was more than that. Nothing more we can do?"

"Not a damn thing. The sea isn't rough and we're near the American coast. Ever read St. Augustine? Once, lying on some beach, I read where he says: 'Rejoice, for one of the thieves that was crucified with Christ was saved. Despair, for one of the thieves died.' "

"What the hell are you talking about, Homer? I really think the welding gas got to you."

"Rejoice," he said. Lather almost closed his red-rimmed eyes he rubbed so hard on his cheeks. "We can be saved, but remember we can end up in the sea. Give me a towel. I've got soap in my eyes."

"Try and get some sleep."

But Homer was too keyed up. "Maybe ninety million gallons can spew out if enough tanks rupture. Wallie, old man, can't you just see the California and the Mexican coast—from Acapulco to San Francisco—eight hundred miles of coast being gummed up with a fifty-two-mile-wide invasion of crude oil, eh? All it would need is a frigging wind behind it from the west. Oh, yes."

"Save it for your novel," Wallie said, inspecting his bruises.

Homer rubbed his face dry, then gave his hair a brisk toweling. He began singing, a verse remembered from his orphanage days that the older boys used to torment him with:

> Liar, Liar,
> Pants on fire,
> Nose is as long as
> A telephone wire!

Wallie decided Homer was still off his trolley.

"We're both bushed," said Wallie. "Let's get some sleep."

"Unless the captain rousts us because the crew panics or he wants more leaks inspected, I'm going to cork off and leave no morning.call."

Wallie combed his hair back, studying his image in the mirror. Any signs of psychological warp? "I think I'll take over Achilles' cabin."

"Suit yourself. But it is written, there is no hiding place. God will find you even behind a thousand walls."

Yes, Homer was a little addle-headed from his hours at the welding. As for himself, Wallie was afraid Farashah would be waiting in his cabin. He wanted no renewal of their last encounter.

In Achilles' cabin he locked the door, after sending Ping Pong to pick up some gear and clothes for him. Sex was a fucking tyranny, but he'd try and keep his loyalty to Sari—not defile his body by taking pleasures with a surrogate.

Up in the radio room Sparky and Moise were having a frantic time keeping up with the messages going back and forth between *Pallas Athena* and KSL Athens:

CPT. HAMMEL'S LAST REPORT OF DAMAGE SEEMS MINOR HOLD COURSE WILL HAVE LA AGENT CONTACT YOU FOR PORT CLEARANCE AM FLYING TO CALIFORNIA.

IONNES K.

"The big shot," said Moise. "Himself, himself."

"Cut the crackle and get the message to the bridge."

A message went back:

TO KSL ATHENS SUGGEST ORDER BARGES STAND BY TO REMOVE CARGO IF SEAWORTHY PROBLEMS DEVELOP P/A SPEED NOW 8 KNOTS.
                    CAPT. THOMAS HAMMEL.

Wallie felt safe in Achilles' cabin. The medical student and some of the housekeeping crew had already looted it, so Wallie changed the linen himself. (It had already been changed by Gemila.) For a moment he paled in horror at the thought of lying where a man had died.

According to ship's gossip, Achilles had made love here, to Farashah, and perhaps to Alice Palamas. Lord, he thought fluffing up the pillow, the whole world seems drowning in sperm.

He carefully turned the latch. The cabin had a slight smell—something smelling like a mixture of eucalyptus, camphor and fuel oil.

Duck Fong was watching the mechanical meat grinder process fifty pounds of corned beef. As Wu Ting Li came up to him, the cook turned off the grinder.

"They expect corn beef hash on Monday. The palate of the 'Round Eyes' is coarse. No culture that likes white bread is a true culture. . . . Well, honored friend?"

"I have inspected below."

"Ah!" Duck Fong drew Wu Ting Li into the pantry he called his office.

"And so, Wu?"

"As you said, the product is behind the light socket shields."

"Damaged?"

"Only two packets—burned somewhat—and of that, most can be saved."

Duck Fong stared at his very clean, very short finger-nails. "There will be much confusion when we get to port."

"*If* we get to port. What if we abandon ship?" Wu Ting Li made a gesture as if he were cracking a stick across his knees.

"I am inspecting the frozen turkeys in our meat locker. We shall stuff them with the packets."

"Turkeys?"

"I give gifts to certain officials in port. It is well known this cumshaw is expected. One such I know *very* well."

"To whom do you give the fowls?"

"I will let you know later. If all is well we shall be very rich." He puffed out his cheeks, patted his paunch, bowed. "A delectable thought."

"Or we will sit in dungeons eating baked beans for twenty years."

"No, no," said Duck Fong. "Think instead of that twelve-year-old beauty you will buy and enjoy in love."

WORLD OIL NEWS HAS RECEIVED A REPORT THAT THE KSL SUPER TANKER "PALLAS ATHENA" IS IN TROUBLE JUST OFF THE AMERICAN WEST COAST. THE TANKER IS NEARING SAN PEDRO, THE LOS ANGELES PORT. IONNES KYPRIOS, PRESIDENT OF THE KYPRIOS SHIPPING LINE, HAS LEFT ATHENS FOR LOS ANGELES. INTERVIEWED DURING A STOPOVER IN HONOLULU, HE SAID THE RUMORS OF DANGER TO HIS SHIP WERE FALSE. WHILE THE "PALLAS ATHENA" HAD BEEN BATTERED SOMEWHAT DURING THE TYPHOON, SHE WAS NOW SAILING IN SMOOTH WATERS, HER CARGO INTACT. HE DENIED SHE WAS LEAKING OIL INTO THE PACIFIC, ENDANGERING AMERICAN SHORES WITH A GIGANTIC SPILL. THE SHIP CARRIES MILLIONS OF GALLONS OF OIL. THE U.S. COAST GUARD IS SENDING ITS CUTTER "SEA LION" OUT TO MEET THE "PALLAS ATHENA," WHICH IS NOW ABOUT A HUNDRED MILES OFF SHORE. ABOARD WILL BE INSPECTORS, SHIP ENGINEERS AND A REPRESENTATIVE OF LLOYDS OF LONDON, WHICH HAS INSURED THE SHIP FOR A REPORTED SUM OF NINETY MILLION DOLLARS,

Tom turned off the speaker in his quarters. Sarah watched him pacing. "I'm getting dizzy. Stop walking around like Krazy Kat. Remember Krazy Kat? They don't have comics like that anymore."

"I wish you hadn't packed, Dolly. The news is all over that the captain's wife is getting ready to abandon ship."

"Okay, so I'll unpack. The sea isn't too rough, and we're making headway. You can buy me a dinner in Scandia; that's the best food in town, isn't it?"

"I'll buy you diamonds for your nose like a Hindu princess if we ever get to port."

He straightened the photograph of *Pallas Athena*. "I'd like to bring my last ship in. Yes, I would. Call it truculent pride. So what."

"You really mean that. Your *last* ship? It's grapes and the easy life in the vineyard for us two old crocks?"

"It's no easy life in the farm dirt, you'll find out. And who the hell is an old crock? I feel fiesty and nasty; I may knock Ionnes Kyprios' ass over a tea kettle when I see him."

"After saving his ship? You'll get a fat bonus if you keep your fists behind your back and your mouth sewed shut."

Farashah came in with an armful of sheets and towels. "Change the bed, yas?"

"Yes, yes. Oh, and unpack my bags."

The maid went into the bedroom and closed the door. Tom glared at Sarah. "Keep my mouth shut, after what's been done and planned? Like hell!"

"Sweetheart, shut up and listen. Think, don't blow your stack. You told me, you haven't any solid evidence. You make charges and sure as shooting KSL will break your back."

Tom roared. "Wallie, Homer, will back me up in court."

"Your honor," Sarah said, addressing a phantom judge—she had watched a lot of "Perry Mason" on television. There was a mocking tone in her voice, "We have here, your honor, hearsay and conjecture. Two witnesses, Ludwig Ott and Achilles Marrkoras, are missing. The damn Hun is dead or hiding someplace in the South Pacific, and Marrkoras is fish food, buried at sea."

Tom frowned. "What about the false invoices on the Persian Gulf loadings? Sending a Greek officer to scuttle the ship for its insurance?"

"Who trusts a Middle East port's evidence, if it exists and . . ."

"Oh shut up." He grabbed his cap. "I have to live with myself."

"And me, mister. We have a good future, only if there are no court inquiries. No law suits, countercharges. You'll be torn to bits beginning with your not listing your heart bypass."

"Woman, shut up."

He went out, an outraged man who never could face a woman.

Sarah hunted for a cigarette. Sarah's problem now was that Skip had never accepted the truth of her favorite saying: In your struggles against the world, baby, always bet on the world.

In her cabin, Farashah lamented loudly, painfully, beating her head against the wall. *"Unataka ngaki!"* she pleaded to Omkah (God of the Dead of her grandmother's cult, the sand people) to take away the ghost of Achilles and his curse on her.

The dead man in his malicious anger at being done to death had put a curse on her—a dreadful curse that made her unattractive to men. Her one gift in the world had been her desirability; she offered a voluptuousness that was not refused by any well-hung male. Now, she no longer had that lurelike scent of a dog in her that brought males to erection. The officer Ormsbee had actually been able to pull out at the last moment and go off stiff-legged. And he had moved himself into the cabin of the dead man and locked himself away from her. If she were ashore she could offer a goat as a sacrifice to blunt Achilles' ire. Would he accept a frozen leg of mutton? No, she beat her head against the wall again. "*Unataka nini—what do you want?*"

To test her potency she had offered her body to the second engineer, Carlos, and he had said, "No thank you, missee. In the eyes of the Church I am pledged to my wife."

In her despair, she had even reached for Ping Pong, but he remained limp in her fingers and said he was sorry but he had a lover aboard, a kitchen boy, and what he could spare he took down to his darling.

She feared to approach Sieko; his wife carried a dagger. If she failed with Duck Fong, she was too old for Wu; he had said no girl was worth bothering with after she got fuzz on her fig.

Farashah stopped beating her head against the wall and began to wail in Swahili, "*Simamenil! Simanenil! Stop, stop!*" Then she sang a dirge for the dead man, insisting he take his earrings back, take himself away with them; she had not planned his death, and no one is held responsible for a bad deed done in hot blood during a moment of madness. She opened the porthole and flung one red-stoned earring into the sea. As a bonus to the sacrifice she added an ivory-backed hand mirror she had taken from Alice's cabin.

She tried to relax. At last she fell asleep after making love to herself. She slept soundly for two hours and came awake to find Achilles watching her from across the cabin. She told him of the sacrifice and that she had sung dirges so he was properly mourned. Now would he take away his curse?

He said he could understand her fears, for him, too, sex was the vital fire. After all, he was a man cut off too soon from that pleasure, and he could not yet fully forgive her. But he would not haunt her anymore, for the ship was doomed; he did not want a second death. He made her promise that she would order the sacrifice not just of one goat, but two goats *and* six white pigeons, when next she was ashore.

She lay awake a long time, breathing hard. She would ask Chandra Gupta for some pills to calm her. No use offering herself to him; drugs and pills were his only mistress since he took charge of the ship's medical supplies.

Near dawn Farashah slept, purified like a child forgiven, hopeful that all would be as it had been. The ship would not sink, of course, for Onkay was a greedy god; he'd not toss away the promise of two goats (and six pigeons).

CHAPTER | 23

The hull of *Pallas Athena* split just as dawn came up. It was a sudden thing; the hull broke open from the main deck, beginning where the original crack had been welded, tearing out the inch-thick steel hull as if it were tissue paper. At once oil spurted out; three tanks punctured at a time, sending twenty-five million gallons of oil into the sea.

Wallie was on duty. The ship seemed to vibrate and he heard a tearing thundering sound. He knew at once what had happened and punched the alarm button; a raucous warning sound rose up and a series of bells placed strategically around the ship began to clamor. Green lights turned yellow, then red on the control boards.

The phone on the bridge rang before Wallie could try to contact Tom.

"Sir, the . . ."

"I know what's happened," the captain said. "Get the fire-control sections out stringing hose. Prepare foam and water lines. What's our speed?"

"We're proceeding at 14 knots. Wu Li has put guards on the lifeboats—much of the crew are sullen—some hysterical."

"Back him up if he needs help, but act calmly—don't threaten . . . Signal the engine room to reduce speed to zero. Have Homer take a work party to assess the damage. Hell, wait—I'll do it myself."

Below, Tom got into his trousers in the semidark bedroom. He pulled on socks and shoes; no use getting oil burns on bare feet. Sarah was sitting up in bed, eyes half-glazed with broken-into sleep. She reached automatically for a cigarette. She said not a word.

Tom dialed Homer's cabin.

"I'm up, Chief, dressing. It's the bloody hull all right, by the sound of it."

"Get your fat ass up on deck and see if she's breaking. Estimate how much oil we're dumping.

"Yes, sir."

Tom tucked in his shirttail, rang Sieko. "Break out the crew to stand by lifeboat stations, fully dressed and wearing life jackets. Prepare skids for lowering the launch and lifeboats."

"All ready I am assembling crew, sar."

"Don't load or launch. Be sure everyone is on deck, except engine room people."

"Five minutes, all done."

Sarah spoke for the first time. "I better dress."

"Get to your boat station. And Christ, no melodrama, Dolly."

"Yes, Captain."

She kept a tight control of her facial expression, picked up a robe and started for the bathroom. There was a knocking on the door, and Alice came in wearing a yellow rain coat over her pajamas, four film cans in her arms.

"This is it, isn't it?"

"Where is your life jacket?" asked Tom. "Get into a life jacket. Dolly will tell you what's up. First, get dressed."

In the radio room Sparky, who had rushed up from his cabin, was trying to yawn himself fully awake while Moise was pouring coffee into cups. "That was the big one, wasn't it, Sparky?"

"It wasn't the captain farting."

The phone rang. Sparky picked it up. "Yes, Captain, ready to send. Go ahead, sir."

Sparky pulled a pad nearer and picked up a ballpoint pen. "Ready, sir."

"Message to KSL Athens, duplicate to Ionnes Kyprios, KSL office, Los Angeles. Got it? Message is: Tanker damaged, hull ruptured, tanks spilling oil, send barges to unload tanker. Get it?"

"Got it, sir."

"Last reported position sixty-five miles off coast, speed zero, stand by for details. Captain T. Hammel."

"Yes, sir, sending at once."

Sparky accepted a cup of coffee and looked down at his quick scrawl.

"To the trenches, Moise, and clear number *uno* Athens first."

"In code?"

"Hell, no. Direct."

The phone rang again. "Yes, sir, sending. Same message to Lloyds of London? Yes, Captain."

Moise was flipping switches. "Must be the whole magilla if it's time to inform Lloyds."

"We'll relay through Honolulu, Sydney, and Calcutta if we have trouble with the repaired circuits."

Someone had cut in the fog horn and its wail of doom seemed to cut through to Sparky's marrow. His coffee cup shook in his hand as he took a scalding swallow.

In the engine room Carlos was watching the power die out. The steam pressure being released far overhead was screaming from escape vents along the side of the painted KSL funnel. Dials were twitching, and there was a smell of hot metal and overheated oil. For all the din of fog horn and bells, the engine room seemed held in expectant silence.

Carlos crossed himself and addressed the engine room crew. "Be sure all below-deck doors are dogged shut. Don't want any oil from busted tanks flooding in here."

A Malay oiler mopped his wide brow with a clean wad of cotton waste. "We go topside? Get to lifeboat?"

"We stay here, Gullah. They will want some steam kept up, engines ready to make port."

"No like to miss lifeboat."

The phone rang.

"Yes, sir. Engine room under control, Captain. Yes, all doors closed. We can get topside fast if need be."

He hung up and studied the distilled water dial. He had enough clean water for eight hours. If the connection was broken, he'd have to use the drinking and bath water. And that would scale the pipes. If that supply failed— well, maybe a deeper-felt prayer would help. How did one ask God for a continual supply of distilled water?

On the main deck Homer was being lowered in a boat-swain chair over the side; oil was gushing out and pouring into the sea. Already he saw a spreading surface of thickening black, the slight roll of the sea's waves being flattened out by the smothering guk, and the stink was choking him.

"Lower, lower," he called up, as Sieko and four men lowered him a foot at a time. The tear in the ship's side looked like a black, bleeding wound, he thought.

He stopped twenty feet above the surface of the sea. The escaping oil made a steady slurping sound. He studied the tear, judging its width to be about eight to ten inches. He couldn't get too close, he was already being spattered by the black stuff as it was. The tear seemed constant in size, remaining twenty feet above the staining sea. Homer could only guess, but he figured three or four tanks had ruptured. Twenty-five million gallons in each, that left sixteen tanks (perhaps) still intact, and millions and millions of gallons of oil in reserve, ready to pour out.

There didn't seem to be much of a wind, at least from where he hung, like a side of frozen Australian mutton. But any rising breeze from the west and miles of coast could be covered in black mourning cloth: San Diego, Los Angeles, even San Francisco, if malicious currents did their stuff.

His legs were cramping, so he signaled to be hauled up. He began to hum "California, Here I Come."

The kitchen crew were at their lifeboat stations except for those engaged in tasks, like checking the lifeboats' water containers, adding rain gear and sealed food tins to the already equipped boats.

Wallie (the adventure had not yet become an ordeal) came on the main deck, carrying extra blankets and two huge vacuum containers of tea. He moved to Sarah's side: she and Alice were standing by boat position A. Alice said she was getting a migraine from the dreadful odor of fuel oil.

"I see you have blankets," Wallie said. "This hot tea will help."

Alice was juggling her film cans, a camera hung around her neck. "We getting into the lifeboats?"

"No, of course not, more like a drill. Doesn't look like critical damage. Why don't you take some footage of the activities?"

"Jesus, I forgot, with this banging headache."

She adjusted the camera and moved off toward Homer who was being hoisted on board.

Sarah looked at Wallie hugging his tea containers and grinned. "I don't want tea. A snort of Scotch now, *that* would help."

"Sari, I want you to know . . ."

She held up a hand, pointed a nicotine-stained finger at

273

his chin. "You start your daffy games again and I'll drop-kick you overboard."

Just seeing her anger set Wallie's adrenaline flowing.

"I'm just thinking of your safety. Look, if I behave, will you have dinner with me ashore? There's a splendid Southwest Museum I'd like to show you — with marvelous tribal artifacts."

"Stuffed Indians? Not for me. I don't suppose I can smoke?"

"No, of course not. We're leaking millions of gallons of oil. The ship must be flooded with dangerous gases. Can't you smell the fumes?"

She sniffed and put an arm around Wallie's neck. "Go take care of your captain. You're a crazy, know that?"

"You betcha."

He leaned over, kissed her on the cheek, and ran off smiling.

Sarah sighed. So you're lickerish with a persistent sexual itch, you old bag, feeling salacious, but you're not knocking down doors, she mused.

Her maid passed, carrying a bundle in a yellow cloth.

"Farashah, is breakfast being served below?"

The maid adjusted her badly tied bundle. "Oh, something being laid out for eating."

"Good, hold my place on deck here. I'm for grits, eggs, biscuits, and honey."

It was a brave attempt on Sarah's part to appear casual. She looked up toward the bridge. The foghorn had been shut off. A few bells were still ringing. Skip was out of sight, but she could visualize him sending messages, figuring out the hourly loss of oil. A man for all seasons, at sea. There was a tightening in her throat, a wobble in her legs, and she was aware she could desperately use a pee.

Sarah passed Alice filming the activity on the main deck.

"The light isn't bad. It will get better. Great clouds."

"I'm going for the john and breakfast."

"Is it safe to go below?"

She shrugged. "The deck is too public. And never stand when you can sit."

"I'm running out of film. You think it's safe to pop into my cabin and get more?"

Sarah wrinkled her nose. "Phew, that oil smells."

The odor was just as strong below in the dining area. Even with the air conditioning blowing there was the smell of fuel oil, not overpowering but present, like a ghost hovering. You didn't see it but the spook was there.

"I wonder how long there will be power in the air conditioning."

Duck Fong and his assistants had not gone on to their stations with the rest of the kitchen staff. Fong was in the cold storage area, inspecting a small food locker. Sides of beef, sections of lamb, and a whole hanging ballet of pork, loins, ribs and hocks hung above him.

The small food locker usually contained caviar and truffles. He opened it and inspected four plucked, obscene-looking turkey bodies; their long, dark feet ending in yellow claws. He slapped a stiff body, and brooded. He had a problem. The packets of drugs were skillfully sewn inside the carcasses. Had he been too smart? How would it look, his getting into a lifeboat with four turkeys? Somehow he would have to. And how would he and Wu Ting Li figure out how to save some of the valuable packets if the ship suddenly broke in two?

From a life full of prudence, slyness, comfort, he was now a victim of the sea's ingratitude.

He heard the door to the food section open. Chandra Gupta came in, bumping into swinging carcasses, pushing them out of his way, and entangling himself in coils of sausages hung like garlands from a rack.

The medical student looked stoned to the ears, and no

wonder, Duck Fong thought; ever since Chandra had been put in charge of the ship's medical supplies he had been taking whatever he could gulp down, uppers, downers, blue and red devils, barbiturates, even mainlining horse and sniffing crystals. He was a tottering wreck. The damn hophead, his skin was bluish and his teeth gaped from a drawn mouth.

"Duck Fong, I have a message from the Vimala Vasahi. It is that the Princess Sudariani is aboard. She has brought us a copy of epic *Ramayana*."

"You stuffed, to the nose with velly bad things."

"No, no, I am raised to the power of the three strides of Vishnu. Over the ship there are creatures flying and the Vidyadhara talk to me . . . you must obey."

Duck Fong turned the key in the small lockers. He'd have to remove the turkeys later.

"Go have coffee, Gupta, like good fellah. No more use needle."

The medical student made a foolish grin and tottered off. The sound of oil pouring seemed louder.

"NBC TODAY CUTS INTO ITS MORNING NEWS WITH A SPE-CIAL REPORT FROM THE WEST COAST BY BARRY WASSERMAN.

"THIS IS BARRY WASSERMAN, NBC, BURBANK. THE WORLD'S LARGEST SUPER TANKER, THE 'PALLAS ATHENA,' FULLY LOADED WITH IRAQIAN OIL, LIES DAMAGED AND BE-CALMED SIXTY MILES FROM THE LOS ANGELES HARBOR AT SAN PEDRO. SHE IS IN DANGER OF BREAKING UP AND MIL-LIONS OF GALLONS OF FUEL OIL ARE POURING UNCHECKED INTO THE OCEAN, THREATENING TO FOUL THE CALIFORNIA COAST, BLACKENING BEACHES AND HARBORS ALONG A HUN-DRED OR MORE MILES OF SHORELINE. IT IS POTENTIALLY THE BIGGEST SPILL ON RECORD.

"NEARBY FISHERMEN WATCH HELPLESSLY AS THE GIANT SLICK SMOTHERS THE SOURCE OF THEIR LIVELIHOOD, POSSI-BLY FOR YEARS TO COME.

"AS CRITICAL HOURS TICK BY, THE FLOW IS AS YET UN-

STEMMED. AN ESTIMATED FIFTY MILLION GALLONS HAS ES-
CAPED FROM PUNCTURED TANKS, AND FOUR OR FIVE TIMES
THAT MUCH OIL REMAINS INTACT IN TANKS. THE SHIP CAR-
RIES POLLUTION INSURANCE FROM LLOYDS OF LONDON, BUT
THE AMOUNT IS NOT IMMEDIATELY KNOWN.

"THE WORST SPILL ON RECORD WAS TWENTY-NINE MIL-
LION GALLONS FROM THE SUPER TANKER 'TORREY CANYON'
WHICH BROKE UP OFF SOUTHWEST ENGLAND IN 1967. THE
OIL WASHED UP ON ENGLISH AND FRENCH BEACHES.

"THE MAYOR OF LOS ANGELES DECRIES THE FACT THAT
NOTHING HAS BEEN LEARNED FROM PREVIOUS SPILLS. SOME
ANALYSTS PREDICT THE SPILL , A TIME BOMB TO THE COAST,
COULD PUSH ECOLOGY-MINDED VOTERS—A POTENT POLITI-
CAL FORCE—TOWARD THE LEFT IN UPCOMING ELECTIONS.

"HIGH-VOLUME PUMPS AND TECHNICIANS FROM TEXAS
ARE BEING AIRLIFTED TO THE SCENE TO HELP WITH THE
CLEANUP. AUTHORITIES HOPE TO HAVE PUMPS IN PLACE
SHORTLY AND TRANSFER THE REMAINING OIL TO SMALLER
TANKERS OR BARGES BEFORE THE SHIP BREAKS UP.

"THERE ARE FOUR WOMEN ON BOARD, BUT CAPTAIN HAM-
MEL REPORTS ALL ON BOARD ARE SAFE. IONNES KYPRIOS,
WHO ARRIVED IN LOS ANGELES FOUR HOURS AGO, SAYS THE
DAMAGE AND DANGER ARE MUCH EXAGGERATED."

It was amazing to Wallie how soon people in peril
could accept the closeness of impending disaster. Even
now they were meeting in groups to chat and compare
notes and drink in the wardroom. Ping Pong was serving,
helped by Gemila and a Chinese boy. There were a few
moments of silence as someone pondered what the next
few hours would bring. A sense of intimacy prevailed.
Wallie sat with Alice and Sarah over drinks. He felt he
had some task to do; but what?

"There should be something I should be doing . . ."

"What?" asked Sarah, "The engines are turned off, the
boiler fires are being cooled. We are drifting and the shore
people know what our condition is. So all we can do is
wait. No power even to see a lousy movie."

Alice was sulky. Her bright yellow cashmere sweater

277

was stained with oil and a blotch of what might be gear grease scarred the thigh of her pale orange stretch pants.

"I'm nearly out of film. I asked the captain to relay to shore to bring me out a few hundred feet of 16mm."

"He'll do it, don't worry," said Sarah. "Skip always keeps his promises, tries to anyway."

"It's been a cockeyed voyage," said Wallie. "I mean, two officers lost, Ott and Achilles, and something odd about the way things have worked out."

"What?" asked Alice.

"Nothing," said Sarah, jingling her blue-stoned bracelet and giving Wallie a head signal to keep his mouth shut. "Just the usual hassle you find running a ship."

Wallie nodded, "Yes, I suppose so. A sort of isolated family life. I hope I don't sound unctuous."

Alice looked from one to the other. "What the hell are you two signaling to each other? What is it I shouldn't know?"

"Now, honey, you just go on taking your leaping snapshots," said Sarah.

"You mean the rumor that maybe Achilles was stabbed by some sailor after he made a pass. A rotten, low-down thing to lie about."

"You're right, Alice," said Wallie. "Not a hint of truth that he was gay."

Sieko came into the dining area and motioned to Wallie. He spoke in a confidential tone. "I feel, sar, you should know some of the crew are acting up. Not just pilfering, you understand. Chandra Gupta has been passing out strange pills. Barbiturates, Dexedrine, Tuinal."

"Damn him, get a couple of hands you can trust and have him locked up in a cabin with a strong door. Any drinking?"

Sieko smiled, "The Muslims are drinking seventy-proof 'fruit juice.' I have locked up what bottles I could find."

"We'll try and send off most of the crew and kitchen staff as soon as we get a ship alongside."

"I hear that sound again. Metal protesting from the bulkheads and the crack. Very clearly heard now."

"Think she'll break in half?"

"I will keep my ears open, sar."

"Yes, do that."

The problems on board ship were escalating in a steadily ascending curve. It was so different from what he had imagined; no rushing about, no true state of panic, just furtive stares from the crew. Meals were being served at odd hours, mostly sandwiches because the captain had ordered the kitchen ranges turned off. The peculiar stench of fuel oil was in everyone's nostrils. Homer declared that the accumulation of gases could be dangerous.

Wallie walked out on the main deck. He looked down at the oil spreading on the sea. A red-eyed seagull was dying in the stuff; its wings gave a last feeble shudder. From the gummy, reptilelike head, two round eyes, like marbles he had played with as a boy stared. Dead fish, too, were surfacing, belly up, and as far as he could see on the eastern horizon, an expanding band of oil widened. It was a pall little troubled by the sea, which now and then broke listlessly into a wave. The ocean was covered with a black skin that now and then heaved like a flexing muscle. Some planes were penciled in the sky. The sunshine remained constant.

CHAPTER 24

Chandra Gupta came out on deck into the sunlight. He had shaved his head and his egg-shaped skull was scarred by cuts. His features seemed like a stretched mask, his eyes opened unnaturally wide. His loose yellow robe, broad red sash, and bare feet would have attracted attention had there not been a Huey helicopter overhead, hovering just a hundred feet above the bridge. Large painted letters CBS and an eye showed from its underside.

A woman with a bullhorn in her hand was leaning out. "This is Snow Williams of CBS News . . . ," but beyond that nothing could be heard above the steam whistling from the boilers of *Pallas Athena*. Fragments of speech came from the Huey ". . . first to contact the disabled tanker . . ."

The medical student went to the rail where the gushing oil flowed into the sea and flung up his arms. *"Juyli!"*

Wallie yelled, "Get the hell away from there!"

". . . Snow Williams speaking to you over the sea of black desolation . . . returning you to New York . . ."

Chandra Gupta paid no attention to anyone, he was reciting, "I am the voice of the three triumphant: Brahma, Vishnu, and Siva. Now for Brahma's four heads I speak . . ."

The helicopter was pulled away. Homer moved toward Chandra Gupta. "The fucking bugger is stoned to the gills."

Sieko motioned to some of the crew, "He is in a holy trance. Do not harm him. Bind him."

Chandra Gupta turned to glare majestically at the people circling him. He cried out, "Siva the destroyer from Mount Kailas, having defeated Jambhavvat, King of the Bears, speaks through me. See how the holy river Ganges sprouts from his head. I must go now to bathe, bathe in Mother Ganges."

He climbed the rail, and as Wallie and Sieko grabbed for him, he extended his arms and jumped feet first into the oil pouring from the split hull, riding from it onto the shiny oil-thick maelstrom of the sea. For a moment he was hidden from sight. Then a blackened arm and his head appeared. A cry like a strong, hilarious howl came from his mouth.

Homer flung a life preserver to him, but the figure made no move to seize it. The oil reached as if to smother some vocal climax of strangling madness. For a moment, his shoulders appeared as if Chandra Gupta were climbing out from engulfing darkness. Then he sank as one seized from below, his head going under with one last convulsive thrashing of his arm. The oil closed over, smoothed itself out leaving not a ripple to show where the messenger, Brahma's voice, had been swallowed up.

"My God," said Wallie.

"The poor sonofabitch," added Homer. "He was so whacked out he didn't feel much. You don't last long with your lungs full of oil."

Another helicopter circled the ship. Two barges and a boat with Coast Guard markings came into view.

From the bridge Tom had witnessed the death of the medical student, but he remained impassive. He was past shock. He had retreated deep within himself, showing no emotion to Moise who came up to him. "Sir, ship-to-shore phone standing by."

He offered the phone to Tom. "All set, sir."

"Hello. Captain Hammel, *Pallas Athena,* here."

The voice of Ionnes Kyprios sounded cheerful and very close to Tom's ear. "Good morning, Captain. Ionnes Kyprios here. At the harbor."

"Morning to you, sir."

"I'm coming out on a harbor boat."

"Are there more barges? Only two in sight."

"Two more left here half an hour ago. May I congratulate you, Captain. You have brought our ship through a storm and great danger. KSL is grateful."

Was there a grain of irony in the Greek's voice? Smooth deceit, Tom wondered. "Yes," he answered dryly. "We did that. The crew, the engine room people, my second officer."

He tried to keep an icy edge to his voice. "She's still afloat and losing oil from at least four ruptured tanks. Eighty million gallons so far, that's a rough estimate."

"We'll pump out the remaining tanks. Will she hold?"

Tom grinned. "She'll not sink. We may puncture more tanks if the sea gets rougher." He smiled. "We may even break in half and float the two parts in."

"No, no, she mustn't break now. The weather is good, nothing but a light breeze."

Tom looked out at a flapping flag. "From the west, it's moving the oil toward the coast. It must be miles long now, and a mile or two wide, judging from the bridge."

"They are putting up booms around the marinas, the harbor mouth."

Tom gave a short laugh. "If that wind rises and we pour out another eighty million gallons, they can close up San Pedro, San Diego, and maybe even San Francisco if there's a northerly coast current."

The Greek remained calm. "Captain, stand by the ship. I'll see what can be done on the coast. Has the Lloyds of London man been on board?"

"Nobody has tried to get through the oil spill. It's thick and sticky."

"I'll be out in three or four hours. Keep in contact, Captain."

"Yes, do that," said Tom, as Ionnes Kyprios hung up.

He looked out at the Coast Guard cutter to the west beyond the mat of floating oil. The cutter was avoiding getting its shiny pearl-gray paint stained, like an old maid, Tom thought, keeping her high button shoes out of a muddy puddle.

Pallas Athena lay dead on the water, not drifting much, turning slowly in a half circle away from the shore, and then by some freak play of the sea turning back toward the coast which lay about sixty miles away.

Already the horizon was dotted with the creeping shapes of ships, small boats, and cabin cruisers, threading their way through strands of trailing oil. The wind was rising but to no great degree. Slightly, very slightly, *Pallas Athena* moved eastward.

Tom rang the engine room. "Carlos here," Carlos answered.

"Do we have any steam pressure?"

"No, Captain. All fires out. Fumes heavy down here. Any flame might set off an explosion. I hear that fellah he jumped into the oil. Crazy."

"Most likely. We're drifting eastward. No way to get up enough power to steer her by?"

"Don't know none, sir. Might put a launch over the side with a towline and pull her around. Mr. Bowen is on deck now, checking the launch."

"I'll think about it. The strain might cause her to break apart."

There was a cheerful answer. "Sure, Mike, always that

chance. Bringing the crew up, sir, engine room fumes (a cough) getting thickish."

"Yes, of course. Radio and phone contact still functioning?"

"There's a battery standby in the radio room. Barges, sir, damn it. Why aren't there more here?"

"On their way. Left some time ago. Get your gear and the engine room people on deck. I'll try and send you off with the ladies and the kitchen staff."

"If you need me, sir, I stay."

"If I need you, Carlos, I'll ask."

"FROM LOS ANGELES ON SPECIAL ASSIGNMENT, THIS IS SNOW WILLIAMS REPORTING THE LATEST NEWS. AT THREE THIS AFTERNOON THE WORLD'S LARGEST OIL TANKER, 'PALLAS ATHENA,' IS NOT MOVING—IT LIES IN THE PACIFIC SIXTY MILES OFF THE CALIFORNIA COAST AND HAS DISCHARGED NEARLY A HUNDRED MILLION GALLONS OF CRUDE OIL INTO THE SEA. HER CARGO VALUED AT 45 MILLION DOLLARS IS INSURED FOR 39 MILLION; THE SHIP HERSELF IS INSURED FOR BETWEEN 80 AND 90 MILLION DOLLARS.

"EXPERTS ESTIMATE THAT POLLUTION DAMAGE COULD COST INTERNATIONAL TANKER OWNERS AND OIL COMPANIES AS MUCH AS 60 MILLION DOLLARS.

"TWO BARGES ARE PREPARING TO PUMP OUT THE REMAINING OIL, WHILE THE COAST GUARD CUTTER 'SEA LION' PREPARES TO REMOVE THE CREW AND FOUR WOMEN PASSENGERS. THREE OFFICERS WILL REMAIN ON BOARD TO DIRECT THE UNLOADING.

"CAPTAIN HAMMEL, RELYING ON AN INSPECTION BY ENGINEER HOMER BROWN, HAS STATED THAT THE TANKER IS NO LONGER IN DANGER OF BREAKING IN HALF. IONNES KYPRIOS, PRESIDENT OF KSL AND ITS MAJOR STOCKHOLDER, INSISTS THE SHIP IS SEAWORTHY. REPORTS OF A CRACKED HULL ARE EXAGGERATED, HE DECLARED. THE PROBLEM, HE EXPLAINED, IS TO FIND A SHIPYARD BIG ENOUGH TO CONTAIN THE HUGE TANKER WHILE IT IS BEING EXAMINED AND REPAIRED.

"ONE DEATH HAS BEEN REPORTED AMONG THE CREW—A

The tugboat, *Helen S. Wurdemann*, came alongside *Pallas Athena* after circling and probing the fringes of the oil slick on the west. Its rubber buffers banged lightly against the ship's side. Ionnes Kyprios looked up at the steel staircase positioned for him to climb. He was neatly dressed in a dark, chalky-gray suit and a blue topcoat, and wore a darker blue homburg. Under one arm he held a dispatch case. He hesitated as the ship stirred in the oil mulch.

Wallie, leaning over the rail, shouted, "All secure for boarding, sir."

The Greek waved and began to ascend the steeply inclined stairs set flat against the hull as if he were trying to avoid appearing ludicrous.

Wallie gave a short salute as Ionnes got to the deck. "Second Officer Ormsbee, sir."

"Yes, yes," Kyprios shook Wallie's hand and looked with a patriarchal gaze at the activity on the deck. Several huge hoses, like extended elephants' trunks, were sucking up oil and transporting it over the rail onto the barges. Two men in British tailoring were examining the cracked hull. Wallie said, "Insurance people."

"Of course. Have the ladies been removed yet?"

"Coast Guard vessel has been delayed for a customs clearance. Something about an immigration ruling."

Ionnes smiled, patted Wallie's arm.

"Red tape is the same the world over."

The Greek looked about him at the stained deck, the salt-encrusted bridge, still white-rimmed from the lashings of giant waves. The slack lines and the twisted remains of the catwalk railing completed the scene. "Poor *Pallas Athena,* a fine lady, in the gutter. Look at her, it breaks the heart, no?"

Wallie nodded with assurance—the bastard seems very cheerful about it all, he thought. But one never knew about Greeks—a wily people; they danced and broke dishes, cooked with grape leaves, and read Plato.

"Sir, the captain is waiting for you on the bridge. He'd have come down to meet you, but he's had to fill out papers for the Coastal Protection Commission."

"Oh I'll come to him. Protocol, you know. He's still in command."

Ionnes looked out at the spreading spill. "Do you think, Ormsbee, it will reach the beaches?"

"Not for me to say, sir. The spill is twenty-eight miles long, and one report estimates it's four miles wide. The stairs are this way, sir. Sorry, the elevator is not working. Captain shut down the engine room and our electric generators are not functioning."

"Of course." He took Wallie's arm. "Tell me, young man, it must have been exciting this voyage?"

"Harrowing, mostly."

Ionnes, turned his dark eyes on Wallie, with a charm that had almost a fervor to it. "I always wished to take to the sea as a young man. But family matters came first."

He waved an arm toward the staircase. "It takes so much effort, time, energy, to keep things active. The captain is well?"

Wallie answered, "Yes, tip-top" (and to himself, he hoped the Greek bastard had a heart attack on the long climb up).

CHAPTER 25

I command a wounded creature, Tom thought, as he paced the bridge. Perhaps, a dying animal.

The Coastal Protection Commissioner, Ellen Harris, had just left. A remarkable woman: she knew so much about environmental factors—tidal damage, public abuse of coastal formations, what the oil spills were doing to wildlife, birds, fish, sea otters, seals.

Alone on the bridge, Tom considered the canvas-covered teak wheel and compass bowl. The sonar and radar screens, blind faces, stared back. He decided not to indulge in small talk with Kyprios. He was prepared to function, he hoped, at his full potential, with the decisiveness necessary for a face-off, eyeball to eyeball. Would he charge KSL directly with the attempt to sink *Pallas Athena?* Or, would it be smarter to sit back on his hunkers and let the Greek carry the talk? "Testing the wind," an old sailor might call it, before putting up his sails.

Tom wore his best uniform, the white cap with the burnished gold braid and the shiny peak. Sarah had insisted he wear a starched white shirt and a neat tie with a hint of golden-orange sheen.

Ionnes came in, followed by Wallie. He held out a hand. Tom shook it.

"Welcome aboard, Mr. Kyprios."

The Greek cocked his head to one side as if he wondered whether the captain was being facetious. However, he grinned. "Not under the conditions I'd prefer. But she is afloat and the wound is not mortal, eh?"

"We hope not. Mr. Ormsbee, pull up two chairs."

Wallie moved two comfortable captain's chairs into the space before the windows.

Tom indicated a chair for Ionnes and dismissed Wallie. "Mr. Ormsbee, will you leave us now and see that no one disturbs us for the next half hour."

"Yes, sir." Wallie gave a short salute. He would have loved to stay. He left the bridge, closing the heavy glass and steel door behind him. The barge pumps below sucked up oil with a hungry slurping sound.

The two men sat facing each other. The late afternoon sun searched their features. Ionnes took a leather cigar case, about the size of a book, and held it out to the captain. Clear nail polish shaped his neatly groomed fingernails.

"No, Captain?"

"No."

"Oh, no flames. Dangerous."

"Could be."

"Yes, well," Ionnes leaned forward. "You performed miracles bringing *Pallas Athena* through this voyage."

"I acted as any captain would."

Tom paused, as if trying to put the Greek in a position of defense, but Ionnes remained tranquil in his absorption, turning the cigar case over in his hand.

From below, the noise of pumping could be heard—a sucking, hoarse sound. Voices, cursing, carried from one of the barges.

Tom spoke softly. "You must be wondering what my report will be?"

"Wondering? I've been anticipating it, almost writing it in my mind."

"It's not that simple for me. We're two different kinds of men. I know you do what is best for your enterprises, the terms and methods of modern times. I don't judge you. I just want to clear the deck for frank talking."

"Our worlds are not so far apart as you think, Thomas. We depend on one another. We're like two wrestlers, we seem to be grappling but really we hold each other upright."

"That's fancy horseshit talk," Tom seemed suddenly bored. But he had to go through with it. "You'll never understand the sea, the essence of ships. This ship, it's alive and in agony for me."

He held up a hand as the Greek tried to speak. "Let me go on, I want to cough it all up. I'm not a perfect man. I've cut too close to the knuckles at times, but I can't condone what you have planned and done."

"What have I done?" He seemed serious; no charm was on display now. "Just *what* are you driving at?"

Tom frowned sarcastically. "You hired me, knowing I had not fully declared my medical record."

"Your disabilities."

"Yes, disabilities. This made me, in your eyes, a bit of a rascal, one you could handle. Use. You planned to have the ship sunk, broken in two by the unbalanced load we took on in the Persian Gulf. When I balked at your route plan, you had Achilles take over."

Tom shifted in his chair. He placed his fingertips together and touched them to his lower lip. "He was a fine man, Kyprios, a good officer. Splendid. Very likable. But you had corrupted him."

"Let us say he understood certain problems. He was loyal."

"A gathering of eagles is usually at a carrion pit. And what of Ott, did he manage the false loading?"

"A German. You know the breed. Culture and bloodlust. A goosestepper and when they lose, they cry in their beer. Tell me, what did happen to Achilles? His mother took it very hard."

"An accident in the storm. A sliver from a glass table that shattered entered his lung. We had no real medical aid for him. You should have provided a proper ship's doctor."

There was a twinge of contrition in the answer. "Should have . . . should have, Captain? The world is full of impractical should-haves. What *are* you writing in your report?"

"No, not yet. But to give it to you straight, I'm thinking of telling the whole truth."

"Didn't some Roman proconsul ask 'What is truth?'"

Ionnes put away the cigar case. "Listen to me. I know you're not a man to take a bribe, but, of course, you and the officers will get a bonus for saving the ship. You've earned it. I don't say this to flatter you either, you're not the man for a snow job."

It was·clear the slang pleased the Greek; as if it could partially blend his world with the captain's.

"Now, Captain, I'm going to talk to you as a lawyer. Whatever you claim happened, you haven't a shred of evidence to back it up in a court of inquiry. Admitted?"

"You sure?"

"Sure? I am positive. Take the loading records. The Iraqians are known liars, notorious for taking bribes. Ott, you may know, distorted the loading figures. I'm not sorry to tell you, he's dead. We traced him through Interpol. Poor fool, he drowned on a reef trying to cross coral formations in the dark. Achilles, God rest his soul," Ionnes crossed himself—as Tom saw it, from tie to fly, pocket watch to golden fountain pen—"he can never testify about anything."

"No, he never will."

"If there was a plot—as you seem to think—a court would ask for solid evidence that KSL knew about it. Now we both cherish our public reputations . . ."

Tom smiled for the first time in their meeting. "You are going to tell me, as a man looking after what are my interests, that I am a hero, I am news, headlines. Famous for a while anyway."

"You save me the bother, Thomas."

Tom wondered why he continued the conversation. "I am an old man. How fine for me to retire with your blessing and a bonus—a man respected for my years at sea. Not a stain or whisper against me."

"Your wife, your friends would want it that way."

Tom stood up, walked to the window and looked down. A heavily loaded barge was inching across the black liquid surface; it threw up no wake.

Tom spoke without turning. "I may have no legal evidence. Your lawyers can make a mockery of anything I claim. I may even be dismissed from the Sea Captains Association for supplying you with incomplete health records."

"False records, creating a doubt that you were physically able to run a ship safely."

"Yes, yes. My name would be mud, as my grandfather used to say. I clearly see my position. I see yours, too."

Ionnes held his hands wide apart.

"I don't ask you to lie or invent. KSL will be pleased with an accurate report of the storm and your heroic efforts to weld the crack caused by the unusual conditions. These details, just the details of what happened in the last few days will satisfy us, Lloyds, and our stockholders."

"Your hope is in what I leave out?"

"Hope? In this world, my dear Captain, hope pays no dividends. I'm asking you to think of yourself. Even if all this is to our mutual benefit, we must live in the world as it is, not as we would want it to be or as we once thought it was. You're a wise enough man to think this through rationally and act on it."

He stood up and joined Tom at the window. They watched the Coast Guard cutter approach.

Tom said, "The wind is coming up from the west. The crap will be hitting the beaches and harbors by morning."

"That's part of the price the world pays for its efforts. I, too, dislike the destruction of nature and beauty; mostly I pity the birds," Ionnes sighed. "I am not at all the man you think I am, Captain. I have duties too. I, too, have emotions. You can say I relate to things. Yet I have issued orders that gave great pain. I suffer from that self-aware-ness, but I go beyond myself. Our culture, the whole world, depends on firms like KSL. You, too, depend on us for work, for civilized comforts, for the welfare of those you love. Don't feel so goddamn superior. We're other brothers, that's all."

"Cut the moral chatter, Kyprios. Long ago I found out that right and wrong are only too easy to define by what you think they mean. But look close, I am what I am, you are what you are. Yes, I think your world, much as I dis-like it, is struggling, you're stumbling along the best you can. You may be right, trying to save the Judeo-Christian tradition from the sons of bitches in the Kremlin."

Tom held up a hand, to keep Ionnes from speaking. "I'm an old work horse; I can only do what I have been taught—remain with my own naive values. As for the *Pallas Athena* voyage, I'm going to tell everything I know as I know it."

Ionnes did not react. He spoke calmly. "Think it over, fully. As a song puts it, 'I like a man that takes his time.' Is fighting the KSL worth destroying your reputation?

Can your heart stand years of courtroom appearances, being battered by relays of lawyers—the meanest cocksuckers alive—flaying you?"

Tom said dryly, "I'm signing my death warrant?"

"I'd take bets on it. I have one request . . ."

"Slip it under my door. We've said everything."

"No. No. I just ask that you talk this over with your wife, once more. I only met the lady once, but, forgive me, my friend, I am a good judge of character. She is on our side. She is aware of the times, she knows, as someone said, a terrible truth of existence—'What does it all matter as long as the wounds fit the arrows.'"

Tom made no answer. The Greek held out his hand and Tom took it. "Kyprios, you're much more clever than I am, but as you see, I've made up my mind."

"Then there is hope. One can't examine a position that's being formed. Now that you've reached your answer it can be examined, its weaknesses spotted."

Tom said nothing. He wanted to hear no more. He watched Kyprios move toward the door. Nothing awkward or defeated in this well-tailored Greek. Hell, that character wouldn't break down, even if I went over and set fire to his hat, Tom thought.

After descending the steep stairs to the main deck, Ionnes stood at the rail, deep in thought. He needed the pungent aroma of a good cigar to focus his thinking. But he would have to do without that particular comfort. To begin with, Thomas Hammel was a man of principle, fanatically held principle. In short, he was not open to logic or reason. That kind of locked-in superiority kept him from seeing the actual flow of life.

Ionnes watched the black hoses, their great rubber snouts nosing into his ship for oil. His gaze wandered over the length of *Pallas Athena;* she was solid for all her battering, except for her now leaking entrails. How he had loved her (still did). He recalled how he and his brother Paul and the whole Kyprios clan had gloried over the first blueprints of her. And the joy they shared in her actual launching, the almost filial piety with which her voyages were charted.

Now she was a tragic queen. And he was the one who had planned, as royalty often did, for the good of a kingdom, an assassination that had failed. Did she feel resentment, plan retaliation? Nonsense—steel was steel. Engines were engines, charters were charters, was he being contaminated by that goddamn captain's talk?

The way to overcome principles was to pit them against other principles. If the captain were an ancient hero in some tragic epic, he would be unreachable; but Thomas Hammel lived in the immediate present, where there were real doubts about the validity of moral conduct.

Find the conflicts and let them assault the rigid captain. Yes.

Alice was sticking masking tape labels on film cans: AT SEA CALM, STORM FIRST DAY, SKY AND SEA ART SHOTS, CREW MSC ETC. There was a quick tap on her cabin door, Ionnes Kyprios came in.

"Ah, Alice, busy, my dear."

He kissed her cheek and looked down at the film cans. "Splendid."

"I don't know if the damn film footage will be worth all the effort. Some of it may be overexposed."

"Nonsense, my dear girl, I'm sure it's up to your usual high standards. Was it a very bad voyage?"

"It wasn't dinner on the grass in a royal park with caviar and champagne."

He sat down facing her. "No, I'm sure it wasn't. You know your film of this trip is going to make you famous, rich, too. A whole career is opening up. How grand."

Alice eyed the man, as he beamed with benevolent caution. "The film is yours, the KSL's," she observed.

He waved that off. "The fabulous voyage of the *Pallas*

Athena, eh? Good title? Feature length, of course. And *all* yours."

Alice made a humming sound, locked her fingers together, and said nothing. Whatever was spinning through that sleek Greek mind, she wasn't going to put her foot into it just yet, whatever the trap he was setting.

He said, "It's a gift. And in return, of course . . . Greeks bearing gifts are suspect, yes?"

He patted her knee; his unblinking eyes focused on her face. "I want a favor."

"Oh," she said. She felt better. It was as her mother would have said: *Tochis afn tish.* Putting it more politely, you are putting your proposition on the table.

"You mean the rumors about how Achilles died?"

"That and some private matters. How did Achilles die? Never mind, you can tell me later. You are friendly, I'm sure, with the captain and his wife, a charming woman, don't you think? Practical, and a good head on her."

"We have been, well, yes, like a family I suppose. Can I offer you some white wine, some vermouth? Would you . . . ?"

"Not just now. I am certain you can be a good influence on the captain, through his wife perhaps. It would be unfortunate if the captain's report caused KSL problems. We'll have enough turmoil with the repairs and insurance investigations."

He stood up. "Alice, we understand each other. The film is yours. I trust the report will not disturb the peace of mind of KSL. Am I frank enough?"

"Yes, Ionnes. I do not forget I am employed by you."

"We have always exchanged loyalties."

He rose, patted her behind and went out. Alice looked down at the film cans. She knew she didn't have any reason to hope the captain or Sarah could be influenced by her but she would try. How far would she go, using friendship to exploit people for her own advantage? Her

Cambridge lover once quoted an old poem. How did it go? Yes, "The wounded deer leaps highest."

FROM THE NOTEBOOKS OF HOMER BOWEN:

These are the last notes I shall make on Pallas Athena. It is near midnight. Work lights from the barges are blazing in the night; the last of the tanks are being emptied. I shall be going ashore in the morning. I borrowed a dynamo from one of the barges to keep us in radio contact and give some light on ship. We have drifted many miles toward the coast.

It has been a hard day, messy. The news from the shore is not good. The slick has reached the coast and harbors. Marinas have rigged booms, sprayed chemicals, and surface sweeping has begun. Work crews have been recruited to spread straw to sop up oil, and beaches are being scraped.

The spill is forty or fifty miles long and the tides and wind are still herding it north and south. It is the greatest deluge of oil the world has yet known—as the media gleefully report—making the notorious English and French coastal spills take second and third place. Sarah says this is a record, we could have been spared.

The empty ship has a sort of after-the-ball-is-over feeling. Sparky and myself, the captain, Wallie, and Sarah (she refused to leave with Alice and the two native women), are the only members of the original group who sailed from that damn Persian Gulf port.

The tear in the hull has not widened, and the ship itself should be fully salvageable after some costly repairs. But that doesn't matter to me. All the investigations and procedures of the customs officers, federal officials, and insurance people have made this voyage a horror. As an abrasive climax, the damage to the sea life, birds, and the coastal areas is still going on.

Whether the kitchen staff or the crew were taken off first, I couldn't make out. I remember Duck Fong and his bundles though; he had four huge turkeys from cold stor-

age which he presented to one of the officials; they seemed to be old friends. "Always we muss give little gifts in ports. Most happy custom. Also, it only spoil to leave big chickees on ship," he explained.

Wu Ting Li carefully inspected the crew's baggage. (Wu is an honest fellow; he made them cough up ship's linen, typewriters, table lamps, and cutlery.) "Belong to ship and KSL. No take what is ship's. Ah no."

Leaving a ship after a long voyage always makes me sentimental, shows I need a good drunk.

Alice left, hung with her camera gear and film, like a comic soldier off to another war. Somehow, I sense she will never quite realize herself. The native maid, Farashah, dressed like she was going to a ball, in a bright crimson robe with long earrings swinging from her head, wiggled her cruppers as she passed me. She was in charge of the captain and Sarah's baggage, seeing it ashore.

I must say Ionnes Kyprios has taken this rather well. He watches all the activities, has conferences with the captain on the bridge, and keeps his smile in place under those suspicious eyebrows.

Ping Pong, before going over the side, presented me with an eight-year-old bottle of Scotch, saying, "In our life, we always will remember this ship, yes?"

I said yes, we certainly would.

Wallie and I opened the bottle and sat in my cabin, taking a few nips. Not getting boozed, just getting ourselves sadly mellow. After the second round, he began to talk of the scandal there would be when the true story of the voyage and the attempt to scuttle Pallas Athena got out.

I said to him, "You're still wet behind the ears, boyo. I've had a serious chin-chin with Tom. He hasn't got one solid fact, and you and me, remember this—yeh, pour—are under the captain's orders. If he doesn't file a report, we keep our clappers shut, you understand?"

"But we can't just forget, Homer. I mean—Jesus Christ Almighty—isn't there such a thing as justice?"

"Sure there is, on paper."

I refilled his glass. Unless the captain files a report and we are called as witnesses, we're just good old boys who did our duty.

I tried to get through to Wallie my ideas on the individual and his problem getting lost in the old power game of the have and have-nots grabbing for money, but I gave up. Like so many intellectuals, he seeks knowledge, but that's not the same thing as understanding experience. As the Yank Navy men used to say, "Doesn't know shit from Shinola."

He is looking forward to getting ashore. The captain will stay on board until the pilots take over and tow the tanker into dock. Wallie is going to take Sarah to Scandia and shop on Wilshire Boulevard.

I have put the cork in the bottle. Have to save myself for the big drunk ashore. Not a really big one. I want to bring myself to begin serious writing. There is a hell of a story forming in my mind. I feel I can turn the voyage of Pallas Athena (names changed, of course) into a big solid theme . . . a kind of sea epic. How would Conrad or Melville have tackled it? What would they make from this accumulation of events? But they sailed in wooden ships and carried clean cargoes, like wheat or whale oil. That must have smelled better than crude oil, and it never soiled shore lines, encasing sea birds in black, sticky death. Yes, yes, a modest drunk ashore, and then to work. Words, skillfully manipulated to the form and pattern of a voyage.

I keep thinking of Grand Da telling me, when I came back second engineer on an ore boat from Venezuela: "You swing through life, laddie, thinking there is a net underneath. There isn't. Everything seems possible when you're young, until the day you discover, no net."

CHAPTER 26

Their bags were ashore with the maid, the few personal pictures were removed from the wall.

"Now don't be a horse's ass," Sarah said.

"Maybe I was born one. Ever think of that?"

"And stop your pacing. You're not on that damn bridge."

He looked at her. Dolly had courage. She, better than he, took in stride the inequities and absurdities of life. He could wear an impenetrable facade of Presbyterian sternness, but he was still holding on by his fingertips, keeping the world from seeing his true and more tortured self.

"I would be giving up my integrity."

"Try eating integrity, buying clothes with it. Look, Skip, I'd like to tell the Kyprioses to go fuck themselves, but it's all wasted motion. The world will go on. And you're guilty too. You'll drop dead; that pacemaker in your chest will go haywire, facing courts of inquiry. And for *what?* So some fat insurance company or Exxon or Dutch Oil will screw the public to make up the piddling costs of a lost cargo?"

He was listening, somnolently. Then he flared up. "Damn it, I don't want good reasons from you."

"No." She came to him, put her arms around him, kissed his rough cheek. "No, you want me to pat you on the head and say you're a good boy and do what's right and honorable? Well, mister, what's right for us—me, you—is what lets us go on living in a world that doesn't give a shit about us. Open your eyes. We have only a few years left together. Be selfish. You'll be able to hold your head up, if you don't get entangled in a mess you didn't make. Walk away from it . . . with me, Skip. God, I'm begging. I'm what you owe your loyalty to. I'm an old bag, but I'm *your* old bag."

"Don't put it like that . . ."

"Want me to sing 'September Song'? That Greek bastard is waiting for you on the bridge right now. Tell him thanks for the bonus. Tell him off, if you want. He won't mind if you call him every dirty, lowdown name in the book, it will only slide off his greased back. But you'll feel better . . . go bite the bullet, lover."

Tom walked to the door and stood, one hand on the knob, like a man waiting for his doom.

"Why have words like 'honor,' 'faith,' become foolish? I'll not kiss ass. I'll not be a good boy." He pointed angrily in her direction. "I'm going to tell him I'm sticking to the truth."

"Don't try to explain integrity to him. I knew you'd be stubborn, sweetheart. Just go and tell him to piss up a rope."

Tom opened the door and walked out with a hoarse laugh.

Sarah sighed. He still has *cojones,* but the laugh of honor is bitter, she thought. Very bitter. That man goes far on his principles—God I forgive him . . . I'm out of cigarettes, too.

All day planes, helicopters, small boats, and ships had been circling the oil spill. Their spiraling movement outlined a black sea dotted with doomed pelicans and cormorants.

Now under the rising moon, this strangling death was killing marine worms, sea squids, amphibians, reptiles and many birds. Small mammals died in agony; generations of crabs, shrimp-anchored tunicates, and mollusks were made lifeless in the thick oil. Sea anemones choked; great kelp beds with thirty-foot-long stems were turned to greasy mops of rot.

Despite the efforts of thousands of technicians and volunteers manning strung-out booms, spraying foam from the air and from boats, dumping hay by the ton on soiled beaches to sop up the reeking stuff, the devastation was overwhelming.

"Fifty, sixty miles by morning, perhaps, of the most valuable shoreline in the world," one national television newscaster put it. Snow Williams, "is devastated." All day, she had broadcast the figures and facts totaling millions of dollars and miles of real estate, itemizing the costs of clearing, estimating the insurance evaluations. Snow Williams was tough; she did not break down easily at the sight of news photos showing dying ducks and acres of dead fish.

In her Holiday House motel room she spoke into her tape recorder, rehashing what she would say on the morning news. "Man has yet to discover the practical balance between the cost of progress and the value its possibilities offer for the future." She sipped her drink, played back the last section, "Correction—change possibilities to achievements."

Chandra Gupta buoyant and at ease, outlined in the bone-white light of the moon—a moon suspended over a black expanse of sea—floated face up. Limbs extended, his body glistened in the shiny black lacquer of the spill, as if he were suspended between matter and faith on his

301

way to be united with the cosmos of the God, Vishnu, reincarnated as Krishna. The body floated beyond fear, beyond myth, beyond good and evil, moved by the endless force of the sea itself. The thick film of oil carried him like a man laid out on a bier to the realm of Yang, king of the dead.

Around him, a crowd of dying dolphins, rock bass, sand sharks, and tarred seagulls struggled to free themselves. Insects scattered like offerings about him. The wind thrust the dead man eastward, murmuring as if to remind him that everything has its price and the payment is always part of our life.

For those whose business it was to acquire and ship oil, the power brokers of wealth and other men's livelihoods, Chandra Gupta was not worthy of notice.

Yet, in the higher clarity of understanding that rules the illusion of our physical existence, there is no wall between the living and the dead. The floating body, bobbing on the dark surface of the undulating sea, was part of the awareness of the God Vishnu guiding us all, Vishnu, the preserver of the world. Destroyed at the end of each cycle of time, Vishnu, in the shape of Krishna, brings the universe back into being again, making each ending a beginning again.

KAMIKAZE SUBMARINE
By Yutaka Yokota with Joseph D. Harrington

PRICE: $1.95 LB723
CATEGORY: War (Non-fiction).

This is the true story of Japan's fantastic secret
weapon during World War II—the kamikaze Kai-
ten torpedo. It was designed to be piloted on a one-
way trip to death by men who volunteered their
lives in a desperate attempt to smash the United
States fleet in the closing months of the war.
Yutaka Yokota, a survivor, tells how the operation worked and reveals the gripping drama of the
men who volunteered for the most fanatical combat group in the history of WW II.

THE TERROR ALLIANCE
Jack D. Hunter
(Author of "The Blue Max" and
"The Blood Order")

PRICE: $2.75 LB808
CATEGORY: Novel (Original)

Will an assassin in Munich decide the outcome of
America's most crucial election?

Not if CIA agent Roger Wagner can help it. When
the Agency gives him 10 days to uncover an assassination plot against the President, Wagner finds
himself on a frantic search which leads from
German underworld thugs and neo-Nazis to
glossy jet-set salons and the highest levels of
government.

The New York Times calls Jack Hunter "A major
contender in the spy field."